THE

FLAMES

BOOK 2 OF THE FEUD TRILOGY

KYLE PRUE

Copyright © 2017 Kyle Prue
All rights reserved.

Cartwright Publishing, Naples, Florida

Electronic ISBN: 978-1545348642
Paperback ISBN: 978-0-9994449-0-0

Cover design by Ashley Ruggirello www.CardboardMonet.com
Interior formatting by Ashley Ruggirello www.CardboardMonet.com

Library of Congress Control Number: 2017944996
The Flames / Kyle Prue

Printed in the U.S.A.

DEDICATION

For David and Courtney

Now that it's dedicated to you, you have to read it.

VOLTERIA

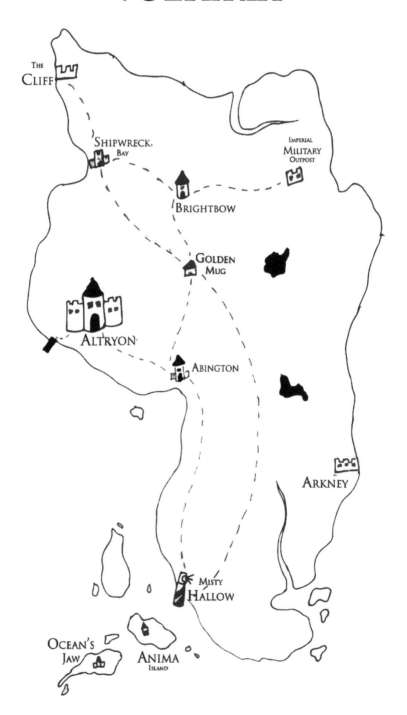

The
CLIFF

SHIPWRECK.
BAY

IMPERIAL
MILITARY
Outpost

BRIGHTBOW

GOLDEN
MUG

ALTRYON

ABINGTON

ARKNEY

MISTY
HALLOW

OCEAN'S
JAW

ANIMA
Island

PART ONE

"Man is a collection of base animal urges. To act on them and experience sinful pleasure would be morally no different than taking a breath."

- Thomas Hobbes

Chapter One

VOLTERIA
NEIL VAPROS

IN JUST SIX MONTHS NEIL HAD ALL BUT FORGOTTEN THE FEELING OF sleeping soundly. He didn't remember what it felt like to walk a crowded street, or attend a party, or even make eye contact with a stranger without panicking. This is how it must always be for escapees on the run, he supposed. For fugitives, life wasn't a march; it was a sprint from cover to cover, where terror squeezed your lungs and held you by the throat. Neil dreamed of a day when these feelings would be a distant memory. In that coveted future he could awake lazily, instead of in a cold sweat, gripping the sheets in terror.

Somehow, facing his enemy head on didn't cause Neil the same terror. It ignited a fire within him. It felt nice to hunt for once instead of being hunted. He stood at the top of a ravine with his back to the glowing moon above him and waited in silence. Every once in a while he lit a flame in his hand and watched it dance in the wind. It wouldn't go out if he concentrated on feeding it with a constant stream of energy. Expelling flames was a lot like exhaling. He could push the fire out of his hands all at once in a giant gasp, or he could set the flames out in a less powerful stream, little by little.

Neil could see the carriage miles away on the horizon, and his eyes narrowed. This mission was an intricate one, and Neil felt his pulse quicken as he thought of how complicated the situation could become. He needed the Imperial Order from within the carriage, and no one could know he'd taken it. At least those were his brother Rhys' instructions. While he watched the convoy of Imperial soldiers roll through the ravine, Neil was once again struck by how gorgeous the fields of Volteria looked in the light of the far- off rising sun. Months ago he'd been living in a giant walled city, Altryon, with no scenery to speak of. Now, outside of those walls, he was greeted by endless stretches of colorful landscape. It was breath taking.

Neil could now hear the soldiers' voices. Their conversation echoed up the walls of the ravine. "Okay, fine," one guard huffed. "Maybe I couldn't win a fight with Darius Taurlum, but I'd snap Neil Vapros in half, no problem. Vapros are known for being easy to break."

Neil's ears perked up. Apparently he was the subject of a discussion. Now that he could see the convoy clearly, he formulated a plan. There was a driver and a few guards on each side of the carriage, sitting ducks in this ravine.

Once the battalion of soldiers was beneath him, he materialized to the carriage roof. Luckily the ancient Vapros ability of teleporting was mostly silent. The wooden roof strained slightly under his boots, and he hoped that no one on the sides of the carriage would notice. He grabbed the driver and materialized back to the top of the ravine. Normal people weren't used to materializing, and often it disoriented them for full minutes at a time. It was a new and frightening

experience to feel your matter disassemble and then reassemble somewhere else. The driver tried to stand, but he fell to the ground and
vomited instead.

The horses, no longer being whipped, stopped in the center of
the ravine. The soldiers fanned out, looking for their coachman. Neil
waited until they were out of each other's sight lines for his next
strike. He materialized down and back up again four or five times
until no soldiers remained in the ravine.

Neil pulled the last one up with a bit of satisfaction. "Is this the
part when you snap me in half?" he asked.

The soldier didn't respond. He was too busy emptying the con-
tents of his stomach onto the ground.

Neil appeared in front of the carriage by the horses. He patted
one gently on the neck and walked to the carriage door. It only took
him a few seconds to find what he needed. General Carlin's wax seal
was easily recognizable among all the common documents. Neil
pocketed the Imperial order and closed the carriage door.

He heard the blade slicing through the air just in time to dodge
it. He threw himself backwards and the soldier's sword embedded
itself in the carriage. Neil struck with a fireball that knocked him off
of his feet. The soldier tried to stand, but Neil's hand began to glow
again and that deterred him. The soldier glared at him. "We're gonna
find you and your little friends. The Emperor won't rest until your
heads are on a pike."

"No need. The revolution will find him first." It took Neil a
moment to decide whether or not to say the next part. "Free Volteria!"

Neil and his friends hadn't officially joined the revolution, but he
knew their battle cry well. He'd heard it whispered enough times. The
soldier pulled a small vial from his coat pocket and popped off the
cork with one hand. "Long live Saewulf and long live the Emperor."

Neil materialized in front of him and seized the poison before the soldier could swallow it. He materialized back to the doors. "Those are some choice last words. But let me make something clear: saying 'long live Saewulf' on your way out is pretty foolish. They're probably still scraping bits of him off the walls of the Imperial Gate."

The soldier leapt forward faster than Neil had anticipated and his sword stretched up towards Neil's head. The soldier only managed to nick his neck before Neil could launch another fireball into his chest. Neil regretted risking his life for a conversation with the guard. He also regretted not counting the soldiers more carefully before starting his mission. That mistake could have been fatal.

The soldier frantically rolled on the ground, desperately trying to extinguish his flaming torso. "Give up," Neil commanded. "Keep pushing us and we'll abandon our aversion to killing."

He drove his heel straight into the soldier's nose and heard the telltale crack. Neil materialized down the road in the direction of the Golden Mug as quickly as possible. He'd taken his time with the guards and would have to move quickly to get back by dawn. He couldn't resist opening the letter as he walked, but reading it didn't ease his panicked nature. He shoved it back into his pocket.

As Neil continuously dematerialized and rematerialized farther down the road, he fell into a mindless rhythm on the long trek back to his hideaway. It seemed impossible that it had only been six months since the Emperor had sent his troops that fateful night, attacking the homes of the three most powerful families in Altryon. Even the Taurlum with their skin of steel and superior strength, and the Celerius with their lightening speed, had fallen to the same fate as the mighty Vapros: all the family members were either killed or imprisoned. Except Neil and his friends. Neil half smiled at the thought of calling Lilly Celerius and Darius Taurlum his friends. Months ago he could have been commanded to assassinate either of them at a moment's notice.

Every day the Empire drew closer, or it just barely passed over them, and every day Neil's resolve to fight weakened slightly. He grew a little wearier. As he bolted up the final path to his secret home, out of breath and over excited, he thought about the future once more. Being on the run had taken its toll. All he wanted was a life away from the fear and worry of being a fugitive. But if something was going to happen, it had to happen soon. He was too tired to slip through the Emperor's long cold fingers forever.

Neil learned to walk silently long ago. When he and his siblings were little they were given a training exercise that made them light-footed. The goal was to descend a set of stairs into the training room of the Vapros bunker without their father, Sir Vapros, hearing them. If he heard the slightest noise, he would turn and fire a bolt with a metal ball on the tip. The arrow always hurt, and sometimes even sprained body parts or fractured bones. Neil still had a small scar on one of his hipbones where he had been struck one afternoon.

Sneaking into the Golden Mug didn't prove to be a problem. He drew a small key from his coat and pushed it into the lock silently. It clicked open and Neil entered the bare bar. In the dark he wandered past the tables and chairs and into the kitchen. He knew the Golden Mug would be open for business in a few hours. He also knew not to touch any surfaces in the bar. It was a mad house during business days and he was sure that sticky, dried alcohol covered every surface even after its cursory nightly cleaning.

Once at the back of the kitchen, he pulled open the latch and materialized into the pitch-black attic. Here were the secret rooms he and his companions had made their temporary home. Neil could see that the only visible light was came from underneath his door. He opened it and sidled past his younger brother. "We're gonna run out of oil."

Rhys was squinting at a book that was nearly his size. "I guess you'll just have to be our new light source then." He gestured vaguely at Neil's hands.

"It worked." Neil let his coat fall to the floor and he into his miniscule bed. "I got it."

"What did it say?"

"The Empire is sending their men in waves. They're redirecting their efforts toward maintaining their hold on Brightbow. The majority of the Imperial force is officially heading west. Now we just have to look out for random patrols and wandering squadrons."

Rhys exhaled in relief and sat up. "I suppose we're in the clear temporarily. No one saw you, did they?"

Neil was silent for a moment. "They did."

"I asked you to be careful."

"I was. You try taking on an entire convoy of soldiers on your own."

Rhys glanced up from his bed. " You have a cut."

"What?" Neil asked. "Oh, right. This thing."

"Were you being cocky again?" Rhys asked with genuine concern in his voice.

"What? No," Neil said, "When have I been cocky? I was all business. I just miscounted the number of men, that's all."

Rhys peered at him through the dark. Neil peered back. "Why don't you ever use your head?" Rhys asked.

Neil wanted to be mad, but it actually sounded like a legitimate question. Rhys's words were completely free of judgment. "Why are you more of a parent than Dad ever was?"

"This just looks like a long road ahead. Little cuts add up."

"Afraid I'll be less pretty by the end of this?" Neil asked.

"No. I'm sure you'll be a very pretty corpse," Rhys said and picked his giant book back up.

Neil pulled out his pillow and beat on it to give it a little fluff. Rhys was definitely an old worried parent trapped in a fifteen year-old's body. "I'm not going anywhere, kid. Get used to worrying about me."

"I'm used to it," Rhys said quietly.

Chapter Two

THE GOLDEN MUG
NEIL VAPROS

Neil woke to someone's hand on his shoulder. He whipped his knife out from under his pillow and waved it wildly. "Calm down!" Rhys whispered urgently, materializing back a few feet. "I just came to wake you up!"

Neil blinked sleepily up at his brother. "Sorry," he said, stowing the knife and rubbing his eyes. "What time is it?"

"Sun went down a few hours ago. We can come out now." Rhys headed toward the door. "And hurry," he groaned over his shoulder. "Josephine says it's *haircut* night."

Neil smiled. Josephine was the closest thing to a mother he ever had. Years of singlehandedly running this bar had left her rough and coarse, but there was a kindness in her eyes that made Neil feel as if for the first time in his life, he was unconditionally loved. When he and his fellow fugitives had knocked on her door one night, begging for shelter from pursuing soldiers, she had let them hide in a few secret rooms in her attic, no questions asked. For months now she had kept them well fed and well hidden, and if all she asked for in exchange was help cleaning up after hours and to let her give them haircuts once in awhile, well, Neil could think of worse ways to live. "I can't wait to see her cut Darius's hair," he said enthusiastically as he followed Rhys out of their tiny bedroom.

Rhys frowned. "I hope he doesn't throw another tantrum."

Darius, Lilly, and Rebecca had gathered in a clump at the top of the stairs. "What's the holdup?" Neil asked.

"Can't go down yet," Lilly said. "There might still be people."

"Oh, come on," Neil rolled his eyes. "The place must have closed an hour ago. We're fine."

Rebecca shook her head and tucked a lock of brown hair behind her ear. "I was down there helping Josephine close up, and there were still some soldiers," she whispered. "They're probably gone, but I don't want to risk it."

"Soldiers?" Neil pushed a hand through his hair. "Were they searching? Or just drinking?"

Rebecca offered him a smile he could barely make out through the dimness. "They were too drunk to walk straight. I doubt they were looking for a fight."

Next to her, Darius squirmed restlessly and let out a little moan. "Can we *go*?" he whined. "I want to *go!*"

Rhys patted his friend's shoulder. "Be patient," he said calmly.

"Why are you so eager anyway?" Lilly snapped. "You hate getting your hair cut."

Darius kept his eyes fixed on the bottom of the stairs. "I just don't like waiting. The suspense kills me." He turned to Rebecca. "Go check again."

Rebecca wrapped her hand around the banister and moved carefully down the stairs. Putting her finger against her lips, she got down on her stomach and slowly lowered the hatch in the floor. She only left it open a few inches, but light flooded into the dark attic space, making her squint. Neil watched her peer through the crack and scan the kitchen below before letting the trap door fall open all the way. "All clear," she announced, and then dove out of the way as Darius charged down the stairs and jumped through the hatch.

He landed with a *thud* that shook the whole bar. Lilly winced. "Let's try not to cause an earthquake, shall we?" she said as she jumped through the hole and landed lightly on the balls of her feet.

Neil heard Darius reply, "Flesh of steel, kids. It's not exactly known for being light."

Laughing, Neil materialized down into the kitchen. He instantly regretted it; he'd grown accustomed to the darkness of the attic, and this new bright light blinded him. He threw his hands over his eyes and groaned. Behind him, he heard Lilly laughing. "Behold," she said playfully, "Neil Vapros's greatest enemy has appeared. Beware the light!"

"Shut up," he said, opening his eyes gingerly. "We're nocturnal now, remember?"

Rhys materialized next to his brother. He'd had the sense to keep his eyes closed. "Are we all here?" Neil glanced up at the trapdoor and saw Rebecca's face looking back at him.

"Need help?" he called.

"I can jump," she said, but she sounded less than enthusiastic.

Neil materialized back up to her, relishing the darkness. "I'll help," he insisted. "Don't want you to hurt yourself."

She smiled and put her arms around him in preparation for the materialization. "Thanks."

"How'd you even make it up here?" Neil asked, focusing his energy. He made sure to close his eyes this time.

"Rhys helped me," she said, then squealed as they materialized down to the floor. "He was the only one awake," she continued, de-tangling herself from Neil. "Does he ever sleep?"

Neil shook his head.

"Why not?"

Neil lowered his voice. "It's dark up there. Rhys has trouble fall-ing asleep in totally dark places."

"Oh." Rebecca looked troubled. "Can't he just. . . ."

Neil knew what she was trying to say and he shook his head. It was a travesty that Rhys' advanced ability worked on everyone but himself. "He can put other people to sleep fine, but it doesn't work on himself. He's tried it."

"Oh." She glanced at Rhys, who was chiding Darius for steal-ing a loaf of bread from a basket on the counter. "Poor thing," she murmured, then disappeared into the other room to find Josephine. Rebecca was Josephine's manager of sorts: she waitressed and helped in the kitchen. According to Rebecca, the village where she'd been born, Abington, was under Imperial occupation. Her parents had been executed for "conspiring with the rebellion" when Rebecca was just a child. Josephine had found her wandering in the woods two weeks later, feasting on tree bark and berries to survive. Josephine had been fostering her ever since. Neil casually swiped some bread of his own from the basket and went to join the others.

"Ugh," Neil said, wincing as he swallowed a bite of his bread. "Darius, is your loaf stale?"

Darius looked at his half-eaten loaf for a moment. "Yeah," he decided as he bit off another mouthful. "It's really stale."

Lilly shook her head in disbelief. "Are you actually eating a stale loaf of bread?"

"Josephine could never serve this. It's disgusting. She was just going to throw it away. I'm taking care of it before she does. This is charity."

"I like that," Rhys announced. "I always thought Taurlum were idiots. But you, my friend, always have an answer."

Darius swallowed with difficulty. "When your siblings eat like elephants you learn to justify taking food," he said as he ripped off a huge piece.

This was absolutely true for Darius. He loved to eat, more than almost anything. Occasionally Josephine would send them to go collect fruits from the nearby forest, and then she'd cook them in a mixture of alcohol and molasses. It was more delicious than any of the cakes Neil had ever had in Altryon, but he was never able to eat more than Darius, who scarfed down more than the rest of them combined. Rhys had once theorized that Darius liked the cakes so much because they had the aftertaste of liquor.

Rebecca poked her head back into the room. "She's ready for you." Darius pushed the rest of his loaf into his mouth and struggled to chew it as he led the way into the closed bar.

Neil couldn't help but admire the mess. Whenever they went to sleep, the restaurant was spotless. Now the tables and chairs were strewn haphazardly around the room, and cups and specks of food littered the floor. "Looks like a busy day here at the Golden Mug," he said to Josephine, who was wiping down a counter.

She looked up at him tiredly and retied her frizzy ponytail. "I wish I could hire you during working hours," she said. "It would be nice to have a Taurlum lifting the heavier orders." She looked Darius up and down.

Rebecca grabbed a rag and began to help clean off the counter. "I can lift the heavy orders," she said, scrubbing hard at a sticky stain left by someone's spilled drink.

Josephine smiled and ruffled her adopted daughter's hair. "You're quite the waitress," she said, wringing out her damp cloth in the sink. "But you can't claim to be as strong as our blonde giant!"

Darius laughed and slid a table back into its proper position. Talking to Josephine had an odd effect on him. Something about her turned him into a helpful, obedient child. "People inside the walls used to call me Golden Boy," he remarked fondly. "I think I like blonde giant even more though."

Josephine yanked open a cabinet and pulled out a long pair of scissors. "It's probably because you've never met anyone as creative as the women in this house." She set the scissors on the counter and dragged a chair into the middle of the room. "Okay, the barber is in business," she announced, retrieving her scissors and opening and closing them rapidly. "Who's first?"

Darius's eyes grew large. The group shifted uncomfortably, trying to avoid Josephine's eyes. She noticed. "Oh, come on," she said, grabbing Lilly's arm and pulling her toward the chair. "It's a haircut, not a death sentence!"

Lilly shifted anxiously in her chair. "I'd rather not let anyone touch my hair," she said stiffly.

Josephine gently stroked Lilly's silky locks. "I'm not going to butcher it," she promised softly. "You'll still look as noble as ever." Lilly didn't seem convinced. "If you don't like it, there's a money back guarantee," she joked.

No one said anything. "Look," Josephine said. "Every soldier in Volteria is carrying around your wanted posters in their back pockets. If you're spotted for some reason, it might be a good idea to not look exactly like they remember you." She pointed at Lilly with the scissors. "Survival takes precedence over what's fashionable."

Neil came to Lilly's rescue. "I'll go first," he offered, and Lilly jumped from the chair as if it had burned her. He took her seat. "Just don't make me bald."

Josephine snapped her scissors a few more times. "No promises," she said and began to cut.

Chapter Three

IMPERIAL PALACE
VIRGIL SERVATUS

VIRGIL RAISED THE GLASS OF WINE TO HIS LIPS AND DRANK DEEPLY JUST to give himself something to do. He'd been waiting here all day for someone, anyone, to return with news. The war room was unlit, but Virgil had memorized the location of every weapon in the room. If anyone tried to attack him, he could easily reach for a sword and slice the enemy in half. Not that anyone was going to attack, he reminded himself, taking another swig from the glass. As second in command of the Imperial army, he had every right to wait here.

He swallowed the wine without tasting it. In spite of everything he kept telling himself, Virgil felt uneasy about being alone in this room, especially since he knew one of his greatest comrades, Anthony Celerius, had been stabbed to death in this very chair a year ago. He couldn't shake the feeling that he was somehow trespassing, that he was being watched. . . .

The war room was flooded with light as the door burst open. Virgil's hand twitched toward a sword, then relaxed as his ally General Carlin, marched into the room. "Drinking alone?" the General observed, taking a seat next to Virgil.

"Waiting for news," he replied. "How was your journey?"

Carlin dropped his sword on the table and put his face in his gloved hands. "We certainly have our work cut out for us. Why did we ever exile anyone? Why didn't we just lop our enemies' heads off?"

"It seemed cleaner to just send troublemakers into the wilderness," Virgil suggested.

"Lot of good it did." Virgil noticed that Carlin had accumulated plenty of grey hair in the last month alone. "Now he has us running around the wilderness trying to track them down. We're never exiling anyone ever again. We had the Wolf in our clutches and we just…" Carlin waved his hand through the air. "let him go."

Virgil swirled his glass around idly. "It could be worse," he offered. "We could be spending our time crawling in the sewers looking for old, dying assassins."

Carlin didn't acknowledge the joke, or maybe he just didn't like it when his grandfather's killer, Nikolai Taurlum, was referenced. Virgil had a complicated relationship with Carlin. Carlin had killed Anthony, and Virgil wanted to hate him for it, but Virgil had only ever had two friends: Anthony and Carlin. If the General ever died, Virgil would be completely alone in this world. Carlin was the only man who knew him personally and not just his methodical way of following orders. Virgil had escaped from an abusive father as a child, and he remembered how terrible it felt to be on his own, solitary. Losing Carlin would put him right back in that position. It didn't help that he was also taunted for being a "savage." At least the

General defended his lieutenant's honor whenever the circumstances of his birthplace arose.

"I don't think the Lightborns will be a problem for much longer," Carlin said. "Not now that we have the assassin contractor on it."

Virgil shuddered. "Your guy seems like a little bit of a maniac."

"I don't like it, either, but the Doctor's our best option. He's the best equipped to take care of the fugitives." Carlin said, reaching up to massage his temples. "We have too much on our plate. We're spread between tracking the four kids who escaped last year, plus we're fighting the Wolf and his rebels, not to mention the Tridenti are getting more aggressive. It's best if I take care of the Wolf while the Doctor takes care of the fugitives."

Virgil put a hand on Carlin's shoulder sympathetically. He started to say something but he was cut off.

"Carlin." The voice came from a large figure standing at the door. "How was your little trip?" In the Emperor's tone, Carlin's military occupation sounded more like a play-date.

Carlin's posture stiffened and he muttered something under his breath as he stood. "We didn't find them, The Lightborns, or the Wolf," he said stiffly to the Emperor. "We checked two villages. We couldn't make it to the other three. The Wolf's men are attacking our convoys. I'm back until we can regroup."

The Emperor's eyes were duller than usual, as if he had missed countless nights of rest. They seemed to lack the spark of life. "Just remember," he said calmly, "I want results, Carlin. What is the objective?"

"To win the war." Carlin said.

"No." the Emperor snapped. "What's the objective?"

Carlin clenched his jaw. "Eliminate the Lightborns."

"Without their precious heroes, the rebellion will dissolve. That's how you win the war Carlin."

Finally there was something they agreed on. "No problem. The Wolf is growing tired. And we'll have the fugitives any day now."

"You can have all but one," the Emperor said.

"I know," Carlin said, glancing at Virgil. "We all know."

The Emperor blinked his eyes a few times. Carlin had responded a little too quickly and a little too forcefully. "Let me reiterate, then, General, because sometimes you don't get it right on the first try." He licked his lips and stared into Carlin's eyes. "I want Neil Vapros. I want him dropped at my feet. Nothing would make me happier. And I do like to be happy. Is that all clear?"

Carlin inched away from the Emperor and bowed slightly in his chair. "Understood, sir," he said, reaching for the bottle Virgil had been drinking from and pouring himself a glass. "I won't pretend I know what's going on with your rule, sir. But you've seemed drained since the psychic was..." he struggled to find the right phrase, "since Saewulf was removed from your service." Removed from his service was the polite way of saying, 'was killed by a servant with a grenade.' Is there anything you need from me?" Carlin continued.

The Emperor smirked, then laughed out loud. Carlin had to stop himself from jumping out of his armor. "You think you can help me, boy?" he said almost gleefully, life dripping back into his expression for an instant. "The things that you don't know could fill a library, General." He shook his head as if disappointed. "I don't care who finds them, Carlin. I just want to see their heads on the pikes in front of the palace. Until then, I want to know where they are. Search every village. *Every village*, Carlin! Slaughter everyone who opposes you. This is not war," he added as he approached the door and threw it open with a hard push, "we're hunting rats. I will not rest until every remaining Lightborn has been killed or imprisoned."

Carlin watched until the Emperor was out of sight, then sank into his chair. "Your father seems to drift in and out of our world," Virgil whispered.

"It's curious business," Carlin said dully.

Virgil raked his hand through his hair. "The next time you go on a mission outside the walls, I'm joining you."

Carlin laughed a little and shook his head. "I need you in the city."

"You need me with *you*. You're exhausted. You can't keep up with all the emperor's missions. Let me come with you. Let me help you."

Carlin looked at his friend in silence for a moment. "I need someone in the city," he repeated.

Virgil rose and marched for the door. "I'm going with you," he announced without looking back. "Don't worry about the fugitives, sir. The Imperial Doctor is coming for them. And I'm sure he'll bring the full force of with him."

Chapter Four

THE CLIFF
THE PACK

AT ONE POINT IN HER LIFE ANASTASIA HAD COMMITTED HER assassinations barefoot. It was an odd strategy, but high profile targets were skittish and paranoid. Announcing your presence was a good way to end up dead. Her expert acrobatic ability, partnered with the element of surprise, made for quick, clean kills. She always kept her chain spike tight, without any slack. Otherwise the links in the chain would rattle.

Now she was older and wore thin silk slippers. They slid across surfaces like a water droplet along a blade of grass. She almost felt freer than she did when she went barefoot. Of course, it didn't matter today. There was no sneaking up on the Imperial Doctor. She'd tried a few times, but he always knew when she was coming. He heard everything. Knew everything. Anticipated everything.

If she were trying to sneak into The Cliff, his fortress, she'd take out the guards on the roof and climb down the mineshaft into his workshop. She was almost certain she was the only one small enough and acrobatic enough to accomplish it, but she didn't try. Today she was fulfilling a contract. She carried Donovan through the giant double doors and dragged him through the workshop.

The Doctor was leaning over one of his tables. From behind he almost looked normal, but Anastasia knew his deformities well. She saw them in every nightmare. He turned around and his copper jaw glinted in the light. According to him, his lower jaw had been removed due to an infection, a complication from being tortured as a child. Every finger on the doctor's hand was a different length, some were missing entirely. One arm vibrated sporadically, as if a current constantly ran through it. His lower jaw lifted and she thought he might be smiling. "You brought him in alive," the Doctor slurred. "Lester also brought in his contract alive. We get to play a game."

"The Hyena brought one in alive?" Anastasia tried not to sound too surprised. The Doctor was very partial to his adopted son, and critiques weren't taken lightly.

"Indeed," the Doctor said as he turned back to fiddle with something on his desk.

Anastasia could hear snickering toward the window. "I caught him right after breakfast, so I wasn't hungry." The Hyena trotted into view. He was grinning ear to ear and his metal veneers were in full view.

Lester, better known as The Hyena, was just over four and a half feet tall and was heavily muscled. Under any kind of clothing, he looked like a child, or a dwarf. Currently he was shirtless, though, and his rock hard frame was visible. His arms were unusually long so when he walked he trotted on all fours. "Hi, Anastasia." He laughed her name out of his lips.

She smiled and tried not to look queasy. "Hi, Lester."

The Doctor brushed past them. "Can we get our injections?" Anastasia's hands were already quivering and she'd been coughing and short of breath for days. She wasn't used to cutting it this close.

"After we play," the Doctor hissed.

Anastasia lugged Donovan after the Doctor. Donovan groaned. He was finally awakening. She'd drugged him into sleep with a mixture of some berries and roots that she'd found. She wondered if he'd hallucinate when he woke. She didn't always get the dosage right.

The Hyena's target looked familiar. The poor soul was bound to a large rusty hook, and dangling with his feet a few inches off the ground, his arms fully extended. His shirt flapped open, exposing a message written on his chest in blood. *To: Dad. Love: Lester.* The Hyena loved to entertain himself. The captive must have been drugged; no one could sleep in that position.

The other hook was lowered and they tied Donovan's hands to it. They hoisted him up so that he hung next to the Hyena's target. Donovan blinked the sleep from his eyes and started kicking in panic when he saw the Doctor.

"Where am I?" he slurred. "What's going on?"

"You're waking up," the Doctor explained. "You're emerging from a drugged sleep. You might feel a little groggy. Perfectly normal."

"I don't know what you ruffians want," he huffed, "but you will not receive it from me."

The Doctor pulled a knife from the tool belt that encompassed his waist. "Jeffery Donovan," he mumbled to himself. "You are the Imperial Judge of Abington, a proud father of four children, an upstanding member of the community…"

"All true." Jeffery Donovan said. Somehow he puffed out his chest while hanging from a hook.

"And a spy for the rebellion," the Doctor said, finishing his list.

The blood drained from Donovan's face. "No…. No. You are confused. Your information is wrong."

"My information has never been wrong before."

The Doctor approached the other captive and poked him lightly with the knife. The man's eye shot open and he yelped. "Logan Barrister," the Doctor said, "you are a highwayman, a bachelor, one of the most sought after criminals in the land… and you've been targeting Imperial supply convoy's for the rebellion."

Logan stared at the Doctor with pure hatred. "I don't know who you are, freak, but I can promise you that the Barrister gang is coming for you."

The Hyena snickered. "No, they're not."

Anastasia tried not to think about what had happened to Logan's men. They were probably the reason the Hyena wasn't hungry enough to eat Logan. Anastasia didn't know if the Hyena was even paid for his services. For all she knew, the Doctor was just enabling his cannibalistic adopted son.

"I don't see the point in—" Donovan started to say.

The Doctor sliced him with the knife. "Do not interrupt!" he demanded. Donovan howled. "Here's the game. One of you is going to tell me where the Wolf has built the stronghold of his rebellion. The other will go into the cage."

He pointed with the stub of a pointer finger on his right hand. They tried to turn their heads, but couldn't. Built into the wall of the workshop was a series of iron bars. Anastasia didn't know exactly what was behind them, but she knew that men who entered didn't exit. Her personal theory was that the Doctor had a bear locked up behind the gate. She'd never been bold enough to check. "What's in the cage?" Logan Barrister asked.

The Doctor said, "One of you is sure to find out. You have one minute, or you both go in. Lester, start counting."

"You can't expect us to be frightened of something we've never seen," Donovan said.

The Doctor cocked his head. "Why of course I can. What could be more terrifying than the unknown?"

"Fifty seconds," the Hyena said.

"You don't know what's in there. You don't know how many times I've heard human bones crack in its mouth. Would it help to tell you that the beast eats its prey alive? Would it help to know what it sounds like?"

He threw a knife from his belt and it struck the metal gate. A deep inhuman roar came from within, and the hostages whimpered in fear. "Thirty-five seconds," the Hyena said.

"Would it help to know how long it takes? Seconds, minutes, hours, or even days? Would it help to know if he plays with his food?"

"Twenty seconds."

"Would it help to know that your death could be painless? All you'd have to do is point in the general direction of the Wolf."

"Shipwreck Bay!" Donovan screamed before the Hyena could finish his countdown.

The Doctor raised an eyebrow in what was probably amusement. It was hard to tell with his face. "That was unexpected. The judge becomes the hangman. Very well."

The Hyena scampered over to the cage and used a crank to open it slightly. Then the Doctor lowered Logan Barrister to the ground. He tried to struggle, but the Doctor struck him in the neck and deterred his efforts to escape. With alarming strength, he dragged Logan over to the gate and with a mighty heave he threw the young man into the cage. The Hyena lowered the gate before Logan could come to his senses and escape. Anastasia didn't watch any further. She didn't want to know what was going to happen to Logan Barrister. It was hard enough to listen to the screams.

The Doctor hobbled past her and over to a circular wooden table in the center of his workshop. He waved her over. She approached with some trepidation. There was a half completed bomb on the table. Or at least it looked like a bomb. He started fiddling with it. "How have your injuries been healing?" he asked a moment later.

She touched her stomach. "I'm good as new."

He made a noise that could have been a laugh or simply his attempt at breathing, she couldn't tell. "Good, very good. I have a new contract for you."

"What kind of contract?"

"You remember the fugitives?"

Yes. "Fugitives?" she asked, feigning ignorance. She definitely didn't want a contract involving them.

"The Lightborns who escaped," he replied absently, tinkering with his bomb. "The ones General Carlin can't find. I'll pay you a hefty sum to go after them."

Anastasia raised her eyebrows. "You want me to find the people who tried to kill me?"

"Is there a problem?"

"No," she said, a hint of a frown playing at her lips. She narrowed her slanted eyes. "Not at all."

"This job is a little different. There are specific instructions."

"How many others have you already hired?"

"Two others," he replied. His attention was still focused on the bomb in his hand, "Plus I put out a public notice to nearly every assassin in the land. Just for fun."

"Two others," she repeated. "The Marksman and the Hyena?"

"Correct," he said, putting his experiment on the table and meeting her eye. "You're all receiving the information at roughly the same time."

She folded her arms. "Why do you need me then?"

"Consider it a race." He glanced back over his shoulder to see how far along Logan Barrister was in the process of being dismembered and eaten. "The rules are simple. The Celerius girl isn't worth anything unless she's delivered to General Carlin, dead or alive. The Taurlum is fair game. I'd recommend killing him as quickly as possible. The eldest Vapros is not to be killed. The Emperor wants him alive for some reason."

Anastasia pursed her lips. "I haven't said yes yet."

He waved his hand. "You will, you will. I would especially like the younger Vapros alive. For personal reasons."

"You want the one who stabbed me? Why?"

"He's quite the intellectual, I've heard," the Imperial Doctor said. "I want to challenge him and test him for something."

There was a roar from the other side of the workshop. The Doctor clicked his tongue. "It's okay, my pet. Just enjoy your dinner."

Anastasia shuddered. He noticed. He lifted his copper jaw into a grin. "It's a thing of beauty. It's art," he said lovingly.

She tried to look convinced. "You want me to go after the fugitives? They've beaten me three times before. I don't know if I'm up for it."

He pulled his gaze away from his monster and examined her. "Do you know how all this," he waved his misshaped hand over his body, "came to be?"

"Your injuries?"

He went to retrieve something from a nearby cabinet. "I was abducted from my home at a very early age. I was forced into the imprisonment of a mad doctor. He specialized in torture. And he made me his science experiment."

Anastasia gulped, then regretted it. She didn't like it when he knew that she was afraid. He pulled a small wooden box out of the cabinet, and she exhaled. It was her injection.

"He turned me into a monster," the slurred voice continued evenly. "He broke my jawbones. He cut off my fingers. He studied my reactions carefully, recorded them in a little book. He wanted to see what I would do, how I would feel. He was trying to create something called a pain index."

Anastasia didn't like the sound of something called a "pain index." The Doctor often scribbled in a tiny book. She wondered if they were one and the same.

"Now, you must understand something, Anastasia." The Doctor came closer and grabbed her arm. She didn't flinch and was proud of herself for that. "I was strong as a child. Unusually strong. I am a Lightborn after all. If I had met this man under any other circumstances, I would have been able to kill him with my bare hands. But in our particular *situation*, he had the upper hand. He had *dominance*." Anastasia could feel the Doctor's breath on her face. He slipped the needle into her vein on the first try. "Of course, eventually, my strength won out. I broke free. I caught my doctor and strapped him down and used everything I had against him. He'd piqued my curiosity though… a pain index. How unique. I'm still completing mine to this very day. He begged me to kill him in the end. And so in that moment, I felt something incredible. Complete control. Complete dominance."

He pushed the plunger on the end of the syringe, and she gripped the table. Finally. She felt her sickness subsiding already. "That feeling of control inspired me to become the man I am today. It made me the Doctor. I also made a promise to myself on the day that I killed him. I would never feel powerless again. I would exercise complete control in every aspect of my life. That includes my assassins and the contracts that they take on." He pulled out the syringe and set it on the table. "Do you really think that I'd send you if I didn't have absolute confidence in your abilities? Do you think I'd send my sons into danger?"

She was almost certain that he didn't care about the lives of her or his sons, but she stayed silent. "I have faith in you, Anastasia. I know you won't disappoint me."

She still didn't say anything. She didn't want to accept this assignment. She'd have to stab quite a few backs to get it done. When she didn't reply, his face turned sour. "I fixed you up, Anastasia." Her name sounded harsh in his accent. "I made sure you lived. Do this for me, or I will make sure that gift does not last."

She looked at him fiercely. He didn't back down. "Then I suppose I have no choice," she said in a low voice.

The Imperial Doctor smiled and went back to tinkering with his explosives. "The Marksman should get there first," he said without looking at her. "I think he had a lead of some sort."

Anastasia furrowed her brow and ran one thumb across her chain spike. "So do I," she said as she turned to exit.

"And Anastasia!" the Doctor called. She eyed him suspiciously, "Just remember, if you turn on me, no more of your precious injections. You will rot from the inside out. Your entire body will turn on you and consume itself. I have studied pain my entire life. The way you will die if you betray me tops the scale."

"Okay… I get it," she said quietly, placing a hand on her stomach. She corrected her posture and exited with her head held high.

As she entered the mineshaft elevator, she heard The Hyena calling to the Doctor. "I guess I'm going to Shipwreck Bay!"

He was probably going to try to find the Wolf and use him to find the fugitives. That way was too slow for her. She only had a month before... she didn't want to think about it. She had a way to find the fugitives that was quicker. It had to be. She knew that her life would end at some point, but she'd finish her business before it did. Time would not be the one to strike her down.

Chapter Five

ALTRYON
THE PACK

THE MARKSMAN PEERED THROUGH THE MULTITUDES OF SWIRLING, intertwined couples toward the other side of the extravagant ballroom. A man and a woman stood by the bar, flirting and drifting subtly closer. The man sported a red coat and a seductive smile. She donned a puffy white dress and a feigned sense of security. The Marksman growled under his breath. *Disgusting,* he thought.

"You have a contract for me, correct?" the Marksman asked patiently staring off into the distance at the couple.

"How the hell did you know I was behind you?" Quintus asked.

The Marksman didn't turn to face him. Instead, he looked down and admired the noble costume he had removed from a corpse that was probably yet to cool in the alley outside. "Do you know why the nobles dress so nicely?" he asked.

The Marksman clearly wasn't going to turn, so Quintus walked around him, blocking the Marksman's view of the courting couple. "Why?"

There wasn't a spec of emotion in the Marksman's eyes. "It's because they can. Because they want people to know that there is a line that separates them from the poor. They want people to know that they are better than the masses." He wrinkled his nose.

"The poor disgust you," Quintus accused as he grabbed a wine glass from a travelling servant.

"No," the Marksman said, "humans disgust me. All humans. Washed or otherwise."

Quintus raised his eyebrows. "Okay. How did you know I was behind you?"

"I assume you acquired your wardrobe the same way I did?" Quintus shifted uncomfortably and the Marksman smirked. "I get it. A few months ago you could just go into your closet and pull out your nicest coat, right? That was before the Vapros burned down your house. Now things are different. You work for my father, the Doctor. Money is scarce. Is there a missing noble lying naked in a street somewhere?"

The Marksman expected Quintus to recoil or squirm, but he didn't. He simply smiled. "I don't need the Emperor or your father to provide for me anymore. I can provide for myself. As you can see."

"I assume the shoes didn't fit."

Quintus looked down at his tattered boots and understanding dawned, "Oh."

The Marksman looked smug, even with a stone-cold expression, "The soles are worn down. Your footsteps are audible yet they don't have the same ring as shoes that are only brought out for extravagant parties."

Quintus scowled, "Okay, zip-up Marksman, we're done measuring."

The Marksman smiled for the first time that night. "You asked."

"Well, now I regret it," Quintus said as his smile contorted into a sneer. "You just want people to marvel at your little 'gifts.' Same as all Lightborns."

The Marksman's eyes dropped from their faraway gaze and onto Quintus. The bookkeeper nearly swallowed his tongue. The Marksman cocked his head. "My gifts are not what make me superior to you, Quintus."

Quintus puffed up his chest and tried to straighten his posture, even though the Marksman was a full head taller than him. "Care to repeat that? I'm not afraid to attack you, Victor. There's one less noble in this city because of me."

"It takes mere savagery to stab someone in an alley while their back is turned. I'm sure it made you feel like a man," the Marksman said whilst examining his fingernails, voice thick with sarcasm.

"That's it!" Quintus barked. "Working with you is the single worst part about my job! People used to respect me! I was an advisor to the emperor and I won't be belittled by—"

The Marksman's hand shot off in a blur and pressed into the side of Quintus's neck, then slightly to the side of his shoulder. Quintus reached for his throat. "Settle," the Marksman whispered. "Your body should be tightening and your airway should be constricting, provided I struck the right pressure points. Which I did. Your heart has stopped temporarily. You're probably feeling very ill, so don't attempt to speak." He grabbed Quintus by the shoulders and dropped his body onto the table behind him. Quintus's large rump crushed several plates of hors d'oeuvres. "Listen closely, simpleton," the Marksman said, staring down his associate. "If you look far off to the other side of the ballroom, you'll see a couple. The man is wearing red and the woman is wearing white. Don't they look civilized, Quintus?"

Quintus tried to nod, but all he was able to manage was a low gurgle. The Marksman continued. "They look polished and well behaved. But one of them is pretending. One of them is hunting." A drop of drool fell from Quintus's lip. "She thinks him to be a proper human, but the powder that he's slipped into her drink suggests that his intentions are far less… civilized." Quintus's eye twitched. "I am superior to you people because I hunt efficiently and without deceit. I don't lie. I don't deny my instincts and I certainly do not befriend my prey before I kill them. You may stand in front of me and tell me that you're a big strong killer, but I can assure you, coming from someone who appearss so…" he looked Quintus up and down, "stout and delicate… Well, it does no good." He slowly released the pressure, and Quintus' color improved as oxygen flooded back. Quintus moved his undamaged arm slowly to his chest pocket. He struggled to remove a letter. The Marksman pulled it out for him. "Is this the target?"

"Targets," Quintus corrected through a shuddery breath. "You'll have to leave the city. You should have the necessary papers for the Empire to let you through the wall."

The Marksman pocketed the letter. "That's fine. I'm headed out anyway. I've got two more men to kill first before I go after the fugitives."

"Who?"

"I've been watching the man in the red coat for a reason. He's worth quite a bit of coin. Dead."

He cocked one of his guns under his coat. "Then I'll head outside the wall to kill Sean Beaton. You should consider leaving the city as well, Quintus. As a member of the Pack, it's best to stay on the move." Out of the corner of his eye he could see the civilized couple beginning to leave the party. "Goodnight," he said to Quintus, following the couple he'd been carefully tracking before they could leave the crowded ballroom. The girl in the white dress stumbled slightly and the man had his hand on her side and was sliding his palm downward. The Marksman wrapped his left hand around the pistol in his coat, "Sir!" he called.

The noble and the woman turned around, "Yes?" the noble asked skeptically as he examined the Marksman's coat. He probably wanted out of the party as soon as possible.

The Marksman extended his hand and the noble hesitantly reached out for it. The second the Marksman entered the handshake, he removed his pistol from his coat, placed it under the noble's chin and fired a shot straight through his head. The corpse dropped to the marble so hard that the Marksman estimated such a fall might have killed him, if he weren't already dead. The girl began screaming as she stared down at the spots of red on her white dress. The other nobles stared in horror and few cried. The music stopped. "Be at peace," the Marksman said to the girl in white. "You'd thank me if you knew the extent of his plans for the evening."

He pocketed his pistol and turned to the room of nobles. "Don't pretend you care," he said to the partygoers. "He's no better than any of the citizens dying in your slums. He's just dressed better." He patted his hands on his coat and went through the back door of the party and into the streets. He ducked into an alley, leaving the young girl to weep over the body of her would-be assailant.

VICTORY LIES WITHIN
THE ASHES

Chapter Six

THE GOLDEN MUG
NEIL VAPROS

JOSEPHINE PUT DOWN HER SCISSORS AND SMILED. *"WHAT DO YOU THINK?"*
she asked, leaning against the counter. "Worthy of family standards?"

Rhys pushed his hand through his newly cut hair. "I'm satisfied
with mine," he announced. His hair had remained long on top, but
the sides had been cut short. Neil and Lilly mumbled their agreement. Only Darius remained silent. He was pouting in the corner,
staring mournfully at the long locks of blonde hair on the floor. His
new haircut consisted of short spiky strands; Josephine had wanted
to dye it brown, but Darius had leaped from the chair and run away
when she suggested it.

"Good to hear," Josephine said, closing her eyes. "I'm beat. Can
I count on you to clean up around here?"

Neil suppressed a groan. Rhys nudged him. "Of course," Neil
said, and Josephine smiled gratefully and wandered off to bed.

Once she was out of earshot, Darius got to his feet and gently touched the top of his head. "I hate it," he moaned.

Lilly rolled her eyes. "You look fine."

"You're one to talk," Darius pouted. "Celerius hair grows back in a flash."

He was right. Lilly was a Celerius and because of her regenerative qualities, her hair grew alarmingly fast. It would be back to its old length in no time. For some reason, she still fought Josephine every time she produced her shears. The honorable Celerius men back in Altryon had always kept close-cropped hair. Neil wondered if they had weekly, or even daily, haircuts.

"You really look fine," Neil said. Darius didn't seem convinced.

"I think it's an improvement, actually," Rhys offered.

Darius looked down at him. "No, it's not."

Rhys persisted. "Longer hair is impractical. Keeping it short like that is a good idea. Your flowing golden locks aren't exactly inconspicuous." Darius said nothing, but looked slightly less murderous after that.

"Okay," Rebecca said, examining the mess in the room. "Rhys, I want you to straighten all the tables and chairs. Lilly, why don't you clean the floors and tabletops? Darius can fetch some water, and Neil, you can finish up the dishes with me."

Darius started for the door. "Of course Neil gets the soft job," he muttered.

Rebecca heard him. "You're stronger than Neil," she insisted. "You can handle harder jobs. Neil is delicate."

"Delicate," Darius repeated with a grin.

"*Delicate?*" Neil looked at her incredulously. He was definitely bigger than Rhys and Lilly. "I'm a trained warrior, Becca!"

Lilly snorted. Rebecca smiled. "Forgive me," she said with a mocking bow. "Would you like to go fetch the water, then?"

Neil sighed. "Did I mention . . . I'm a very delicate trained warrior?"

Rebecca laughed. "That's what I thought." She walked back to the kitchen. Neil followed at her heels and began to scrub at a plate with a rag. Rebecca was humming one of Darius's Taurlum drinking songs under her breath. She and Josephine both liked to sing while they worked. While Neil normally didn't mind listening, this song drove him crazy.

"A lot of business tonight, huh?" he said, hoping to spark a conversation and end the humming.

Rebecca submerged a mug. "People really like Rhys's beer. They can't get enough of it."

"Yeah, back home the Vapros are in charge of alcohol. We owned all the bars and made all the drinks. It was a good business strategy." He picked up a new dish. "Because people always want beer, you know? In good times, they celebrate with it. In bad times, they use it to forget their troubles. We were more successful than any of the Taurlum market stands."

"Isn't it funny," Rebecca said, "that you all used to be so competitive?"

"'Funny isn't the word I'd use," Neil said.

Rebecca laughed. "But look at you now! You're all cleaning Josephine's restaurant and singing each other's songs."

"*You* are singing his songs," he corrected. "I have never sung about the 'Mighty, mighty Taurlum and their mighty, mighty might.' Most idiotic lyrics of all time."

"I like them. They're catchy."

"So is smallpox," he grunted and began to scrub as hard as he could against a tough stain. It didn't budge. He quickly let a small flame leap from his hand and burned it away. Rebecca yelped, and Neil quickly doused the plate in water. "Sorry about that," he said, examining the plate. He'd left a few scorch marks, but the stain was gone. "I forgot you aren't used to that."

"It's okay," she said, still stunned. "You ruined the plate, though."

"Yeah," he said tossing it into the sink. "Sorry."

"It's fine." She wouldn't meet his eye. "I've ruined plenty of plates before. No big deal."

"I keep forgetting you aren't used to people like me."

"What, men?" Rebecca laughed shakily and threw herself back into dishwashing. "I've known plenty of men, I can assure you."

"I meant people with *abilities* like mine," Neil said.

"Oh!" Rebecca's face flushed. "Right. I mean . . . I've heard things about people like you. But I've never met any Lightborns before your gang arrived. I don't know if I've met anyone from the Industrial City before now."

It took Neil a moment to remember that the Industrial City was the name those outside the wall had given the walled city where he had grown up. Those within the walls just called it Altryon. He'd once thought that Altryon was the word for the entire realm, but once again he and the people had been misled. The people had dubbed the greater landmass Volteria, even though the Empire insisted on leaving the outer reaches nameless. Rebecca had taught him many new terms in his weeks outside the walls. People out here were dubbed "Outsiders" by the Empire. They also commonly used the slang term for family members, Lightborns. Neil had heard that word inside the walls but far less frequently than they used it out here. "Well, here we are." He quickly burned away another stain while her back was turned. This time he was careful not to damage the plate itself. "Most of what you've heard is probably just rumors, though. There are a lot of myths that aren't true. We Vapros don't eat children, for instance."

She laughed. "Does anyone actually believe that?"

"You'd be surprised." He smiled fondly at a memory. "What kinds of things do they say about us out here?"

She thoughtfully dried her hands on a cloth. Her half of the sink was empty; she'd finished before him again. "The Celerius can catch arrows," she said finally. "Is that true?"

"Probably."

"The Taurlum are huge drinkers?"

"Very true. Darius used to be an insufferable drunk, before he decided to join us."

She pushed him aside and started to finish his half of the dishes. "The Celerius are afraid of heights?"

"I'm not sure about that one," he said after a moment. "You'll have to ask Lilly. You don't have to finish these," he added, taking a mug out of her hand. "I can do my part."

She backed off. "How about . . . the Taurlum can't read?"

Neil let out a laugh. "Darius can read!" he insisted. "At least . . . I think he can." He paused. "Well now that you mention it, I've never actually seen him read anything. Might be worth investigating." He dunked another mug in the sudsy water and began to scrub at its sticky handle. "We've heard a lot of rumors about you people, too."

"Outsiders?" Rebecca asked.

Neil dried the mug and set it aside. "And the outside world in general. It's different than we were told."

"How so?"

"We were told that it was a wasteland out here, but it's not. It's beautiful, and it's peaceful. We were also told that the people out here were savages."

She frowned and he remembered that these people didn't like that word. The Imperial Army used it too often to belittle and degrade the people of Volteria. They were tired of hearing it. "But if anything, the people out here are kinder than inside the walls. They're less polite, but definitely kinder."

"I'm sorry that we're so rude to you," she teased. "Would you like me to curtsey every time you enter a room?"

"Now that you mention it, that would certainly make me feel more at home."

She slugged him in the arm playfully and doused it with soap and water. He thought about using a flame to dry it, but thought better of it. He was using his powers too frequently. It was a thing to be hidden.

"Well if you ask me," she said playfulness fading, "the Imperial meatheads are the real savages. People outside the walls respect each other. It's only when those soldiers come around that things get messy."

She was absolutely right. Volteria had its bad eggs, but not nearly as many as he'd encountered in Altryon. Maybe it had something to do with packing people together in an enclosed space. People in Altryon were practically tripping over each other while citizens of Volteria were given ample room to keep their own space. If Neil wanted to, he could run off into the wilderness and not see another human for weeks. It really hadn't taken him long to understand the need for revolution outside the walls. The Empire imposed exorbitant taxes and their soldiers never missed a chance to demonstrate excessive force. No one had ever shared with Neil what started the current rebellion. According to Rebecca, they'd been revolting since the walls had been built to keep them out of Altryon.

"What about the Vapros?" Neil pressed. "What do you hear about my family?"

She smiled. "The Vapros are liars?" she tried. She was trying to look nonchalant, but he could tell she was afraid to hear the answer.

"Sometimes," he admitted quietly. "When we need to be."

"The Vapros are ruthless womanizers."

He stopped washing. "You know that's not true," he said lightly. "Look at Rhys. Rhys could never be a womanizer. He's too shy."

"What about you?" she asked.

"I wouldn't say I'm *ruthless*," he said carefully. "There's been a fair share of girls, but only one that's mattered."

There was one dish left in the sink. They both reached for it, but she got there first. "Was it the girl who left the city with you?" Rebecca asked when the dish was clean. "Your girlfriend? Where'd she end up?"

"She's not my girlfriend," Neil said automatically. Then he glared at Rebecca. "Did you do that on purpose? Did you plan that last question?"

She didn't meet his eye as she dried the dish and put it away. "What do you mean?"

"That last question. Was that something you asked so you could get me to talk about Bianca? Because I've refused to talk about her before, and I'm not about to start now."

She met his eyes. "Never mind, then," she said quickly. "Forget it."

He leaned back against one of the counters and stared at the floor. "I don't know where she is," he said finally. "But I can only assume that she's cutting through a soldier or burning something down."

VOLTERIA

Chapter Seven

LT BLACKMORE'S CABIN
BIANCA BLACKMORE

Bianca knew exactly what was waiting for her in the deterio-rating cabin. Word travelled surprisingly fast through Volteria and Bianca was famous for being able to track people down. She patted her torso to make sure her throwing knives were within reach and her leather breastplate was securely fastened. It was a useless precaution. What did she have to fear from a corpse? She entered the cabin without making a sound. Even the rustiest of hinges went silent at Bianca's expert touch.

"Hel---" Bianca had a knife at the ready before the middle-aged man was even finished with his greeting. He raised an eyebrow at her. "You're the one breaking and entering, Bianca."

Bianca's heart raced. The scene inside the cabin was a lot to take in. In the center was a table. Seated at that table were the middle-aged man and the body of a man with ivory colored hair. The living man was examining her politely, but he had his hand on the hilt of a rapier. The dead man was all too familiar. His eyes were closed, but his skin gave him away: it was grey and lacked the hue shared by living things. "Why are you here?" she asked.

"To pay respects to one of my oldest friends." His voice had a deep richness. It was the voice of a much younger man.

Bianca stared. He wore a long dirty coat over thin leather armor and he had wavy auburn hair. Despite the fact that his head was without a single gray hair, his face was covered in a thin layer of grey stubble. Some of his features looked oddly familiar, and Bianca could feel old memories resurface. *Who did he look like?*

"How do you know my name?" she asked cautiously nearing the table. He looked trustworthy, but Bianca knew never to judge based on appearance.

"Well, when I found out my old friend Paul Blackmore had finally passed, I knew I had to come visit to say goodbye one last time. Funny thing is, I've been looking for you for weeks. So I didn't see any harm in waiting a while with him to see if his daughter would show." The man spoke carefully. "They call me The Wolf."

Bianca's jaw fell. *The leader of the revolution?* Bianca knew that if she tried to talk she would end up stuttering, so she opted for stunned silence instead. He grinned at her knowingly. His eyes shifted to her father's body and his smile vanished. "Do you know how he went?"

"I could wager a guess," she said cynically. The smell of alcohol was palpable in the must of the cabin. "He wasn't a good father. And it's been years. I just thought I might as well come see him one last time."

The Wolf patted the dead man. "He and I have been on opposite sides of this thing for a while now." Bianca realized he was referring to the war for Volteria's independence. "I thought this would be a good last meeting for the two of us. Friends again. Sharing a drink."

"He had a few too many before you got here, it seems."

The Wolf chuckled. "Paul was always a few drinks ahead of everyone."

The name sounded foreign to Bianca. She'd never heard anyone call her father by his first name. It was always Lieutenant Blackmore. She sheathed her throwing knife and sat at the table. He didn't seem surprised. "How did you know him?"

The Wolf delicately turned the body's head to show the tattoo on the back of his neck. *IHS.* "Your father and I were part of a very special club."

"He's had that since before I was born," she said.

The Wolf unbuttoned the shirt underneath his leather breastplate and exposed an identical tattoo just below his collarbone. "I've had it since before you were born too. General Carlin's got one too, on his forearm. It's short for Imperial Hunting Squadron."

They sat in silence. She couldn't help but wonder if it was in remembrance of her father or if he simply couldn't find the right words to say. She didn't really want him to say anything. She didn't need to be comforted, she didn't need words of wisdom, and she didn't need a friend. She'd come to see the body. That was all. As always, Paul Blackmore wore his Imperial lieutenant badge and cape, but it was fastened over beige pajamas. Bianca stared at the badge for a moment before pulling it from his corpse. She unclipped it from the crimson cape and draped the cape over her father's body. She pocketed the badge. The Wolf acknowledged this action with a nod of his head. "Why have you been looking for me?" she asked.

"Well, it started when I heard that you were looking for me."

"I am. To join the revolution."

"Then I heard whose daughter you were and your story, so I made it a point to meet you."

"My story?" Bianca asked.

"You were with the Lightborns who escaped the city and made it through the wall, correct?"

"Without me, they wouldn't have made it." Bianca had told Neil when she learned of the secret back gate through which they had all escaped.

He leaned toward her urgently. "Did Lilly Celerius make it out?" he asked. "I know Jonathan died. I need to know. Is Lilly alive?"

Bianca didn't flinch. "Are you an enemy of hers?" she asked fiercely.

He shook his head and rubbed his forehead, closing his eyes. "Hardly." He wiped a smudge of dirt from his faded blue coat. Something about that coat stirred Bianca's memory. "I've been trying to find her for months," the Wolf said. He picked up his glass and drained it with three gulps. He met Bianca's eyes, and for the first time she saw pain in his piercing stare. "I'm her uncle."

Chapter Eight

HOME OF SEAN BEATON
THE PACK

THE MARKSMAN ADMIRED HIS RIFLE FOR A MOMENT AND THEN CHECKED to make sure that all of his pistols were in working order. He set his sights on the village a few miles below the mountain on which he stood. He glared down at the entrance to his target's home with his incredible sight and patiently waited. Sean Beaton was his target. And Sean Beaton was a former friend, a friend with a daily schedule. This made him an easy target, despite his extensive security detail.

After hours of waiting, any normal assassin would have drifted off. Not the Marksman. He was always focused and ready for anything. That's how his kind operated. Not only did they all possess super human senses, but they also had razor-sharp focus. Their brains always functioned on a higher level, and they never turned off.

This was one of the reasons that the Marksman despised being around people. In nature everything smelled, felt, sounded and tasted as it should. People complicated things. They added spices to their foods. They perfumed themselves. They sang songs. They wore makeup. They denied the basic genius and perfection of nature. Even thinking about it made Victor nauseated.

Finally he saw the troops making their way through the streets to Beaton's home. The Marksman double checked his weapons and stood from his crouching position. He smirked and proceeded down the mountain. It was time to make his living.

Beaton hobbled into his lavish home and threw off his coat. A guard picked it up and tossed it onto a coat hook on the wall. "All right, everyone. I'm going to sleep," Beaton grumbled as he started towards his staircase. "Keep a perimeter. Those Imperial bastards won't repel themselves."

Suddenly the Marksman leapt through a glass window and rolled into Beaton's atrium. Before any of the guards could react or prepare weapons, he was drawing pistols and firing. He pulled two guns from the two holsters at his hips and fired them into the guards at Beaton's side. He quickly dropped the guns and pulled out two that had been strapped to his back. He quickly unloaded them into Beaton's remaining guards and whipped out his prized rifle to execute the final sentry.

Beaton gasped as he realized his entire group had been disposed of in less than ten seconds. "Damn, Victor. I know you're killing for the Empire, but somehow I thought you'd leave me out of it."

The Marksman began to relax. "It's not the Empire who wants you dead. Well, actually it is. But the other arms dealers in the area are paying me. You can't sell to the rebels and expect the competition not to be savage."

Beaton glanced around his home with a sentimental look in his eye. "You really have the guts to put a bullet in me?"

The Marksman drew a pistol from a holster on his chest. "Of course not," he said. His eyes settled on the chandelier above Beaton. "I could never do that to my old friend."

He fired straight through the chain holding the chandelier. It fell and crushed Beaton as if he were an insect. The Marksman didn't even blink as it fell. He strutted over to his weapons and began to reclaim them; he stopped once he heard coughing coming from the pile of crystal where Beaton had been. "You're still alive?" he asked. Beaton replied with a cough. "I'm glad I remembered. We met in Abington about a month ago and you'd stopped in a pub for a beer. Do you remember what the establishment was called?"

Beaton dragged his crushed body out from under the broken chandelier. "The... Golden Mug...?" he asked. He coughed up a good deal of blood.

"That was it," the Marksman said thoughtfully. "Your breath smelled like rosemary, honey and citrus. I didn't think much of it at the time."

"So?"

"Those are some of the secret ingredients used in the Vapros Classic beer. Most people wouldn't be able to tell, but as you know, I have a very refined palate." An idea struck him and he mused to himself. "The road between Abington and Shipwreck Bay is also near Altryon. It makes sense that they might have hidden there."

Beaton tried to stand, but flopped back onto the floor. "You're going after the Vapros?"

"Yes," he said casually, reloading his favorite rifle, "I'm not the only one hunting, but I've got something the other assassins don't."

"What's that?" Beaton coughed.

The Marksman pointed his rifle and fired it into the back of Beaton's head. "None of the other assassins are Lightborns."

Chapter Nine

THE GOLDEN MUG
LILLY CELERIUS

LILLY FINISHED HER LAST BIT OF CLEANING AND WANDERED OFF TO THE side of the restaurant to watch Rhys and Darius complete the rest of their chores. She curled a lock of her hair and focused her energy. She began to send it out in waves through her feet and soon had a clear look at the Golden Mug and its surroundings. In her mind she could feel Josephine settling upstairs. With further concentration, she deduced that Neil had retreated into the depths of the large attic. She began to feel the earth around the bar and she tensed; it was harder to extend over bare ground. The Golden Mug was almost five miles away from the nearest village, so she couldn't feel any other buildings. She stopped when she reached one of the large hills that loomed in the distance.

Her powers weren't of much use right now, but they calmed her. Unlike the others, she found the world outside the walls abrasive. The Lightborns had always been told that people outside the walls were savages, and while that wasn't exactly accurate, people weren't civilized in the way that she was used to. They hardly ever ate with silverware, they rarely cleaned their bed sheets, and they didn't bathe as often as they should have. The boys had taken to it immediately, but she needed more time. It didn't help that she was naturally restless nowadays. All she could think about in her moments alone was killing Carlin Filus, the murderer of her brothers Anthony and Thomas. Sometimes the only way to feel at peace and in control was to use her powers to survey the surroundings.

"Lilly?" She heard Rhys's voice and pulled her focus back to the pub.

Rhys and Darius lounged at one of the bar tables, eating a loaf of bread. "Yes?" she asked.

"Everything all right?" Rhys asked. "You looked to be in a trance of some sort."

"Just observing the area." She improved her posture and wandered over to the table.

"Well take a night off," Darius said as he took a massive bite. "Rhys and I are discussing our siblings. We'd like you to weigh in, Miss."

Her eyes narrowed when she heard her title. Darius had a way of saying it that made it sound pretentious and unneeded. "What about our siblings?"

"Just what they could do and everything," Darius said. "I heard your brother Thomas could read minds."

"That's true," she said and took a seat next to Rhys. "I do admit it was hard to be around him sometimes. He had a habit of making his findings known."

Rhys said, "I never fought him, but I was careful to keep my distance. Strategically he was a nightmare."

Before she could answer, the door to the kitchen opened, and Rebecca entered the room. "Hello," she said, pulling up a chair.

"Where's Neil?" Rhys asked as he tried to get a glance into the swinging kitchen door.

Rebecca visibly reddened. "He's upset."

Darius chuckled. "Let me guess, you tried to talk to him about his sweetheart?"

Rebecca let out a long breath. "That was not a good idea."

"No it was not," Rhys mused. "Maybe he just needs some sleep. I'll check on him in a bit."

Rebecca nodded silently. Her eyes slowly settled on Lilly. "Are you afraid of heights?"

Lilly smoothed her military coat. "Pardon?" she asked trying to keep her voice level.

"Are you afraid of heights?"

"No," Lilly said cautiously. "Anyone who has told you otherwise is a liar." She glanced around the table and realized Darius was a moment away from busting into laughter.

Rebecca's head turned to Rhys. "Are you a ruthless womanizer?" she asked.

Rhys gave her a startled look and shook his head. "No, Rebecca. That trait never grew on me."

Lilly cocked her head in confusion at Rebecca's strange attitude. She wanted to respond to all of it, but Rebecca was ready with more questions. "Can you read?" Rebecca finally asked Darius.

Darius's smile fell. "Yeah," he said as he took another huge bite of bread. "Of course I can read."

The others at the table shared nervous glances. Rhys looked like he was about to say something, then decided better of it. Lilly opened her mouth to speak, but a loud crack of thunder interrupted her. A smile made its way around the table. The group had learned early on that storms outside the Industrial City were powerful and often lasted for quite a while. A storm in the middle of the night usually meant that the bar would be inaccessible to the nearest village; therefore, closed for business. "Maybe we'll be able to spend a day downstairs," Darius said hopefully.

Rebecca leaned on an elbow wistfully. "And then Josephine and I can get some real sleep for a change. It's getting colder. Maybe we'll get snow."

"So Darius," Lilly cooed with a suppressed smile. "What's your favorite book?"

He shoved the remaining half of the loaf into his mouth. He made a grumble that sounded sort of like the words, "I don't know."

Rebecca gave Lilly a nervous look. Darius scared her. If he even threw a little bit of a temper tantrum she would need to find a new place of employment. Lilly responded with a wink. Nothing scared Lilly. Except for heights apparently. "Well then, what was the last book you read?"

Darius chewed. "You get mad at me when I try to talk with my mouth full."

"Rhys, hand me your little strategy book," she demanded.

Rhys sighed and pulled a tiny notebook from his pocket. "I don't condone this." Underneath his façade, his eyes alit with curiosity.

He handed the tiny notebook to Darius, who palmed it in his massive hands. It was a wonder if he'd even be able to turn the pages. "You want me to...?"

"Read something." Lilly said.

"No problem, Miss."

Suddenly, the door from the kitchen was thrown open and Neil arrived with a skip in his step. He seemed to have recovered quickly. "What's going on?" he asked and surveyed the table.

Rebecca motioned subtly with her head toward Darius who was desperately looking at Neil for help. "Tell me this is what I think it is," Neil snickered.

Darius's needful expression turned to one of exasperation. "You pests want to see me read?" he shouted. "Then you're gonna see me read."

He flipped a few pages and found one he liked. "Billy had a little job/ That kept him clothed and fed/ The Emperor had him fired/ So his friend could work, instead. / So Billy got some paper/ And a letter he did write. / And he took it to the Palace - / (Billy's head is on a spike.)"

The group stared at Darius who looked mighty pleased with himself. "What was that?" Rebecca asked.

"Did you seriously just quote *Little Billy*?" Neil said on the verge of uproarious laughter.

"What's Little Billy?" Rebecca asked.

"Little Billy was a propaganda campaign that was launched about thirty years ago. Every new parent in Altryon was given a book called *Little Billy's Nursery Rhymes*. It was a cultural phenomenon for a while," Rhys said. "But it was essentially just a list of precautions. Family members don't really partake in reading it, as the nursery rhymes are mainly used to disparage the families."

Darius shrugged. "Well there you have it. I have the ability to read. Let's move on. Have you heard that the Vapros eat children?"

"Not so fast," Lilly said. "You expect me to believe that Rhys Vapros, of all people, has written a piece of the Emperor's propaganda in his precious strategy book?"

Rhys put out his hand and Darius returned his book. "I'm fascinated by the idea of propaganda. Especially Little Billy, because they were making a mental impression on every child to respect the empire or not to trust the families or to fear what was outside the wall."

"This wasn't as funny as I'd hoped," Neil said. "Did we ever find out if Lilly is afraid of heights?"

"No," said Lilly.

"Yes!" said everyone else.

Within a few hours the storm had become violent enough to warrant a day outside of the attic. Rhys and Neil went to check on the production of the newest batch of ale and Rebecca tagged along to watch them. With Josephine sleeping, Darius and Lilly were left in the atrium with only the entertainment of each other's company.

"You know," Lilly said delicately as she approached the bar, "no one learns to read on their own. The Celerius family has always had a tradition of teaching letters and literature well past common proficiency."

Darius glared at her. He and Lilly got along fine, but this was the kind of stuff he hated. She didn't even realize she was being condescending. "That's real fascinating, Miss." Darius rubbed his temples. "Now if only they could teach you to manage your fear of heights."

She just about hissed at him. "I was trying to be nice, Darius. Maybe you should just realize that people could actually..." she trailed off.

"Finish their sentences?" Darius offered.

"Someone's coming up to the door," she whispered.

"In this storm?" Darius asked.

"Apparently."

At that exact moment the door was thrown open and what looked to be five Imperial guards entered. They were dripping wet, yet appeared to be in high spirits. "Five ales, girly!" called the one in the front.

There was a palpable second of tension as the guards stopped laughing and examined Lilly's coat. Then their eyes drifted to her face. She'd been foolish in protesting the haircut. Despite the trim, she still looked like a Celerius. *They should have cut it all off.* Darius thought. That auburn color was unmistakable.

His hand dropped behind the bar and palmed a metal mug. The guards looked at each other and their hands drifted to the hilts of their swords. The one in the front gulped audibly. "So… five drinks please." A small drop of sweat slid down his face.

Lilly glanced back at Darius questioningly. "Are you really going to pretend that this isn't about to become a bloodbath?" Darius asked the trembling guards.

The first guard stepped forward and tried to whisper under his breath, "Briggs, back to the outpost. Go get reinforcements."

A guard in the back bolted through the door into the rain. The guard in front tried to take a commanding stance. "In the name of the Emperor you two are both--"

Darius heard enough. He sent the metal mug straight into the guard's face. He fell to the ground, bleeding from his head. "Get the runner!" Darius called. He leapt over the bar and in front of the remaining three men.

Lilly bolted past the men. One tried to stop her, but she expertly ducked under his hands and off into the rain. Darius used the distraction to charge them. By lashing his arms out in a wide arc, as he tackled them, he was able to send the guards flying. He selected a nearby chair from a table and smashed it over the back of one guard who attempted to stand. He peered out into the rainy landscape for a moment. "I'll just wait here," he murmured.

Lilly wiped her hand over her eyes to clear them from the pouring rain. She anxiously turned, looking for the missing guard. If he made it back to the outpost, the entire Imperial military would soon be brought down upon them. She let her senses widen and absorbed the landscape. She could feel him riding the convoy less than a mile down the road toward Shipwreck Bay. He was probably trying to throw her off by taking a trail that didn't go to Abington, where the nearest outpost was located. She let her senses narrow and was bolting after the guard along the trail. It was a common topic of debate in Altryon. What was faster: a Celerius or a racehorse? The debate usually always ended the same way, with a chuckle and the affirmation that it would depend on the horse and the Celerius in question. When it came to Lilly and these horses, there was no question that Lilly was the faster party, mostly because she didn't have an Imperial convoy to pull.

Within a minute she could see the carriage in the distance. She silently cursed herself for leaving her sword back at the Golden Mug. She would have to fight this one with her bare hands. With her chest heaving and feet bleeding in her boots, she gripped the back end of the convoy. In an attempt to pull herself into the open back, she stumbled. The convoy dragged her through the mud and tore the skin from her knees. She cried out.

Lilly cursed herself once again as she pulled her bloody body into the open end of the convoy and felt her skin re-stitching together.

After a moment of rest, she looked around for a weapon to kill the guard. All she found were two pikes and a broadsword. Neither of them were suitable for her level of strength. Any thinner swords were apparently already in use. After a bit more rummaging, she found a small dagger and set out to finish her mission. She pulled herself up to the roof of the convoy with a grunt. Suddenly, she felt an Imperial boot kick her to the brink of consciousness. Apparently the guard had heard her scream earlier. He swung his sword at her and it nicked the side of her face. She rolled to the edge of the convoy. The guard swung down hard on the place where she had been a moment before. "I served your brother!" he cried over the sound of the pouring rain and hoof beats. "I mourn his death. But I know my duty."

She recognized the man. Briggs had been one of Anthony's close friends, long ago, and she remembered that her brother used to speak of his swordsmanship highly. He was quick, sure, but he was no match for her speed. Lilly stabbed the dagger into his foot, effectively pinning him to the roof of the convoy. He howled in pain and thrust his sword at her. She summersaulted out of the way and bolted to the front of the carriage. "Don't waste your pity on my family. I have none to give in return."

She jumped down to the platform where the reins dangled unattended. She grabbed them and tried to calm the horses. Suddenly she felt cold steel open her back and dropped to the platform in horrendous pain. The guard stood above her with a bloody sword and a murderous look in his eyes. His next few attempts to stab her were awkward and weak, as she was on the platform below and slightly out of reach. Her back was healing slowly. This was a deep cut.

She glanced at the horses pulling them ever closer to the outpost where she could expect an army of new adversaries. The guard threw the dagger that was messy with his blood at her. It embedded in the platform beside her. She considered stabbing one of the horses because she didn't have the ability to dodge the guard and manage the reins, but dismissed the idea quickly. She found the strength to cut down Imperial soldiers, but a horse was different. There was no way Lilly could ever kill a horse.

In another frantic thrust, he dipped the blade into her shoulder. She cried out as he let it dig deeper into her. She knew that in a few more moments he might stab her deep enough to nick her heart. That would be the end of her. Suddenly, the sword clattered to the ground next to her. Through the monotonous pounding of the rain she heard a thumping noise, as if his body had collapsed. She took advantage of the moment of peace and used the reins to pull the horses from a gallop into trot, then to a halt. She rolled off the platform and into the grass on the side of the pathway. She took the Guard's sword with her. Her vision was blurred and her head swimming, but she kept an eye on the roof of the convoy. If the guard came lumbering off, she would attempt to stand and face him. Otherwise, she would lie on the sturdy ground and let it support her.

After she could see clearly, she stood and used her free hand to feel her back. There were no open wounds. That was lucky. She skeptically wandered back to the convoy. She could see that the guard's body was lying still, one hand hanging off the edge. She pulled it hard and his body slipped off the convoy into the mud. She quickly found the affliction that had hindered his attempts to kill her. There was an arrow buried up to its feather in his forehead.

Lilly paled. She could very well still be in range of this mystery archer. She looked up and around at the uneven landscape of Volteria. She didn't see a soul, but it would be incredibly easy for the archer to hide behind a ridge or on the other side of a hill. She pulled the arrow from the guard's head and wiped it clean on the grass. Then she began the long jog home. The Golden Mug was safe, for today at least.

VOLTERIA

Chapter Ten

MISTY HOLLOW
BIANCA BLACKMORE

MISTY HOLLOW WAS KNOWN FOR MANY THINGS. FOR INSTANCE, IT SOLD large red lanterns with depictions of its heroes on them. Ancient mayors and warriors adorned their streets in the form of brightly glowing lanterns. The lanterns were necessary, of course, because Misty Hollow was constantly draped in a think layer of fog. No one knew exactly why. Many citizens claimed the city was cursed because it had once unjustly executed its mayor after mistaking him for a common criminal. Others claimed it was due to the fact that the city was beneath a mountain and also happened to be on the seashore. In recent months, though, Misty Hollow became known for something entirely different: its strong military presence and the Imperial Light-house. Of all the burdens bestowed upon the people of Misty Hollow, the Lighthouse was by far the worst. It was continuously manned by a series of troops and tall enough to observe all "misdoings" in the village. It had turned the Imperial occupation into a rebel slaughter. A city once lit by colorful lanterns now had a very dark center.

Luckily Bianca Blackmore also had a dark side and she'd travelled to Misty Hollow for one reason and one reason only: to take control of the Lighthouse and loosen the Empire's grip on Misty Hollow. There was a lot at stake for this mission. The Wolf had promised her a Lieutenant's position if she could drive out the military forces occupying the lighthouse without using rebel reinforcements.

She crept through the city and made sure to keep out of the lighthouse's gaze. It took nearly an hour to make it to the building across the street from the lighthouse. She readied her knives and steadied her breathing. After a quick glance around the corner, she gathered that there were two guards outside the main entrance lazily standing watch. She bolted around the corner silently and threw two knives as she ran. Each found its way into a guard's neck. She made it to the door and held up their bodies so that their armor wouldn't clang when they fell. She used her heel to knock on the main door and held her breath. The door opened. "Your shift isn't over for--" The soldier screamed. Bianca dropped the bodies and spun away so she could throw her next knife. The soldier at the door fell to the ground and she bolted in. She threw her last five knives once she reached the center of the room. The three guards inside didn't stand a chance. Their bodies clattered to the ground. She collected her knives and started for the staircase, but before her foot hit the first step she heard a cabinet open. A soldier popped out with a rifle in hand. "No moves, girly!" he yelled.

Bianca growled audibly. It was stupid not to check the room fully before heading upstairs. "Drop the knives," he commanded.

She did. He laughed. "Let me guess? One of the Wolf's protégés? I'll send you back to him full of holes."

Bianca prepared for the worst. Instead she heard the guard groan in pain and crumple to the floor. She turned and saw a spike sticking out of his chest. Anastasia pulled it out of him and rewrapped it around her wrist. "Are you getting slow, Bianca?"

Bianca glared at her. "What are *you* doing here?"

"Can't a sister just drop by to say hello?"

"No," Bianca said and hurried up the stairs.

"Can a sister drop by to help you waste these Imperial fools?"

Bianca paused. "Yes."

They climbed the spiral staircase quickly and approached the next door without making a sound. Bianca kicked in the door on the first try. There was only one guard inside. He managed to dodge Bianca's first knife, but her second found his eye. Anastasia's spike silenced him before he could scream in pain. Bianca walked into the room, cautiously this time. She made sure to check all corners and side rooms. The room had a ladder in the center that led to a wooden hatch. Clearly this led to the very top of the lighthouse. "After you," Anastasia said.

Bianca scowled and climbed. She was aware of how terrible this situation was tactically. There was no possible way to open the hatch and also get a jump on whoever was up there, unless they were looking completely away from the hatch. She opened it slowly and peered through. She saw an Imperial pair of legs facing the other way. If she were quiet enough she'd be able to get the jump on the soldier. She began to climb through the hatch when the hinges creaked. She winced. The soldier turned and stomped down on the hatch, effectively knocking her through the opening, off of the ladder and onto the wooden ground below. She howled as her shoulder cracked on the ground. The soldier peered down and readied his gun to finish Bianca off. Anastasia threw her spike upwards. "You might want to roll to the side," she said to her sister. With one yank of the chain she pulled down the newly impaled soldier.

Bianca rolled out of the way and the soldier's body slammed into the floor. Bianca sat up and glowered at Anastasia. "What?" Anastasia asked panting for air. "I warned you."

Bianca looked like she was about to tell her sister off when suddenly bullets began to fly through the ceiling. Bianca somersaulted under a table and Anastasia backed against the wall. The remaining soldiers were shooting through the floor in an attempt to kill the intruders.

"They're about to reload. Follow my lead!" Anastasia yelled.

The second bullets stopped flying Anastasia was up the ladder. She was able to dodge the sword waiting for her and she hurled her spike. Her offenses proved to be enough to distract the guards. Bianca followed up to the top floor and sent her knives flying. That was enough to eliminate the remaining soldiers. Anastasia pulled the one she'd hooked with the spike forward and knocked him unconscious with a jab from her elbow.

The two sisters fell to the ground in synchronized exhaustion. They lay there, breathing heavily and struggling to let the adrenaline pass. "Why are you here?" Bianca asked.

Anastasia continued to breathe heavily. She didn't answer.

Bianca staggered to her feet and examined the top floor.

"What are you gonna do?" Anastasia asked.

"I'm gonna take down the Imperial flag and put out the light so that the rebels can take the lighthouse and form a stronghold here."

"You know the Empire's gonna be pretty upset, right?" Anastasia asked as she looked over the balcony.

"They're already pretty upset," Bianca said. "Why are you here, Anastasia?"

"Look, I know you're upset that I went after those Lightborns a few months back. I'm sorry. I didn't know they were your friends," Anastasia said.

"You tried to kill my best friend's little brother." Bianca shuddered as she remembered the night Anastasia had tried to help Michael Taurlum kill Darius and even Rhys when he'd tried to help. Even today, Darius was suffering from the shock that Michael, his own flesh and blood, had hired Anastasia to kill him over the family inheritance. Bianca still reeled when she thought of how close Neil came to losing Rhys that night too. She had not forgiven Anastasia for her part in the whole mess.

"I didn't know it was him," Anastasia growled. "And, anyway, I'm still paying for that one." She pulled up her shirt and exposed a stitched wound on her stomach. "I'm here to make it up to you, Bianca."

Bianca narrowed her eyes. "You helping me clear the lighthouse doesn't do it."

"Your Lightborn friends are in trouble. And so are you."

Bianca chuckled. "Because the empire is looking for us?"

"No, because the Imperial Doctor is looking for you. And so is the rest of the Pack."

Bianca stared at Anastasia disbelievingly. "Oh," she said quietly.

Anastasia rewrapped her chain and stared at her sister. "Yeah. Oh."

Chapter Eleven

THE GOLDEN MUG
DARIUS TAURLUM

DARIUS HOBBLED BACK INTO THE GOLDEN MUG. APPARENTLY EVERYONE had gathered in the kitchen. "It's done!" he called.

Rhys popped his head out. "Any sign of Lilly?"

"No," Darius said. "If she didn't take care of that guard we're gonna be in real trouble though."

Rhys walked over hesitantly. "This is probably the wrong time but…" he paused, "I don't have any 'Little Billy' in my strategy book."

Darius glared at him. "I seem to remember one."

"You really can't read, huh?" Rhys asked.

"And you can't keep your voice down, can you?" Darius hissed. He could feel his cheeks reddening. "I appreciate you covering for me, but a good friend would stop there."

Rhys furrowed his brow. "Well… Um…" He snapped his fingers. "Lilly."

"What about Lilly?" Darius asked.

Rhys sat down at the table with Darius despite the fact that he was growling under his breath. "You and Lilly bicker constantly. You think she's gonna let this one go?"

Darius shook his head and began a sentence, then decided not to finish it. "She's..." he said. "I proved it."

Rhys winced. "Really? Not everyone who can recite Little Billy is exactly a literary genius."

Darius groaned. He didn't want to draw attention to this conversation. "Do you have a solution or are you just here to make fun of me?"

"I'm not making fun," Rhys persisted. "I'm offering my services. I can teach you."

"To read?" Darius asked.

Rhys wasn't shaken by Darius's unenthused tone. "Absolutely. I can teach you within a few weeks. Best of all, you can prove Lilly wrong."

"I've tried before. Letters don't come easily to me."

Rhys opened his strategy book and pulled out a stack of loose papers fastened together by a ring in the corner. "Cheat sheets," he said handing them to Darius.

"Look, little buddy... I appreciate this but—" Darius stopped as he noticed the drawings on the cards.

"There's a weapon or something related to battle which represents each letter of the alphabet. A is for Axe, B is for Battle, C is for Catapult..." Rhys went through each card explaining the picture and pointing to the letter at the top.

Darius stared at the little cards, flipping through them as he quietly repeated Rhys's words. Darius was obviously fascinated by the drawings. "You are quite the artist, little buddy." Darius drummed his fingers on the table, deep in thought. "Fine," he said. "We can practice when no one's around."

"Deal." Rhys said. "You'll be a scholar in no time." He grabbed Darius' hand that was drumming absently on the table and placed it on his forearm. Darius opened his mouth to object, but Rhys interjected, "Wait! Drum your fingers on your arm as you read the cards."

Darius stared at Rhys in confusion. "Are you messing with me?"

"No! I would never do that! I take this very seriously. I tutored a lot of people when I was in school and I developed a theory."

Darius chuckled. "I should have known there was going to be a Rhys Vapros theory involved."

Rhys raised a finger for emphasis and said, "Yes, but it's more than a theory really. I had unusual success as a tutor, so I know it works in many cases. Tap your fingers on your forearm as you study. It activates areas of the brain involved in—"

"All right! All right!" Darius interrupted, " I don't need a science lesson too. I'll drum my fingers. Anything else? Stand on my head and sing?"

"Well actually, music can be quite helpful—" Rhys stopped as the front door was pushed in and Lilly reappeared, drenched and panting. Hearing the door, Neil and Rebecca exited the kitchen.

"Are we in trouble?" Darius asked Lilly as he quickly slid the cards into his pocket.

Everyone besides Josephine had gathered in the main area. Miraculously, she'd slept through the fight. This was a blessing. She'd be furious to see that they were engaging in rebel acts. She wanted them to stay far away from the fires of war. Lilly was soaking wet and looked exhausted. Her royal blue coat looked navy blue when it was drenched in rainwater. She wasn't answering the question. Darius rubbed his forehead nervously. "Because if I have to pack up all two of my belongings you should tell me now."

Lilly dropped the arrow on the bar and crossed her arms. "He's dead," she said definitively.

Rhys examined her. "Where's the arrow from?"

"Someone was looking out for me," she said. "This has happened before. There's some mysterious archer who's been protecting me since we were in Altryon."

The group looked at her skeptically. "Did you see him?" Neil asked. Lilly shook her head. "Any chance there's just a lot of archers with incredibly bad aim?" Neil asked. "You saw how difficult it was for us to get out of the city's walls. What are the chances that someone snuck through to protect you?"

Lilly was speechless.

"Well I carried those soldiers down to the shed by the river," Darius said, changing the subject. "We've got an Imperial prison going now. Are we still pretending that we're not part of this revolution?"

No one said anything. "Just asking," Darius said. "I'm fine with living in denial."

"If the danger's over I'd love to hit the hay," Neil said. "If that's alright with you all."

The rest of the group murmured in agreement. "At least you guys keep this place interesting," Rebecca murmured as she trudged off into the kitchen. She always liked to stay and spend time with the Lightborns, but she also worked during the day, which wreaked havoc on her sleep schedule.

Once the main bar was empty, Darius fished the cards out of his pockets. He rubbed his eyes and then stared at the letters with new perspective. He was the kind of man who could lift ten times his weight and punch through solid concrete. How hard could learning twenty-six letters be?

Chapter Twelve

SHIPWRECK BAY ARMORY
THE PACK

THE BELL ATTACHED TO THE WOODEN DOOR CHIMED AS A CUSTOMER entered Shipwreck Bay's highest end armory. The smith sat behind the counter and barely looked up to see who had entered. He was writing in a ledger. "Sword or shield?" he asked.

The customer giggled, then suppressed it with a fake cough. "Don't you sell armor?"

"It's a cute little saying," the smith said unenthusiastically. "Do you want armor or weapons?

"I'm curious." There was clearly something wrong with the customer. He was shaking. "Do you know what the best type of armor is for sneaking around?"

"I'd recommend no armor for being silent," the smith said, glancing up from his work.

"No," the customer said. "The best armor for sneaking is leather armor."

"Why's that?" asked the smith.

"Because it's made of Hyde!"

The smith looked up at the customer and the stranger erupted into furious laughter. The smith's eyes narrowed. "That's funny," he said without humor.

"I see your fingers reaching for a weapon," the stranger said. "I'm curious. Is it because you remember me? Or because you hated my joke that much?"

The smith's eyes widened in surprise and stayed wide as fear began to set in.

"We were best friends once, Tyler," the customer said.

The smith scrambled backwards. "Lester Buchwald," the smith said, recognition finally dawning. "You unholy demon. I will kill you if you take another step forward."

The Hyena shook his head and bared his metal teeth. "No one outside my family calls me Lester anymore, not since the orphanage. Out here they call me something else."

The smith grabbed a sword. "What do you want, Hyena?"

"I just want to catch up!" the Hyena giggled. "I want to talk about the orphanage. I want to talk to you about your life! Consider this our twenty-year reunion... After all..." His eyes shone with evil intent. "Everyone who made it out is here."

The smith pointed the sword at the Hyena's chest. "I always wondered if I'd get the chance to see you again. To slice you in half for what you did."

The Hyena was bouncing now with furious excitement. "Didn't you always wonder about Wallace?" the Hyena asked. "That kid with the cleft lip? I was always curious... Who adopts the ugly ones?"

"No one adopted anyone," the smith said. "Because of what you did to them."

The Hyena took a fast step forward and the smith swung at him. The Hyena ducked under it and lunged up with his head. He head-butted the smith under the chin and the smith was thrown back into the wall. The Hyena shook his head. "No one ever wants to hear my side of the story," the Hyena pouted. "People say that I was bullied and that I stole the kids away one by one. People say that I became a cannibal because I was driven to madness by the bullying by the other children. They say I'm the reason the orphanage closed."

"That's exactly what happened," the smith whispered.

"I know," the Hyena said. "But no one asks to hear it from me!" He cackled and then shrugged overdramatically. "So how have you been? How are the kids?"

"I don't have kids," the smith said.

"That's good," the Hyena said. "You don't have to be worried about who they're hanging out with. Or whether they're eating the other kids."

"If you're here to finish what you started, then do it." the smith said.

The Hyena dragged a chair from the corner of the room and sat down. It was noticeable once he climbed into the chair that he wasn't a very tall man. His feet dangled in the air, inches above the floor. "I'm not going to kill you to check you off some imaginary list, Tyler. You just happen to own this store and I just happen to need it. You also just happen to be the one person who knows how it was back then. We're like soul mates, Tyler." The Hyena blew him an over the top kiss and when he did his metal teeth were clearly visible, center stage. "You should find peace in knowing that I was adopted eventually, even though the orphanage closed." The Hyena spoke wistfully. "By a nice man. He even gave me these!" He grinned widely to show that his lower jaw had been outfitted with enough metal to make a sword. "So I guess someone does look out for the ugly ones."

The smith had been waiting to attack unexpectedly, but spontaneity was the Hyena's specialty and he dodged the attack easily. He leapt at the smith and with one quick chomp his prey lay still. The Hyena giggled to himself at a private joke and pulled the body into the back room where the forge was. The Hyena then began to prepare his new shop. For a moment he stopped and reflected on the fact that he was now the sole survivor of the Abington Orphanage. He smiled at his reflection in a polished shield and twirled around as joy overcame him. "Now wherever I go, it's a reunion!" he sang out loud to himself. He scampered over to the forge and admired the smith's tools. "It's time to prepare for some guests."

Chapter Thirteen

THE GOLDEN MUG
NEIL VAPROS

Neil didn't know where he was.

He was in some kind of forest, that was for sure, but he couldn't quite remember how he got there. Trees and fog surrounded him; if he hadn't known better he would have guessed these were the orchards of Altryon. But he'd left Altryon behind months ago.

A warm light cut through the fog. It glowed more brightly than the sun. Neil shielded his eyes from the glow and took a few steps backward. "Hello?" he asked skeptically.

A thousand voices answered him in unison. "Neil Vapros," they chorused. Neil clapped his hands over his ears. "Step forward."

Keeping his ears covered, Neil took a wary step. He couldn't remember if he had his knife with him. "Who are you?"

Silence, although the light continued to shine.

He took a deep breath and tried again. "What are you?"

The chorus boomed with laughter. "Decide for yourself."

"That's helpful," Neil muttered as he peered further into the light. "Can you give me a hint?"

The light began to shift and collect itself, realigning until it outlined a human form. "Do you understand now?"

The honest answer was no, but the longer Neil looked, the more familiar the scene became. "You're . . . the Man with the Golden Light?" he guessed. "The one from the legend? The one who gave my ancestors their abilities?"

The outline bowed its head once in a nod. Hesitantly, Neil got to his knees and bowed.

"Stand, Neil," the outline commanded. "I want to speak to you face to face."

Neil stumbled to his feet, trying not to stare. He didn't really know where the man's face was supposed to be. "Your Majesty," he began uncertainly. Was that how one addressed the Man with the Golden Light? "Not to sound ungrateful or anything, but why are you here?"

"You need help," the outline answered. "You need guidance. You all do."

Neil shoved his fingers through his hair. "You could say that. You asked our families to protect Altryon and we failed." A terrifying thought occurred to him. "You're not going to take away my abilities, are you?"

The outline shook his head. "I won't blame the children for the sins of their fathers." He brushed past Neil and began to glide through the forest. Neil followed closely at his golden heels.

"So why are you here, then?" Neil asked after a few seconds of silence.

The Man with the Golden Light slowed to a stop. "I am here to offer you guidance. If you choose to accept it."

"I'll accept any help I can get," Neil said bluntly.

"Outside the walls of Altryon, the feud is over, Neil Vapros," the outline said solemnly. "The families are at peace. If you choose to let the feud *live, you will doom your descendants. You must let it end, Neil Vapros. You must let your wounds heal. Lightborn against Lightborn is not the way to a better world."*

Neil furrowed his brow. "So, what about the rebellion, then?" he asked. "You don't want us to join?"

"The rebellion is a just cause. My people are oppressed by the Empire. They need to free themselves. You can join and you can fight, but do not make this war about the families. Make it about the common man." The outline began to dissolve. "We will speak again, Neil Vapros," he said as he faded into the fog.

"But--wait!" Neil called. "I have so many things to ask you!"

"In due time," the man whispered as he disappeared into nothing. The ground began to shake violently. Neil's knees gave way and he crumpled to the soft forest floor.

Neil cleared his eyes in the middle of the night and sat upright. It was just a dream. All a dream. When he looked to his left he realized in horror that Rhys wasn't in bed beside him. He clutched his chest and tried to keep from panicking. The Golden Mug was closed until the storm subsided so they'd actually started to sleep during the nighttime again. Rhys was probably just up at odd hours, as he was known for having insomnia. Neil crept out of his bed and into the hallway. He materialized out of the hatch and into the kitchen. He could hear conversation in the bar.

"I ended the paragraph here," he heard Rhys say.

"Why?" Darius replied.

"Because I wrote some dialogue. Every time someone speaks you jump to the next paragraph," Rhys said.

Neil grabbed a slice of cake left over from dinner that evening. Josephine had prepared a special feast in celebration of her day off. They were all in extra good moods since they were able to be awake during normal hours for a change. It was unlike Darius to leave any leftovers, so Neil smiled at his luck. Neil pushed his head through the kitchen door and saw the two of them hunched over a dimly lit candle and Rhys's strategy book. "Right away?" Darius asked his teacher.

"No. Not always right away," Rhys said. He pulled the book back toward himself and flipped through more pages. "Let me show you some examples."

"This is a confusing scene," Neil said, swallowing a bite of cake.

The two of them turned in shock and a little too much fear for the mundane nature of what they were doing. "Darius was just reading through my strategy book," Rhys said.

"That's nice," Neil said. "Why is he doing it in the dead of night though?"

"You try keeping a normal sleep schedule in this place," Darius grumbled.

Neil sat down and propped his feet up at a table. "Fair enough. I gotta say for someone who can read, you sure need a lot of things explained."

Darius glared at him. "What are you saying, Vapros?"

Neil chuckled. "Come on, Darius," he said. "It's okay if you can't read. No one thinks you can anyway."

"Well they're wrong. I'm an academic type, like Rhys," Darius said. "Now shut up or I'll crush your head in the palm of my hand."

"How academic," Neil said licking a bit of frosting off his fingers. "Like you, Darius, I was an avid reader of Little Billy as a child. One particular rhyme springs to mind."

"Neil, knock it off," Rhys said. "That was a mean one."

Neil held back his desire to rattle off the nursery rhyme. "You know which one I'm talking about, right?" he asked Darius.

"Little Billy had a friend/ A Taurlum, big and strong. /And the Taurlum couldn't read/ Because his brain was just too small," Darius recited. "Billy tried to teach him/ How to read instead of punch, / But the Taurlum couldn't learn/ And ate the boy and book for lunch."

"Yeah," Neil said. "That's the one."

"Moral of the story is, don't make me angry or I'll eat you," Darius said with a grin. "And this book."

"That's my book," Rhys said.

"I'll get my own book. And then eat it. Along with you. For being a jerk."

"You're a barbarian," Neil said with a chuckle. After he stopped laughing, Neil realized something. "I don't hear any raindrops."

"Yeah," Darius said. "Storm's over. We gotta head up soon. Before people come looking for drinks."

Suddenly Neil heard the window behind him crack and a bullet ricocheted off of Darius's back. "Did someone just try to...?" Rhys asked.

Instinct drove Neil to materialize in between Rhys and the window so that his brother would be out of the line of fire. Before Rhys even knew his brother was protecting him, a bullet tore through Neil's back and he fell to the ground screaming. Darius flipped the table and the three of them hid behind it as another bullet struck the weak wood and splintered it. Neil's back was on fire. As he collapsed he could feel Rhys pawing at his back to remove his shirt and assess the damage. "Darius!" Rhys said. "Can you handle this?"

"Why me?" Darius asked.

"Because you're bulletproof," Rhys said.

Darius gave one last look at Neil's writhing form and leapt over the table. He pulled the front door from its hinges and charged out into the night. Neil felt blackness descending on him as the pain pulled at his consciousness. "Rhys…" Neil groaned in pain.

Rhys crawled behind the bar and came back with a knife and a bottle of alcohol. "It's okay!" Rhys said. "I'm gonna fix this. I think it just missed an artery. It could just be a flesh wound."

Neil was hyperventilating. It certainly didn't feel like a flesh wound. Before Neil could protest, his little brother, now his surgeon, was going to work on his back. He grabbed a large fragment of the table and bit it with all his might. "You took a bullet for me," Rhys breathed.

"And you're gonna cut it out of me," Neil said through the fragment of wood. "Deal?"

Neil heard Rhys gulp. "Deal."

Chapter Fourteen

THE GOLDEN MUG
THE PACK

THE MARKSMAN CURSED HIMSELF SILENTLY AS HE WATCHED HIS BLONDE-
headed target flip a table and obscure his next shot. It had been
foolish to shoot the blonde one first. He'd been told about his iron
skin, but he'd assumed that the back of the neck was a kill shot for
anyone, tough skin or otherwise. He reloaded his prized rifle and
fired another shot into the table, effectively splitting off a fragment
of wood. He sighed. He'd lost the element of surprise. Maybe it was
time to escape into the woods and wait for them to lower their de-
fenses again. He'd shot one of the fugitives in the back. Maybe that
one would be dead by morning.

He stood up and brushed off his knees. With a final look down
at the pub, he realized with horror that not all of his targets had
stayed pinned down. The blonde one tore the front door off of its
hinges and charged out of the building with murderous purpose.
The Marksman fired his rifle and struck the boy in his kneecap. His

enemy didn't even falter and charged at him with renewed determination. The Marksman backpedaled and fired shots from the pistols at his sides, but they bounced off the target's unprotected legs like raindrops. He had fewer weak spots than the Marksman had anticipated. Darius closed the distance between them and swung the door like a club. The Marksman ducked under it with his extraordinary flexibility and rolled backwards. "You're going to pay for every bullet you fired here today," Darius spat from behind his door.

"You're incorrect," the Marksman said. "I'm going to *be paid* for every bullet I fire here today."

Darius swung again. Just like before, the Marksman retreated out of striking distance. This time he turned around and fled into the forest with his attacker at his back. He grabbed a tree branch and within a few seconds was up in the branches. With a mighty cry, Darius shattered the tree's base and it fell to the ground with The Marksman in its branches. The Marksman landed without hurting himself, but not in time to escape his pursuer. Darius caught him by the foot and pulled his flailing body back toward him. The Marksman spun around and jabbed his hand into Darius's weak navel. Darius paled and dropped both the assassin and the door. The Marksman scanned Darius's body, absorbing this newfound information. "Pressure points work on you. How interesting. Now I know where your weak spots are."

Darius raised his fists. "Listen, friend," he growled. "To me, every piece of your body is a weak spot."

The Marksman lunged at Darius and ducked under both of his rapid-fire punches. The Marksman jabbed Darius right underneath his arm and it seemed to go limp. The Marksman retreated out of range before Darius could fully recover. Finally, a tactic that worked. On his next attack the Marksman delivered a snap kick to the inside of Darius's thigh where several nerves met in the average human. However, there was no weak spot here and the force of the Marksman's kick, redirected back onto him, cracked the bone. He bit back his scream but his motion was limited. Darius stepped in and smashed his elbow across his face before he could recover from the fractured bone. The Marksman collapsed and the next feeling he experienced was the cold ground against his face. He tried to look around, but his eyes seemed out of control and sank into the back of his head.

He felt the boy pick him up and hoist him over his shoulder. He babbled in protest to no avail. He knew for a fact that if his father, the Doctor, learned of his failure he'd be denied the elements that were essential to his life. Before darkness could set in, he focused his energy and manually cleared his mind. He needed focus if he was going to escape this. He shifted his weight and realized that the Taurlum's grip was as tough as his skin. Despite how hopeless this situation might seem for someone else, the Marksman remained calm. He knew what it took to escape a trap: patience and an undying sense of self-preservation. Fortunately, he had both.

Chapter Fifteen

THE GOLDEN MUG
DARIUS TAURLUM

"**WHAT IN THE NAME OF ALL THAT IS HOLY HAS BEEN GOING ON DOWN** here?" Josephine cried as Darius entered with the body of a semi-conscious assassin draped over his shoulder.

"We have a rather aggressive customer," Darius said.

Darius surveyed the room. The table was still flipped, the windows were shattered, and the door was missing. Neil was lying on the ground unconscious from pain, and Rhys was behind the bar, rummaging through drawers and cabinets with blood soaked hands. "I've told you," she said as she knelt next to Neil and checked his pulse with two fingers, "I won't have revolutionary activity in this house. You told me you wanted solace from that."

"We do, Josephine," Darius said. "Believe me. Most of us want to move on from all this. But it seems the Empire is coming to us."

The Marksman groaned in his arms. Darius dropped him onto the floor with a thud. "An assassin?" Josephine asked.

"Looks like it," Darius said.

The Marksman had a short military haircut and a weather beaten face. Scars covered the visible parts of his skin and his eyes, though dull from near unconsciousness, were a bright hazel that glowed yellow in the light of the Golden Mug. His entire outfit looked like it had been assembled one piece at a time on the run, a shirt here, a vest there, pants somewhere else. His choice of style was chaotic and looked hastily put together, but paid assassins were never the fashion-forward types.

Lilly and Rebecca entered from the kitchen. "Do you have a good reason for waking everyone in the pub?" Lilly asked. She paused when she noticed Neil's body. "Oh."

"Yeah 'oh.' Does nearly getting murdered make the list of things you'll roll out of bed for, Miss?" Darius asked.

"Easy there," Josephine commanded. "Rhys, what's the status with Neil?"

"He's alive and he'll stay alive," Rhys said. "Provided I can stitch him up. This guy was using small bullets. Probably for the sake of precision. If Neil hadn't materialized in front of me, I'd be dead."

The room was silent. Darius noticed that Rebecca was shaking violently. Even though she was from outside the walls, she clearly wasn't used to seeing trauma. A friend on the ground with a bullet-hole in his back was second nature for the fugitives. Or maybe it reminded her of what had happened to her parents. He was astounded at Josephine's unshaken resolve. She had clearly seen her fair share of action. Suddenly the assassin on the floor began to speak. Everyone in the room jumped, Rebecca the highest. "You can mop up that blood and stitch up that boy, but it will make no difference. The Pack is coming for you. More bullets will follow. If you're lucky enough to die before you meet the Doctor himself."

"Not a single word of that made sense to me," Darius said. "I elect that I crush his ribs with my foot right now. All in favor say, aye."

"Aye," said Lilly.

"Don't!" Josephine said. "I know what a few of those words mean. This man is a Venator."

"That's not good," Rhys said. "I think."

"No," Josephine said. "It's not."

"What's a Venator?" Darius asked.

Josephine looked conflicted about answering. "We can discuss the Venator later. For now we need to focus on the task at hand. This man has answers you need. The Pack never sends one assassin to cover an important job. They're a unit. We'll need to know more."

"I thought revolutionary acts were forbidden in the pub," Rebecca said. Her voice was equal parts fear and fascination.

Josephine tied the curly mess that was her hair into a ponytail and approached the Marksman. With one swift kick she knocked him straight out. "I'm willing to make an exception for uninvited guests," she said. "Tie him up well and tight. He shouldn't be able to breathe properly. Store him in one of the back rooms and lock the door. We'll interrogate him later." She pointed at Rhys. "There's a needle and thread in the kitchen in the same place where we keep the matches. Move Neil into one of the public rooms. I want us to be able to keep an eye on him in case of infection."

The entire room stared at her. "What?" she asked. "You think I just serve drinks and give haircuts? Come on. Let's get to it."

With that the room sprang into action. While Darius and Lilly argued over the best way to tie up the Marksman so he wouldn't be able to slip away, Rhys and Rebecca discussed the best form of sterilization so that Neil wouldn't be able to slip away in an entirely different fashion.

Chapter Sixteen

THE GOLDEN MUG
NEIL VAPROS

NEIL AWOKE PEACEFULLY FOR THE FIRST TIME IN MONTHS. FOR A FEW seconds he felt serene peace as the soft blankets wrapped him and caressed him. That is, until he woke fully and the searing pain in his back reached the pain receptors in his brain. He shifted slightly and resisted the urge to whimper. "You were shot," Rhys said from the small bench at the side of the bed.

He looked liked he'd been just staring at Neil with his big jade eyes, awaiting his awakening. "Yeah, Rhys. I know," Neil said hoarsely. "I was there. Everything hurts."

"It wasn't serious," Rhys said, bringing a mug of water to Neil's parched lips. "I don't exactly have the expertise of a real surgeon, but I was able to save you."

"I could have died, Rhys," Neil said after swallowing a few long gulps. Even though it was directed at Rhys, it sounded like he was saying it to himself. "That could have been the end."

"You've almost died lots of times," Rhys said. "You've probably almost died twenty times at least."

"Not since we left the city," Neil said. "Not since I decided that I didn't want to be part of the revolution. I thought I'd live a long happy life outside of the walls and away from the Empire."

Rhys balled up his hands and pushed them against his chin reflectively. "Two things," Rhys said. "To start, you say you don't want to be part of the revolution, but you still act like you're getting ready for a war sometimes. When I wanted someone to go fight those guards by that ravine you were the first one out the door." Neil didn't say anything. He just stared at the ceiling. "And second of all, you still could die. We all could. Whether we want to be a part of this or not, the Emperor is coming after us. Apparently now he's enlisted the help of an elite group of assassins."

"What happened to the one that shot me?" Neil asked.

"Darius caught him and now we've got him tied up in the back room."

"Is this a front room?" Neil asked as he tried to sit up. He'd been wrapped tightly in the blankets and he found it hard to pull out of them in his wounded state.

Rhys gently pushed Neil back to a lying position. "Josephine is closing the Golden Mug until we can decide what to do." He paused. "We're probably going to have to leave, Neil. We can't endanger Josephine and Rebecca."

Neil had been fighting that truth for a long time. They loved staying at the Golden Mug, but every day they slept there brought their hosts closer to the Empire's wrath. "That's fair. But where do we go?" Neil asked.

"Maybe Shipwreck Bay?" Rhys wondered. "I've heard it has the least amount of Imperial soldiers."

Neil blinked a few times and realized that he was sweating heavily. He pulled his arms out of the blankets. "If you want to join the revolution I want you to just tell me," Neil said firmly.

Rhys sighed. "It's just... you didn't join because you didn't want to lose any more people after Jennifer. Darius didn't want to kill anyone after he killed Michael, and Lilly was grieving Jonathan. We all had perfectly good reasons to avoid the revolution at first..."

"And now?" Neil asked.

"Now, you could lose people no matter where they are. We're being hunted. Lilly seems to have recovered well enough. In fact, she seems anxious. And angry. Darius is jumping right back into combat again. Maybe we're ready," Rhys said. "I know you wanted a life away from this, but they're ripping it away from you piece by piece and soon they'll do it person by person."

Neil pursed his lips. "I have to think about this. Just a little more."

Rhys patted him on the shoulder. "Sure," he said. "I'll let you sleep."

Rhys stood up to leave and Neil felt something push its way out of his mouth. "We have to tell Lilly."

Rhys didn't turn around. "I thought we were gonna wait."

"I thought I'd have time, or that we'd have time, but if we're really getting back into the action, I don't want to die without her knowing."

Rhys looked around a few times, as if they were being spied on, and sat back down. "I'm not saying that I'm against this, but if I were I'd have two reasons for it," he said quietly. "One is that the alliance between Lightborns is already fragile. Lilly and Darius are at each other's throats all the time. You fight with Darius sometimes. I'm just saying. It might not be the best thing if she knows about Edward."

"Look," Neil said more forcefully. "She told us that she hasn't been able to sleep properly since Edward was killed. When she does she has terrible nightmares. Maybe she'll appreciate the fact that we're getting ahead of it and telling her face-to-face."

Rhys laced his fingers together. "The second thing we need to worry about is Jennifer's legacy."

Neil tried to sit up but quickly laid back down as pain shot through his back. "Look, Jennifer told me and only me because she felt like she had to with Victoria being gone. I then made the decision to tell you because I felt you needed to know more about why she was the way she was. Doesn't it help to know it? Don't you understand her better? She killed the only boy she ever loved. Her legacy will survive if others know how pained she was."

Rhys didn't look convinced and Neil wondered what his little brother thought of Jennifer's memory. Rhys said, "I understand. I'm just saying that this might not be the best time to come clean about Jennifer's history with Edward. We talk about her a lot. It's nice to keep her memory alive through stories. Once Lilly knows, that all stops. Can you imagine trying to tell a story about Jennifer after Lilly knows that she killed her brother?"

"I just want to consider coming clean," Neil said. "I know it might not be the smartest decision, but I just almost died. I want to know that if that were the end, you'd tell Lilly at some point. All she talks about is tracking down her brother's killers. How long can we deny her the truth? Not knowing is tearing her apart. Isn't this the right thing to do?"

Rhys rubbed his eyes. "We can talk about this later," he said. "I want to come back to this with fresh minds. Lilly won't see Jennifer's pain and grief over Edward as justification for killing him. We'll forever just be related to the girl who killed her brother. It'll renew our place as her enemy in her mind."

"Isn't the feud behind us?" Neil persisted, even though he was growing fainter.

"I want to think it is," Rhys said. "But I think we should wait for our friendship to cement before we put more tension on it." He opened the door and lowered his voice before he left Neil to sleep. "Lilly will be okay for now. I'll keep putting her to sleep when I can. I can't do anything about the nightmares though."

"The nightmares aren't really what I'm worried about," Neil said. "I mean, have you seen that girl on the battlefield? She can handle a few bad dreams."

Chapter Seventeen

THE GOLDEN MUG
LILLY CELERIUS

Lilly was walking through an unfamiliar marketplace when she heard a familiar voice drawing her in. "I can carry that for you, Lilly," said the voice.

Lilly turned around and her heart nearly stopped. There was Jonathan, standing at attention as he always did for her. "Jonathan?" she asked. How can you... How are you alive?"

"You need me!" Jonathan said happily. "I'd do anything to serve you. I can carry that for you."

She looked down and realized she was carrying an expensive looking roll of fabric. She handed it to him and he wrapped it under his tiny arm. "Let's move on!" Jonathan said.

She continued through the market and marveled at how new stands appeared as she passed by the older ones. Periodically shopkeepers would hand her goods and ornate delicacies, which Jonathan would pull from her hands. She never paid much mind to the shopkeepers, but there was *something off about these merchants. They looked to be wounded in battle. A merchant with a bloody chest passed her a golden plate. Next a man with no eyes handed her a delicious looking plate of pears. Jonathan once again carried it for her. "I can carry something Jonathan!" she said without looking behind her.*

"No, Miss!" Jonathan said. "You shouldn't be made to carry anything."

Eventually she realized that there was less and less on the merchants. Some were now missing arms, or legs, or heads. At a point she stopped and looked to Jonathan, but he was completely buried under the massive pile of goods he carryied for her. "Jonathan?" She began to tear away her presents to find him in the rubble.

When she finally did he was bloody and his coat was torn. A small metal circle was clutched in his hand. "What are you doing Jonathan?" she asked.

"I would do anything for you," he persisted.

With that final, cryptic message he pulled the pin on the grenade.

Lilly screamed as she awoke, then clamped her hand over her mouth. "Not again," she muttered.

She tried to calm herself, but her body wouldn't comply. Her chest heaved and sweat poured from her forehead. She rolled onto her front and pressed her hands into the mattress. She sent waves through it and through the walls of the Golden Mug until she could feel the presence of everyone inside. Next-door was the assassin who almost killed Neil. One more room over, Rebecca slept soundly. She let her senses expand until she could feel the main rooms where Neil lay injured. Rhys was with him. From what she could feel it seemed like the boy was just watching his brother sleep. It had probably been traumatizing for him to almost lose his only remaining family member. She felt for Rhys and his renewed paranoia. She reached out and her senses told her that Darius was in the main serving room with a book and a candle. She sighed. Maybe it was possible that he could read. She wished she could feel far enough away to find Carlin. She'd leave right now if she knew where he was. Despite all this talk of the revolution, that's all she really wanted. She couldn't image the peace that would come from his death. Would she be able to sleep soundly again? Or would her brother Edward still plague her mind?

Suddenly, she stiffened. She could feel two people creeping near the door outside.

Lilly bounded out of bed. With her Celerius speed, she was down the hatch and into the kitchen within two seconds. She opened the door with her shoulder. "Darius!" she whispered.

Darius jumped. "What?"

She pointed at the front door. "I think someone is here. We need to—"

If she weren't so focused Lilly might have missed the dark shadow that slipped in through the broken window and crawled into the shadows. Darius stood up. Evidently, he'd seen it too. He tore his way across the room and flipped a table in the process. The girl creeping around was none other than Anastasia: the assassin who had tried to kill him multiple times when she worked for his brother, Michael. Darius recoiled in sheer surprise. "Listen," she said. "I know how this looks, but—"

He knocked her across the room and charged at her, ready to beat her into the floor. Undeterred by the massive blow she had just taken, Anastasia whipped her chain-spike across Darius's neck and, as it was unprotected, she hit the right spot to make him bleed. Darius's hand found his neck and Lilly realized that he was in a rare situation of danger. He kicked Anastasia away, but with her next chain-spike attack, she wrapped it around his neck and leapt onto his back as if she were riding a bucking bronco. He swung her off and she cartwheeled into a standing position, acrobatically. She moved unlike anyone Lilly had ever seen. Before Darius could charge again, another form slipped through the window. "Enough!" Bianca said.

Lilly looked to Anastasia and then to Bianca. "Bianca?" Lilly asked.

"Hi, Lilly," Bianca said. "Fists down, big guy. She's not here to hurt you."

Darius didn't lower his fists. "In my experience, that's never been true."

"Believe it or not," Bianca said, "Anastasia is here to help you all."

"I'm going to go with not," Darius said without breaking eye contact with the assassin.

Lilly rubbed her palms together. She knew from her experience with Darius that if he broke eye contact he would usually calm down. "Darius!" she said. Darius turned his head to her. "I think we should at least hear her out. Bianca trusts her. And we trust Bianca."

"Do we?" Darius asked hostilely as he turned back to glare at Anastasia.

"Yes." Lilly said. "Fists down, Darius."

"I'm gonna put my fists down her throat."

"She doesn't stand a chance against the two of us. Let's at least ask a few questions first," Lilly persisted.

Darius lowered his fists slowly, but kept his eyes laser focused on Anastasia. "How well do you know her?" Darius asked Bianca.

Anastasia laughed and Darius looked like he wanted to raise his fists again. "She knows me pretty well. After all we have the same father."

Chapter Eighteen

THE GOLDEN MUG
NEIL VAPROS

RHYS SAT AT THE DOOR, BRANDISHING HIS KNIFE. "SOMEONE'S HERE," HE said. "I heard," Neil said in his dazed state. "What do you think we should do?"

Rhys opened the door a slight crack and peeked through. He studied for a few moments and then turned back to Neil. "I think it's Bianca."

Neil sat up. "Are you sure?"

"Ashen hair," Rhys said. "Definitely looks like her. And it looks like Anastasia is here too."

"The assassin?" Neil asked. Rhys nodded even though his back was turned to Neil and it was hard for him to see. "Is Bianca tearing her apart?"

"No," Rhys said. "They actually look friendly with each other."

"I must be hallucinating," Neil said. Suddenly a thought struck him. "Do you think Bianca is gonna come up here at some point?"

"Of course. She wouldn't come here and not see you."

Neil shook his head and tried to clear it of the pain that had been chipping away at him. "I want you to do me a favor, buddy."

"Okay."

"Tell her I'm way worse than I am," Neil said.

"Neil, you're gonna be okay," Rhys insisted.

"I know that," Neil said. "But maybe if she thinks I'm already gonna die she might not stab me."

"This seems dishonest," Rhys said.

"That's because it is," Neil said. "I feel bad about it, but I want to fix things with her. This will make it easier."

"Okay," Rhys said after a while.

"Also make sure Anastasia isn't here to murder us," Neil said.

"That, I'm happy to do," Rhys said as he exited the room, knife in hand.

Neil waited and stared at the ceiling. He tried to formulate the perfect response to whatever Bianca might say to him. He didn't have to wait long before the door opened and he heard her light footsteps. "Neil?" she asked.

He pretended to be startled. "Bianca?" he asked. "What are you doing here?"

Tears brimmed her eyes and her face had lost all color. She clutched his hand. He was struck by the fear on her face. Bianca was never afraid of anything. She put her hand out to feel his forehead. "Rhys says you're not looking so good."

Neil wanted to go with his previously established white lie, but knew he couldn't. She looked too upset, concerned and a whole bunch of other things that he hadn't expected. "It's really not that bad," he insisted. "Not much worse than a flesh wound."

She dropped her hand from his cool forehead, grabbed his hand again and stroked his palm. "Really?"

"Yeah," he said. "I'll be okay."

She shifted her jaw as if mulling something over. "Then we should talk."

"Actually it might be worse than I'm making it out to be," he said quietly.

She dropped his hand and sat on the bench that had been vacated by Rhys. She raised an eyebrow. "Does this mean I have to go first?" Neil asked.

She just sat back and waited, her face blank. *That's a wonderful sign,* Neil thought sarcastically to himself. "So..." he said. "I'm sorry." She cocked her head at him and narrowed her eyes. "For everything," Neil said. "I'm even sorry for the things I'm not wrong about."

She straightened and he was prepared for her to use him as a dartboard. "And what aren't you wrong about?" Bianca asked.

Neil gulped. There was no way out of this one. Other girls were so easy to talk to. Everyone was easy for Neil to talk to, especially Bianca, on most days. But not when she was upset with him and not when he was trying to reconcile. "I'm sorry I didn't come with you," Neil said. "I really am. I miss you."

"Neil, I'm not angry that you decided not to come with me."

"That doesn't feel like the end of that thought."

"I'm mad at you because you told me we'd be together and that we could have a life together," she said. "But then when I went to join the revolution, you deserted me. I left Altryon to join the revolution and I was glad that you were coming too. I wanted a new life for us out here."

"I wanted that too," he persisted.

"Then why didn't you meet me? We had a plan, Neil. We were going to meet in the forest and join the rebels together. You didn't have to join. You didn't have to follow me into the unknown. But you told me that you would and then you just abandoned me with no explanation whatsoever. Just the way my father abandoned me." She blinked rapidly and Neil felt his stomach tighten. "I wanted to know that you still felt something for me, even if I decided to leave."

Neil was speechless. He closed his eyes and leaned his head back. How could he be such an idiot? He never thought for a second that she would compare him to her worthless father. "You can't love someone only when it's convenient for you," Bianca continued. "You have to show dedication for people. I wanted to see that you had dedication to me, not even as a—" she hesitated. "Even outside of all the romantic stuff. We've been friends since we were kids, Neil. I wanted to know that you'd still care about me despite the fact that I made a choice that didn't fit in with your vision for you new 'perfect life.' You didn't have to come with me, but you also didn't have to lie and say you would."

Neil sat up again and tried to ignore the stabbing pain as the bandage pulled at Rhys' fragile stitches. He had to fix this with Bianca, but his head was swimming from just that small movement. "Look, Bianca, I'll always care about you. And I always have. You are the most important person in the world to me, other than Rhys." He shook his head, trying to clear his mind so that he could explain in a way she would understand . "That night when you left, I had every intention of showing up… I wanted to go with you, but you seemed like you had this whole plan about where you were going and what you were doing. It didn't seem like I fit in. I felt like I'd never fit in."

She clearly wasn't ready for that. Her eyes widened and then she blinked. "Really...? Are you...?" She clearly hadn't formulated an end to that sentence.

"I didn't want to hold you back," he said. "And it's never been easy to change your mind."

She placed her hands on his arm again and he felt himself relax back against the pillow. "What about now?" she asked. "Do you still want this normal life, away from the revolution? Do you want to have a nice happy family somewhere far away from the Industrial City."

Neil rolled his arm over and gripped one of her hands. "I can't stop thinking about Jennifer. When she was dying she told me she didn't want me to be an assassin. She didn't want me to have to take lives. She wanted safety for me. And I want that for me and for everyone I love too, but I was shot in the back yesterday. Not being a part of the revolution isn't a guarantee of life."

Bianca tussled his hair gently. "That's actually why I'm here. I used to think Saewulf and the Emperor went after the Lightborns because they wanted complete control. They wanted power. But now... Seeing how things are out here. It seems pretty clear that they're only after one thing for the Lightborns."

Neil didn't have to wonder what it was. "Extinction."

"The emperor isn't just trying to win a war. He's trying to exterminate a race." Neil remembered that the Emperor's father had been killed by Nicolai Taurlum, and since then he'd detested Lightborns. He shivered as the reality of the situation hit him once more. Bianca continued, "You don't have to join the front lines, but this war is coming to you whether you like it or not. The Pack is coming for you."

"I'd probably be more afraid if I knew what that was," Neil said, his eyes heavy.

Bianca pulled back. "The Pack is a vicious group of assassins. Run by two Lightborns called Venator. Rest up. Soon the Wolf will be here. He'll explain everything."

"You've got to stop saying things I don't understand." He curled into his pillow for sleep.

"Well, then we wouldn't have anything to talk about," she said with a wink.

He was able to get one last glimpse of her before he drifted off to sleep. He was sure that his dreams would be pleasant for once.

Chapter Nineteen

THE GOLDEN MUG
THE PACK

THE MARKSMAN HAD BEEN AWAKE FOR TWO DAYS STRAIGHT. HE KNEW he was inadvertently torturing himself but didn't care. He knew he wouldn't be able to kill everyone in this house and he had to escape before his time ran out. Despite the fact that he was the Imperial Doctor's son, The Marksman was also given one of the Doctor's trademark injections. That had been twenty-seven days ago, and in another four he'd die from the withdrawal. The only way he could possibly convince his father to give him another dose was to pay for it with information. Luckily he had superhuman hearing to aid him. So far the only juicy bit of gossip he'd developed was that the Vapros boys were hiding a secret from the Celerius girl about the death of her brother. Along with that, he'd discovered some simpler secrets. The Taurlum couldn't read but was telling everyone he could. Based on the breathing patterns of the woman who owned the bar, she had what sounded like a throat infection. When Josephine told Bianca and Anastasia that they could stay for the night, he heard the tightness of her lungs in her voice.

He was curious as to why Anastasia was here. From his calculations she was due for another injection fairly soon also. He knew her tactics for assassination well. She was acrobatic and limber but not particularly strong. She was famous among the members of the Pack for befriending her enemies, then executing them in the dead of night or tricking them into the Doctor's web. He could hear her claiming to be Bianca Blackmore's sister. He wondered if that was true. If so, it meant her father was the once honorable Paul Blackmore of the Imperial Army. He didn't have to wait for more answers, as a few hours later Anastasia snuck into his room. He drilled his eyes into her accusingly. "What's your strategy here?" he asked.

"What's yours? I've never seen anyone take you down in a fight. Ever."

They were both speaking quietly enough so that no one would even hear the faintest whispers. "I underestimated these fools," Victor said. "Although they are clearly from inside the Industrial City. 'What's a Venator?' 'What's the Pack?'" he mocked. "For Lightborns they aren't very educated about their own race."

"I think the barkeeper woman is keeping certain details away from them. It's clear that she doesn't want them joining the revolution. I just can't figure out why." Anastasia sat down on the bed opposite. "My strategy is to befriend them and lead them into the Doctor's clutches. I'm using my connection to Bianca to do it."

The Marksman gritted his teeth. "Is that true? I've met Paul Blackmore. You didn't exactly inherit the ashen hair."

"It's true," Anastasia said. "Lieutenant Blackmore was in and out of the Industrial City. He had one wife inside and one wife outside.

Before long he had two daughters. He took me inside the walls a few times and that's how I met her. We've never been close."

"And you're willing to offer her up for the Doctor's needs?" the Marksman asked.

"I don't have a choice."

"You need to cut me," the Marksman said. "Draw blood."

Anastasia recoiled. "Why?"

"Advanced ability. If I bleed I can morph my body to become more… animalistic."

"Really?" she asked. "I've never seen you use that power."

"I've never needed to," the Marksman said. "It's not very far advanced because I don't practice with it. But if you cut me I can grow some claws on my right hand and cut my way out of these binds."

She cocked her head. "Why don't you just ask me to cut the ropes?"

"They'll be able to tell if the ropes are sliced evenly with a knife. Or a spike." He indicated her weapon. "If I can escape on my own, they'll hear from the Wolf about my special ability. Is he really coming here?"

He smelled the fear on Anastasia. The Wolf worried every morally decrepit citizen of Volteria, no matter how tough they were. "Bianca sent him a letter and he said he'd arrive soon. He was starting riots in Abington."

The Marksman stiffened. "I want to escape before he arrives. I can't be sure that he won't kill me on sight on behalf of the Venator."

Anastasia stood up and rubbed her chin. "If I free you the same night I get here, what does it say about my cover?"

He glared at her. "You're not setting me free. You're going to prick my finger. That is all."

She shook her head. "No. I don't think I will." She approached the door once more. "You're a smart man, Victor. You'll figure it out."

She left and he resisted the urge to scream in fury. He quickly centered himself and went back to listening. He'd escape. It was only a matter of time.

VICTORY LIES WITHIN
THE ASHES

Chapter Twenty

THE GOLDEN MUG
NEIL VAPROS

THE NEXT MORNING EVERYONE WAS GATHERED IN THE KITCHEN FOR A meeting of sorts. Bianca sat at the head of one of the tables and the rest of the fugitives gathered around. Josephine and Rebecca sat behind the bar. Even Neil was in attendance although he was heavily bandaged and didn't look to be fully focused on what was going on. Lilly drummed her fingers nervously at her Celerius speed. She probably hadn't seen her uncle since before she could remember and she couldn't know how living outside the walls had affected him. Maybe he was an animalistic ruffian now. Neil was still trying to grapple with the fact that Bianca and Anastasia were half-sisters.

"Let's start with why the Wolf is coming here," Bianca said. "The revolution has been in trouble recently, but things finally look like they're on the upswing again. So he actually has time to educate you all on how to deal with the Pack and what the Pack is."

"How does Anastasia know that the Pack is after us?" Darius asked with a little too much suspicion in his voice.

Anastasia opened her mouth to answer, but Bianca stepped in. "Anastasia was working with the Doctor out of necessity a while back, but once she saw that he was planning to kill all of you, friends of her sister," Bianca indicated herself, "she decided it was time to leave his service and warn us of his plans."

"So who is this Doctor?" Rhys asked.

"The Imperial Doctor," Anastasia said. "He works for the Empire. Every month they send him a list of who they want dead through a bookkeeper named Quintus."

Neil laughed and the group looked at him. Rhys grinned giddily. "You're familiar?" Bianca asked.

"With Quintus?" Neil asked. "Yes. He and I are very familiar. I assume his demotion to bookkeeper is because of me."

"Well, anyway," Bianca continued, "after the month is over the Doctor tells Quintus how many are dead and then the Emperor pays him. This month all of your names are on the list."

"So the Doctor's group of assassins is called the Pack?" Rhys asked.

Bianca nodded. "It's a small unit and it used to consist of the Doctor's son, Victor Venator—known as the Marksman--- he's your hostage upstairs, Anastasia, and a deranged fellow named the Hyena. You've met two of them so far, it seems. He has others, but they don't work outside the walls."

"So we only have one more assassin to worry about?" Neil asked.

"And the Doctor himself," Anastasia said. "Trust me. You don't want to underestimate him. Don't underestimate the Hyena either. He's a type of crazy that you've never even seen before."

"Have you met General Carlin?" Lilly asked.

"I have," Anastasia said. "Carlin is angry daddy-issues crazy. The Hyena doesn't even have a grasp on reality any more."

"Then why does the Doctor choose to work with him?" Rhys asked.

Anastasia seemed to be considering her words very carefully. "The Hyena is also known as the Demon of Abington. He used to be at the Abington Orphanage and eventually… kids started going missing. He escaped the inquisition by joining a circus as a clown. The Doctor found him and trained him from adolescence. They're very close."

"How long will it take for you to deal with this threat?" Josephine piped in. "How long until these kids are safe."

"They'll never be safe until the Doctor is dealt with," Anastasia said. "He doesn't miss targets, and he never gives up."

The room went silent for a moment. That wasn't the answer Neil wanted to hear. "This Doctor is a Lightborn?" Neil asked. "Of the Venator family?"

"Yes," Bianca said. "But he doesn't have his powers anymore."

"What?" Rhys asked. "How is that possible?"

"The oaths?" Bianca asked the room. "How have you been living outside the wall for four months and have never heard of the Venator?"

"We don't get out much," Darius said.

"They don't get many chances to interact with the people of Volteria, what with hiding and all," Josephine said.

"You're telling me that it never occurred to you to tell them?" Anastasia asked.

Josephine planted her hands on the bar. "These children have made the decision not to join the revolution. I figured they'd come to learn about the Venator in their own time when they went off on their own. Believe it or not, being new to these lands is a huge transition."

"Still," Bianca said, "the Venator are a family that emerged roughly a hundred years ago. Legend has it that there was a husband and wife that led a large tribe when the villages were forming, yet they had no means to protect themselves from the beasts of the land and no means to protect themselves from the Empire controlling the oceans. The Man with the Golden Light granted them each a different power. The husband was given control of the land on the condition that he followed eight sacred rules."

"What would happen if he didn't follow them?" Lilly asked.

"His powers would fade," Bianca said. "It holds true for them even now. Anyway, it was their duty to protect the land and the citizens of Volteria with their abilities of super-human senses and aim. They're essentially the unrivaled hunters of these lands. They make it their priority to keep the people safe. The wife was given control of the water on the condition that she'd lose her powers on dry land. They had to leave each other, tragically, but two new families of Lightborns were created for the betterment of Volteria. The man's family are Venator and the woman's family are Tridenti."

"Wonderful story," Darius said. "Any idea what these eight rules are?"

"I don't remember them, precisely," Bianca said. "The Doctor has lost his powers because he broke the most important one: Venator do not kill for sport."

"What about our little friend upstairs?" Neil asked. "He's still got pretty good aim."

"Victor Venator has managed to keep his powers by using loopholes to exploit the rules. For instance, he never kills anyone unless he can get money out of it. Technically it's not for sport, no matter how immoral it is. Venator are also forbidden from hunting in packs, so he only spends a day at a time in the presence of his father so that his powers won't fade."

"The guys who are forbidden from hunting in packs decided to name their murder group the Pack?" Neil asked.

"It's their way of antagonizing the Venator who actually follow the rules," Anastasia said. "The Doctor is their greatest scourge and he wants it to be known."

Neil racked his brain for questions. He didn't like the sound of going up against "the Pack." He wanted to see less action, but now was being hunted by a pack of crazy assassins. He just wanted peace and quiet.

"What can you tell me about Steven?" Lilly asked, interrupting Neil's thought process.

"Steven?" Darius asked.

"The Wolf's real name is Steven Celerius," Lilly said. "I don't know why he's called the Wolf now."

"That comes from a legend about the Wolf," Bianca said. "People in the rebellion practically tell it once per hour. The Wolf was once General of the Imperial Army, but when he saw first-hand how the soldiers were mistreating the villagers, he decided to confront the Emperor. Instead of listening to his grievances, the Emperor stripped him of his titles and exiled him. According to legend, the Emperor said, 'I don't need to kill you. I'll throw you to the wolves and they'll take care of it.'"

That does sound like the Emperor, Neil thought.

"So Steven, after wandering for a year or so found the Venator," Bianca said. "They're not allowed to have families, but they do have a central lodge where they all rest in between journeys. He actually trained Victor Venator, the man in your attic. Soon though, the Wolf found out that his wife had been killed by the Empire."

Lilly stiffened, but didn't interject. Bianca continued. "The Wolf, enraged, rounded up a group of villagers and destroyed a few convoys that belonged to the Empire. They sent a spy after him, but the Wolf caught him and sent him back to the emperor with a message. He told him that—"

"I told him," said a voice at the door, "that the best way to survive being eaten by wolves is to become one."

The man at the door was exceedingly tall, even taller than Darius. His hair was perfectly styled and combed despite how weathered the rest of him looked. Neil's eye was drawn to the sword at his back and then to his knee length blue coat. "Thank you for setting up that exciting entrance, Bianca," he said.

Bianca saluted him. His eyes settled on Lilly and he opened his arms wide. "Lilly!" he said. "I never thought I'd see you again. I never thought I'd see you grown."

She looked momentarily paralyzed by his sudden arrival and ragtag appearance, but she stood up and was across the room to him in a flash. He hugged her tightly for what was probably an entire minute. When they parted, she had tears in her eyes. Neil remembered that she had lost most of her family members in the last year. As he left the hug, the Wolf examined the group before him. "I also never thought I'd see so many young Lightborns working together. It's nice to meet you boys."

He extended his hand to Darius first and Darius took it with excitement. Rhys was next and Neil was last. The Wolf smiled at each of them. Neil was almost caught off guard by how white his teeth were. Even while living on the run, somehow he'd managed to keep his dental hygiene pristine. *He really is Lilly's uncle,* Neil thought. From across the room Josephine cleared her throat and the Wolf stood up straight, showing off that famous military posture. "Josephine Belmont," he said. "I didn't realize this was your business."

"Well, now you do," she said. "So you'd do well to be on your way as soon as possible."

"I apologize for being so sudden with my entrance," the Wolf said. "But, I couldn't exactly knock." He pointed to where the missing door had once been.

With its polished wooden interior and scattered glowing candles, The Golden Mug typically felt warm and inviting to all who entered, but Neil could tell that the Wolf wasn't welcome. "Just remember that these young ones aren't soldiers. They're not your pawns. They're children." Josephine gave them all one last fierce look and went into the kitchen. Rebecca nervously stayed behind the bar for a moment and then followed Josephine.

"Do you know everyone outside the walls?" Bianca asked to break the silence.

"It seems so," he said. "Regrettably. Her son was in my squadron during the early days of the revolution."

"Josephine had a son?" Darius asked. "Where is he now?"

The Wolf gave him a look that was enough of an answer. No wonder Josephine was always so protective of them. The Wolf walked past Anastasia. "Anastasia Blackmore," he said. "Our woman on the inside."

"I'm not exactly on the inside anymore," Anastasia said. "The Doctor knows I've crossed him. His son is upstairs. My cover is dead."

The Wolf stiffened. "What did you say? Victor is here?"

"Yeah," Darius said. "He shot our friend, Neil. We caught him and tied him up in the attic."

The Wolf looked to Bianca. "That's worrisome. Did anyone fill his ears?"

"Fill his ears with what?" Bianca asked.

The Wolf went to the bar and grabbed a candle. "How do I get up there?" he asked.

"Through the kitchen," Neil said. "I'll show you."

"You shouldn't strain yourself," Rhys said.

"I'll be fine," Neil said. "I want to see the man who shot me."

Neil led the way and the mysterious addition to their gang followed. Josephine and Rebecca were working in the back, but Neil was sure it was just to seem busy. The bar was closed for now and no customers would be coming anytime soon. Neil materialized up into the attic and the Wolf climbed up, showing great athleticism for a man his age. They went to the room with the Marksman in it and the Wolf entered briskly. "Steven, I've missed you," Victor managed before the Wolf was pouring hot candle wax into his ears.

Neil hadn't seen the Marksman face to face yet, and now that they were together the assassin terrified him. The scariest thing were his eyes, wide and unblinking like a feral cat. Something else bothered Neil. He'd touched candle wax before and knew that having it poured into your ear holes would be an excruciating experience, but the Marksman took it silently and without flinching. Steam drifted from either side of his head, but the Marksman remained stoic. Soon his ear canals were filled to the brim with wax and the remnants were dripping onto his shoulders. The Wolf slapped him across the face for good measure. He seemed satisfied and turned to face Neil. "This man is the most ruthless and shameless killer in all of Volteria. I wouldn't recommend that anyone approach him unless entirely necessary."

"You just slapped him in the face," Neil pointed out.

"That one felt necessary to me."

Even though his ears were blocked, the Marksman still spoke. "I'm glad to see that you're all right Neil Vapros. I was given instructions not to kill you. Perhaps the Emperor plans to do it with his own hands."

Neil paled and resisted the urge to look at the Marksman. "Trust me. I'm aware of how dangerous he is." He indicated the bandages wrapped around his body.

"I'm glad you're aware," the Wolf said. He shifted past Neil respectfully and exited the attic at a speed that amazed Neil, even after living with Lilly who exhibited the Celerius speed daily.

Neil followed the Wolf through the kitchen and back to the main room. The General pulled off his blue coat and laid it over the bar. "I've stopped him from eavesdropping on you."

"He was listening to our conversations?" Rhys asked.

"I assume so," the Wolf said. "Don't be concerned, I don't plan to let that man live to use the information. I'm taking him to face justice at the hands of the head of the Venator family. But you should know that anything you've said in this house over the last two days is no longer a secret."

Neil looked to Rhys and then they both turned to Lilly. They had discussed the matter of Edward's death and the Marksman had been listening. Hopefully that wouldn't be an issue later on. "Anyone have anything to share?" the Wolf asked, noticing more than a few shifty gazes around the room. No one answered. "Well good," he said. "It's not easy to fight beside people you don't trust."

"Not all of us are interested in joining the fight," Neil said. "I'm perfectly content outside of this war."

"Really?" the Wolf said, surprised. He adjusted, "Well, that's understandable given all you've lost." He sat down at the table and rolled up the sleeves on his yellowing shirt. "Just out of curiosity, after learning of the challenges you face, who is still interested in staying out of the fight."

Neil raised his hand, confident that his friends would follow. To his surprise, he found that he was the only holdout. "That's awkward," Anastasia said.

"Really?" Neil asked the table.

"You should be the angriest of all," Darius said. "You're the one who got shot."

"And I was lucky to live," Neil said. "I'm just not convinced that this fight is best for me. It doesn't feel like my purpose."

The Wolf leaned back and rubbed his stubbly chin. "Neil's always been sort of... sentimental," Bianca said.

Neil's cheeks grew flushed. "I'm not being sentimental. I'm being honest."

The Wolf raised his hands. "It all makes sense to me, Neil. Really, it does. You've fought through more in your young years than most ever have to." He patted a small hair back into place. "But let's not make all of our decisions today. I'm tired, you're tired, and we're all tired. Let's start with the Pack and worry about the Empire later."

"Agreed," Bianca said. "Anastasia and Victor are here, so that means the Hyena is the only remaining assassin."

"Let's not forget the Doctor himself," Anastasia said.

"Of course not," the Wolf said. "Bianca, my horse is outside. Retrieve my book, will you?"

Without a moments hesitation she exited through the gaping threshold and returned seconds later with a large leather-bound book. "I'm actually excited to meet all of you for many reasons, and not just revolutionary ones. This," he said, "is a project I've been working on since I first joined the army. I call it *A Rough History of Lightborns.* It's essentially an atlas of Lightborns."

He dropped it on the table. Rhys had his hands on it before it even hit the wood. The book had hundreds of illustrated pages overflowing with the Wolf's scribbles. Rhys was mere inches away from the paper when the Wolf approached him from behind. He handed Rhys a small pair of spectacles over his shoulder. "Would you like to borrow these?" the Wolf asked.

Rhys's eyes lit up. "Are you sure?" he asked.

"Of course," the Wolf said. "You look like you need them even more than I do."

"Father mentioned this book once when I was younger," Lilly said as she pulled it from Rhys's hands. "You wrote down everything you knew about every Lightborn."

"Indeed," the Wolf said. The word would have sounded pretentious coming from any other Celerius, but there was something about the way he clearly knew the word didn't fit in his mouth that made it amusing. "Despite the fact he's not actually a Lightborn, the Hyena is in there. I decided that he qualifies based on the fact that the Doctor adopted him."

"You think reading this book is going to help take this guy out?" Darius asked. "No offence, but I don't usually prep for battle in the library."

"You should," the Wolf said as he flipped to his handwritten section about the Hyena. "I can guarantee you that the Doctor has studied each and every one of us. If we walk into a battle with the Pack uninformed, I assure you, no weapons will help us and no armor will protect us. An armored man with an empty mind is naked."

"I love that," Rhys said.

"You would," Neil said with a grin.

"That was so deep," Darius said, unimpressed.

"I for one am ready to learn," Lilly said pointedly at Darius. "And we've got nothing but time."

The Wolf laughed. "I appreciate your enthusiasm, but the Doctor is most likely building his web around us. Time is one thing we don't have."

It had been four hours of rigorous studying, and Neil wished that he could succumb to his injuries and die already. The Wolf had a deep rich voice. It was interesting to listen to, but only for so long. He'd understood the basics after the first hour. By now he felt like an official expert on the Venator family. He had the eight sacred rules of their family written out in front of him along with the family crest. The Venator's crest boasted a forest green octagon with a spider upside-down in the center. Neil read the rules one more time:

Venator do not hunt in packs.
Venator do not kill for sport.
Venator die. They do not retire.
Venator do not marry.
Venator do not indulge in unhealthy vices.
Venator must remain on the mainland.
Venator put their mission over emotion.
Venator put protection of the land above all else.

Even though the only remaining free assassin wasn't a Venator, Neil felt equipped to deal with him. Lester Buchwald, the Hyena, was a perfect killing machine, complete with a lower jaw made of metal fangs. The maniac specialized in killing his enemies up close with his teeth. What made Neil confident was the fact that apparently the Hyena couldn't resist laughing when he stalked his prey. Neil was hard to sneak up on at any given time, and if his enemy was cackling like a maniac, it didn't exactly help his chances.

"That should do for today," the Wolf said, snapping Neil out of his trance. "We've learned a lot."

"We're not going to talk about the family from the sea?" Rhys asked, disappointed.

"Unfortunately," the Wolf said as he pulled his book across the table. "I don't know half as much about the Tridenti as I do about the Venator. Remember, I was trained by the Grand Master of the Venator, but I've never had the pleasure of meeting someone from the Tridenti family."

"I think we've learned enough today," Neil said. He kicked Darius who was napping quietly. He cursed himself for doing so. Kicking Darius was like kicking someone's shield.

Darius's eyes flickered open. "I… What?" he asked.

The Wolf smiled at them. "I know that this was a strange and unexciting way for us to meet," he said. "These circumstances are not ideal, but I'm glad I had a chance to meet you all. Tomorrow we will hopefully finish up our lessons on the Doctor and his allies. Then we'll be properly equipped to end his business once and for all."

"And after that?" Lilly asked.

The Wolf stood and grabbed his coat from the bar. "It's up to you. You might wish to join the revolution and me. Or not. The decision is yours. Either way, I'm tired and headed off to sleep."

He walked toward the front door. "Outside?" asked Josephine as she entered from the kitchen. She'd been in and out of the main room all night. "I have rooms inside."

The Wolf didn't turn around. "I know you don't want me sleeping in one of your beds."

She crossed her arms. "You're right," she said. "But you may."

"I grieve for your boy, Josephine," he said. "But I don't regret his service. And I won't regret theirs should they decide to join." He gestured to the Lightborns and the Blackmore sisters. "We shouldn't regret it if the people we love choose to give their lives to make our world a better place. They understand that the world is better for having them."

"You might not regret it," Josephine said, close to tears. "But I do."

"I know," the Wolf said. "That's why I'm going to be sleeping outside. Goodnight everyone."

He left and Josephine went to her room upstairs, pounding her feet on every step the way up. They waited until she was back in her room. "I didn't expect that to happen," Lilly said.

"Revolution is bloody," Bianca said. "And most of the time it takes a while for people to come around."

"I feel bad," Darius said. "I want to join this guy and his revolution, but I don't want to hurt Josephine."

"She'll live," Anastasia said. "Her fear of losing you is a terrible reason to stay out of this fight."

"I don't know," Neil said. "She has the right to be upset. She's lost someone close to her. That kind of thing changes you."

Rhys stood up and yawned. His spectacles slid down his nose and he pushed them back up. They actually looked perfect on him, like they'd been missing his entire life. *He should have been born with them,* Neil thought to himself, amused. "She's got the right to be sad, but not to tell us how to live our lives out here," Rhys said. "I like the Wolf, and I can understand why people follow him."

Neil wanted to agree, but the same thing as always held him back. Sure, the Wolf was charismatic and wise, but he also represented a life that Neil wasn't sure he wanted, a life outside the Golden Mug. "I need rest," Neil said.

"I'll help you back up," Bianca said.

Neil wanted to protest at first and say that it would be much easier for Darius to carry him upstairs, but then he remembered how long it had been since Bianca had been close to him. She helped him up and together they ascended the staircase. The rest of the Lightborns went through the kitchen to the secret rooms. Once Bianca got him to his bed, he slumped into it violently. "He's really something, isn't he?" Bianca asked.

"He's certainly not like any Celerius I've ever met," Neil said. "They're not the type to sleep outside."

"He doesn't like to owe anyone anything," Bianca said. "He's got a pretty strict moral code."

Neil was trying to listen, but he felt himself drifting off. "Like the Venator," he said in a moment of random word association. "Except he keeps his powers if he breaks his code."

Bianca pulled the blankets over him. "He doesn't even use his powers very often. Apparently he has the same advanced power as Lilly, but he can channel it into a super scream."

That was interesting enough to keep Neil awake for a moment longer. "Really? That sounds incredible."

"The rebels call it, 'The Howl.'"

"Of course they do," Neil said.

The last thing he remembered before drifting off was Bianca asking him a question. "Are you any closer to changing your mind about joining?"

He fell asleep before he could answer and he was thankful for that. Truthfully, he had no idea how he would answer.

Chapter Twenty-One

THE GOLDEN MUG
THE PACK

THE MARKSMAN KNEW MANY THINGS WELL. HE KNEW EVERY SINGLE pressure point on the human body. He knew how to survive in the woods for years on end. He knew how to filet every creature native to Volteria's forests. But better than all these things, he knew the feeling of withdrawal and the sickness that arose in his stomach when he was without the injection he needed to live. Now was one of those moments. His stomach churned constantly and sweat dripped from every pore. On top of the fact that he would soon be dead from the withdrawal now the Wolf, his old enemy, was here. He relished the fact that even if he didn't escape, he wouldn't live long enough to face justice at the Grand Master's hands. The Grand Master was the head of the Venator, and not exactly a friend. The Marksman had committed too many crimes against the Venator. In doing so he'd lost the right to an honorable death. Just as the Marksman knew how to filet a bear, the Grand Master knew how to filet traitors. The Marksman would not survive a trial with the Grand Master.

Even with the wax in his ears, the Marksman could hear slightly better than the average human. His days of eavesdropping were over, but he was still able to hear the other Lightborns coming upstairs. He waited until he could hear the girls go into their room and the young intellectual go into his. The blonde giant, Darius, was right next-door. "Simpleton," the Marksman said, just loudly enough for someone to hear him through the door. "Simpleton," he said again.

The door opened a crack and Darius poked his head in. "Did you say something, prisoner?"

The Marksman shook his head. "I didn't say anything, simpleton."

Darius entered the room. "You want to go another round?" he asked.

The Marksman raised his arms, which were still bound tightly together. "Like this? That doesn't exactly sound fair."

"You're barking up the wrong tree," Darius said. "I'm not going to untie you. You can't provoke me."

"You're right," the Marksman said. "In order for me to provoke you, you'd have to understand the words coming out of my mouth."

"Excuse me?" the Marksman noticed that Darius's hands were curled into fists.

"Oh, should I speak slowly?" the Marksman asked. "Maybe I could write it down for you." He bit back a sinister grin. "Oh wait. That wouldn't do you any good either."

Darius looked over his shoulder instinctually, then back to the Marksman. "I'm not going to do this," he said. "You can't taunt me. You can't get inside my head."

"Apparently knowledge can't get inside your head either. Isn't that right, simpleton?" He could almost see the rage bubbling up inside Darius. All he had to do was push a little bit harder. "I'm curious, when you killed your brother was it intentional? Or was it just hard to control those big stupid fists of yours?"

The Marksman saw the punch coming and leaned into it at the perfect angle. Blood sprayed from his nose and splattered over the wall behind him. "Done talking?" Darius asked. "Or do you want more?"

"No," the Marksman said, "that will be sufficient."

Darius stared at him and the Marksman saw a shadow of regret pass over his face. He didn't yet know what he had done, but the Marksman would make him aware, just as soon as he escaped. "Get some sleep," Darius commanded. "I'm sure the Wolf has big plans for you."

The Marksman bowed his head in mock defeat. Once Darius was gone, he focused his energy and channeled it through his hands. One of his fingers began to mutate and the bones began to realign. Soon a claw grew from his fingernail and he was able to use it to tear at the ropes binding his hands. Strand by strand, they tore. He knew he'd be free by morning. The Marksman grinned to himself internally. The Marksman knew many things, but few better than pressure points. With Darius he knew exactly where to push.

Chapter Twenty-Two

THE GOLDEN MUG
LILLY CELERIUS

To Lilly the morning felt like a bizarre combination of chaos and serenity. Being with her uncle again was a dream come true, but Bianca continually pulled him aside with rebel business. Neil had pushed himself too much and was now on mandatory bed rest. Anastasia drifted between rooms, fueled by anxious energy.

When Lilly reentered the bar, Rhys and Darius were passing the Lightborn book back and forth. According to the Wolf, *A Rough History of Lightborns* was a work in progress and he was always looking for more information to include in it. "Cassie Taurlum..." Darius dictated as Rhys wrote. "She was well known in the slums for sneaking into underground boxing matches, disguised as a man."

Lilly set her sword on the table. "Is that true?" she asked. "That's one secret that never made it into the Celerius rumor mill."

"You bet it's true," Darius said. "She would wrap her hair into some weird circle braid."

"Do you mean a bun?" Lilly asked.

"Hell if I know," he said. "But she would cover her hair in a brown scarf and put on some makeup that looked like dirt. She'd go a few times per week." He smiled to himself. "No one could take Cassie in a fight. If she'd been old enough to join the feud… You guys might not be here." He winked.

Lilly wanted to scoff and talk about how her speed would out-match Cassie's strength, but she didn't. "Do you miss her?" Lilly asked.

Darius's face fell. "Yeah, I do." He turned back to the book. "But I'm going to save her. The second I get her out of the Emperor's dungeon, she's gonna be back to her sparring. I just know it. Maybe I'll let her get a few swings in at the Emperor himself."

"If she fights like her brother, then the Emperor's going to be in trouble," Anastasia said from the balcony above them. Lilly didn't know how long she'd been there.

Darius smiled at her comment, but stopped when he realized whom he was smiling at. Anastasia noticed and sighed. "Maybe she'll take a few swings at you too," Darius said. "I doubt she'll be happy to hear about Michael…"

Anastasia leapt over the balcony and swung down fluidly to the floor below. There was no denying her acrobatic prowess. She reminded Lilly of a leaf in the wind the way she bounded weightlessly from balcony to table to floor. She made only the slightest sound and drifted as if controlled by the wind. Lilly even felt a twinge of jealousy. Despite her unmatched speed and extraordinary skill with her weapon, she had never been light-footed and she couldn't help but go a little green when she saw someone like Anastasia move. In addition, it was hard enough to pretend that jumping down from the attic didn't fill her with vertigo, dread, and fear. She'd never be the "leaping off of balconies" type. "I'm sorry that the wrong guy paid me, Darius," Anastasia said. "But you'll have to get over it if we're working together. It was just business."

"Oh you're right," Darius said. "Maybe I'll pay Cassie to beat you down. That makes it business, doesn't it?"

Anastasia scowled at him and exited the room through the gaping front door. Bianca walked in past her. "What did you do?" she immediately asked Darius.

"I let her live through the night," Darius said nonchalantly. "You're welcome."

Something pulled at Lilly's mind and she grabbed Bianca's arm. "May I speak to you?" she asked in a low voice, quietly enough so that Rhys and Darius couldn't hear her.

Bianca glanced over at them and silently indicated the kitchen. They walked in only to find it occupied by Josephine. "Oh…" Lilly said. "Apologies, I thought the kitchen was empty."

Josephine was chopping potatoes but she set the knife down when the girls entered. Despite the fact that she now had an unwelcome guest in her home, she was still preparing dinner. "What are you girls plotting?" Josephine asked. She grabbed a tomato and diced it swiftly. "Should I leave?" she asked.

Lilly hesitated, knowing Josephine's apprehensions about the Wolf. Maybe this was something she needed to hear too. "I just wanted to ask Bianca something," Lilly said. "Yesterday you said that the Wolf's wife was killed by the Empire?"

Bianca glanced over at Josephine, who hardly appeared to be listening. "I did. Why?"

"Well…" Lilly said. "That's not exactly true. She didn't die. She was just expelled from the Celerius family."

"I don't understand."

Lilly explained. "Maybe I'm mistaken, but I'd always been told that the Wolf was exiled for crimes against the Empire. We were forced to sever ties with him, so his wife wasn't allowed to live in the house anymore."

"What happened to her?" Bianca asked.

"I was told that she died of pneumonia a few years ago," Lilly said. "She's still dead, but not in the way my Uncle was told."

Bianca's fingers twitched. "I would keep this to yourself, for now," she said in a low voice. "Let me do some digging. I'll find out what really happened. There's no need to distract him if we don't need to. He's the most important man outside the walls. I'd hate to divide his attention."

Lilly patted Bianca on the arm in agreement. "Understood."

She liked Bianca more and more every time they talked. At one point Bianca had been rash and impolite towards her, but since leaving the walls she'd demonstrated not only an incredible amount of bravery, but also an enviable emotional intelligence. Bianca was still from the streets, but she'd adapted to this new world well. The two of them had formed a friendship in the short time they'd spent outside the walls together. Bianca squeezed her hand and left the kitchen. Lilly could hear her yelling at Neil. "Get back in bed!" Bianca commanded. "You're wounded."

"I just want to go outside for five minutes," she heard Neil whine. "I'm bored in here."

Lilly wanted to join the argument, but she remembered that Josephine was still in the room with her. "I hope that I can trust your discretion about…" Lilly faltered. "About my uncle's wife."

Josephine smiled at her. "I love you very much, Lilly," Josephine said and slid the diced tomatoes into a pot. "I'm not petty enough to share secrets with someone out of spite."

Lilly released a breath that she didn't remember holding. "I was very sorry to hear about your son."

Josephine didn't look up from the meal she was preparing. "So was I," she said. "Being a mother and then suddenly not being a mother... It changes you."

Lilly wanted to say something, but nothing seemed sufficient.

"Maybe I'm not being fair towards your uncle. I understand how important he is to the people. It's just hard to watch the man who convinced my son to fight lead you all down the same path."

Lilly walked around the counter and hugged Josephine. "I wish we had a choice. I wish we could have whatever life we want."

Josephine laid her hand on Lilly's head and hugged her back. "I know I can't be, but I wish I could be the one to give it to you. You kids deserve that."

Lilly noticed that Josephine was wiping tears from her eyes when they parted. Josephine went to add the vegetables to whatever she was cooking, probably a stew.

Lilly felt relieved that she could reconnect with her uncle and stay close to Josephine as well.

"Do we have carrots?" Josephine called.

"In the store room," Lilly said.

She'd been in charge of stocking it a few days ago. Lilly heard shifting in the floorboards above her and an odd thought ran through her mind. *Who could be moving upstairs?* Neil was outside with Bianca and the Wolf, Rhys and Darius were in the bar area, Josephine was in the kitchen, and Rebecca was bringing food to the Imperial prisoners at the shack by the river. The only one upstairs was... Lilly's eyes widened. Before she could scream or alert her friends, the trapdoor to the attic swung open and the Marksman dropped down. He swept her feet out from under her instantly and placed his foot on her throat.

She tried to alert someone, but he was pressing too hard for her to make any sound other than a pitiful gurgling. Josephine was only a room away. Maybe she could manage a scream.

She clamped her hand down on his leg in the hopes that she could channel energy through him, but the lack of oxygen made it impossible to focus her energy. The Marksman pressed a finger against his lips, a silent command to subdue and allow him to escape.

Lilly saw Josephine rush at him with a knife. He maneuvered around her swings, disarmed her, then slammed her head into the table. She fell to the ground, groaning in pain. As Lilly's consciousness slipped away, the Marksman admired Josephine's knife and flipped it in his hand, ready to resume his hunt.

Chapter Twenty-Three

THE GOLDEN MUG
NEIL VAPROS

*N*EIL *WATCHED PATIENTLY AS B*IANCA *AND THE W*OLF *SPARRED. S*HE *WAS* fast, faster than he'd ever seen her, but that didn't help her with the Wolf. He parried easily and blocked each punch without an ounce of effort. He actually looked half asleep as he partook in combat that would kill a normal man.

Suddenly Neil heard heavy footfalls behind him and realized that their prisoner was escaping. The Marksman was bolting from the Golden Mug and charging up the nearest hill toward the tree line. His rifle was strapped to his back. Apparently, he'd recovered it from Rhys somehow. "Wolf!" Neil cried.

The Wolf was already looking. It was as if he'd sensed the presence of a new body in the open air. He tore after the Marksman with his Celerius speed. The Wolf tackled him to the ground, but the Marksman quickly rolled over onto his back and delivered a strong kick to the Wolf's nose. Blood spurted out and the Wolf staggered to his feet. Neil bolted over as fast as he could. He knew it was only a matter of time before Bianca retrieved her throwing knives. The Marksman stared at them, obviously tired; after all, he'd been kept in a dark room with little food or water for the last week. Desperation crept into his eyes as he backtracked slowly.

Neil let his hands ignite. "This isn't gonna end how you want it to, Marksman."

The Marksman studied him for a moment, then turned to look at the Wolf, who kept his fighting stance strong. The Marksman drew his trusty rifle. Neil threw a fireball. He wasn't going to wait for the Marksman to shoot.

Victor dodged the fireball in one fluid movement. He corrected his stance he fired his rifle at the Wolf. The Celerius seemed to be anticipating it and weaved out of the way letting the bullet seamlessly pass by.

"Looks like you missed," Neil said.

The Marksman almost looked sad as he shook his head. "Missed the old man, maybe."

Neil turned and realized that the Marksman must have accidentally fired his gun straight through the open door of the Golden Mug. While Neil's head was turned, the Marksman continued his dash towards the tree line. Neil and the Wolf exchanged looks when they realized their predicament: Go after the Marksman or see what damage the bullet had done. The Wolf raised his arm to feel the surroundings around him. "Is someone dead?" Neil asked.

"I don't know."

"Should I-"

The Wolf's eyes widened. "Do you have any medical knowledge?"

"No," Neil said.

The Wolf ran back toward the bar almost without waiting to hear his answer. "Don't lose him!" the Wolf called over his shoulder. "Follow but don't try to fight him."

Neil wanted to debate the Wolf's decision to run back to the pub. Clearly that's what the Marksman wanted: the strongest fighter out of the picture, but Neil decided that he could take Victor alone. He couldn't be worse than Saewulf. Neil's fiery hands propelled him up the hill. He was hardly running anymore. He was flying. He reached the tree line and let his hands extinguish themselves. He stepped into the forest, but anxiety weighed on his mind. If what the Wolf said was to be believed, chasing a Venator into a forest was a dangerous act. It didn't help that this forest was so different from anything Neil had ever seen. Inside the city, trees were planted in an orderly fashion and well kept. Nothing grew to excess. Outside the wall it was a different story. Trees grew randomly and sporadically wherever they wanted.

The Marksman was probably long gone by now. Neil saw a hint of movement in one of the tall trees. Without a second's hesitation, he launched a fireball into the canopy. The Marksman leapt from the tree acrobatically and caught onto another nearby branch. He slid down it without difficulty and dodged Neil's next fireball with a somersault. He rolled onto his feet and stood to face Neil. "You came to fight me alone?"

Neil glared at him. "I don't need anyone else. Last I checked, Darius was alone when he nearly killed you."

"Your friend is impervious to bullets. If I'm not mistaken, you can't say the same," the Marksman pointed out.

"If I'm not mistaken, you're out of bullets," Neil said and hurled another fireball.

"You're not easy to beat because you can be killed by a bullet," the Marksman said without emotion. He twirled out of the way of the fireball and with his next step closed the distance between the two of them. Neil tried to burn him to death, but the Marksman twisted his arm behind his back before his hands could ignite. Neil felt the Marksman kick him in the back and heard a popping noise. Sharp pains shot through his arms and chest and his airways felt like they were collapsing.

Neil tried to summon some fire, but none sprung from his damaged arm. He yelped in pain as the Marksman grabbed his other arm. "You're easy to beat because you're cocky. You think fire is the eternal problem solver, when in actuality there is no refinement to it. No finesse. It's destruction."

Neil's other shoulder popped and he began to scream. His arms sat uselessly by as the Marksman stood over him. "I figured without proper control over your arms, your abilities would be useless. I suppose I was right."

Neil couldn't breathe and his mind was racing. What else could he do other than throw fire? The Marksman pulled a kitchen knife from his belt. "I've been told not to kill you." The Marksman sounded conflicted. "But I don't suppose you need your hands."

Neil gasped. He then remembered he was still in possession of the paramount Vapros ability. He materialized a few feet away from the Marksman and closer to the tree line. He stumbled to his feet and bolted as fast as his legs would carry him. The Marksman caught him and slammed him into the nearest tree. He jabbed Neil in the stomach and Neil stifled a scream. The Marksman held Neil to the tree by his neck. "I have no anger towards you, Neil Vapros," the Marksman said. His voice never changed from its monotone delivery. "If you're going to give me trouble on our way to see the Doctor, then I'm going to hurt you very badly."

Neil wanted to talk but he was more focused on trying to breathe.

"A common side effect of having your shoulder dislocated is the inability to breath correctly. It will pass."

Without warning the Marksman coughed violently onto Neil's face. Neil would have been disgusted if he weren't so frightened. The Marksman then released Neil and continued his coughing spasm. He took a step back as it worsened. Neil didn't try and run. He just stared. The Marksman glared back, as usual not making full eye contact. "It seems I've run out of time, Vapros," he wheezed. "I'll be back for my bounty. You can be sure."

He straightened his back and calmly escaped deeper into the woods. Neil fell to the ground and tried not to sob into the frosted forest floor. He could hardly breathe; he couldn't move his arms and his pride had been shattered. Neil couldn't tell which was worse, his injuries or the idea that he couldn't protect his friends. The Marksman was told not to kill him. Under different circumstances Neil would have been dead. Then where would Rhys be? Alone. He'd be the last hope for the Vapros family. That started the tears.

Neil sat with his face buried in the grass until he heard the Wolf calling his name. He called out in pain until the old General found his broken body. "Neil…"

"No lectures," Neil whispered as he tried to wipe his tears away on the grass.

The Wolf stared at him. "Neil…I…" He couldn't finish his thought for some reason.

"My shoulders are dis-something," Neil said. "Please tell me they won't stay like this forever."

The Wolf grabbed Neil's right arm and placed his foot on his back. "So?" Neil asked. "That kind of hurts. Do you just hold my arm there and then eventually it—"

The Wolf popped Neil's arm back into its socket. He screamed and the Wolf sighed. "Did no one tell you about dislocated shoulders when you were training to be an assassin?"

Neil flexed his hand and realized his right arm was working again. "No, they taught us to kill people. Not how to give people shoulder discomfort."

The Wolf snapped the other arm back into place and Neil howled in pain again. The tears were back too. "That might be the loudest I've ever heard a man scream," the Wolf said. "Are we experiencing shoulder discomfort?"

Neil rolled over to face the Wolf and felt the sweet rush of air into his lungs. After a few deep breaths, he felt well enough to talk without pain. "I wish I could tell you that the other guy looks worse but..." Neil's words died in his throat.

The Wolf also had tears on his face. Neil had never seen a man that old cry before. "What?" Neil started.

Then he remembered how the Marksman had fired his gun into the Golden Mug. Neil reached his feet at near Celerius speed. "Who?"

The Wolf looked like he wanted to speak but his mouth wasn't obeying him. Neil was down the hill and through the door of the Golden Mug before he even realized he was running. His eyes landed on Darius first. He was slumped up against the wall with a knife sticking out of his side. Rhys was crouched in front of him providing the necessary medical attention. He would live.

Then Neil's eyes shifted across the room. She was propped up against the bar. Neil felt his heart stop. She was standing somehow, as if she were a drunken patron who was holding onto the bar for support. The blood seeping from the back of her head pointed to another conclusion entirely. Josephine had worked at her bar, slept at her bar, and harbored fugitives at her bar. She'd died there too. Everyone else was already gathered, but Neil hardly noticed them. He collapsed numbly to his knees. For the second time in his life he experienced one of the worst feelings of all: being without a mother.

Chapter Twenty-Four

THE GOLDEN MUG
NEIL VAPROS

THE DAY OF JOSEPHINE'S FUNERAL ALSO BROUGHT THE FIRST SNOWFALL OF the year. Snowflakes drifted over the mourners gathered around the makeshift grave behind the Golden Mug. The fugitives had built the coffin and dug the grave with their own hands. Every light in the Golden Mug was out, and when Neil looked at it, he couldn't help but feel they'd gotten it killed as well.

Josephine's tombstone boasted one messily written sentence: *She was a mother to all who needed one.* The Wolf stood next to it, the others in a collective heap before the grave. Neil would have been cold on any other day, but the tears that slid down his face were warm, boiled from within by anger. "I don't know if Josephine would have objected to me speaking at her funeral, but I spoke at her son's," the Wolf began. "I have also spoken at too many other funerals in my time, but never have I known what to say so definitely as I do now. She was not a vengeful person. I am told she was forgiving. I hope she will forgive my need to express our sorrow at her passing. We make decisions in our lives about who we wish to be. Sure, the moments we experience change us, but we get to choose how. Life pushes us to crossroads and then we decide which path to walk down. When life takes people that we love from us, we are faced with the greatest challenge of all: do we realize that the world is unforgiving? Do we abandon those closest to us in fear of having them ripped away? Do we pursue our own selfish desires? Those are understandable options, and Josephine could have walked that path, judgment free, given what she lost. There is another path, though, and it is the one that she decided to walk. When she realized the cruel nature of the world she didn't close herself off from others. She welcomed them in because the world has been, and is, cruel. She watched over all of you purely out of kindness and love. She ignored the danger to her own life to protect you." The Wolf paused and laced his fingers together. "We are also now brought to that same crossroads."

His eyes settled on Neil who looked away out of awkwardness. The Wolf was imposing and regal, despite his ruffled appearance. Even though he represented a life that Neil didn't want, Neil felt the need to impress him. Or to be strong. Surely a man who had seen half a century of combat didn't want to see tears on the face of a sentimental boy. "We are faced with her same decision, which path do we walk? You've been asked before and you will be asked again. Make a choice and choose who you will be for the rest of your life. Will you close yourself off from a cruel world because it will hurt you again? Or will you choose to be there for others because the world will hurt them? Either way Josephine made a choice. She made an admirable one that not all of us are strong enough to make. She was an exceptional woman, and I know she is together with her son and will remain with us all."

It was a shame that none of the fugitives had offered to speak for Josephine, but the guilt strangled them. Neil had also never even been to a funeral. Even though his family had suffered endless casualties, they chose never to dwell. It made them seem weak. He was willing to bet that Darius and Lilly had never held funerals either. Neil didn't even know where he'd begin to honor Josephine's memory. He was used to stringing together long streams of sentimental dialogue, but today he knew it wouldn't be enough. Neil was a socialite, and Josephine deserved something more. She deserved what the Wolf had given her, a speech that honored her memory and at the same time steered them forward. Josephine would have wanted them to move forward. Despite the loss of her son, she'd still saved all of their lives. She hadn't crawled into a ball and died from sorrow. She'd lived well.

They paid their respects one by one and eventually dispersed. Rebecca pulled on Neil's arm gently and led him away from the group. He followed until she was just out of earshot. "I'm going to Misty Hollow," she said with shaky breath. "There's nothing left for me here."

Neil's guilt grew stronger now, gripping him by the throat. "I'm so sorry. We brought this into your house."

Rebecca shook her head. "No. Josephine knew what she was doing. She knew the risks. Don't let this consume you."

Neil was having trouble with that. "You can't reopen the Inn?"

Rebecca repositioned herself to face the Golden Mug which loomed in the distance. "Not alone," she decided. "And it doesn't seem like you'll be sticking around much longer. Misty Hollow was liberated recently. I'll try and go work in a bar there."

"Maybe I could stay," Neil mused. "Working at the Golden Mug doesn't sound so bad."

Rebecca patted the side of his face and he blushed. For a brief moment he wondered what that would look like to Bianca who was a few yards away. "You're special, Neil," she said. "You're being called to battle. To a higher purpose. I'd answer a call like that, if I could." She hugged him. "But the revolution, Volteria, it's not calling my name. It's calling yours."

They parted and she trudged down the hill to the Golden Mug, presumably to pack her things. "Wait…" Neil said. "So that's it? The Golden Mug closes? Forever?" He wanted something, anything, solid to remain of Josephine.

"Not forever," Rebecca said. "I'll reopen it one day when the war is over. I'll fix it up good as new, and maybe take in some wayward souls of my own. I owe her that much."

She smiled at the thought, then turned away. Neil stared at the snowflakes drifting over the grass by his feet. "She's right, you know," the Wolf said. He was still using his funeral voice. It was delicate, as if everyone around him was fragile and ready to crack at the slightest use of force. "You're special, Neil."

Neil looked up at the Wolf but didn't respond. He kicked his foot through the swirling snow.

"You see him, don't you?" the Wolf asked. "You've spoken to him."

Neil's eyes widened. Somehow he knew exactly what the Wolf was talking about. "They're just dreams," he whispered.

The Wolf chuckled. "You've spoken to the Man with the Golden Light, Neil. It doesn't matter if it's a dream. You should listen to what he's telling you."

"Have you seen him too?" Neil asked.

The Wolf looked off at nothing and smiled. "Once when I was very young, I saw him. Like your encounter, it was in a dream. He was completely transfixing and spoke with millions of voices, like the legends say."

Neil tensed. The Wolf could be lying to him. That's how everyone described the Man with the Golden Light. But something in his voice sounded pure and hopeful, like the voice of a man who had gazed into the face of a god. The Wolf continued. "We spoke about the path that the families were on. We really have strayed."

"He didn't seem as judgmental when we spoke," Neil murmured.

The Wolf examined Neil closely and it made him uncomfortable. "Do you have any tattoos?" the Wolf asked.

Neil had answered this question too many times. "No. I've never assassinated anyone."

"In your experience, what is the purpose of the Vapros tattooing ceremony? What is the purpose of the tattoos in general?"

This was clearly a loaded question, but Neil didn't care. He just wished that the Wolf could teach without playing word games. "They're trophies," Neil said. "It's how someone shows off their resume in our family."

The Wolf patted him on the shoulder. "There it is," he said tiredly as he sat in the cold grass. "We've strayed so far. We continue straying even now."

Neil grunted as he sat down as well. "I figure that was the wrong answer?"

"No, actually it's exactly what I wanted to hear. It wasn't always like that. They weren't always trophies. At least, not according to a few books that predate your father's lessons."

Neil wanted to leap to his father's defense, but he held back. Maybe it would be nice to hear what his ancestors had in mind for the tattoos before any needle touched his skin. "So…?" Neil asked impatiently.

The Wolf had a roundabout way of teaching things. He always waited for someone to finish his or her thoughts before he continued. It was as if he wanted to give the gears in their heads room to spin. "They used to be a terrible burden. It used to be that a Vapros would tattoo himself for every life he took, not in arrogance, but in remembrance. The ink on your skin was supposed to signify that you carried a terrible weight on your conscience and those with more tattoos were meant to be given sympathy for the crimes they'd committed against their own souls."

Without hesitation Neil thought of his sister Jennifer and how she killed the only boy she ever loved: Edward Celerius. After doing so, their father had tattooed a skeletal hand clutching a heart on her chest. The Wolf was wrong about one thing. Not everyone had strayed. Jennifer's tattoo was a burden on her soul, not a trophy. He couldn't speak for the other tattoos, as Jennifer had many, but that one certainly must have killed her to see in the mirror everyday. She must have felt like the hand inked onto her chest gripped her heart, unrelentingly. "I understand that," Neil said. "Luckily, I don't have any tattoos yet. No burdens on my soul."

"I disagree," the Wolf said finitely. "I believe that you're burdened with a great purpose."

Neil watched as a snowflake desperately tried to cling to a leaf on a nearby flower, but was forced into the sky by the wind. "How am I burdened with purpose?" Neil asked.

"You want a normal life," the Wolf said. "I understand that. You want to have a family. You want to be at peace. You want to know that people are in your life for good and that they won't be ripped away."

"That's exactly right," Neil said.

The Wolf plucked a flower from the ground and studied it. Neil was prepared for an inspirational speech, but the Wolf didn't stand, or turn to face him. He didn't raise his voice or make it swell like music. He sat there examining his flower. "What happened to Josephine, and what happened to you," he pointed to Neil's injury with the flower. "It's happening every day. All over this nation. Children are left fatherless and motherless by the hour in Volteria. Running from this fight, despite how much you want it, is no guarantee of safety. You could die in your new home, along with Bianca. Your little Lightborn children could go just as quickly. You won't ever be safe. Not truly."

Neil wanted to protest the idea that the Wolf had assumed Bianca would be his partner for life. Bianca had bigger dreams and aspirations to fulfill. The Wolf, once again, was waiting for the gears in Neil's head to stop turning. When they did, he continued. "The Man with the Golden Light once told me that one Lightborn was going to change everything. He told me that the revolution was a just cause, but without one Lightborn it would be completely without meaning or true victory. He said that his life would bring about our new nation."

"What's the new nation?"

"I'm not entirely sure. I like to think it's Volteria. It's a nation controlled by the common people and protected by Lightborns. I know we've strayed. I know we've made mistakes. But there are more good Lightborns than bad ones, and we don't deserve to be driven into extinction. I like to hope that with the help of that Lightborn we can restore our purpose as guardians, and the people can finally be liberated."

Neil was quiet for a moment. He didn't know what the Wolf was suggesting. "You think I'm that Lightborn?" he asked.

The Wolf released the flower and it rolled down the hill, spurred in its leaps and bounds by the breeze. "I asked if I'd know him when I saw him. The Man with the Golden Light, as deities do, left me with a cryptic message."

The Wolf stood and pointed down to the Golden Mug. Darius, a spec against the landscape, lumbered toward the open threshold. "I'd like to make sure he doesn't do anything he regrets. It's no longer safe here. We can speak on the way to Shipwreck Bay."

"What's at Shipwreck Bay?"

"The heart of our little rag-tag army."

Before the Wolf could get too far away, Neil cried out to him. "Okay, I give up! What did the Man with the Golden Light say? Is it me?"

"I honestly couldn't tell you," the Wolf said. It sounded like he meant it. "He told me that the Lightborn would be like a phoenix. Reborn in fire. Forged in fire." He pointed at Neil's hands. "People tell me you changed quite a bit once fire entered your life."

Neil shook his head. "I don't know if I believe you."

"Trust me, I don't believe it either," the Wolf said. "It's just something to think about. I'm not trying to sell you. I'm saying this and only this: you were given this extraordinary power, maybe it forged you, and maybe it didn't. Maybe it's a curse to you because it means you can never live a completely normal life. You have always had the ability to help more people, to liberate more people. You're a Lightborn. You were born with a purpose and you can run from it if you want. If safety and peace is what you're after, the only way past this is through it. You want to make a better world for yourself? You want to make a world where people won't be ripped away? Then use that fire inside of you to forge it. That's your burden. That's your purpose."

The Wolf didn't wait to see the change come across Neil's face. He went down the hill in pursuit of Darius, one more broken child to inspire. Neil leaned back for a moment and inhaled deeply, as if he could suck in the north wind and extinguish the fire inside of him. But he knew that he couldn't. He raised his hand and a small flame burst to life within it. He watched and saw his own spirit reflected back. He'd have peace, he'd have a normal life, and he'd one day be with those he loved. Until then, he was burdened, like Jennifer, and like every Lightborn had been before, with grief and purpose. One day the fire inside would dim into an ember, but not yet. There was a nation to shape and it would be forged. Until the day when he could be at peace, the flames would roar inside him, ceaselessly and ever growing.

Chapter Twenty-Five

THE GOLDEN MUG
DARIUS TAURLUM

DARIUS PUSHED HIS WAY THROUGH THE NON-EXISTENT DOOR OF THE Golden Mug and made a beeline for the bar. He jumped over it seamlessly and crouched down to raid its cupboards. When he stood up with a bottle of gin, the Wolf was standing there almost as if he were a paying customer. "Are you sure about that?" he asked.

"I can control it," Darius said.

The Wolf extended his hand to give Darius a handshake. Darius took his hand with a look of confusion. The Wolf dug his thumb into a pressure point that Darius hadn't known about. As Darius winced in pain, the Wolf lifted the bottle from his hand. Darius slammed his hands on the table in fury and the wood cracked. "Give it," Darius said.

The Wolf was silent.

"You're really going to try and stop me? You really think you can imagine the guilt I feel."

"I don't think you know how many lives are on my conscience."

Darius wanted to debate, but something in the Wolf's eyes proved that he wasn't kidding.

"I want to tell you a story," the Wolf said.

"I want to snap you in half," Darius retorted.

"One story. And if you listen I'll give you the bottle and you can drink yourself to death."

Darius wouldn't have listened if gin weren't his alcohol of choice. He placed his elbows on the bar and sarcastically set his chin in his hands like a child awaiting a bedtime story.

"I used to know a man named Robin Tuttle. When I originally met him, he was a merchant and probably weighed about one hundred and fifty pounds. He barely scraped by every week until his wife left him."

"Then he became depressed and drank a bunch?" Darius asked.

"No," the Wolf said. "He actually improved his business with his extra time. Eventually he bought a few more shops and stopped manufacturing with his own hands. He allowed young businessmen to run branches of his shops and made enough money to keep him comfortable for the rest of his life. As time went on, he began to host large dinners and invited everyone on his block. Through this combination of not working and overeating, he ballooned up to three hundred pounds."

"Wow," Darius said with the least possible amount of amusement.

"But a few weeks later he ran into his wife in a market and became disgusted with what he had become. So he began to restrict himself. He ate perfectly for an entire month at every meal except one. And at that meal he ate to his heart's content. Before long, he was back to his old fighting weight."

"I get it," Darius said. "You think I should restrict myself as well. To a glass per month?"

"No," the Wolf said. "The story isn't done. Tuttle's plan wasn't exactly foolproof. He thought he could have it both ways. He thought he could be at his healthy weight and also fill the void in him by over-eating. He didn't change his weight because he wanted to be healthy. He wanted to be happy, and his plan didn't account for the possibility that there was something he had to confront outside of his weight. Six months after getting back to one-fifty he was up to four-hundred."

"Where is he now?" Darius asked.

"He drowned in his own bathtub," the Wolf said. "It took a few weeks for anyone to find him, too."

Darius glared at the Wolf. "So what?" he asked. "I'm Robin Tuttle because I want a drink?"

"You're Robin Tuttle because you're not being smart about dealing with your emotions. I know about your past with drinking. You think you can limit yourself because one drink will end your pain. It won't. If you down a cup of this," he shook the bottle, "that's fine, but you have to have an endgame in mind for your emotions. Because if you just drink to end the pain, it'll never end, and it'll suck you down deeper and deeper. You'll drown in it. This won't bring Josephine back, and it certainly won't end your pain or your guilt. I need you to be useful, Darius. The revolution needs you to be useful. I have a feeling this won't help." The Wolf placed the bottle on the bar where Darius could reach it if he wanted to.

Darius gripped the bar and the parts underneath his thumbs splintered. "I hate this. I hate you," he murmured.

"That's all right. So long as you've heard me."

"I hear you." Darius stepped away from the bar. "Any other sage advice?"

"Stay away from bathtubs?" the Wolf said with a shrug.

Darius opened the door to the kitchen with one hand. "What about sleep?" he asked. "Can I sleep this off?"

"I'd actually recommend it," the Wolf said.

Darius shook his head and walked off into the kitchen. As he climbed into the secret rooms, he could hear the Wolf pouring out the alcohol into the sink. At first he felt angry that the Wolf didn't trust him, but as he settled into bed he felt relieved. Because he didn't trust himself either.

Chapter Twenty-Six

ROAD TO SHIPWRECK BAY
NEIL VAPROS

WITH EVERY HOBBLE AND LURCH OF THE CARRIAGE, DARIUS GRUNTED. Neil was counting them actually. The grunts. Today they were at three hundred and twenty four. It was as if he hated to have his feet off of the ground. He didn't exactly have a right to complain. The reason they were taking carriages in the first place was because of him. The Wolf had spent a few days procuring horses for them only to realize that no horse in existence could possibly bear Darius's weight. They hadn't tested it, by Darius's suggestion. All he'd said was, "I swear, if you put me on that horse's back, its little horsey legs are going to snap under my metal ass."

This comment earned a horrified gasp from Lilly and a new strategy for going to Shipwreck Bay. The Wolf returned the next day with two carriages. Darius, Neil and Rhys rode in one with the Wolf at the helm. Bianca led the second carriage with Lilly and Anastasia. It had been a few days and things were going smoothly, but Neil knew it wasn't going to last. Tension was flowed rampantly through the group. Anastasia showed the worst of it. The way she looked reminded Neil of how he felt when he was living as a fugitive on the streets of Altryon. She was always on edge and never sat still when she didn't have to. She had become an uncontrollable force of kinetic motion. Based solely on her anxious nature, Neil was willing to bet that there was more to her story. Or maybe this "Imperial Doctor" was as bad as she said. Maybe he really was the embodiment of pure analytical evil.

The carriage stirred to a stop and Rhys jutted awake. "Bathroom break?" he asked. Rhys never seemed to go in and out of sleep gradually. The dream world didn't cling to him like it clung to everyone else. Neil heard the Wolf step down from the seat on the front of the coach. He opened the door and stepped out into the midday sun. He saw the problem immediately and held his hand out to convince Rhys not to exit. Their way was blocked by six vicious looking highwaymen, all armed to the teeth. The one in front was huge, maybe even bigger than Darius. He held a deadly looking club covered in spikes. His head was shaved, lazily so. Knicks and scars were visible through the stubble that covered his square head. He grinned at the Wolf who approached him fearlessly.

Bianca hopped off of her carriage. Lilly and Anastasia also exited the coacharriage without delay. Neil quickly realized how much firepower they were packing between five Lightborns, one assassin, and Bianca. The Wolf waved them away. "Nice carriages," the leader of the highwaymen said.

The Wolf turned around. "They're all right," he said. "You wouldn't like them. Not enough leg room for a man your size."

"I think I'll take them anyway," the highwayman said. "I'll take that sword too."

The Wolf smiled at him, flashing his pearly whites. "Oh you'll take it."

"You think you're funny," the highwayman said. He whistled by placing his two meaty fingers in his mouth. Three of his men appeared out of the forest on either side of the carriages with arrows notched. "How do you do under pressure, old man?"

"Neil, Bianca, Lilly!" the Wolf commanded. With one fireball from Neil, the men on the right side of the road scattered. Neil blasted the only remaining man before he could fire off an arrow. From what he could hear, Lilly and Bianca had dealt with their side of the carriage. The Wolf smiled at the man, wider this time. "I do all right."

"You're the Wolf? Aren't you?" the highwayman accused.

"I am," the Wolf said.

"You think you're different than the Empire, but you're not. We don't want you either. Volteria is free. We're free to do what we want. Don't suck us into a war."

"And you're free to do what? Rob and kill your brethren?"

The highwayman swung his club without warning. The Wolf ducked under it and dodged the backswing fluidly. There was something entrancing about the way he moved. When Neil was younger, his father had hired dancers to perform at the more lavish parties. The Wolf moved like a dancer. When he was in combat he had no bones, and never resisted an enemy. He simply bent around their weapons. He drew his sword after the highwayman's third swing and with one more elegant twirl, the criminal's head was off of his neck. His men tried to overwhelm him but, step-by-step, he sliced through them, the way Josephine used to slice through vegetables. Before Neil could fully register what was happening, the road was cleared of enemies.

The Wolf turned and noticed everyone staring at him. "If you have a quicker way to clear a roadblock, I'm open to suggestions," he said. "Darius!" he called.

Darius poked his head out of the carriage. His eyes widened when he realized what he'd missed. "Would you be a friend and clear the road for us? They might be in pieces, but they're still heavy."

Darius lumbered out and went to work without a word. He knew better than to argue. He hadn't had to kill anyone. As he went to clear the road, the Wolf walked back to the carriages leisurely. When Neil stepped back into the carriage he saw the Wolf cleaning the blood from his sword with a handkerchief. "What was that?" Rhys asked.

"Steven Celerius and the Wolf are very different people," Neil declared as he sat opposite his brother. "The guy who's been giving us helpful advice and who's been supporting us is Steven Celerius. There were highwaymen blocking our way."

"And?" Rhys asked.

"And they met the Wolf," Neil said.

Chapter Twenty-Seven

SHIPWRECK BAY
NEIL VAPROS

ACCORDING TO THE WOLF, SHIPWRECK BAY HAD MANY DIFFERENT ORIGIN stories despite how young it was. The giant overturned pirate ship in the center of town certainly warranted some discussion. The Wolf's story was that it had been brought to shore for maintenance and barnacle removal. After the ship was propped up, something peculiar happened to the sea and the tides. They didn't come back in. So the ship was left outside of the ocean and the men had no way to push it back out to sea. Once they realized there was no other alternative, the settlers hollowed out the ship from its sides and turned it into the town hall.

Now the group walked through the crowded city that had been built at the foot of this marvelous ship. People saluted the Wolf and dropped whatever they were doing to cheer for him. Some even tried to grab his hands and coat as he walked through the streets. It was clear, the revolution was strongest in Shipwreck Bay and the Wolf was their patron saint of freedom. "Where are your men?" Lilly asked.

The Wolf smiled at a private joke. "Where else? The pirate ship. Formally she's called Annalisa. After some captain's wife, presumably."

The Annalisa loomed in the distance. They journeyed toward it through the last stretch of buildings and civilization. Once they arrived, Neil realized that the Wolf's forces were smaller than he'd imagined. Five or six tents were set up around the entrance. The entrance was created by the absence of a few planks, but Neil could see men busy with activity inside. Neil was sure he'd get vertigo working in a fortress propped up on a beach. Everything must have been shifting diagonally inside.

When the Wolf and Bianca approached, the mere forty men outside began to cheer. He smiled at them and turned to his new troops. "This is smaller than I expected," Anastasia said.

The Wolf examined his tiny operation. "That's the idea. We focus our energy on staying hidden. We attack like the Vapros are trained to."

"What?" Neil asked.

"We spring from the shadows and deliver crippling blows. Then we vanish into thin air," the Wolf said. "Nearly half of the citizens out here support us and will fight for us, but stay hidden right under the Empire's nose. These are just my strategists and analysts."

"Half of the people in Volteria support you?" That number seemed a little high to Neil. Looking around at the Wolf's scarce numbers made him nervous. He'd just agreed to join a revolution. It would help if that revolution involved more than forty men.

Without a word the Wolf turned back toward the denser parts of town and planted his feet. With a cry loud enough to start an earthquake, he howled out the words, "Free Volteria!"

It took a few moments, but voices began to sound off in the distance. Dozens of cries, turned to hundreds, and perhaps even thousands at its loudest. The chorus yelled the same thing. "Free Volteria!"

Neil's breath of awe faded to one of relief. The revolution might have been well hidden, but it was certainly forceful and formidable.

The Wolf turned back to the group and smirked. "We have more than enough power to cripple the Empire. We just need to figure out where to apply the pressure. I'm sure I'll be needed." The Wolf gestured to his men. "But I'd like to give you some assignments first."

"All of us?" Neil asked immediately.

"Well, not Bianca," the Wolf said. "She's done her time on my training ground. Not Anastasia either. Not to offend you, my dear, but I doubt you'd fight for us without proper payment. Despite being well organized, we are not well financed."

Anastasia said, "No hard feelings, Wolf. I'll keep myself entertained."

"Probably by killing people," Darius muttered.

"Probably," Anastasia agreed. She trekked off toward town.

The Wolf frowned. "Maybe I should have sent someone to keep an eye on her." He thought for another moment. "I definitely should have."

The Wolf gave a subtle wave of his hand and a rebel soldier shed his blue coat. Beneath it he wore a thin white shirt. Neil was surprised by the instant transformation. He looked like just another civilian. The Wolf was a proponent of stealth and cleverly devised attacks meant to cripple enemies. It probably helped that his soldier could become anyone just by abandoning a coat. The young rebel trailed behind Anastasia until they both disappeared from view. "As for the rest of you, I have some training planned for the next few days. In one week, we'll be visiting my arms dealer friend and picking up some new weapons. Then we'll go after the Doctor. Rhys, you'll stay here today."

"I don't get to train?" Rhys asked. He looked hurt. He'd never been known for his skills as a warrior, but it was always nice to be included.

"You're training here," the Wolf explained. "You're going to study my battle strategies and suggest your own. We're putting that mind of yours to use."

"Oh." Rhys was at a loss for real words. "Oh. Yes." He tried again. "Yay!"

The Wolf gestured to his men. "The big tent has my war maps. Unleash yourself. I'll be back soon."

Rhys bounded over to the largest tent in an uncharacteristically excited fashion. The Wolf signaled for the rest of them to follow. They went away from the Annalisa, and away from town until the Wolf found a dusty path in the dirt. It circled the entire town of Shipwreck Bay and ended on the other side of the Annalisa. "Lilly," the Wolf said, "it's your turn. This path is about ten miles from end to end."

Lilly stomped one of her feet, testing the dirt underneath her boots. "You want me to run it?"

The Wolf pulled a pocket watch out of his coat. "Yes. You have twenty minutes."

Lilly stalled. "That's a mile every two minutes. I'm a Celerius but I'm not—"

"Go," the Wolf said and clicked the top of his watch.

Lilly's scowl was nothing but a distant memory as she shot down the path, sending up waves of dust in her wake. Neil was always amazed by the way she moved, mostly because he could never see her feet. She always looked like a torso and head surrounded by a blur.

He wondered how she looked to the other Celerius. "Onward?" Neil asked. He was already nervous about what his training would be.

"Onward," the Wolf replied.

They went past the path and within a few clicks of the Wolf's watch they were at his next destination. They came upon a giant carriage that was turned over and buried halfway into the clearing. If Neil didn't known any better he would have said that the ground itself reached up and was swallowing it. "Darius, meet your opponent," the Wolf said.

Darius cracked his knuckles and flexed his muscles. That was his favorite thing to do, Neil had noticed. Even though Darius wasn't as muscular as he had been back in the glory days of the families, he was still big enough to show off. He cast a glance at Bianca as he stretched his arm. Neil felt heat pooling in his fingertips, but he didn't say anything. "You want me to pull it out of the ground?" Darius asked.

The Wolf indicated with an open hand. "I want you to try."

Darius practically skipped over, brimming with confidence, and wrapped his fingers around two popped out windows. He bent his knees and heaved with a mighty roar. The carriage didn't budge. He tried again, with a less mighty roar and turned around, embarrassed. "I don't understand the point of this," he said. "I'm the strongest guy walking around in Volteria. Why do I need to be stronger?"

The Wolf nodded as if absorbing the information, but Neil knew he wasn't. "Were you stronger than that gate at the secret entrance?" the Wolf asked.

The look on Darius's face indicated to everyone there that he was remembering how he released the gate and stopped Lilly from going after Jonathan. "How do you know about that?"

"I make it my business to know everything," the Wolf said. "Knowledge wins fights. Not brute strength. Pull this carriage out of the ground. You're not allowed to use tools either."

It was a demand now. Darius, ego bruised, went to the other side of the carriage and pulled it in a different direction experimentally. The Wolf silently led Bianca and Neil away from Darius and his task. Nearby was one more clearing and the Wolf took them to the center. He pulled two balls of tape from his coat and tossed them to Neil. Neil caught them and tried to resist burning them to pieces. "You want to box me?"

"No," the Wolf said. "I want you to box her." He cocked his head in the direction of Bianca. "Wrap your hands."

"You can't be serious," Neil said. "I'm not gonna hit Bianca."

"You're right," the Wolf said. "You probably won't hit Bianca. But that's no excuse not to try."

Neil noticed that Bianca's hands were already taped. They usually were, seeing as she was a close combat fighter whenever she wasn't throwing knives. He grabbed the ball of tape and began rolling it over his knuckles. "Are you sure about this?" he asked Bianca.

She looked a little too sure and Neil remembered that just recently they'd been fighting. Maybe she was simply waiting for her chance to have a go at him. "Don't worry, Neil," she said. "It'll be fun."

"There are ground rules," the Wolf said. "Neil, no powers."

Neil's heart rate spiked. He hadn't been trained to fight hand to hand without powers. Based on the Wolf's expression he knew it. "Why do I need to learn this?" Neil asked. The moment the words left his mouth he realized he sounded a lot like Darius.

"In one week, you'll spar me," the Wolf said. "I'd suggest getting ready for that fight."

The Wolf left them to it and Neil watched him stride into the distance like some sort of phantom. Neil finished wrapping his hands. "Okay," he said as he punched his opposite palm. "When do we start?"

Neil was suddenly on the ground, his face caressed by the short grass. He blinked and realized blood was pooling in his mouth. "Did you just...?"

"Win round one? Why, yes Neil. It looks like I did." Bianca danced back and forth and jabbed the air.

Neil stood shakily and raised his fists for round two. Hopefully, this one would last a little longer.

Chapter Twenty-Eight

THE CLIFF
THE PACK

EVEN THOUGH THE DOCTOR'S POWERS HAD FADED OVER TIME, HE STILL had an extraordinary sense of hearing. Even now, over the roaring of his personal forge, he could hear the Marksman sneaking into his workshop. His son was no doubt searching for another hit of the Doctor's special concoction. "You won't find it, Victor," the Doctor said.

His son limped into view. He was pale as snow and sweat poured from his brow.

"Are they dead?" the Doctor asked. "Did you earn it?"

"I don't have time for this," the Marksman said. "I need it. I need it now. I have moments."

"If you didn't manage to kill a single one of them, then why should I renew my contract with you?" The Doctor didn't even face his son. "I don't need dead weight in my Pack."

If the Marksman was offended he didn't show it. He pulled his pistol from his side and positioned it against the back of the Doctor's head. "If I feel my heart giving out, I'll pull this trigger."

"You don't have the spine for it." The Doctor continued assembling a wooden box, with a triggering mechanism inside. "You want to live? Earn it."

"The Vapros boys are hiding secrets from the Celerius girl. She's also hiding secrets from the Wolf. Both the Celerius girl and the Wolf have the same power: they channel sound waves through the air. The street girl is Anastasia's sister. Anastasia and the street girl are both spawn of Paul Blackmore."

As the Marksman rattled off information methodically the Doctor tightened a screw on his metal jaw. "That last detail is particularly interesting," the Doctor said. "Has Anastasia wavered?"

"I don't know," the Marksman said. "She told me she's using her connection to lead them to you directly."

The Doctor laughed, or coughed. "Of course she is. She's a survivor and she's running out of time. I estimate that in a week she'll be in the same situation you are now."

The Marksman tightened his grip on the gun. "I'm going to do it this time."

"I know you're not one for boasting," the Doctor said. "I know that if you're saying it, you really mean it. My last question for you is this, Victor: are you ready to enter the void?"

Victor cocked the gun. "I've been ready for a while."

The Doctor pulled a wooden box from the inside of his coat pocket and passed it to Victor. His son lowered the gun and fumbled with the box until it opened and a syringe fell out. The Marksman caught it before it hit the ground and jabbed it into his neck. He injected the chemical and collapsed in relief as the withdrawal subsided. "Is Sean Beaton dead?" the Doctor asked conversationally.

"Yes," the Marksman said. "I'll share the payment."

"No need," the Doctor said. "Your friend, your contract, your money."

The Marksman rested his head on the stone floor and exhaled evenly. They waited in silence as the Doctor finished his contraption. "I saw your brother last month," the Doctor said.

"Lester?" the Marksman asked.

"No," the Doctor said. "The other one."

This shook the Marksman from his trance. "Are you sure?"

The Doctor set the box on its side and wiped his hands on his apron. "I am. He's in the Industrial City. Working. His powers are gone."

"Broke his oaths?"

"I assume so. Not all Venator want to remain Venator."

"You know that better than anyone."

The Doctor's upper lip, his only lip, curled. "Go to sleep, Victor. Tomorrow you're going to build a machine with me."

"A machine for what?"

The Doctor looked into the bannisters above them. "We're building a web, Victor. This particular strand is for the Celerius. They'll be wrapped up. Like flies."

Chapter Twenty-Nine

SHIPWRECK BAY
DARIUS TAURLUM

Darius looked like he'd been swimming, he was sure. Sweat dripped from every iron pore and, for the first time in his life, he felt sore. For the thousandth time that day he grabbed the carriage and heaved with all of his might. It didn't budge. Again. He groaned in frustration. Maybe he could tear the carriage to pieces and deliver it to the Wolf in a thousand different parts. After another unsuccessful attempt he stood straight, only to find that Anastasia was sitting cross legged on top of the carriage. "Get off," Darius growled. "I don't need this thing to be any heavier."

She didn't move. "Take a break?" she recommended. "You've been at this for two days."

Darius waved her away as if she were nothing but a bug. "Taurlum get stronger the angrier they get."

"So I must make you very strong," Anastasia supplied. "Seeing me must make you lift like nothing else."

Darius scowled, but didn't respond. There was actually some logic to her backwards thinking. He flopped onto his back and pushed with his legs. The carriage still didn't budge. "Maybe I don't make you as angry as you say," Anastasia said. "Maybe you actually like seeing my face around."

She spoke mostly too herself, but it was enough to infuriate Darius. "I don't know if you've noticed, but none of us are exactly glad to have you around," he said. "You're an assassin. How can we charge into battle with you when we don't even know what side you're on?"

"Bianca trusts me," Anastasia said.

She didn't sound completely certain. Darius had found a weakness. He didn't have an endgame in mind aside from hurting Anastasia. It was petty and he knew it, but he wanted her gone more than he wanted the strength to move this carriage. "You think Bianca trusts you? I'm pretty sure I had a friendlier relationship with Michael. And he tried to kill me. At least Michael and I exchanged words."

Anastasia narrowed her eyes. She knew what he was doing, he could tell. "I suppose you're right," Anastasia said. "Bianca and I have never been close."

Darius paused. He'd expected a battle and not getting one was frustrating him. "Why not?" he asked.

She gave him a look that said, *you don't really want to know. You're messing with me.* He shrugged and went back to pushing up against the side. "Our father was a truly terrible man. His name was Paul Blackmore."

"I've heard the name," Darius said. "He's a lieutenant in the army."

"*Was* a lieutenant in the army," Anastasia corrected him. "He drank himself to death a few weeks ago. Good riddance." She murmured the last part while looking up to the sky.

"What did he do that was so bad to you and Bianca?"

"He didn't do anything to Bianca," she said. "He didn't turn her into a killing machine."

Darius punched the carriage, which dented it, but not much else. "Bianca turned into a killing machine all on her own, then," Darius said more to himself than to her.

"Our father used to be a part of something called the Imperial Hunting Squadron. They were responsible for going after anyone out here with a body count over ten. His job was to research the land beyond the walls before the rest of the group came out to join him. He would meet the locals in an area and map out the journey for the rest."

"So he was in charge." Darius slammed into the carriage shoulder first. Nothing.

"Actually the Wolf was in charge."

Darius took a moment to remember that the Wolf had once been the General of the Imperial Army. He seemed like an Outsider through and through. "So the Wolf and your dad had their own little club. One thing leads to another, and now you kill people for money."

She looked annoyed. For a moment he was sure that she wouldn't continue the story. "It wasn't just the Wolf and my Dad. Carlin was part of it too. And so were Anthony Celerius and Virgil." Her hand rested on her chain spike and Darius tensed up instinctually. "Carlin, Anthony and Virgil were just firepower. They were the real hunters. The Wolf was in charge of directing them and my father would feed them information. He loved it outside the walls. He loved the people. He found an Outsider woman and seduced her."

"Your Mom?" Darius guessed.

"Good Darius," she said. He was close enough for her to pat him on the head condescendingly. "You're listening very well. Nine months later I was born. My mother wanted to keep me, but Paul Blackmore loved the idea of having an Outsider child. So he took me around all of Volteria. I went on every scouting mission. I even got one of these." She pulled her shirt up and exposed a small tattoo on her flank. *IHS.* It looked slightly stretched and morphed. It was clear that it had been given to a much smaller girl. "Everyone in the hunting squadron had one, so my father gave me one too."

"How old were you when that happened?" He indicated the tattoo.

"Five," she said. "Bianca was born that same year. My father would never take me inside the walls, and then I knew why. He had another wife, and she'd just birthed another daughter. Once I found out I threw a few tantrums, so he took me inside to meet her whenever he could. We spent a few years seeing each other every couple months. My father didn't care for her as much and only came by when he had to. She was spared."

"Spared what?"

"He wanted to turn his Outsider child into a soldier. Like he was. So he taught me everything. He made sure that I knew how to kill. Eventually he stopped taking me on his missions and started giving me my own. Eventually Bianca's mother died of sickness and we stopped visiting her altogether."

"So you just left her all alone?" Darius asked.

"You never met my father. She was better off. No one took him seriously because he was always drunk, but he was secretly vicious and calculating. When he was without drink his temper only got worse."

Darius wanted to mention that vicious and calculating was how he saw her, but he found it difficult. He didn't want to hurt her anymore. It was always easier to hate someone you didn't know.

"When I was sixteen I failed one of his crucial missions and he attacked me. That was the last time I saw him. I found my way back inside the city by forging documents and started using the only skill I had to make money."

"So how did you fall in with the Doctor?"

Her grip on the spike increased and he saw her knuckles turn white. "After Rhys stabbed me, I needed medical help. All assassins are told about the Doctor. I was able to find him before I bled out and he promised to help me if I promised to join the Pack." She stared into nothingness with fury. "I've spent a lot of time killing for men who made me think I had no other choice." She slid her hand over the side of her spike as if to wipe off the Doctor's imaginary blood. "But you can be certain, when I send this spike through the Doctor's body, it'll be for me."

One look into her eyes told Darius that she believed it. He was silent as he continued to push and pull at the carriage. "You have to dig it out," Anastasia said.

"The Wolf said that I couldn't use tools."

"You don't have to. You have super strength. Dig around the sides until the whole thing is unearthed. Then pull it out."

"And that will work?"

"It'll work better than throwing your weight against it like an ox."

Darius chuckled under his breath and went to work digging. She watched him, unblinking, but now he didn't mind. He was sure about one thing as he threw handful after handful behind him. He felt sorry for her. Part of him understood everything she'd done to him. She might help him carry the carriage out of the dirt, but not by provoking his anger. He'd already wasted too much of that.

Chapter Thirty

SHIPWRECK BAY
LILLY CELERIUS

LILLY SPOTTED VIRGIL AS HE PULLED HIS CLOAK OVER HIS HEAD IN THE town square. She'd just failed her sixth run of the week and was jogging back slowly. So far she hadn't even come close to the Wolf's twenty-minute cap. She was stuck near thirty minutes for each run, some faster, some slower. On this particular run she'd tripped over a branch and pulled a muscle in her leg, so she was taking the more direct route back to the ship. The route happened to put her on a collision course with someone she badly wanted a word with. She waited until he exited the more populated area of town and tailed him through the streets. She bolted from alley to alley as she pursued him and made sure her blue coat was never visible when he turned around to search for a tail.

She'd known Virgil over the course of his rise to lieutenant. After all, Anthony had practically adopted him. He was always skittish, his head constantly in motion. Every time she came within a hundred yards, he'd turn to search for a tail, and she'd have to dart into hiding with her Celerius speed. He eventually reached the outskirts of town and she realized that her chance was slipping away. She had no weapon, but that wasn't an issue. She planned to commandeer his. She advanced quickly and reached out for the knife at his belt. He seemed to anticipate her and yielded to her attack. She tumbled past him and onto the ground, but recovered immediately. She wouldn't let him have the upper hand. "I've waited a long time to see you again, Virgil," she spat.

He pulled his knife from his belt and held it in a defensive position. "I've awaited it as well. I regret what happened to Anthony. I think about it every day, but I have a new purpose. I can't be made to dwell on Anthony's death."

"Your purpose was assigned to you by a psychotic murderer," Lilly said. "I'm interested, Virgil." She pronounced his name like it was a curse upon him. "When you think about Anthony, do you think about the fact that he pulled you out of poverty and made you a soldier? He used to talk about how he turned you, a savage, into a man of honor. Anthony practically adopted you."

"And I love him for that," Virgil said. "But he made his choice. What was I to do? Fight him? Stab Carlin through the heart?"

"It would have been a good start," Lilly said.

Virgil shook his head. "Your brother loved you more than you know, and I'm sure he watches over you from beyond the grave. Leave Shipwreck Bay within the week. I have no choice but to report what I've seen here to General Carlin."

"You have no choice," Lilly said with a humorless laugh. "That would make a good family motto for you."

Virgil placed his hand over his weapon cautiously. "I'll consider it."

He turned around and walked away down the road. He did it calmly, too. Lilly wanted to scream at his arrogance. He somehow knew that he could defend himself well enough or that she wouldn't go after him. She wanted to find a rock and bash his head in from behind, but it wasn't in her nature. She wasn't a scoundrel like him.

She turned back to report his presence to the Wolf when something occurred to her. Virgil had been exiting a store. She hadn't taken the time to look at what store it was exactly, but chances were that it had something to do with whatever assignment Carlin had given him. She hoped that it wasn't just a bakery or something ridiculous. She considered going back to get assistance from the Wolf and her friends, but there was a fire burning within her and she had to release her rage somehow. An investigation seemed like a good place to start.

She returned to the square and went to the corner store. She could tell it was an armory from looking in the dusty windows. She opened the door and a small bell attached to the frame rang. "I'll be just a moment!" came a cry from the back.

She examined the swords and noticed that a few looked to be expertly made, with intricate golden handles. Surprisingly, a few others looked like a man with no arms had forged them. The metal was bent and unpolished. When she ran a finger over the blade it wasn't even sharp enough to cut her. She used her abilities to feel her way around the store. An incredibly short man was in the back fiddling with a sword. She could also feel another mass in the closet nearest her. It was dense and crumpled, but she couldn't figure out what it was. She wanted to open the closet but decided to wait until she met the owner. The man walked out of the back and she was stricken by his size. She had always been tall for her age and gender, but this man looked to be in his thirties and rested at four-and-a-half feet tall. Despite this, he was muscular enough to look formidable. He had a sizable cloak and it concealed his face in shadows. "Are you looking for anything in particular?" he asked.

She instantly determined that something wasn't quite right. There was something off about this man. He looked like he was vibrating in anticipation and his entire body looked tense and rigid. "I'm just browsing," she said sternly.

He grinned beneath his cloak. She was certain that she could see the glint of metal in his mouth. Something stirred in her mind but she ignored it. He probably had a gold tooth. Nobles in Altryon sometimes did that. "Do you forge these swords yourself?"

He looked at them in confusion for a moment, then smiled widely. His smile glinted in the light, but his mouth closed before she could take note of that. "I do. I love your coat. My most famous customer has one just like it."

She blinked and looked around the store. Was this the infamous arms-dealer that the Wolf had spoken of? His craftsmanship didn't exactly seem up to par with the weaponry that the revolutionaries needed. "You work with the Wolf?"

"I do!" the tiny man said, once again shaking. "We're good friends. Would you like to see one of the new swords I'm crafting for him?"

"I suppose," she said on the verge of walking straight out the door. This wasn't sitting right with her. "Let me see."

He went to the back and returned with an unpolished sword. She looked at it with disdain. He noticed. "Just hold it in your hands. Then it will be clear."

She grabbed the sword and felt something poke her finger, sharp enough to draw blood. Her second observation was that the handle was wet. She dropped the sword and pulled one of the better looking ones off of the wall. "What did you just do?"

"Who me?" the man said as he shook furiously. "All I did was invent the triple edged sword. Not even the user is safe from its sting. You can have it. I'll give it to you for a steal."

"What?" Lilly asked. Suddenly her vision began to go blurry and the floor shifted under her feet. "What is...? I..." Her tongue turned to concrete in her mouth.

The small man threw off his cloak and erupted into unbridled and insane laughter. Even in her woozy state, Lilly realized that he had been shaking as a result of trying to suppress his cackling. "I was so close!" he screamed through his hilarity. "I did so well! I just couldn't resist. I gave it to you for a steal! Get it? Like steel?" He placed his hands on his knees and continued losing his mind over his terrible joke.

Lilly dropped her weapon. "What did you do?" she managed.

"You really can't hold your cyanide, can you?" he giggled. "What a lightweight."

She gasped. She knew that Celerius could resist low doses of poisons, but it was never an easy journey. "Lester Buchwald," she said as she realized who he was. "The Hyena."

"I can't believe you came in here!" the Hyena cried. "I wanted you the most! Even on your wanted poster you look like a knockout!"

He lifted her arm and smelled it. "You can have the sword. I might charge you an arm and a leg for it, though." He winked and took an exploratory bite of her arm.

In her drugged state she almost didn't feel it. He pulled back and the skin on her arm healed itself. "Just as I thought!" he said. "The Celerius are my favorite Lightborns. I could eat all your fingers today and have a new batch by tomorrow." He turned very serious. "Should we end world hunger, Lilly?"

Her head began to clear and she knew that her body was recovering. He picked up her pointer finger in his hand and jeered at her up close with his shiny metal teeth. She lashed out and kicked him in the groin. He let out a noise that sounded half-scream and half-laugh. "Feisty!" he growled as he stumbled to his feet.

She grabbed the sword and used it to keep the Hyena at bay. "I've had just about enough of your stupid jokes," she said. "Where's the man who owns this shop?"

The Hyena pointed at his stomach. "Lower intestine?" he said. "I mean, most of him." He stepped backwards to the closet and opened it. Lilly realized the mass that she had felt earlier was a half of a man. The Hyena closed the closet. "Anyway," he said, "I can't exactly let you leave here, Lilly. I don't want you speaking badly of me and driving away future customers."

She swung her sword and he ducked under it. She followed with a thrust, but he managed to dodge this as well. She felt the effects of the poison and clearly couldn't attack at her usual speed. He tackled her and wrestled the sword out of her arms. In the struggle he cut her arm deeply and she yelped in pain. It healed over before The Hyena could claim the sword for his own. By the time he had it in his hand, she was ready for battle again. He swung it at her a few times, but she evaded it easily. It was clear to both involved that the sword was too large for someone his size to use efficiently. He tossed it to the side and pounced on her viciously. He snapped at her a few times, but she managed to throw him off. She bolted for the sword with all of her speed, but when she turned to face her opponent again he was gone. She pushed through the door after him. Somehow he'd escaped into the crowds. She cursed and threw the sword to the ground. How could she expect to eventually end Carlin's life when she couldn't even handle a miniature lunatic with a sick sense of humor? She trotted down the road in hopes that he would appear and she could eliminate another assassin from the Pack. Unfortunately, he had the good sense to disappear. She slowed to a walking pace and changed course so that she was directed toward the rebel hideout. One thing would be absolutely certain upon her return: the Wolf would be very disappointed in her time.

Chapter Thirty-One

SHIPWRECK BAY
NEIL VAPROS

Neil took special notice of Bianca's boxing skills, particularly the way she blocked oncoming attacks. Whenever he swung at her, she simply slipped around his arm like a snake or redirected his arm and set him off balance. The Wolf had clearly trained her recently. He saw the Wolf's elegant swordplay and delicate touch in every swing. He hadn't even come close to winning a fight yet and they were three days into training. At least she'd stopped hitting him. Now she simply pushed him away or tapped him on the side of the head. "To prevent brain damage," she'd teased. "You need what remains."

One day she'd shared with him some useful advice, but he still wasn't winning any fights. "Do you know why I don't lose fights to men twice my size?" she'd asked.

"Why?"

"Because every time I square up against an opponent they think they can end me in one swing. If they miss, or don't knock me out with that first punch, they have no plan. They're not ready to face the consequences of a real fist fight."

Neil saw Anastasia lingering by the edge of the clearing on certain days. To his advantage, her presence distracted Bianca. He landed his first strike, an open faced jab, on the end of day three. It was light, but it was a hit. "Finally," he cheered.

"Great," she said. "The score is ten-thousand to one. Should I be prepared for a comeback?"

Neil glanced over his shoulder to find that Anastasia was gone. "If your sister sticks around, you should."

Bianca's eyebrows travelled south and he knew that he'd upset her. But he had the right to be upset. "You always told me your family was dead," Neil said pointedly as he prepared for another round.

Bianca tried to sweep his leg, but Neil had been prepared. That was her favorite move and she used it often. "Dead to me," she supplied.

"Come on," he grunted as he tried to hit her with another open jab. A little of her fancy footwork prevented his attack from succeeding. "You had a living father and sister and you never told me?"

"They stopped visiting when I was very young." Bianca spun out of the way of another punch. "My father never loved me like he loved her. She got to travel all over the world and I was left alone in Altryon. In the slums." Her nose crinkled reflexively when she said the word "slums."

She lashed out with a simple punch, which Neil blocked. She then kicked his ankle with her right foot. He gasped and tried to retreat, but she knocked him off his feet before he could. "Ten-thousand and one to one," she said.

"I've heard about your father," Neil said. "A guy who hunts humans for a living doesn't sound like the perfect father figure." He didn't try to get up.

"What father? He was never a father to me." She pulled him to his feet. "At least Anastasia wasn't alone."

Neil tested his ankle. It was sore. "Right, but look at her. She's a killer. One who's worked for the Pack. You're a revolutionary. You're..." She stared at him expectantly. He struggled for the right words. "You turned out the way you did, with or without him. You're extraordinary and somehow you ended up that way on the streets."

She threw her head back and laughed. "Neil, you must really be in love with me."

"What?"

"I can beat you half to death for three days and you'll still tell me how extraordinary I am. I should have started hitting you a long time ago."

Neil laughed. "Okay. Round ten-thousand and three. This one's mine."

They sparred until the sun went down behind them. "Maybe I should try and reconnect with her more," Bianca said as she undid the tape on her hands. "It wasn't her fault that our father was obsessed with her."

Neil knew it would be best not to push too hard. Bianca hated being told what to do. "It might be a good idea if we're going into battle with her."

"What about you? We're going into battle together. You're not mad that I'm beating you to a pulp, are you?"

"Of course not." Neil's smile began to fade. "You're not the one I'm worried about. I saw what the Wolf did to those robbers."

"He's not going to cut your head off."

"Do you think he's capable of punching it off?" Neil asked.

"No, I don't think that's…" Bianca paused and then shrugged. "Well, I guess we'll see, won't we?"

Chapter Thirty-Two

SHIPWRECK BAY
LILLY CELERIUS

LILLY'S NEWS ABOUT THE HYENA HAD SHAKEN THE CAMP. THEY'D LOST their provider of weapons and it showed on the Wolf's face. She hated being the bearer of such unhappy news. Especially because it didn't end with her returning with the Hyena's decapitated head. She remembered exactly what the Wolf had said when she told him about her confrontation with the lunatic. "Maybe he's smarter than he seems."

It was a clever enough plan. The Hyena didn't know where to start looking for them, so he decided to steal a shop where the Wolf would come to buy weapons. He'd gambled that the Lightborns would be with him. Then when they were all in the same place he'd spring a trap. "Real question is, how did he know where the hideout was?"

That question had two possible answers: either someone had reported their presence in Shipwreck Bay, or they had a spy in their midst. It was clear everyone suspected Anastasia. These were the thoughts that filled Lilly's head as she sprinted down the dirt path in pursuit of the Wolf's impossible standards. She glimpsed the finish line in the distance and slid through it, sending up a cloud of dust. The Wolf was waiting for her, as always. "Twenty-five," he said as he put his pocket watch away.

That was all he needed to say to crush Lilly's hopes. There was no possible way for her to shave off that much time. "We go to see the Doctor tomorrow night. I'd prepare for your last run."

"I don't know what I can possibly do!" Lilly exploded as her energy returned. "I can't break twenty minutes."

"I have," the Wolf said. "After much practice."

Lilly wanted to collapse into a fit of tears and frustration. "How'd you do it?" she begged. "Is there a trick?"

The Wolf approached and slid his hand across the shoulder of her coat where a few specs of dirt lingered. "I, for one, was not wearing a five pound military coat."

She looked down at it and then back to him. "I'm not supposed to be seen without it," she resisted automatically.

"Really? Whose rule is that? What ancient custom are you adhering to?"

"In Altryon," Lilly persisted, "Father always—"

"This is not Altryon," the Wolf said. "And I am not your father. I am a broken version of any noble Celerius that you knew. The Empire has made me a ruffian, Lilly. I follow no rules. I am not an honorable fighter, and that's because I've lost everything. I have been made a desperate man, and I have abandoned old honor. If you want to survive out here, you have to do the same."

"Celerius are known for their honor!" Her face grew red. She couldn't imagine these words coming from any other Celerius's mouth. "Our motto is 'Highest Honor!'"

"I didn't say that I've abandoned honor altogether," the Wolf said, keeping his composure. "I've abandoned old honor. Old customs. I understand now that the highest honor is sacrifice. I have sacrificed the man I used to be in order to create who I am now: a leader, a fighter, and a rebel. You have to sacrifice this perfect lady. You have to abandon her, Lilly. Your enemies won't care about your perfectly tailored coat, or your immaculately styled hair. They'll care about filling you with blades and bullets."

Lilly felt a war emerging inside her. She was a lady *and* a warrior. She'd balanced them so well over the years. How could the Wolf tell her to abandon a part of herself? But he had a point. The Wolf indicated his face. "Gentlemen don't wear war paint. I am an honorable man, but I am no longer the same man. You've lost so much, Lilly. Don't you feel the need to change? To grow? To become something stronger?"

She knew her father would hate her for it, but she held her hand out. "Do you have any of that war paint on you?"

He grinned and pulled a tin from his coat pocket. She opened it and smeared two blue steaks under her eyes. She pulled the Wolf's handkerchief from his coat pocket and wiped her hands. Then she pulled off her coat and folded it over the Wolf's outstretched arm. With a quick pull she rid her blouse of its sleeves. "Shouldn't you wait until your final run tomorrow?" the Wolf asked.

"No," she said. "I'm going to do it right now."

She tied her perfect hair into a tight bun and bounced at the start of the path. Her lungs regenerated quickly, but performing this run two times in a row would be a strain on her. Somehow in removing the coat and tying up her hair, something changed within her. She felt lighter and hungry for something. Maybe it was glory, or liberation. Either way, she knew she could channel that hunger into a run. She heard the Wolf remove his pocket watch.

And she was gone. Over the hills and through the landscapes, she let all thoughts exit her mind. She didn't worry who might catch a glimpse of her bare arms, she didn't worry about washing off the paint later, and she didn't worry about the nightmares that were sure to plague her in sleep. She ran. The world seemed to bend around her and she felt heat warming her body as the air pushed against her. After a few minutes it didn't feel like running anymore, it felt like flying. She passed the finish line and slid into a kneeling position. The wind bent around her as she stopped and sparks appeared in the air. She didn't even feel the need to breathe heavily. She'd lifted a weight from her shoulders and arose new. "Thirteen," the Wolf said. "Thirteen!"

She smiled. "So am I tough enough to join your war?"

He pocketed his watch and admired her evolution. "I think you might be tough enough to end it." He looked proud. She almost didn't remember what that looked like. "You always had this inside of you, Lilly. You just needed to give yourself permission."

She walked past him toward the Annalisa, and the Wolf followed. "You're trying to teach us all a lesson, right?" she asked. "So my lesson was what? Abandon my honor?"

The Wolf laughed. "I wanted you to learn that you are more than just your honor."

The giddy feeling of soaring along the road didn't leave Lilly's stomach for a great while. She'd found something incredible and no one was going to get in the way of her unleashing it. She thought of what she could do to Carlin with her new speed and smiled. It certainly would not be honorable.

Chapter Thirty-Three

SHIPWRECK BAY
DARIUS TAURLUM

DARIUS TURNED, ROLLED OVER IN HIS BED AND GAVE OFF A DISCONTENTED growl. Earlier, after Darius's lifting sessions, he'd told Rhys he was going to take the Lightborn book and read it before bed. Rhys had told him that *A Rough History of Lightborns* was incredibly complicated and he wasn't ready to read it alone. Who was Rhys to tell him what books were too hard for him? Darius was making incredible progress and he knew it. *A Rough History of Lightborns* was just another book like *Little Billy*. It was uncomplicated letters strewn into slightly more complicated words that made partially complicated sentences Darius could absolutely read, if he wanted to, of course. He sat up. This was stupid. He could have the book done by morning. He lumbered out of bed as quietly as his iron skin would allow and hobbled out of his secluded room in the Annalisa. It felt weird to sleep in the rooms of a hollowed out ship, especially one that was on its side. Darius knew that vibrations travelled unnaturally well on this ship. With little difficulty he descended the staircase. In the darkness Darius stubbed his toe, which resulted in the wall of the Annalisa cracking. He exhaled slowly. It was a good thing they weren't at sea.

He found his way to the large tent and grabbed a nearby candle. He pulled a splinter of wood off of the deteriorating table and rubbed it furiously against his hand. Eventually a flame emerged and he transferred it to the candle. He crushed the splinter and applauded his own ingenuity. He pulled the book close to him and opened it to a random chapter. He examined the heading of the chapter and realized that he was reading from recent family history. He could tell from the illustration that the man pictured was a Venator. He picked a random sentence and attempted to read it out loud. "We first met the Horseman while hunting for Nikolai Taurlum. His ability was to train animals with his mind and use them as his servants. He took offense to our killing of one of his animals and he hunted us for a few days. In our first encounter he had mental control of a deer, a spider, a bear and a..." Darius stopped.

"Stal... Stall... Stallion?" He stared at the word intently. "Stallion?" he murmured. "What the hell is that?"

He looked for a footnote, but found nothing. He glared at the page. "The Stallion was several feet taller than even I was at the time. It was a glorious animal, that is, until Carlin Filus killed it to prove a point to the Horseman."

Darius rubbed his forehead. Well, the guy was called the Horseman, so maybe a Stallion was a type of horse? Why be named the Horseman if you didn't at least have one horse on your payroll? That was probably right. Darius pumped his fist in the air.

His celebration was cut short when he heard light footsteps coming from the Annalisa. He looked down at the book and remembered how much the Wolf loved it. He probably wouldn't appreciate someone reading it in the dead of night. Especially someone who could accidentally rip it in half if he sneezed while holding it. Darius put out the candle's flame between his fingers and crawled under the table. He saw small black boots maneuver out the open door of the Annalisa and through the array of tents. Darius crawled out and scratched his head. *Was that Anastasia?* he wondered.

He followed her out into the expanses of Volteria and saw her jogging down the road in the direction of the main town. He shrugged to no one in particular and followed her. After nearly half an hour of Darius darting behind buildings and into alleys to remain unseen, Anastasia reached a seedier part of Shipwreck Bay. He followed her through it, fully aware of how stupid it was. Shipwreck Bay didn't have a strong Imperial presence, but it did have outlaws of every cut and creed. She stopped at a small and unmarked shop and knocked on the door. A sketchy looking gentleman in a hat extended his hand to her. She gave him something white. It looked sort of like a letter but could easily have been any other type of parchment. The sketchy man listened to what sounded like harsh instructions and closed the door. Then Anastasia pivoted and made her way to an unmarked door a few streets over. She knocked on it and a man who looked even sketchier opened the door. He smiled at her through rotting teeth and handed her a small pouch. She handed him a pouch of her own and the man closed the door. Anastasia turned and bumped straight into Darius's iron chest. She didn't look surprised to see him Darius noted, but then again, she hardly ever looked phased by anything.

"Why hello there," she said as she rubbed her head with one hand and patted Darius's chest. "Been lifting your carriages, I can see."

He stared at her skeptically. "What are you doing here?"

Anastasia glanced around. "Just came to pick up some things. Loose ends are being tied up."

"What's in the pouch?" Darius asked.

"What's with the interrogation?" Anastasia countered.

He stared at her. She was up to something, he could tell. "What's in the pouch?" he repeated a little louder.

Anastasia glanced around, clearly not wanting to start a scene. "It's called Nature's Scream," she said. She pulled the pouch open to reveal a red powder. "It's made from a rare flower that grows on an island somewhere. When it's ground up into a powder it produces the hottest spice imaginable. One small bit can leave a grown man in tears."

"And you bought it so you can... what?" Darius asked. "Make us all dinner?"

"It's for interrogation," she said. "Obviously."

"Obviously," Darius repeated.

She smiled. "So I paid those weasel-faced gentlemen for a dose. I usually always carry some on me. But I've been running low recently."

"What about that other guy? The one you gave a letter to."

Anastasia didn't answer straight away. "I could answer questions all night, Blondie," she said affectionately. "What do you want from me? I'm sorry I left the ship? Am I a hostage now?"

Darius looked over his shoulder at the first building she'd knocked on. Maybe he should knock on it too and then, for good measure, knock a few heads. That was the quickest way to find out what she was doing with all those papers. He walked toward it, and she gave an overly exaggerated sigh. "Fine!" she said. "You got me!"

Darius turned around. "I did?" he asked. "I did," he decided.

She sauntered towards him. "Look, I knew you were following me. You're not exactly the stealthiest fellow. Sure I wanted some of this," she said indicating the bag of Nature's Scream, "but what I really wanted was to get you away from the others."

"Why?"

"So no one would catch us," she said nonchalantly.

"Doing what?"

In lieu of answering, she pulled him into a deep kiss. The iron Taurlum tried desperately to avoid turning into butter. He kissed her back passionately and forgot his concerns. He pulled away. "Oh," he said. "Awesome."

She gripped the back of his neck as she pulled him in for another. He thought he saw her eyes drift over his shoulder to the shop where she'd dropped off the parchment. His suspicions washed away during this next kiss. Despite what he'd thought a minute ago, something was absolutely different now. For this wasn't some halfhearted kiss with nothing behind it. This was a real kiss. A passionate kiss. Darius was absolutely certain of that, and that alone.

Chapter Thirty-Four

SHIPWRECK BAY
NEIL VAPROS

Neil was sure that he knew the secret to not getting his teeth knocked out. Whenever he swung at Bianca during sparring, he noticed that she never looked at his first directly. She didn't focus her vision. Every move he made was always in her periphery. He would swing and she would evade. When he was slowing, she would deliver an attack somewhere unexpected like his ankle or the inside of his thigh. Finally she'd finish him off with a strong punch or use his weight to flip him over her shoulder. She always won, but Neil wasn't trying to hurt her. He was trying to learn everything about how she fought because the Wolf had taught her and he was coming next.

In the back of his mind, as he parried punches and kicks, he tried to discover what the Wolf meant to teach him with this. Lilly had been changed from head to toe by her exercise with the Wolf. She seemed less tense now, more sure of herself. Maybe she was even free of the nightmares that plagued her night after night. He could see the Wolf on the outside of the clearing and knew it was time. "Is he ready?" the Wolf called to Bianca.

She delivered a swift roundhouse kick, but Neil was ready for it. He ducked and hit Bianca with her signature leg sweep. She never hit the ground fully, but he knew that he'd won the round. "Looks like he might be," Bianca said to the Wolf.

She left and Neil's new opponent circled him. His hands were already wrapped and he'd come without his coat. His thick cream colored oxford shirt was rolled at the sleeves and made him look like one of the boxers that occupied the slums of Altryon. "Are you ready, Neil?"

Neil raised his fists and let his mind go blank. If he were going to learn a lesson, it wouldn't come from being beaten senseless. The Wolf didn't raise his fists. He was clearly waiting on Neil to make the first move. Neil experimentally threw a few punches and the Wolf blocked each one effortlessly. He struck Neil's arms in a way that slowed them and made them tense. He could feel his tendons and muscles tightening all the way through his shoulders and chest. The Wolf struck Neil once. That was all it took for the Wolf to knock him out cold: one punch. "Again," the Wolf said. This wasn't the voice of Steven Celerius. This was the voice of a savage. It was the Wolf. "Get up."

Neil stood up and raised his fists again. He didn't attack this time; he waited for the Wolf. This tactic proved to be a mistake, as the Wolf could land ten punches within a second. Neil fell to the ground, coughing violently. "Again," the Wolf repeated.

Neil stood and fell six more times before sundown. The Wolf was too fast, and Neil had never seen anything like it. No wonder this man had evaded capture for years. He was unbeatable. The Wolf rubbed his stubble. "Again."

Neil stood and hoped that his organs would decide to stay inside of him. He inhaled sharply. Maybe if his guard were strong enough he could get in a few punches after blocking the Wolf. This strategy proved slightly more successful. The Wolf's first hits were blocked, but Neil's next swing was caught, and the Wolf used a pressure point in his wrist to bring him to his knees. "I suppose that is enough," the Wolf said.

He released Neil's arm and walked away. Neil's mind began to race and even more sweat poured from his brow. It couldn't end here. He needed that lesson. "Again," Neil said.

The Wolf turned around. "You're hurt."

"Again."

The Wolf squared up against him and this time actually prepared a proper guard. He could see the fire in Neil's eyes. Neil intentionally led with a slower swing in the hopes that the Wolf was too quick to notice the difference. While the Wolf was distracted with his block, Neil's left foot pivoted and he delivered a snap kick into the Wolf's thigh. The Wolf exhaled in surprise and stepped out of range of any more attacks. This time he was going to lead with the offensive, Neil could tell. The Wolf closed the distance between them in a flash. Neil did the only thing he could remember. He let his peripherals do the work. He didn't focus on the Wolf's hands; he just let the swings come. By some miracle, Neil blocked one punch with enough force to set the Wolf off balance. Before the next swing came, Neil nailed the Wolf with a solid uppercut that sent him staggering backwards. Neil expected the Wolf to berate him with crushing blows, but instead the man threw his head back and laughed. "That was excellent, Neil," he said. "No one's landed a swing on me since I was a lieutenant." He patted Neil on the shoulder and the young Vapros dropped his weary stance. "You're certainly fit to join us."

"Wait…" Neil said. "Wasn't I supposed to learn a lesson?"

"I don't know," the Wolf said. He leaned back expectantly. "Did anything sink in?"

Neil didn't say anything. He just panted lightly, still exhausted from the fight. "Neil, I've said it before and I'll say it again. I believe that you are burdened with purpose. Maybe you're not this chosen one, but you still have this extraordinary strength and power within you. I wanted to see how much you would take and keep going."

"Did I really land that hit or did you just let me?"

"It doesn't matter. The reason you won is because you stood up again and again. Even after I stopped pushing you. Revolution is a long road that breaks many people. I wanted to see if you could be broken."

"And?"

"There's no end in sight. You might just be him. You might just be forged in fire."

Neil wanted to smile or buckle under the pressure. But whatever his revelation would be, the Wolf left him to contemplate it alone. "Wait," Neil said. "Why couldn't I use my powers? Why hand-to-hand combat?"

"I wanted to see you prove that you could do it without them." The Wolf cocked his head back and forth as if weighing a decision in his head. "Also, Bianca told me she wanted to hit you a little bit."

Neil laughed. So did the Wolf. "She likes you," the Wolf said.

"She likes hitting me." Neil said, collapsing to the clearing floor for a rest.

The laughs subsided. "Seriously though, she really cares about you. You two might not ever have a normal life, but you might still have a life together."

Neil sat until the sun disappeared completely from view. Something warm was growing in his heart and he couldn't tell if it was a terrible happiness or a terrible longing. No one set him on fire like Bianca.

Chapter Thirty-Five

SHIPWRECK BAY
DARIUS TAURLUM

DARIUS FINISHED THROWING HIS FINAL PILES OF SAND OUT OF THE PIT JUST as the Wolf approached him. Anastasia had been watching and he made a little extra show of the labor. He'd stretched his muscles just a little bit more than necessary. Something was off about her though. She was coughing often and looked like chills racked her body despite Shipwreck Bay's warm climate. He couldn't help but look up at her from the hole he'd dug every few moments. The Wolf arrived and whistled. "Someone figured it out."

Darius grinned. "Are you ready old man?" he asked.

The Wolf bowed to Darius like a caricature of an old gentleman. "After you, youngling."

Darius placed both hands under the side and lifted with all of his might. He could feel the blood rush to his face and was sure it was as red as one of Josephine's tomatoes. The muscles under his iron skin tensed and nearly tore under the weight of the behemoth steel carriage. "All this for nothing?" he heard Anastasia tease.

He could feel warmth building in his chest. With one last burst of adrenaline, he lifted the carriage off the ground and onto its side. Darius roared in triumph.

"Well, well," Anastasia said. "He's conquered the mighty carriage. What a warrior."

Darius climbed out of his hole. "I did it," he said. He raised his hand for a high five and the Wolf returned it slowly.

"Did you learn anything from trying to move a carriage for a week?" the Wolf asked.

"I learned how strong horses are," Darius said.

The Wolf raised an eyebrow and Darius tried to avoid paling. This guy didn't like making jokes. "I learned that there are limits to my strength."

"And when you encounter those limits what must you do?"

"Apply intelligence?" Darius asked.

Those were big words for him. And he knew it. "Seems you learned what you needed to," the Wolf said. "And you also learned some humility in the process. Those are certainly pleasing results."

"Am I in?" Darius asked.

"Everyone's in," the Wolf said. "I'm not charging into battle with the Doctor without a Taurlum at my side. Follow me to the strategy tent. Neil and Lilly should be there already."

They walked down the paths of Shipwreck Bay until they reached the Annalisa. As expected, Neil, Bianca, and Lilly were waiting there. Rhys sat at the front with spectacles perched on his nose. Darius snorted. They kept slipping off of him. The kid either needed a bigger nose or smaller spectacles. "Tomorrow night is the night," the Wolf said as everyone gathered around. "Rhys, shall we discuss the plan?"

Rhys beckoned them to come closer. "You guys are going to want to listen very carefully. I've taken all of your special talents into consideration here."

"Rhys designed the plan?" Neil asked.

"What do you think he's been doing all this time?" the Wolf asked.

Rhys continued with his strategy. "According to Anastasia and the Wolf's spies, the Doctor is holed up in a military base called the Cliff."

Neil snorted. "People sure are simplistic outside the walls. The Cliff, the Wolf, the Doctor, the Marksman."

"What did your family name its opera house again?" Bianca asked.

"The Vapros Opera House," Neil said without thinking.

"Right," Bianca said.

"It's not Outsiders that are simple," the Wolf said. "It's the Venator. We don't do real names at the lodges. Everyone goes by their hunter name. That's where they came up with the Marksman, the Doctor and, of course, the Wolf." He indicated himself.

"Can we get back to nicknames later?" Anastasia asked. "I want to see if this plan is going to get us killed."

A few people smirked. Rhys did not, which worried Darius. "Okay, so this thing is huge and built into the side of a cliff. Which is the point. No one can come or go without using a special pulley system on top of the cliff." He pointed to the top of his schematic. "The doors are iron and reinforced; it's the only way in." Rhys shifted the drawing so that everyone could see. "But there's a small balcony off the main office. It's where Carlin stays whenever he visits." He said that in the direction of Lilly and her eyes flared at the mention of her archenemy. "They don't expect anyone to be able to rappel down the cliff because it's guarded at the top and you'd need hundreds of feet of rope."

"Are you sure we couldn't just force our way into the shaft?" Lilly grumbled. "Darius could rip those iron doors right open." The idea of rappelling down a mountain made her skittish. She hated heights.

"If someone tries to go through without sending the correct signal, they drop the cart and it falls hundreds of feet. Darius is strong, but a fall like that would even turn him into a paste," Rhys said. "The balcony is the best way for our initial entrance. You won't even be the one going through the balcony. Neil will."

"I will?"

"Neil you can fly. You can just land on the balcony," Rhys said.

Neil's eyes widened. "I can't actually fly. I can just give myself a boost. Accelerate."

"If you can accelerate then you can decelerate," Rhys said. "You can make a controlled descent to the balcony. All we need to do is get you through the guardhouse at the top of the Cliff."

"Who clears the guard house?" Anastasia asked, peering at the drawing. "They'll probably have alarms." She sounded confident about that.

"Darius will lift the gate for Lilly and the Wolf. They'll clear the room before anyone can signal the alarm."

"Are you sure I can life the gate?" Darius asked. He didn't want another carriage situation on his hands.

"You'll be fine. It's a crank gate, more for show than anything else." Rhys pushed his spectacles up his nose again. "Anastasia and Bianca will clear the sentry guards on the roof of the guard house."

"How do we get up to the roof?" Bianca asked.

"Anastasia's an acrobat. She'll be fine. You can take them from far away with your knives. Just do it quietly. Once Neil's inside he'll break the locks on the pulley system that lifts the cart. Darius can then use his strength to operate the pulley from within. Manually. We'll hop in and take it down to the Doctor's workshop on the floor beneath the balcony."

Darius exhaled and placed his head in his hands. "So we are taking the shaft, but I have to carry all of us, not to mention the cart itself."

"Good thing you've been getting so much exercise." Anastasia winked at him and he groaned.

"I hate this," Darius said. "If dropping this thing would turn me into paste, what will it do to you guys?"

"Thinner paste," Rhys said, confident in his answer.

"Well, I suppose we should get a move on," the Wolf said. "To the Cliff we go."

Chapter Thirty-Six

THE CLIFF
THE PACK

THE HYENA BOUNDED INTO THE DOCTOR'S WORKSHOP WITH A SKIP IN HIS step. "Am I too late?" he asked. "Are they here yet?"

"Do I look like I've just dealt with six targets?" the Doctor asked. "They're right behind you, I assume."

"You've prepared a trap right?" The Hyena placed his hands over his mouth to keep from bursting with hilarity. "Are you going to blow anyone up?"

"I might," the Doctor said. "That box over there has a Lightborn Cuff in it. It's for the Taurlum."

The Hyena looked up to see Victor assembling a giant machine in the rafters. "Hi brother," he said. "Father's keeping you hanging around, huh?"

"Hello Lester," the Marksman said. "I actually want to be here. These Lightborns are dangerous. Too dangerous for Father to take alone."

"I met one of them. She deals with cyanide quite well. Well, better than most people I've met," the Hyena snickered.

The Marksman above them cocked his head. "Bodies are falling up above us. I smell blood. Also smoke outside, on the balcony."

"They're here. You can still smell blood, even though we've been together for three days?" the Doctor asked his son.

"Smell lasts the longest," the Marksman said.

The Doctor scribbled a note on a piece of paper and shoved it into his pocket. "Could be useful," he mumbled.

"Is your pet here?" the Hyena asked, unmoved by the news that they would soon be attacked. "The monster?"

"I had it moved to our hideout in Abington," the Doctor said.

"How's it getting fed?" the Hyena asked.

"I left him five or six villagers. It should hold him over."

"You should feed it flesh with a silver spoon. That's what it grew up with." The Hyena crawled up one of the wooden pillars and up to the rafters. He knew the drill. Setting ambushes was all about distributing your troops and your traps. The Doctor liked to call these details strands, and he liked to call the ambush itself "his web." He certainly took to his family's spider mascot. "I'd give it two minutes. I want to play some games with the eldest Vapros and the Celerius girl. If I look like I'm in any real trouble, turn on the machine."

"Yes Father," they said in unison.

From his perch he could see the Doctor leaving an injection out for Anastasia. "Is she still with us?" Victor called.

"I don't know," the Doctor replied. "But if I do have a spy, I'm not willing to lose her so soon. She knows who she belongs to."

The Hyena couldn't help but snicker as he waited with his brother. This was the best kind of joke, his favorite kind, where everyone thinks they know the punch line until the real one appears and whips them across the face. The Hyena ripped off a sleeve from his shirt and curled it into a ball. He shoved it into his mouth to stop himself from laughing during the show. He knew he wouldn't be able to resist; after all, this was his favorite kind of ending----chaos, blood, and fire.

Chapter Thirty-Seven

THE CLIFF
NEIL VAPROS

NEIL'S FRIENDS HAD MADE SHORT WORK OF THE SOLDIERS IN THE GUARD-
house. Lilly and her Uncle swept through the ground units like painters
applying brush to canvas. Everything they did looked so smooth and
calculated. That was probably because their minds worked so quickly.
Bianca and Anastasia cleared the upper units with ease and soon it
was up to him. It was time to make a controlled descent down the
cliff face to the balcony below.

He stared over the edge for a moment and every nerve in his
body tightened. This was insane. He'd never tried anything like this
before, and all of his friends were counting on him. He looked over
his shoulder and saw the others were staring at him. They looked as
nervous as he felt. He curled his hands into fists and began to gather
the power inside of him. Could he really be the Wolf's chosen one?
Forged in fire. Sounds like me, he thought.

But even if it did sound like him, did he really want it? Having these people rely on him was terrifying. He couldn't imagine carrying all of Volteria on his back. "Neil?" the Wolf asked. "Are you alright?"

"Yes," Neil said. "I just need a second."

"Tick tock, buddy," Darius mumbled.

Neil rubbed his forehead. He had to focus on one thing at a time. The expectations he faced would crush him otherwise. The Doctor was his primary objective. The sick, deranged monster in the base below was waiting to see justice. He'd been responsible for Josephine's death and the bullet hole in Neil's back. He turned around and faced his friends one more time. He and Bianca met eyes and he tried to put on a brave face for her. She'd certainly be a better chosen one than he'd ever be. She never wavered, never crumbled, and never showed a lapse in dedication to him.

He knew in that moment that if he made it through the revolution, he'd marry her. He'd keep her safe from a world with men like Saewulf, the Doctor, and the Emperor. Or maybe she'd be the one keeping him safe. Either way was fine, as long as they were together. Without giving himself another chance to second-guess himself, he stepped off the cliff and let his fire slow his descent.

The Doctor had messed with the wrong group of revolutionaries. As Neil landed on the balcony, he felt fire ignite in his chest. He was in the Doctor's web. Now he would burn it away, strand by strand.

Chapter Thirty-Eight

THE CLIFF
NEIL VAPROS

"No one celebrate just yet," the *Wolf* warned as they pushed the Doctor to his knees after cuffing him. "This place is definitely booby-trapped and I doubt we're alone. Everyone spread out."

Things had gone as planned. Rhys really had thought things out well. However, Neil was shocked to see what the Doctor looked like. The man was a collection of deformities, loosely tied together. Neil couldn't see a single part of him that was whole.

"I want a word with him," Neil hissed. "For Josephine."

The Wolf agreed. "I expected as much. Bianca and Anastasia, come with me. Let's make sure there's no one on the ground floor to worry about."

They proceeded out in a tight formation, ready to disembowel anyone hiding in the Doctor's massive workspace. As they drifted away, Neil realized he was now alone with the group that had been living at the Golden Mug with him. These were Josephine's children and they were ready to avenge her. "You're the one who sent that animal after us," Neil accused the Doctor.

The Doctor stared at him. "You should be more specific. Every one of my assassins is an animal in their own right."

"The Marksman. Your son."

"Ah yes." The Doctor smiled as much as he could with his metal jaw. "Victor is all instinct. But when you back someone into a corner, you shouldn't feel offended when their claws come out."

Neil would have punched him if he weren't so sure it was what the Doctor wanted. A snicker came from somewhere in the workplace and the group tensed as they swiveled nervously. The Wolf was right. They weren't alone.

"But the most animalistic of us all is your new friend Anastasia," the Doctor said.

Darius glared.

"You know what truly makes her an animal? It's her instinct for self-preservation, her drive to survive. She loses a bit of humanity every time she tears off a piece of herself to escape a trap. She'll cut you in half if it means securing her safety."

"Shut up," Darius said louder this time. "You're the one who surrounds himself with 'animals.'"

"Because I can trust them," the Doctor said. "Animals are predictable. Nothing makes a man safer than the ability to control something with basic instincts."

"Well, look where that predictability got you."

The Doctor's eyes focused on Neil who felt a chill travel down his spine. "You're animalistic too, Vapros."

"I'm not going to play your games," Neil said.

"Do you struggle to sleep at night knowing that Miss Celerius is wide awake? That she constantly wonders what happened to her younger brother Edward? Your ability to sleep like a baby is animal-istic." Saliva leaked down the Doctor's lower jaw.

Neil glanced at Rhys, who looked equally terrified. Lilly stared at them, eyebrows narrowed. "What do you think she'd say if she real-ized you've known who killed him all along? That you've been lying to her and letting her lie awake wondering what caused his death?"

"What?" Lilly demanded. Her words were angry but her eyes told a different story, a deep wound that had long been open. In a flash, Lilly had her sword pressed firmly against Neil's throat. He couldn't crane his neck but he could see Lilly. She had violent tears in her eyes.

"He's just trying to get to you..." Neil whispered.

"Tell me it's not true, then. Tell me you don't know how Edward died."

Neil stared at her and his eyes flickered to Rhys. *Lie.* Rhys was saying with his eyes. *Don't ruin this mission. Tell her later.* "I can't," he said as he prepared to have his throat slit. "Jennifer," he said simply to Lilly. "My sister, Jennifer. She killed him."

Neil could tell that Lilly was on the verge of breaking down. "Why did she leave the body? Why did we have to wonder? Why couldn't she have just left him in a pile of ashes?" Her whole body was quivering. "I will cut you down, Vapros. Why did she leave the body?"

Neil stared at the floor sullenly. "She loved him."

Lilly blinked. Neil could feel the sword slightly pressing against his Adam's apple. There was no way he'd be able to materialize out of this without being decapitated. "Don't be a hypocrite, Lilly," the Doctor said.

She turned on him. "What did you say to me?"

"Don't. Be. A. Hypocrite." He pushed each word through his metal jaw.

His eyes bore into hers. She pulled her sword from Neil's throat and put it to his. "How am I a hypocrite?"

The Doctor's eyes drifted up. Lilly's eyes went with them. The Doctor's workspace was several stories tall and the rafters seemed to stretch upward infinitely. "You're keeping secrets as well. Doesn't the Wolf have a right to know about his wife?"

Neil looked around cautiously. Not only was he searching for the Doctor's ally, but he didn't want the Wolf to hear the specifics of this conversation. "Lilly," Neil whispered. "You might want to use your senses to find whoever's hiding in here."

"I'm not done with you yet," Lilly barked. Her eyes remained on the Doctor.

"I understand that. However, we might not get a chance to finish this if the Doctor's trap kills us."

She closed her eyes and extended her hands as if she were trying to keep her balance. Neil kept his eyes on the Doctor. She opened her eyes and looked up. "There are two bodies up in the rafters and a pretty large machine of some sort," she called loud enough for the Wolf to hear.

"I'm getting the same thing!" he called back.

The laughter from the rafters resumed and the Doctor joined it with a metallic chuckle. "The Hyena is hard to plan an ambush with. But we can't help but include him. He's just so much fun."

The Hyena laughed harder above their heads. "Whenever you're ready," the Doctor said with confidence.

Suddenly the machine far above them spurred into a low hum and the small lights and dials on its sides revealed the Doctor's two servants spinning dials on either side. "What is that?" Darius asked.

"Wait for it," the Doctor commanded.

The low hum began to go up in pitch little by little as if a cat were walking across a giant piano. Clumsily the makeshift melody climbed higher and higher until Neil could no longer hear it. "I'm done with this," Lilly said. "Your head is coming clean off of—"

She dropped to the ground mid-sentence and began screaming in agony. Across the room the Wolf also began groaning in pain. The Hyena cackled and the Doctor joined him. Only the Marksman stayed quiet. "What's happening to them?" Rhys asked.

The Doctor put his hands up calmly. "They share a special ability that comes with sending vibrations through the air at a certain frequency. We learned to duplicate that frequency and send it right back. Imagine a super powerful dog whistle that weighs half a ton."

"Tell me how to turn it off," Neil demanded as he ignited his hands. "You've still got half of a face to lose."

The Doctor's eyes blazed. They were in his web now. Bianca began tossing knives at the machine with reckless abandon, but they either bounced off or the Marksman caught them before they could hit anything crucial. "Naturally," he said. "The only way to turn it off is with a key. You'd be lucky to find it before their eardrums burst."

Neil began to panic. He could feel his heart racing and his face reddening. In contrast, the Doctor looked calm and collected as the room went to chaos around him. "Where's the key?" Neil demanded again.

The Doctor looked like he wanted to laugh again. "Sorry. I won't be sharing that detail."

Neil's placed his ignited hand close enough to the Doctor's face to inflict pain. "Want to lose what's left of your face?"

"See that chest over there? If you can figure out how to open it, you'll be rewarded with the key."

Neil glared at him. "I'm not playing your games."

"Then your friends will spend the rest of their short lives on this floor screaming. It's up to you really."

"I'll get it open," Darius said confidently.

"Did I mention that breaking the box results in the deformation of the key? Minor detail, Mr. Taurlum. I'm sure you can do it though. I'm sure you're not stupid."

Darius snorted. "You can't bait me."

"It's okay," Neil said. "I'll get it open."

He darted over to the box, but made sure to keep the Doctor in his peripheral vision. This was more than likely a trap. The Doctor actually looked frustrated. He probably did want Darius to try and open the box instead. The box was a simple wooden one with no lid and no discerning features beside steel rivets equidistant apart on either side. Neil picked up the box and noted that it was unusually heavy. There was definitely something in there. Upon examining the bottom he found a small hole just bigger than his hand. He tried to look inside but couldn't see much besides something that looked like a latch. Neil experimentally placed his hand inside the hole and realized his mistake before he could withdraw it. A steel circle about the size of a bracelet latched onto his flesh and the box closed around his arm. "What the?" Neil said as he stifled the whimper of pain that threatened to escape his lips.

The box began to tick loudly enough for everyone in the room to hear. "That box wasn't exactly for you." The Doctor glared at Darius. "But no matter. You've managed to fail all the same. So instead of opening the box, you've got a fire bomb strapped to your arm. I'm sorry. I didn't have time to prepare a more suitable consolation prize."

"A what?" Neil asked as he tried to keep his heart from leaping out of his chest. "Well you've made a mistake. If anyone can handle a bit of fire, it's me."

The Doctor shook his head. "Of course you can, Neil, but what about your friends? What about your friends or your little girlfriend? Is their flesh fireproof?"

Neil tried to materialize out of the hold of the box, but he found himself unable to focus his energy. "As long as that metal band is attached to your wrist you won't be able to use your powers," the Doctor said. "Unless you can manage to get your heart rate over one hundred and thirty beats per minute."

Neil shook his arm violently.

"Neil?" Rhys said frightened.

"You're a monster," Neil said.

"And you don't have much time left," the Doctor spat. "You decided to come into my home and squish the spider. You have no right to feel betrayed when your own stupidity drives you into the web. Isn't that just life? Sometimes you're the boot and sometimes you're the bug." He licked his upper lip. "I wasn't supposed to kill you, but plans change. The Emperor will understand."

Neil turned to Bianca. He could see his own terror reflected in her eyes. "What do you suggest I do?"

"I have a window," the Doctor said. "The quickest way to get away from your friends might just be gravity."

Neil didn't have time to think or to question the horrors of what he was being forced to do. He ran to the floor to ceiling window. He slammed the box against it until it cracked. "Neil, slow down," Bianca begged.

"Neil, don't," the Doctor said. "For all of our sakes."

The window shattered as Neil looked down at the cliff face below. There was no way he'd survive something like that. "Misty Hollow," Neil said to Bianca. "If I'm alive I'll meet you there. One month from today. Town square." He felt like he had swallowed his tongue and now he was choking on it.

"Neil, think about what you're doing," Bianca said.

"I know exactly what I'm doing," Neil decided as he met her eyes. "I'm showing some dedication."

With that final note he hurled himself through the open window into the night air. He plummeted quickly and all the while attempted to dematerialize away. The energy in his body travelled passive-aggressively back and forth through his chest but refused to turn him into smoke. Without warning, the bomb exploded and he burst into particles along with it until he was floating through the air on the wind as if he had never been created in the first place.

Chapter Thirty-Nine

THE CLIFF
THE PACK

THE DOCTOR LOOKED UP AT HIS CAPTORS. IT WAS TIME TO CRUSH THEM in his rattrap. He bolted up suddenly and precisely at just the right angle so that the top of his head collided with the weak spot right under Darius's chin. Before Rhys could escape, the Doctor used an unforeseen flexibility to slip his cuffs from behind his back, under his legs, and out in front of him. He wrapped the chain around Rhys's neck and pulled it tight enough to keep him from escaping. Darius, who had been dazed, lifted his arm to strike the Doctor, but there was no way to get a clean swing in. "Move any closer and I will fracture his tiny neck," the Doctor breathed.

Darius stared him down. "I'm going to crush you, spider."

The Doctor laughed. "I've issued thousands of death threats in my line of work." The Doctor's voice was eerily filled with glee. "Advice from a professional: don't mark someone for dead unless you're certain you can complete the job."

From across the room the Doctor could hear Bianca sobbing. Where was Anastasia though? With a start the Doctor realized that she had used his distractions to go looking for his special needles. He heard footsteps approaching from behind and knew that Bianca was charging him in revenge for how he'd treated her beloved. He dodged the first knife and jerked Rhys around so that his shoulder was nicked by the second. Rhys would have cried out if he weren't being suffocated. This maneuver was enough to distract Bianca and he lobbed a knife from his own arsenal at her. She blocked it, but just barely. "Victor. Take care of her," the Doctor said without raising his voice.

The Marksman leapt from the rafters and landed on all fours. She turned to face him. "You're furious," he noted. "It will make you easy to beat."

Bianca pulled her last two knives from her belt. "I just watched the person I care most about sacrifice himself."

"Things would be different if he were smarter," the Marksman said. "No mercy for fools."

They clashed, but the Doctor didn't have any more time to pay attention. The Taurlum was obviously trying to think of a way to free Rhys from his custody. Rhys was passing out and the Doctor lessened his grip. No need to suffocate his newest toy before the fun could begin.

"Hyena," the Doctor said, "your turn. Take the Celerius to General Carlin."

The Hyena slid down a banister using his claws to slow the fall. He scampered over to Lilly's unconscious body but Darius kicked him away. "You're not taking anyone anywhere."

The Doctor laughed as he transitioned Rhys's unconscious body so that it was draped over his shoulder. "I like you, Darius Taurlum. I have something spectacular planned for you. You're going to die. But you're going to witness true horror before you do." He winked his hazel eye and used his free hand to fumble with some chemicals on the table next to him. Darius charged. The Doctor tossed a mixture of chemicals onto the ground and a cloud of gas swelled up from the ground. "Be careful not to breathe that," he whispered.

Darius, however, was intent on charging the Doctor. He ran through the smoke and, unfortunately, sustained a whiff of it. He collapsed to the ground, wheezing in pain. The Doctor jeered. "Not one for listening, are you? Would you mind rating your pain on a scale of one to one hundred?" he asked.

Darius responded by coughing violently.

"Victor, get to the hideout. Make sure my workshop is ready," the Doctor called to his eldest son across the workshop.

Victor's fight with Bianca had gone well for him apparently, seeing as he had Bianca in one of his special holds. "Yes, father," he said simply.

He pulled her arm out of its socket and she screamed. He dropped her body and bolted through one of the side doors. The Hyena had already escaped with the two Celerius. The Doctor knew that Darius was recovering quickly and he had little time to flee before the beast attempted to crush him into a puddle. He retreated with Rhys through the back door and on his way out saw Anastasia by one of his tables pulling a needle from her belly. She looked up and saw him. Her eyes were desperate and pleading. He nodded at her once, subtly enough to get his message across. *You still work for me.* He didn't have any more injections prepared so she would have to be back at his mercy in one month's time.

He adjusted Rhys's weight so that it was easier on his back and carried him through the deep stone hallways of the outpost. By to-morrow they would be across Volteria and he would be free to begin his experiments. Hopefully this boy was the one he was looking for. Hopefully this boy was his heir.

Chapter Forty

THE CLIFF
DARIUS TAURLUM

DARIUS FELT LIKE HIS LUNGS WERE FILLING WITH BLOOD. HE COULDN'T BE sure but part of him knew he'd drown in it. Suddenly, Anastasia was beside him. "Drink this," she said.

He was nervous at first because the liquid she gave him was in a test tube but he was happy to learn it was water. "Help your sister," he said. "He broke something on her."

Darius leaned his head against the ground and knew he'd be kicking himself as soon as he could. The Doctor had outsmarted them in dozens of different ways and now he had Rhys. Not to mention the fact that Neil was now either dead or in the water hundreds of feet below. He groaned and rolled over onto his hands and knees. Across the room Anastasia was popping Bianca's arm back into her socket. "Where were you?" Darius asked. "While we were getting thrashed?"

"I decided to take a look around. It looked like you all had it covered," Anastasia said. "Should have known better."

Darius bent over and vomited. It made him feel much better. He stood and grabbed his head in his hands. "We have to get to Misty Hollow," Bianca said, tears in her eyes.

"In a month," Darius said. "Going now won't do anything for anyone."

In response Bianca rolled over into the fetal position. Darius sighed. "We have a decision to make. We either go after Lilly and the Wolf or we go after Rhys."

Anastasia gritted her teeth. "We need to go after Rhys."

"He might already be dead," Darius said.

Anastasia shook her head. "The Doctor was promising double the money if anyone would bring Rhys in alive. He's got plans for him. If I know the Doctor it'll be worse than death."

Bianca stood as well. "Even so, how do we know where to find him? The Doctor was sloppy enough to be caught. He won't let it happen again."

The room was silent, aside from the wind blowing in from the broken window. "I know a guy," Anastasia said. "Well, I know a guy who knows a guy who will know where he is."

Darius groaned. "That sounds like it'll be a walk in the park. I'm not convinced we shouldn't go after Lilly."

"Lilly is with the Wolf," Bianca said. "They'll figure something out. I'm sure of it."

"So we're going after Rhys?" Anastasia asked. "Because if we are I'll get in touch with my contact."

Darius stared at the ground. "He beat us. He beat every single one of us: Lilly, Neil, the Wolf, me, Rhys, you guys. None of us stood the slightest chance."

"And?" Bianca asked.

"If we go after him again we might not live through it," Darius said. "We have to accept that now. We are risking our lives for his."

"When have we ever been concerned about risking our lives, Darius?" Bianca asked.

Darius remembered how many times he'd rushed headfirst into battle for less. "Okay. Anastasia get in touch with your friend. We're going after Rhys before the Doctor can break him."

"And if we can't get there in time?" she asked.

"Then we're going to avenge him," Darius said.

PART TWO

"We must be willing to get rid of the life we've planned, so as to have the life that is waiting for us. The old skin must be shed before the new one can come."

- Joseph Campbell

Chapter Forty-One

VOLTERIA'S OCEAN
NEIL VAPROS

In one moment Neil was floating through the wind, then suddenly, without warning, his consciousness reassembled. The force of his mind gluing itself back together was so powerful that if he had been whole, it might have knocked the wind out of him. He tried to open his eyes and look around, but quickly found that not everything was working yet. He was surrounded by darkness. Until a small light the size of a firefly appeared. It grew slowly and took the form of a man.

"Death, right?" Neil asked.

His voice wasn't coming through his mouth, but his mind. The Man with the Golden Light hovered in front of him silently. "That killed me, right?" Neil asked. He knew if he could he'd be crying. "This is where it ends for me?"

"You are not a prophet, Neil," the Man said in thousands of voices. "You are the same as any Lightborn. You've been foolish at times, prideful, selfish."

Neil wanted to argue, but had trouble finding the words. He could be stubborn, but not arguing-with-deities stubborn. The Man with the Golden Light continued, "But you have always been extraordinary in one aspect. Your capacity for hope is unbridled. Unprecedented. It's a great power." He floated closer to Neil and touched his forehead lightly. "Don't abandon that hope. Don't tell me you're even willing to consider that this is the end."

"My great power is… hope?"

"Do you know why you received your advanced ability?" the Man asked. He didn't wait for an answer. "An advanced ability can only be achieved when a person is on the verge of losing hope. It was created to remind Lightborns to be our inspiration and to keep pushing onward. When you're at your lowest, it is never easy to see the way upward. The advanced ability is to clear the way."

Neil let the words wash over him. He thought immediately of how it felt when his ability had presented itself: terrified for Bianca's safety, in pain, and out of options. That night at the gate rushed back. He then thought of his sister Jennifer and how she must have felt standing over Edward, the boy she'd killed by accident. "The only thing worse than pessimism is the total absence of hope," the Man added.

"I'm alive," Neil said. He allowed the hope to grow within him.

"Alive. Yes," the Man said. "You have yet to reform, but I assure you it is coming."

"Reform?" Neil asked. "I remember dematerializing… But I guess for the first time I don't remember rematerializing after."

"Your soul is pulling the remaining pieces of you back together. Soon you'll be one with yourself again. Although, I can't promise you'll feel the same. You'll be new. You'll be confused."

Feeling appeared in Neil's fingertips. It began to stretch toward his torso. The feeling of existence was soft and warmer than he'd expected. "Wait!" he said. "Why meet me now?"

"Your mind is nearly empty. This is the best possible time for learning, re-creation and advice," the Man said. "What's your purpose, Neil?"

"I don't..." Neil trailed off as the feeling of warmth engulfed his legs and feet. "I don't know."

"Then now is the best time for you to realize your meaning. Lightborns were made to protect the people, and each other. Remember now that the right thing is not always the easy thing, but you should always know it to be the right thing."

"The right thing," Neil repeated.

"You must also remember how heavy guilt is. If you decide to carry it, it will break you. Learn from your pain, acknowledge its lessons, ask my forgiveness, and then let it rest. Never carry it."

"Guilt is heavy," Neil repeated. The feeling of warmth stretched over his face. "How do I know...?" With those words his eyes opened and he realized his voice was coming through his mouth again.

He was wrapped in blankets. *That explains the warm feeling,* he thought. He unraveled himself from the blankets and realized he wasn't wearing a shirt. He lifted the sheet and sighed with relief upon realization that he was in fact wearing pants. Even though they weren't his own pants, he'd take that over nothing.

"That's the first thing I'd check for too," said a soft feminine voice from the foot of the bed.

Neil instinctually rolled into fighting position, however he did so while only halfway sitting up, probably ruining his only chance of intimidation. His guest was leaning against one of the bedposts and had her legs casually kicked up on the bed. She raised an eyebrow at him and he lowered his arms. "What's going on…?" he asked as he stumbled out of the bed. He grabbed a nearby cabinet to steady himself.

"Maybe you should tell me first. What's your name?" she asked.

Neil stepped away from her. He swiveled around to examine the room. The floor, walls and ceiling were all completely wooden, as were the bedframe and all the cabinets. Not only was the entire room made of wood, it was also creaking mysteriously. He considered lighting his hands on fire, but instantly realized what a mistake that would be. "You're Imperial," Neil said.

For some reason he didn't know what that word meant. It left his mouth nevertheless. She stood up and approached him. "You'd better calm down," she said forcefully.

Neil heard enough. He used his front foot to perform an ankle breaker the way someone had taught him. Unfortunately his new foe slid her foot back, effectively dodging his attack. She lashed out with superhuman speed and jabbed him just below his chest and above his stomach. The strike sent Neil reeling into the wall, then to the floor. He wanted to vomit, but there was nothing to expel. He gasped for air pathetically until she picked him up. She set him back in the bed and frowned at him with crossed arms. "I thought you'd be nicer," she pouted.

He stared at her, as his vision returned. She was actually strikingly beautiful. Neil hadn't noticed until she punched the air straight out of his lungs. Her skin was unnaturally tan and only served to make her turquoise eyes brighter. Her sandy blonde hair had been pulled into a long braid that reached her mid back. Small golden rings held the braid together. That was the only hint of jewelry she wore.

"You're staring," she said.

Neil was thrown off by her tone. It wasn't judgmental or serious. It simply seemed like an observation. Her voice was harmonic and pleasant, as if she were singing without even trying. "I think you broke every bone in my chest," he said.

"Sorry," she said in her airy tone. "We'll see if you can breathe in a bit. If not I might have to hit you again." She winked. "Knock everything back into place."

Neil blinked a few times. "What's your name?"

"Serena. Serena Tridenti."

"It's nice to meet you," he managed.

"What's your name?" she asked.

"It's…" Neil stopped. "It's…"

Her eyes narrowed. "You don't know your own name?"

"I feel like I must've had one," Neil said. "But for some reason I can't remember."

"When you're feeling well enough to stand we should go see my brother," she said with a scratch of her nose.

"I don't know," Neil said. "I feel dizzy. The room won't sit still."

Serena laughed melodiously. "You really don't have any idea where you are, do you?" He shook his head. "The reason you think the room is moving is because it is," she continued. "Currently you're sailing on the Tridenti family's prized long ship."

The room shifted violently, and Neil was practically thrown from the bed. "Welcome to my crew," she said playfully.

Serena led Neil through the underbelly of her ship without slowing to accommodate his lack of sea legs. She glided through the halls and storage rooms with ease, while he slipped and stumbled into walls.

Neil had never been on a ship before. In addition, he'd only ever seen one boat in his life. Altryon's largest river had a steamboat that could carry goods from the factories in the slums to the stores in the markets. They reached a large door, presumably on the other end of the ship. Serena threw it open and ushered him inside.

Sitting at the desk was a man that looked only a few years older than Neil. Like Serena he had blond hair with sandy streaks in it. Except, instead of a braid his was pulled into a bun. He had a thin beard, the kind that probably needed to be styled and neatly trimmed every morning. He looked up from the papers he was reading. Serena placed her hands out as if Neil was a trophy she was proudly presenting. "I win!" she said.

The man behind the desk smiled, and Neil was struck by how white his teeth were. "It doesn't count if you woke him."

"I didn't!" she said. "He started talking more and more and then eventually he shot up!"

Neil felt awkward. He didn't exactly know how to address Serena or the man behind the desk. "What did she win?" Neil asked.

"We were betting on whether you'd wake up within a week," the man said. "Serena is an optimist and said you'd awake within five days. My estimation, however, was that you'd awake after a week, or not at all."

"I've been asleep for five days?" Neil asked.

"You've been asleep for four," Serena said. "Which is why I'm owed some coin."

The man opened a drawer in his desk and tossed Serena a small sack. "I'm Alexander Tridenti," he said. "If I end up liking you, you can call me Alex. Otherwise you probably won't like me either and we'll call each other whatever we want in secret."

Neil looked from him to Serena. "You two are…?"

"Siblings. Yes," Alexander said. He perpetually had the look of someone who was stifling a smirk. "Do you honestly not know anything about the Tridenti?"

Neil tried to search his mind but found large gaps where knowledge usually waited. "I think I might have. At one point, but… I can't remember much."

"Well, you were fished out of the ocean four days ago by Serena." Alexander said. "We have no idea how you lived or where you came from. Apparently neither do you."

"Sorry," Neil said. "I'm just getting random names and phrases."

Alexander leaned back in his chair and studied Neil. "Does one of those names sound like your own?" he asked.

"He can't remember," Serena said.

"So that means he get's a guppy name," Alexander said.

Serena hopped once in excitement but was serious when she landed. Both of them were staring at Neil intently. "What's a guppy name?" Neil asked.

"Kids in the Tridenti family aren't formally named until they're around ten," Alexander said. "That's so we're sure that the name fits with their personality. So we give them a placeholder name."

"He's got really dark hair," Serena said. "It's almost pitch black. We could name him Pitch?"

"Mamba?" Alexander suggested. "After the snake."

"That's perfect!" Serena said with an experimental touch of Neil's hair. "Are we taking him to Ocean's Jaw?"

"I don't know," Alexander said looking expectantly at Neil. "Are we?"

Neil stared at them. "I don't know what that is. I do remember something about Misty Hollow though. I think I was going to meet someone there."

Alexander glanced at Serena. "Is that on the mainland?"

"I think so," she said. "Bad news, Mamba."

"We can't take you to the mainland. The Tridenti aren't allowed," Alexander said. "Best case scenario, you jump off and swim. Or you wait until we get to Ocean's Jaw where we can give you a small ship."

Neil rubbed his forehead.

"Where are we now?"

"Tridenti ships patrol the sea looking for the Empire's ships." Alexander said. "We picked you up pretty far north, but now heading east toward home."

Neil didn't know what most of those words meant. "I guess I'll stay with you guys, then. I can't even remember if Misty Hollow is where I'm supposed to be anyway."

"It'll only take a few days for us to reach our stronghold," Alexander said. "Until then you can stay in that room we've made up for you. I'll have a crewman bring you some food."

Neil bowed nervously. Alexander and Serena laughed at him. "Why are you bowing?" Alexander asked.

"I don't know. Let's blame it on the fact that I'm confused and don't remember who I am."

Serena giggled. "That might be the first time anyone's ever bowed to you," she said to Alexander. "Maybe he's a servant and is accustomed to bowing to his masters."

Alexander kicked his feet up onto the desk. "Well, maybe you're in luck then. You are a free man. No need to bow. Good to have you along, Mamba. We can talk more once you're fed."

There was something so charismatic about the two of them. They radiated happiness. "Also, is there any way I could trouble you for a shirt?" Neil asked.

Alexander looked up from his papers. "Yeah, of course." He looked at Serena. "Why doesn't he have a shirt?"

She blushed. "I forgot it?"

"Sure," he said. "Get the kid a shirt."

"Fine. Come with me."

Neil followed her back out into the expanses of the ship. Or the hull, Neil guessed. "By the way," Serena said as she pointed to this iron cuff on Neil's arm. "This was hooked onto your arm when you woke up. I wasn't able to pry it off. It was causing you to bleed pretty heavily, but it looks like it's stopped."

Neil stared at it. It was just a small iron bracelet. On the inside were a series of hooks and a latch to hook it on and off. A memory surged through Neil's head. He'd stuck his hand into a small box and it had been stuck on him. He remembered the fear of it all, and quite possibly jumping through a window. He placed his hands on his temples in a desperate attempt to pull out more memories. "You okay, Mamba?" Serena asked.

"Yeah," Neil said. "I think this was hooked on my arm by some-one very bad."

Serena grabbed it from him. "I'd guess so. These hooks are stuck in you." She seemed to notice Neil's discomfort. "I can cut it off you, given enough time."

"I think it did something special," Neil said. "But I don't want to lose my arm."

"Yes, sir," she said mockingly.

"About that shirt?" he said.

She smiled. Her teeth were just as white as Alexander's. "Every-one is so obsessed with this shirt."

Before Neil could reply, he felt the entire ship lurch. Muffled explosions could be heard above deck. The force of the next lurch knocked the two of them off their feet. "What...?" Neil started.

"Someone's trying to sink us," Serena said as she bolted through the hallway, presumably toward a way to the main deck.

Neil shook his head in amazement and followed as quickly as he could. Neil felt very confused by many things but of one thing he was certain. He was charging into battle.

Chapter Forty-Two

CONVOY
LILLY CELERIUS

LILLY ALWAYS KNEW WHEN SHE WAS DREAMING. THERE WAS AN EERIE *silence and calm that she never felt in the real world. She couldn't feel the earth around her or use her powers to see through walls. It was like being a little girl again.*

She was seated at the head of her family's dining room table and a delicious feast sat before her; everything from roasted pigs to trays of fruit and bottles upon bottles of red wine.

Lilly's eyes shifted around the table and she realized she was sitting with her brothers and the rest of her family.. Her father was seated closest to her, calmly cutting his portion of pork with a gold knife.

"Father?" she asked.

He kept staring forward. His posture was perfect, as was the Celerius way, but his eyes were dead. They never shifted or showed emotion. Blood poured from a gaping hole in his chest. "How does the new pony ride, Lilly?" Somehow she heard his voice without him ever opening his mouth.

"It rides well, father," she whispered frightfully.

A laugh came from her other side. "Lilly hasn't been riding," her brother Thomas, said with a closed mouth and dead expression. "She's too fast to get any real thrill out of riding horses anymore. She just runs around the fields on her own." Thomas was doing his mind-reading tricks again.

"I feel bad for you, Thomas." Now her eldest brother, Anthony, was at the table. He was drinking wine, but his voice still resonated clearly through the air. The wine poured out of the wound in his chest. Or maybe it was blood. Lilly screamed. Anthony's voice continued talking to Thomas. "Once you finally meet a woman, you'll know exactly what she thinks of you right from the beginning. You're going to be a lonely fellow, aren't you?"

"Maybe I'll like what she thinks," Thomas said.

"Well I think you're annoying." Lilly gasped as she heard Edward's voice.

She hadn't heard Edward's voice in so long. There he was though, seated next to Thomas and swirling a bowl of soup with a spoon. There were red lipstick marks on his face and blood coming from inside his coat. It was running down his back freely. Or maybe it was wine. "You're not a girl," Thomas's voice said to Edward.

"Lilly, you're a girl," Edward's voice said to Lilly. "Do you think other girls will find Thomas annoying?"

Lilly was crying freely now. Despite this, she could still hear her own voice ringing through the dining room. "I think Thomas is going to have to learn some self control when he meets a woman."

"If he meets a woman," Edward said, stifling a laugh.

"Do you really want to talk about women, Edward?" Thomas asked. "Despite your constant fighting, I can feel the basic emotions. You feel like you're in love, right this very instant."

"Something we should worry about, Tom?" Sir Celerius asked. His eyes shifted slightly. For a moment he almost looked alive, but he quickly descended back into his corpse like state. "A noble family I presume?"

Suddenly Lilly felt a cold liquid dripping down her neck. She brought her hand to it and realized that, like her family, she was leaking wine or blood. She started screaming louder and louder, as if she knew she could wake herself from her dream if she were loud enough.

Suddenly Lilly felt a kick to the back and her eyes snapped open. She was in the Imperial convoy where the Hyena had imprisoned her.

"What happened?" Lilly said groggily.

"You were screaming," the Wolf said. "I've heard of your nightmares but that was, well... legitimately frightening. Are you okay?"

Lilly shook her head. She was hyperventilating. The Wolf was chained up behind her and she couldn't see him, but she was sure that he could hear her having a panic attack. "Focus on my voice, Lilly," he said. "Feel the wood underneath your feet. Feel the chains digging into your wrists. This might not be a ton better, but this is what's real. This is what's happening. Not what's creeping into your head."

Lilly tried to shake herself free of the dream world. "Thank you," she whispered. "I think I'm all right now."

"Being a Celerius comes with quite the stigma," the Wolf said.

Lilly tried desperately to ignore him. After a horrific dream like that she certainly wasn't ready for one of the Wolf's speeches about inner power or whatever he was spewing now. She wanted to clasp her hands over her ears, but unfortunately they were chained to either side of the convoy. She felt like a scarecrow.

"Wounds to our flesh heal so easily that the masses believe we don't understand lasting pain. That we don't understand what it's like to burn from within."

"Do you have a solution?" she asked. She didn't want to cry in front of her uncle.

The Wolf shrugged as much as he could in his chains. "I'm just saying I understand you, Lilly."

She buried her face into her shoulder to wipe away the tears. When she was younger she always felt so strong. People would see her walk through the streets and gape at her in awe. She was a Celerius. She was honorable. Things couldn't have changed more in the last few months; now she wept often and silently, and woke up screaming more nights than not. She could imagine her father's voice in her head: "*There's nothing honorable about self-pity or weakness, Lilly.*"

"There's a way out of this. If you want it," the Wolf said. "Just as soon as you're ready."

"The nightmares?" she asked.

"One thing at a time, Lilly," the Wolf said. "I meant escaping these chains."

Lilly lifted her arm and felt the cool steel pressing into her skin. "That's a good start. How do you suppose we do that?"

The Wolf was clearly becoming more hesitant about his plan. "You're not going to like it."

She sniffled. "Try me."

"Would you say you're partial to the bones in your hands?"

Chapter Forty-Three

TRIDENTI SHIP
NEIL VAPROS

OLD INSTINCTS BEGAN TO RESURFACE AS NEIL CLIMBED ABOVE DECK. HE knew he wanted to do something with his hands and he had an insatiable urge to be somewhere far across the deck. Serena was far ahead of him, though, and immediately upon entering the fray she cut down armored soldiers left and right. Neil tried to get a handle on what was occurring. There was a far bigger ship parallel to the one that they were on. Large hooks connected the two ships and armored soldiers were attacking dirty crewmen in a tight formation. They were being boarded.

Alexander sprung out of the hatch that led to the hull with a large sword in tow. He charged into battle beside his sister and they began slicing through the formation in perfect synchronization. A meaty soldier made eye contact with Neil and pointed with his sword. "Vapros!" he accused angrily.

That name sounded very familiar. The guard didn't wait for a response. He plowed a few crewmen over and ran at Neil with his sword swinging. When the guard grew close, Neil instinctively ducked under it and rolled to safety. The guard turned around and kicked out viciously. Neil fell back onto the ground, but was able to dodge the sword that imbedded itself in the wooden ship beside him. He rolled slightly back and kicked straight upward with all of his force. He made direct contact with the soldier's chin with enough power to knock him unconscious. The meaty guard's unmoving body slammed into the deck and Neil jumped to his feet, gasping for air. Going four days without a meal was not a productive method of preserving energy.

Even in his dazed state he could see soldiers on the enemy boat loading a cannon of some sort and wheeling it to face the Tridenti siblings. They aimed carefully. It didn't seem like either of them was paying attention. "Serena!" Neil called just as the cannon was fired. "Alex!"

Serena turned around and slipped out of the path of the cannonball. Alexander was not so lucky. It struck him right in the back and his body flew straight off the side of the boat. Neil's jaw dropped. The enemy soldiers began cheering and raising their hands above their heads as a way of declaring victory. Neil studied Serena, but for some reason she didn't seem particularly distraught by the slaughter of her brother. She turned around and faced her enemies with a small smile. They turned to see what she was smiling at and their hands fell almost in unison. The guards operating the cannon turned around to find their victim, Alexander Tridenti, standing on the deck of their ship. Although he was soaked, he showed no other signs of being affected by his run-in with the cannonball. He dispatched the guards quickly in one fluid motion. He raised his arms and cheered victoriously. His men joined him in his revelry.

Another guard recognized Neil and took the moment's distraction as an opportunity to decapitate him. Neil's heart was racing so fast, it felt as though it would burst from his chest. Before the guard could slice him in half, Neil felt a bolt of energy fly from his hand. The smoky ball of fire knocked the soldier off his feet. He rolled around trying to extinguish the flames. Fiery pain seized Neil's wrist where the cuff was. He stared at his hand for a moment and then channeled his energy once again. His hand ignited and the people on deck stared at him in awe. He shot the next fireball at the guard at the front of the formation. He skidded to the other end of the boat. Neil's arm felt paralyzed with pain, but it was worth it to utilize his abilities. "Mamba!" Serena yelled. "This entire boat is made of wood! Let's not throw fire around!"

He lowered his hand, embarrassed.

"Stop fooling around, Serena!" Alexander yelled as he leapt from the enemy ship back on to his own. "Finish this."

Serena planted her feet and clenched her fists. She began to breathe meditatively. A guard tried to swing at her while she was in this trance, but Alexander intercepted him and threw him off of the boat with one hand. Serena's eyes opened and she began to sing. Neil was confused for a second. In the next he was on his knees. The entire world seemed brighter and calmer. It felt as if his entire body had been submerged in warm water. He collapsed to the ground and laid his cheek against the wooden deck as if he'd float away if not anchored to something that felt real.

After a few moments of this paradise, his eyes flickered open. The warm airy feeling was gone and he was collapsed on the deck. The Tridenti kids had hogtied many soldiers and a few more were throwing their armor into the sea. "What happened?" Neil asked groggily. The pain in his arm was even gone.

"You got a taste of my favorite song," Serena said. She helped him up.

"You two are…" Neil didn't have a word.

"Lightborns," Alexander said. "And evidently you are too, Mamba. Not a servant, after all."

Neil looked at his hand again. "Yeah," Neil said. "That's surprising."

"Neil Vapros!" one of the hogtied guards screamed. "That boy is Neil Vapros and he will bring the Empire down on your heads!"

"Neil Vapros," Neil said. "That's definitely it."

"Thanks, guy." Alexander said to the guard. "I like Mamba better though," he said to Neil.

"You don't understand!" the guard screamed. "The Imperial Doctor is after him. The entire Empire is after him! Every soldier in the land knows his face. Give him up and you might be spared."

Alexander approached the guard and grabbed him by the hair. "You might see Neil Vapros: fugitive of the empire, but we only see Mamba, our friend from the sea." He dropped the guard. "If anyone from the Empire tries to touch him while he's under our protection, they'll have to deal with the wrath of Mama Tridenti."

The soldier's eyes widened and he began blubbering an apology. "Take their ship and the prisoners back to the Ocean's Jaw," Serena said to a few crewmen. "Rip the ship for parts and put the men under lock and key. We'll meet you there." The men saluted her and hopped over to the other ship.

"Anything else you men can tell us about our little friend Mamba? He's looking for answers," Alex roared to the hostages as they were being unloaded onto the other boat. "Anyone with anything helpful will receive twice as much food for their first month in our prison."

"He's got a brother!" one called. "Rhys Vapros!"

Neil's mind made the connection and in his head he could see his brother clear as day. His short hair and jade green eyes stuck out prominently in Neil's mind. "He was responsible for the death of Saewulf Anima!" another one yelled.

A chill ran down Neil's spine. He couldn't put his finger on why, but the name Saewulf made him want to flee back down into the hull. "Is any of this helping?" Alexander asked.

"Yeah," Neil said. "A lot is coming back to me. Thanks, Alexander."

"Alex is fine," he said. "Glad you're part of the crew, Mamba." He outstretched his hand.

Neil shook his hand appreciatively. Until he could fully remember who Neil was, maybe being Mamba wouldn't be so bad.

Chapter Forty-Four

THE DOCTOR'S WORKSHOP
THE PACK

THE BOY HADN'T YET AWAKENED, BUT THAT WAS TO BE EXPECTED. THE Doctor made his preparations. He was actually nervous. He'd heard much about the boy and desperately wanted the stories to be true. Maybe this one would understand. Maybe this one would grow to seize his mantle. He would finally be free from his undertaking.

"Victor," the Doctor said.

Victor peered up from his workbench where he was cleaning his weapons. "Yes?"

"How many people know the location of this workshop?"

The Marksman thought. "Besides us? Three or so. The Hyena, General Carlin, and Quintus."

"We can lead the remaining fugitives back here when the boy has been converted, but if they arrive sooner it will make me very upset. Quintus is the weak link."

"I understand," the Marksman said. "But we'd get a lot of flack for killing him."

"Just protect him," the Doctor ordered. "They'll go after him for information. Make sure they don't get it before I can turn the boy."

The Marksman began suiting up without a word of confirmation. The Doctor didn't need it. People did what he asked when he asked. "Before you go, bring a body back for the pet," the Doctor continued. "He hasn't eaten in too long."

The Marksman bowed to his father and left the workshop. The Doctor could hear the boy stirring and he knew that if he still had a full mouth, he'd be grinning. It was time.

"Rhys Vapros: scholar, strategist, medical mind. You've got a full list of talents under your belt."

The boy's big round eyes opened as if he'd just left a nightmare, but the terror didn't fade. From one nightmare to the next, he supposed. "Welcome to my workshop, Rhys," the Doctor said. "I have a very exciting opportunity to share with you."

The boy was panicking as expected. The Doctor waited until he calmed. "What do you want with me?" Rhys asked.

"I want an heir," the Doctor said. "I want you to become what I've long searched for: the next Imperial Doctor."

"What?" Rhys asked. He was clearly horrified.

The Doctor stared at his misshapen hands and then over to Rhys. "I never wanted to be this way. I didn't choose this fate. It was given to me by the first Imperial Doctor."

"I don't understand..." Rhys said. "I don't want..."

"I was kidnapped when I was a little younger than you are despite my powers, by a man trying to create a pain index. Can you understand what a pain index is?"

"He wanted to determine a unit to measure pain and then rank what hurts the most?" Rhys asked.

The Doctor had to resist shrieking in excitement. "Yes! Yes, that's it!" He calmed himself and smoothed his blood-splattered apron. "In being tortured to determine this, I realized that my curiosity was piqued. I needed to know. So once I escaped, I strapped him down and tortured him until he expired. I was actually much closer to finishing it. I've spent the last fifty years working on it, but I am terrified that my mission will outlive me. It won't be finished in time. So I need an heir. I need someone to finish this pain index."

"There are humane ways to do this," Rhys said desperately. "You could go to clinics or work to... You don't have to cause the pain yourself."

"I thought the same," the Doctor said. "By the light, you remind me so much of myself, Rhys. I know what has to happen."

"What has to happen?" Rhys breathed.

"The Imperial Doctor is not a title. It's a calling. It's a mantle. You can't choose it; it has to choose you. After I killed him, I continued to hear his voice everywhere I went until it eventually replaced my own. Here is what has to happen: you have to become me. You have to accept the spirit and mind that is the Imperial Doctor."

"That's not possible," Rhys said. "You can't turn me into you. I can't share in your psychosis."

"Big word," the Doctor said, his mood turning. "Psychosis would imply that I have had a break with reality. And yet this is all very real, as you will discover. Here's what has to happen: I will experiment on you and add new procedures to the pain index until I complete a few chapters. Then you will torture me until the pain index has advanced considerably. You have to kill me Rhys, to truly become me."

Rhys stared at him horror. "I can't. I won't. I can't kill you."

"You're only killing me in a way," the Doctor said. "I will be reborn in your mind and in your work. Death will only be the beginning for me. Trust that."

Rhys stared at him unconvinced and uninspired. The Doctor growled, frustrated that Rhys hadn't taken to his calling. He selected a pair of pliers from the workbench and rubbed his metal chin. "Get some rest, Rhys. Tomorrow we begin with sleep deprivation. This can't be rushed. It must be done carefully and with the utmost precision. And don't bother trying to materialize out of that cage. It might be possible if you were only wearing one cuff, but I've never seen anyone use their powers with two cuffs."

He left the boy to cry and ponder the horrors that might await him. The Doctor went to one of his benches and began working on another project to calm himself. He remembered that he hadn't accepted his destiny at first either. It would take time and dedication but he would have his prodigy. This boy was perfect. He could feel it in every remaining inch of his body.

Chapter Forty-Five

CONVOY
LILLY CELERIUS

WITH A SQUEAL OF PAIN LILLY SLAMMED HER HAND INTO THE WOODEN wall of the convoy. The Wolf did the same while grunting quietly. "The tricky part is the speed," he murmured as he brought his fist into the wall again. "You've got to hit hard enough that your bones will break, but at the same time…"

"You've got to go fast enough that they won't heal before the next hit," Lilly said as she heard her own knuckles crack against the wood. "I know."

"What do you dream about?" the Wolf asked.

Lilly never wanted to think about her dreams. She couldn't imagine anything worse than discussing them. "I dream about the dead. Always the dead," she said quietly. "Why?"

"I used to dream about my wife every night," the Wolf said. "Right after I was exiled. It was always the same thing. I'd be comfortable in bed with her and then I would feel her pull away. When

I turned back she would be a few feet away. She was in the same bed and all. She was just beckoning to me from the other side."

"That sounds horrific, Uncle," Lilly sighed.

"I wish that were it," he chuckled sadly. "I would reach out to her and she'd just keep getting farther away. The bed would keep getting bigger. I'd try to push through the covers but I'd find myself tied up in them. The more I struggled for her, the further away she appeared to be. I'd scream and claw, but I would sink deeper into the plushness of it all. Soon the sheets would strangle me or the pillows would smother me. Really bizarre, isn't it?"

Lilly didn't know what to say. "Doesn't it hurt to think about?"

"Lilly, I'm crushing my hands into pulp," the Wolf said.

She grimaced. "Right."

"For a while I found myself pulled between these two worlds. I was either wrestling with pillows and blankets or doing something like this." Lilly couldn't see him but she was sure he was gesturing to his damaged hand. "I always tried to live in the world that hurt less at the time. I was bobbing and weaving. Dodging punches. It hurts to dwell, Lilly. But sometimes it hurts just a bit less than what's right in front of you."

"That's your lesson in recovery?" she asked incredulously.

"No," he said, "That's my lesson in maintaining sanity."

She heard a sickening pop and then what must have been the Wolf ripping his bloodied right hand out of his chains. He groaned in relief. "I got one free."

His hand began to reform as the bones found their shattered fragments and realigned. Within a few moments his hand was starting to look more like a hand again and less like a puddle of flesh.

Lilly's next strike cracked a bone in her thumb and with a pop she managed to free one of her hands. She used her new freedom of motion to wrap her arm around her uncle's shoulder. He returned the hug half-heartedly. "We've still got another hand to go, Miss."

She tried not to whimper as she pulled away. "Well, we're not getting any closer to escaping by talking about it."

The Wolf looked anxious. "If they're taking us to Carlin then we might not have much time left."

"Once we get free we can take the guards by surprise," she said. "They probably think we're asleep back here. We'll certainly have the upper hand."

"I really have to question your choice of wording there, darling," the Wolf said.

Within ten minutes Lilly's left hand was free. She winced in pain as her skeleton returned to proper form and the flesh reshaped. The Wolf had managed to free his other hand as well. "How many guards do you think we're dealing with?" Lilly asked as she scanned the bare caravan for a weapon.

"Two up front managing the horses and then the assassin riding on a racehorse in case anything goes wrong," the Wolf said.

"It's a wonder they didn't put someone back here to watch us," Lilly said.

The Wolf shook his head. "The Doctor was smart enough to know that we could easily overpower any Imperial guard. Chained or not."

Lilly and the Wolf sat waiting in silence while the cart moved on.

After a few seconds of silent meditation, the Wolf climbed up on top of the convoy. Lilly heard a body hit the ground and watched as a soldier was crushed under the wheel of the cart. She dropped out of the back and pulled his sword from his hip. She fought off dizziness from hunger and thirst. The Wolf was disposing of the other guard on the convoy. There were two unbridled horses and that circled around.

The Wolf leapt onto the nearest one and tackled its rider off the horse and into the dirt. The other horse charged at Lilly and she realized the Hyena was the one spurring it along. She lashed out with the sword, but in her attempt not to hit the horse the Hyena was able to dodge her attack and kick her solidly in the head. It certainly didn't help with her nausea and dizziness. She stumbled like a drunkard. The Hyena pulled a knife of his own from his belt. He circled the horse and ran it across her shoulder on the next charge. He then used his momentum to pull his horse next to the escaping convoy. He lashed at the nearest horse's side and in a panic the two horses bolted out of sight, down the dirt road. He threw his knife at the horse the Wolf had pushed the guard from. The Horse fell to the ground and crushed the soldier that had been wrestling with the Wolf. Lilly gasped loudly at the sight of a horse being killed. The Hyena cackled at her. "Why the long face?" he managed through his laughs. He then steered his horse off to make his escape.

The Wolf groaned. "I doubt we'll be able to catch him," he said as he approached Lilly. "Not at this strength."

Lilly debated running after him, but her legs were wobbling just from standing. Their trip in the convoy had taken days and they'd been given nothing but a bit of bread and water. Clearly their captors wanted to keep them in a weakened state. "See that in the distance?" the Wolf said pointing toward the horizon.

For the first time since her escape, Lilly actually examined her surroundings. They were on a basic dirt road that cut through miles upon miles of even plains. For the first time they were surrounded by flat land. Gone were the rolling hills and mountains of the north. In the distance loomed a large village. It must have been one of the big five. "Brightbow?" Lilly asked.

The Wolf nodded. His face always maintained a modicum of quiet dignity, but something was wrong. His lower jaw trembled. "Lilly we are in a great deal of trouble."

"What?" Lilly asked. "We can go to Brightbow, regain our strength and then head back in the direction of the Cliff. It won't be an easy journey, but Brightbow has a strong, secret rebel presence, correct? I'm sure we can find some strong horses."

The Wolf didn't even seem to be listening. He placed his hands over his face for a moment. When he raised his head his eyes were full of fear. "We were better off in the carriage," he whispered.

"What is wrong with you?" Lilly asked. She couldn't keep the discomfort out of her voice.

"Of all the places we could have ended up, tactically, this is the worst. Brightbow is about half rebels and half loyalists. The rebels here are incredibly organized, so most of the loyalists don't even know that they're here."

"I don't understand the problem," Lilly said.

"When I was General, the Imperial Hunting Squadron used to talk about Brightbow a good deal. It was tactically interesting because it's surrounded on all sides by miles and miles of plains. All flat." He gestured around him. "We were hunting a Venator, not unlike the Marksman. He was famous for killing Imperial soldiers with arrows and stringing them up in a forest that used to be on this path."

He pointed down the road. "We didn't know what he looked like, how old he was, or whether or not it even was a he. All we knew was that he'd been shot in the center of the back at some point. The devil was such a problem that we ended up building a military outpost and burning down the forest."

"So he couldn't hide in the trees?"

"Essentially," the Wolf said. "But what we really wanted was to force him out onto the fields. So we could hunt him down and he'd have nothing to use as cover in a firefight."

Lilly looked around impatiently. Carlin could be on his way at any moment. "Did it work?"

"Well our problem was always Brightbow. What would stop him from fleeing into the village? How could we catch someone in a village of thousands if we didn't know what he looked like? He could simply vanish into the crowds or disguise himself."

"And what's to stop us from doing that right now?" Lilly asked.

"Carlin, " the Wolf said. "Before we started recruiting people from outside the wall, the Imperial Hunting Party consisted of Anthony, Carlin, myself, and a few others. Carlin and Anthony both proposed different approaches to finding the Venator if he made it to Brightbow. Anthony would post a reward and send in a few spies. They'd watch the city and anyone who left would be checked for a scar on their back. He'd have to leave eventually so we would just wait him out. In the end it didn't matter because the Imperial Hunting Party was called away to search for Nikolai Taurlum."

Lilly stared at him. "What was Carlin's idea?"

"Carlin insisted that the Venator had a revolutionary spirit and could be drawn out by his hatred for the Empire or his desire to protect people. He would take hostages and destroy property until the Venator stepped forward. He'd close off the city and turn it into a trap."

Lilly's face grew hot. She suddenly understood the Wolf's fear. "We're in the same position that the Venator was all those years ago," the Wolf said. "Carlin is about to know where we are. And the only place we can flee is to Brightbow village."

Lilly felt dizzy. She stabbed the sword into the ground and gripped it for balance. The Wolf looked like he wanted to do the same. "If we're killed, the entire Celerius line, and possibly the revolution, dies with us. But if we go into this city, we're putting every rebel in grave danger. The ones in Brightbow are clever, but not clever enough to stay hidden if Carlin turns this village upside down."

Lilly looked around. "But... exposed out here. No cover. No nothing."

He gripped his sword hilt and gritted his teeth. "We have an interesting moral dilemma to face."

Chapter Forty-Six

TRIDENTI SHIP
NEIL VAPROS

NEIL HAD BEEN ON THE TRIDENTI SHIP FOR THREE DAYS AND HE'D ONLY discovered one more thing about himself. He hated and deeply feared fish. The taste was familiar to him but the look of them certainly was not. Their eyes were particularly frightening, soulless, just recently snuffed out. Unfortunately the Tridenti family only ate food from the sea for both convenience and superstitious reasons. Neil had been watching them in action for the last few days and nothing within his short memory had ever impressed him so much. Their powers were connected to the sea, and so was all of their nourishment. According to Serena, they were immortal when they were in contact with seawater. They could also naturally breathe underwater and swim faster than anything else in the ocean.

"Do you two think fish have unsettling eyes?" Neil asked at dinner one night. He'd always been invited to eat with them in their special dining room.

Alex picked up a fish from the center of the table and flicked its mouth open and shut to mime speaking. "Why don't you love me, Mamba?" he asked through the fish. "Don't you think I'm pretty, Mamba?"

"Stop it," Serena giggled. "You're going to scare him away."

"You don't have to eat fish our way, Mamba," Alex said. "You could just heat it up with your hands."

"You know I can't remember how," Neil said. "I think I can only do it when I'm in trouble or frustrated."

"We could give you some crew work," Serena suggested. "I'm sure that would get your blood pumping."

Neil shrugged. Living on this ship it was doubtful he'd ever be under great amounts of stress ever again. The Tridenti were so carefree. They laughed loudly and never showed any signs of being uncomfortable. Maybe having their life force tied to nature kept them happy and in the moment. "Have you tried teleporting?" Alex asked.

Alex had grilled a few prisoners and revealed the extent of Neil's powers. The Tridenti weren't saying it, but clearly they were dying to see more of his abilities. He was dying to see more of theirs as well. Neil shook his head. "I wouldn't know where to begin."

"I have an idea." Alex stood up and slid his dinner knife off of the table. "How much do you trust me, Mamba?"

"At the moment?" Neil asked. "Very little."

Alex beamed. "Perfect. Stand up."

Neil stood up cautiously. "Are you really gonna do this?"

"Do you know how we teach Tridenti guppies how to swim?"

"Alex, this is a bad idea." Serena said. However, she looked calm and amused as Alex took a few steps back.

"We throw them off our largest boat and into the sea," Alex said. "They all learn to swim."

Neil ran his hand through his hair. "How old are they when you do that?"

"About six months old."

"Just do it," Neil said. "The anticipation is gonna kill me."

Alex threw the knife by the handle directly at Neil's chest. Neil felt his energy dissipate and reform on the other side of the room. Alex and Serena burst into applause. Neil fell to the ground breathing heavily. The area around his cuff throbbed with pain. "Ladies and gents, Mamba knows how to swim!" Alex cheered.

Serena pulled him to his feet. "I thought we were going to have to toss you back in the ocean," she said laughing.

"We would never do that," Alex said. "Not when we could accept that reward from the Empire." He winked at Neil.

Neil sat back down on the bench. "Do you try to murder all of your guests?" he asked as he took a reluctant bite of fish.

"Just the ones we like," Serena said.

There was a knock at the door and a crewman poked his head inside. "Ocean's Jaw is visible, Captains," he said. "Half-hour until docking."

"Thank you," Serena said, dismissing him.

"You ready to see the largest ocean fortress in the realm?" Alex asked.

"Depends. Are people gonna throw knives at me?"

"Only if you're unfriendly," Alex replied.

Neil didn't remember much, but he was completely certain he'd never seen anything quite like the Ocean's Jaw. From the deck of the Tridenti ship he could see most of it laid out before him. Its name was clearly derived from the shape of the island it was built on. The shore was in a semi-oval and large stone triangles had been carved out and laid equidistant, probably to look like shark teeth. Built into the sand and sea was a giant mansion that seemed to cover nearly every inch of the land. Outside of the stone teeth were a series of sprawling docks, each with its own ship and crew. The ship settled about a hundred meters from the shore and the crewmen dropped the anchor. "How are we getting in?" Neil asked.

"You can't bring anything into the Ocean's Jaw," Alex said. "You have to swim."

Neil looked to Serena. "Is he being serious?"

She seemed taken aback by how grave he was.

"I can't swim," Neil said.

The Tridenti shared a glance. "How do you know?" Alex asked.

"There are some things I just know," Neil said. "For instance, I don't think I've ever been swimming."

Serena shared a glance with Alex and then approached Neil. "But you can't be certain…"

"I can be," Neil said.

Serena frowned. "You've gotta get to land somehow, Mamba."

"Come and see," Alex said becking Neil closer to the edge of the ship. "It's not too deep. You could jump in here and upon reaching that point there…"

He pointed far off, and Neil followed his finger with his eye. The second Neil reached the very edge of the deck he remembered what the Tridenti did to guppies. He tried to spin around, but the two seafaring siblings had him by the arms. Seemingly without any effort they tossed him straight off the edge. As he plummeted a few memories came racing to meet him as quickly as the water. Upon sinking into the sea, he remembered looking up from a cobblestone street as a blonde giant stood in a window with a hammer. Neil paddled without coordination and began to sink. One thing was for certain. He was no Tridenti and he certainly couldn't swim like one.

Chapter Forty-Seven

BRIGHTBOW
LILLY CELERIUS

THE WOLF KNEW BRIGHTBOW WELL. WITHIN MINUTES OF ENTERING THE city the two Celerius were outfitted in brown cloaks and disguises from cheap local clothing shops. The Wolf dragged her through uninhabited alley after alley for what felt like an hour. Lilly wished she could use her Celerius speed to make the journey shorter, but she knew the risk. If the Wolf was right, this village was soon going to turn into a slaughterhouse. He eventually reached a small abandoned-looking restaurant and pointed to the door. "Okay, inside," he said as he pulled a key from his belt and slipped it into the lock. It clicked open and he ushered her inside. "Welcome to the Feeding Ground," he murmured.

"The Feeding Ground?" Lilly asked.

"They used to have a variety of dogs that lived here. The rule was when you were done eating you could just throw your remaining food on the ground and they would gobble it up. The Feeding Ground. It's a joke."

Lilly wiped some dust off of the bar. "It looks abandoned. Why did it close?"

"Rat infestation," the Wolf replied.

He gently kicked open the door to the kitchen and stomped his feet on the floor. "It's me. No one needs to hide."

Suddenly the floorboards a few feet away from Lilly lifted from below, exposing a secret trap door.

Two young boys wearing goggles poked their heads up. They looked like frightened church mice. Actually everything about them reminded Lilly of church mice. They had tiny upturned button noses and disproportionately tiny mouths. "Sir?" one of them asked. "What are you doing in Brightbow?"

"There's about to be a mess of trouble, boys," the Wolf said. "I want to know where the rest of the rebel presence is."

The two boys looked at each other sheepishly. "Well... we tried to send word to you," one murmured as if preparing for a scolding. "The rebels in Brightbow left to help in the liberation of Abington. We thought you knew... there's probably only six or seven men left."

Lilly and the Wolf exhaled a sigh of relief. "Boys, that's the best news I've heard in about five years," the Wolf said. "Carlin is chasing my niece and me and he's about to turn this city upside down. Any rebels here would have been decapitated."

"Carlin's coming to decapitate us?" the one in back whimpered.

"Your niece?" the other said flirtatiously as he removed his goggles.

She stared at him. He pulled himself out of the hole and finished removing his giant goggles. She was able to get a better look at him. He was terribly skinny and covered in dirt or maybe it was black powder. He had a red bandanna tied loosely around his fore-head. His most notable feature was his set of big brown eyes. They appeared larger than average and gave him the appearance of a much younger boy. "James Jacobson!" he said proudly, extending his tiny hand overzealously for a handshake.

She shook it hesitantly. He quickly realized that'd he'd stained her hand with his dirty one and retracted it embarrassed. His brother climbed out of the hole behind him. They looked identical aside from the fact that James Jacobson's brother was a few inches shorter. "Jack Jacobson!" he said proudly. But he didn't extend his hand for a hand-shake in lieu of his brother's mistake.

"Your names are Jack and James Jacobson?" she asked.

They nodded eagerly and in perfect sync. The Wolf approached them. "Don't try to tell them apart," he told Lilly. "We don't have enough time." He turned to the young boys who were both still staring at Lilly. "Stop drooling," the Wolf said. They both turned crimson. "What's going on down there?"

"We're doing things," James said.

The Wolf stared, waiting for them to elaborate. They didn't. "What kind of things?"

"Gunpowder things," Jack said.

"Don't blow up the restaurant," the Wolf sighed.

"It would take care of the rats, sir," James said.

"It would also take care of us," the Wolf quipped. He walked to the other side of the bar.

"Are you two twins?" Lilly asked.

They shook their heads in unison. "I'm older by a year," James said.

"Stop socializing," the Wolf said. "Carlin is on his way and we have to stop this city from turning into his plaything."

"Well," James said. "If he's going to try to use the smokehouse method, what we really have to do is break the military presence as soon as it arrives."

"We could use our..." Jack paused. "Gunpowder things to destroy their supply carts and then we could start wounding soldiers."

James rubbed his chin. "You know what would really end the occupation quickly?"

The Wolf's eyes widened. "If we wound Carlin! That's brilliant!"

Lilly's jaw tightened and she crossed her arms. "If we can get close enough to Carlin, we have to kill him. No other option is a real option."

The Wolf raised his hand to stop the inevitable tirade. "I understand, but imagine what happens when Carlin is wounded. There's a commandment in Altryon's military that says during expeditions they have to protect their chief above all else and despite all other orders. In this case, that's Carlin. That's why we were called away from catching that Venator all those years ago. Our chief, the new emperor, was believed to be in danger. If we wound Carlin badly enough, he won't be able to order them to continue the occupation. They're forced to protect him, even if it's against his will. If he dies, the second-in-command will just take over and continue the smokehouse method."

Lilly's stomach knotted. Carlin was the source of all her pain and all her suffering. He was her nemesis. Letting him live would eat her alive inside. Then again, so would letting innocent people die. "Let's say I'm willing to consider this," Lilly said in a razor sharp tone. "How could we possibly get close enough to wound Carlin? Chances are he'll be waiting for us. And chances are, he'll be very well protected."

The Wolf turned to his tiny compatriots. "Where is Carlin most likely to put down roots?"

James hopped over the bar in one fluid motion and snatched a map from one of the cabinets. He unrolled it on the bar. "He's probably going to want to make his message to the city clear the second he arrives. He's going to want as many people as possible to know what's happening."

"So the town square?" the Wolf asked.

James nodded. "That's where it'll be easiest for him to spread his message."

"So he'll set down his roots nearby?" Jack said to the Wolf.

The Wolf ran his fingers over some of the buildings on the map. "Although, in Altryon's military training you're taught not to set your base camp anywhere that isn't easily defensible in a civilized area."

"Which means?" Lilly asked.

"He's going to forcefully occupy a building near the town square. Most likely the strongest fortified one," the Wolf said.

"Right here," James said as he tapped on the map enthusiastically. "The Mayor's house. It's made of stone and it's connected to the town square."

"So what?" Lilly mused. "Once he makes his ultimatum, we destroy their supply carts and sneak into the mayor's house?"

James sat back against the bar casually and scratched his head. "Sneaking into the mayor's house might be tough," he said. "The windows are high up and all the doors are reinforced. Unless you have the climbing skills of an animal or a battering ram, we can't get the jump on Carlin."

"There's always a way," the Wolf muttered. He stared at the map. "As far as we know, Carlin isn't here yet. He think's he's making the trap, but in reality, we'll be the ones setting the trap."

"Isn't that the same strategy the Doctor used on us?" Lilly asked.

"It worked didn't it?" the Wolf said without looking up.

"You have a plan?" Jack asked.

"I do," the Wolf said. "Assemble any rebels currently remaining in this city. Tell them to bring any masks and weapons they have to this hideout." He indicated a place on the map. "It's closest to the square."

"Do you need us to do anything to help you break into the mayor's house?" James asked.

"No. We don't need to break in."

The group looked at the Wolf curiously. "Why not?" Lilly asked.

"Because Carlin is going to invite us in himself."

Chapter Forty-Eight

BRIGHTBOW
CARLIN FILUS

CARLIN'S BOOTS ECHOED LOUDLY THROUGH THE TOWN SQUARE AS HE AND a fleet of armed soldiers took up formation in the center. A palpable tension hung in the air as the villagers who remained were clearly trying to decide if it was in their best interest to run. "You're sure this is it?" Carlin whispered to Virgil.

Virgil glanced around the square skeptically as if looking for possible threats. Virgil's head never seemed to be fixed in one place. He was always on the lookout for something. "The soldier said he saw them run from the road and toward this village. Our men are patrolling the surrounding plains, but this would be an ideal hiding place for them. If they're wandering alone on the plains our horsemen will catch them. And if they're here…" Virgil trailed off.

"We'll hunt them down like the rats they are," Carlin said as he gave Virgil a nod of assent.

"We can send small groups of soldiers into the buildings and clear them one by one in a grid format," Virgil said.

Carlin shook his head defiantly. "Never use a knife when you can use a broadsword."

Carlin pulled his pistol from its holster and fired a shot straight into the bright blue sky. A few villagers screamed and a few others ran, but the shot had the desired effect: all activity came to a screeching halt. Carlin re-holstered his weapon. "Citizens of Brightbow Village!" His voice echoed through the square. "I am Carlin Filus, General of the Imperial Military. It has come to my attention that a few ill-behaved citizens might be harboring fugitives of Altryon's Empire in this very village. I don't know how you're accustomed to doing things in this edge of the empire, but I can assure you, the act of harboring a menace to the public and to your Emperor is a crime punishable by the most painful of deaths."

He could see the crowd of villagers shifting with anxiety. "Each of you take a hostage," he commanded.

The squadron of twelve soldiers silently drew their swords and charged the crowd of villagers. Before long there were twelve sobbing villagers on their knees with swords at their throats. Carlin snarled, "You have two options, citizens. You can leave Brightbow and trek off into the open plains, or you can remain and help us hunt Lilly Celerius and the Wolf. If you make a sizable contribution to their capture or deaths, then you will be paid with your weight in gold."

The crowd was silent as Carlin drew his broadsword and approached a kneeling hostage who sobbed openly. The man looked up to see Carlin coming closer and began to crawl away in terror. Carlin brought his sword straight down through the man's back. The man howled in agony. "I forgot the best bit," Carlin hissed. "Every two hours we kill a hostage and leave the body in this very square. So go, citizens of Brightbow. Whether you find yourself motivated by gold or heroic tendencies, you've got some fugitives to catch. The rest of you will be searched and sent out onto the plains until this business is done."

Carlin pulled his blade from the villager's back and sheathed it. Virgil removed a pistol and fired it into the air. The village erupted into chaos as the masses began to flee for their lives. Carlin assessed his situation. "Virgil, take five soldiers and go building by building. Leave no floorboard unturned. They will be ours."

Virgil saluted and signaled for five men to follow. They darted off down an alley and Carlin paced. Seeing the death of his worst enemies was now a game of patience.

Chapter Forty-Nine

OCEAN'S JAW
NEIL VAPROS

ALEX AND SERENA LAUGHED AS THEY PULLED NEIL ASHORE. HE WAS grumpy, as they'd probably expected. "You both laugh too much," Neil said.

"I swear we didn't laugh half this much before your arrival," Alex gasped between outbursts.

"You bring so much joy to our lives, Mamba," Serena giggled.

"That's just because you like having someone to torture," Neil said with a huff.

"Aha!" Alex slapped his forehead to commemorate a fake realization. "I was trying to figure out why having you around was so much fun. That's definitely it."

Neil watched as the rest of the crew swabbed the deck and lowered the masts on the ship. "Aren't they coming ashore?" Neil asked.

Serena turned around and then back to Neil. "Who? The crew?"

Neil nodded. Once again Serena and Alex shared a look. They seemed to have dozens of silent conversations per day. Neil found nothing more frustrating. "The crew can't come ashore," Alex said. "There's an ancient rule about this island. No more than twenty-five people are allowed on it at any given time."

Neil was silent for a moment. "Well then I'm honored to be here."

"It's not that simple," Serena said. "Last we heard they had twenty-three people on the mainland.

"And the three of us makes twenty-six," Neil said.

Alex and Serena smiled at him hesitantly. He felt like they were about to toss him off of another ship. "So I need to what? Stay with the boat?"

"The ship's going to a secondary fortress where it'll be restocked and prepared for another voyage. So no," Alex said. "How familiar are you with hand-to-hand combat?"

"Any questions that start with 'how familiar are you with' probably aren't useful," Neil said.

"At least you've got a sense of humor," Alex said. "You'll have to challenge someone for their place on the island. There are eight Tridenti, so you'll have eighteen options."

"You guys really aren't going to let me rest, are you?" Neil asked.

"You gotta learn how to swim somehow," Alex said.

Neil didn't love the idea of challenging someone on the island, but at the moment he had no other options. Alex and Serena were his only friends and the Ocean's Jaw was his only hope of fitting in somewhere. "So the challenge is always hand-to-hand combat?"

"You got it," Serena said. "You made pretty quick work of those two guards on the ship. It should be a snap!" She snapped her fingers to illustrate her point. Remarkably, it didn't make Neil feel any better.

"What if I lose?" Neil asked.

"You'll be given a row boat and we can point you in the direction of the mainland," Alex said. "Sorry, Mamba. This is our only option. Trimming the fat keeps all dead weight off of the island."

"I'm dead weight?" Neil asked.

"Not if you prove you're more useful than someone else," Alex said. "Forget about it for now. You can come in, bathe, rest, and eat. Tonight there will be a feast and it's then that you'll have to decide who you want to challenge. We'll discuss it more before then."

"One of you can't challenge someone?" Neil asked.

"Afraid not," Alex said. "Tridenti are guaranteed a spot. It's the guests that need to fight for a room."

Alex stood and Serena pulled Neil up. The mansion was even bigger from his current perspective. The entire thing looked to be made of the same material. It was wooden, but not like the ship. It was polished and smooth so that it shined like the sun reflecting off of the water. The pillars out front were as tall as trees and Neil couldn't help wondering how they'd gotten that much wood onto an island this small. Two banners hung down from a balcony and drifted in the wind. They were copper and teal, adorned with a vicious looking shark. Underneath something was written in small letters. "What's that?" Neil pointed at the banner.

"It's our family crest," Serena said.

"What's written underneath?" Neil asked.

"It's our motto," Alex said. "The shore holds strong."

"And what's that mean?"

Serena looked like she wanted to answer, but Alex jumped on the question first. "It's always been our duty to make sure the Imperials never bring their warships to the shore of Volteria's mainland and no one is ever able to take advantage of outsiders via the sea. The sea has always been neutral territory for all to take advantage of. And it always will be."

"Noble cause," Neil said.

There were giant copper bowls of water set up on either side of the doors. Serena and Alex dipped their hands into the pools. They then pushed the mammoth wooden doors open easily. Neil followed them into the atrium and gasped audibly. The interior somehow looked twice as large as the exterior. They'd put the space to good use as well with shallow pools every few feet and bridges to assist those who wanted to be dry. It was beautifully decorated, but Neil knew the pools had a greater purpose: they were obviously a tactical decision made by the building's architect. The Tridenti were stronger and faster when touching water, not to mention immortal. Anyone who tried to storm this fortress would meet the Tridenti on their home turf where they were at their strongest.

In the very center of the room a woman stood on one leg. Neil could only see her from the back but could tell she was a Tridenti. Her tan skin and sandy dreadlocked hair gave her away. She was slowly alternating positions silently and with perfect balance. Alex and Serena walked right past her and didn't bother to say hello. "This is our Mama," Serena said.

"Mama Tridenti?" Neil asked.

"Yes sir," Serena said.

"Those Imperial sailors seemed pretty afraid of her," Neil said.

"For good reason." Alex said.

"She's violent," Serena elaborated.

He walked around so he could see the front of her. From the back she'd looked like she was in her thirties, but from the front her age was apparent. She had deep wrinkles and he could see the gray streaks that were tied into her dreadlocks. "Yes. She looks quite violent," Neil said.

"She needs to do this." Serena said "Daily."

"Or what'll happen?" Neil asked.

"It restores her patience," Alex said. "When she runs out of patience people…" Alex clearly couldn't find a phrase that sounded good.

"I get it," Neil said. "Stuff happens." He followed them past Mama Tridenti and out of the entry hall. "It's a wonder where you guys get all of your patience. I'd get very tired of trying to explain stuff to me."

They both laughed. "It makes us feel smarter," Serena said.

They reached another giant set of doors and two more copper water bowls. Alex dipped his hands and pushed through into the next room. It led to a room that split off into two directions. He followed them through another series of doors until they reached one of their guest rooms. "You'll find clothes in there," Alex said. "There are soaps and a bath too. We'll come get you when it's time for dinner."

⁂

"I know who you should fight," Alex said to Neil before he was even fully through the door of Neil's room. He hadn't bothered knocking.

"Excellent." Neil said. "Care to share?"

"There's a guy who's been on the island for a few months named George Haxon," Alex said. "He's a nasty scoundrel who's been particularly vocal against certain members of the family. You'll probably gain some fans here if you take him out."

Neil didn't like the idea of fighting anyone for a place on the island, however, he didn't mind so much if his opponent was considered a nasty scoundrel. Neil hopped off the bed with more spring in his step. "Alright," Neil said. "How does this work?"

"Tonight Mama Tridenti will stand up during dinner and give a speech. No one knows what it's about or what it's gonna be. It's normally old stories. After she's done, she'll ask if anyone has anything else to declare. Sometimes someone will stand up and share a story, but it's rare. If no one else stands then it's your turn."

"I stand up? At your family dinner?" Neil asked.

"Exactly," Alex said. "Then you say, 'I dedicate my service to the shore and I demand a seat at this table.' Mama Tridenti will ask whose seat you demand. And you reply with…?"

"George Haxon?"

"George Haxon," Alex confirmed. "Then we'll finish dinner and head down to the fighting pit."

Neil palms were already sweating at the idea of the fight. "Hand-to-hand means no fire right?"

Alex glanced at Neil's metal cuff and he remembered that his powers would be hard to summon anyway. "I'm afraid so, mate," Alex said. "Don't worry though. Haxon isn't the most in shape individual. He's going to try and body slam you. If you can avoid him, it'll be over quickly."

"Awesome," Neil said.

"But seriously, Mamba. Avoid the body slam."

"Yeah, I got it." Neil said. "I'm not too worried. There's no way to be one hundred percent sure, but I bet I've fought bigger."

"That's a big man," Neil almost whimpered upon seeing George Haxon in the dining hall. "He's a giant."

He could tell Alex wanted to make fun of him, but the seriousness of the situation was grounding. Neil was seated in-between Alex and Serena. She leaned forward to hiss at her brother. "You want Mamba to fight Haxon? Are you trying to kill our only friend?"

"Mamba would also like an answer to that question," Neil said quietly.

"Relax," Alex said. "Haxon is Mamba's best way into good standing here."

"Every punch is gonna bounce right off of him!" Serena was obviously trying her hardest to keep her voice down. Luckily the mammoth Haxon and his friends were sitting across the room at a different table.

The setup of the room was devised so that there were three tables making an incomplete rectangle with longer tables on the sides. There was an empty chair that looked regal in nature at the middle table. It was empty and most likely reserved for Mama Tridenti. Neil was nervous about meeting her under these circumstances.

He glanced over the table at Haxon and realized he was staring him down. The man was the largest Neil had ever seen. He reminded Neil of a dress that had been lingering in his mind for some reason. Like the dress, Haxon 's body seemed to explode outwardly in a never-ending waterfall. Instead of being made of blue ruffles and lace, he was made of pure body fat and a sweat stained tunic that looked like it had been a bed sheet at some point. His face was decorated with a thick mustache and dynamic pair of muttonchops. His head was completely bald and polka dotted with tiny beads of sweat. "What if he eats me?" Neil asked his friends.

Alex chuckled. Serena stared at the two of them as if that were a legitimate concern. "You can't tell me you're not worried about this," Serena said to Alex.

"I don't know what to tell you. I'm not a worrier." He patted Neil on the back. "And I believe in Mamba."

At that moment the door opened and Mama Tridenti entered. Everyone hushed as she made her way to her chair. With her eyes open, the bags under her eyes were clearer to see and her actual age was more apparent. She smiled at the room and waved her hands dismissively. "Eat. Relax." Her voice was unnaturally loud and clear for someone her size. "I'll speak after I've eaten and drunk my fill."

As she sat she glanced pointedly at Neil. He was their twenty-sixth and she knew better than anyone that before the night was up he would be challenging one of her men for a place on the island. Neil glanced back over at Haxon instinctively and to his horror the man was eating a fish whole with one hand. The other was wrapped around his next fish. Every time the man gobbled down a fish, Neil paled a bit. Neil consoled himself with the thought that every fish he ate would slow him down a bit. Neil ate slowly and just enough to give him energy. He hated fish.

The tables were covered end to end with plates full of fish of every shape and size. Even the plates that looked to be of some variety were made from octopus or seaweed or some other seafood. Most of the people sitting at his table were clearly from the sea as well, seeing as they shared the tan Tridenti skin and long sandy hair. He was getting strange looks from a lot of them. Hopefully he'd earn their approval in his fight with Haxon. Unless of course, Haxon stepped on his head and crushed it. Or sat on him and crushed him. Or crushed him in a bear hug. Neil gulped and tried to rid all head-crushing thoughts out of his mind.

Mama Tridenti stood up and everyone stopped speaking at once. She smirked at her apparent power. "The goal of meditation is to clear one's mind completely." Her voice boomed even louder than Neil had expected. Maybe breathing underwater for years had strengthened her lung capacity. "However, in the beginning I always find it hard to slip all the way into a meditative state. Worries, obligations and strong feelings rise to the surface. In the early hours of each day, I find my mind drifting to two things more and more often. I think of my children and I think of my empire."

Serena smiled and Alex rubbed his chin thoughtfully. "My rule has been questioned many times since my father passed away," Mama Tridenti continued. "Many also questioned my choice of husband when he was alive. It's easy to let doubt penetrate your mind, and I've always maintained that the best course of action when questioned is to look inward. Others have questioned whether I should lead so I ask myself: what makes a good leader?" She turned and faced her offspring directly. "I believe the traits that make a successful leader are also the ones that make a successful mother. A successful mother is one who disregards her sense of self and remembers the joy and opportunities of her children come first. She remembers that her life's purpose must be to make a world that her children would be lucky to live in. A good mother plants trees even when she knows that she'll never get to sit in their shade or taste their fruit."

She turned from her children and faced the rest of the room. "Ask yourselves when you question your fellow Tridenti, whether it be me or anyone else, how far down the line are they looking? Are they thinking about their opportunities or are they thinking about the lives their children might lead?"

A memory resurfaced in Neil's head. He was small and standing in front of a massive desk. He was being scolded and could feel the guilt and shame arising even now. Despite the fact that Mama Tridenti was described as violent she inspired him. He knew without a doubt that no parent had ever put him first. Mama Tridenti raised her cup into the air and the others followed suit. "I care for you all as my children. I hope you have faith in me and in each other as we dedicate our lives to the shore. If you pledge your lives to your duty, then I will pledge my life to protecting you and toward forging a world that is worth fighting for."

She drank and the rest of the room followed suit. Neil watched her in awe. No wonder everyone here was so carefree. He couldn't imagine worrying when someone like Mama Tridenti was watching out for him. She then turned directly toward him and he nearly choked on his drink. "Does anyone have anything to declare?"

The room was silent for about ten seconds. Neil wanted to stand, but he felt paralyzed under her gaze. His desire to impress her and find a place to call home finally spurred him into a standing position. "I dedicate my service to the shore and I demand a place at this table."

Mama Tridenti frowned slightly. "And whose place do you demand?"

Neil tried not to make eye contact with his adversary. "George Haxon's."

Haxon dropped a half eaten fish onto his plate in surprise. "And why do you demand it?" she asked.

Neil paled. He didn't realize that this was part of the process. He looked at Alex for help, but Alex just responded with a shrug. "He's been vocal against certain members of your family," Neil said. She raised an eyebrow at him. "And also to keep dead weight off of the island."

There was a second of silence and then uproarious laughter from a few Tridenti at Neil's table. Neil realized they thought he was making fun of Haxon because of his weight. Neil wanted to clarify that he had only been quoting Alex, but didn't know if that was part of the process. Mama Tridenti faced Haxon. "Prepare yourself, George," she said. "Eat and drink your fill. After dinner I expect to see you in the fighting pit."

She turned back to Neil and approached him. She leaned in close and Neil's blood went cold. "What's your name?"

"Neil Vapros," he said. "But I have a guppy name."

"What is it?"

"Mamba."

She glanced at her son. "Like the snake?"

Neil tried to hold her gaze. "Yes ma'am. I'm told anyway. I've never seen a snake."

"Mamba has no memory of anything before we found him," Serena said. "Makes him a pretty good recruit, right Mama?"

"If he can hold his own," Mama Tridenti said and returned to her seat to finish her dinner.

Neil nibbled at his fish. Alex patted him on the shoulder. "No turning back now," Serena said.

"You got that right," Neil said. He avoided making eye contact with Haxon who was shaking with fury as he gobbled down more fish. In a few moments, Neil would be an official member of the island or he'd be rowing his way to Misty Hollow. Wherever that was. There was also the possibility that he'd be crushed to death under Haxon's foot. As Neil finished his drink he did his best to purge the thought from his mind.

Chapter Fifty

ARKNEY
DARIUS TAURLUM

Darius was no stranger to bars. He'd been in dozens back in Altryon, and to a few outside the walls. Most of the time, people weren't drinking to have fun; they were doing it because they needed to, because they might go insane under the Emperor's thumb without it. Apparently, bars in Arkney were the exception. Everyone was shouting to each other and roaming unrestricted. Bars inside Altryon weren't like this. Usually they weren't alight with conversation and song. These men were afraid of nothing. "You sure this is the place?" Darius asked Anastasia.

She shushed him. It sounded condescending, but he didn't mind. They hadn't kissed since that night in Shipwreck Bay but he still felt that she had a strong hold over him. "Fine," he said. "Let's just get out of Arkney as soon as possible. I hear everyone here is a fugitive."

"That includes you, big guy," she whispered.

Despite her easygoing attitude he could hear uneasiness in her voice. Arkney was known for one thing only: it had no political alliance. Abington was controlled by the Empire, as was Brightbow, officially. Other cities such as Misty Hollow and Shipwreck Bay had a secret rebel presence that outnumbered the Empire's. Arkney was different in the fact that it was near the edge of the Empire's reach and repelled all tax collectors or military intrusion. Yet it also couldn't be persuaded to join the cause. It sat unoccupied by anyone who wasn't wanted by the law or ousted from traditional society.

The bar they were in was indicative of the whole town. Everyone looked big and dangerous. Some were even bigger than Darius. Bianca descended the spiral staircase silently and approached her friends. "You were right," she said to Anastasia. "There's a group of people playing cards upstairs."

"Okay," Anastasia said. "Then it's go time for us. We're looking for a man named Barlow Venator. His hunting name is the Dealer."

"What does he sell?" Darius asked.

"Nothing. He deals cards," Anastasia said.

"And how is he going to help us find the Imperial Bookkeeper?" Darius asked.

"Rumors say that Quintus is here in Arkney," Anastasia said. "The Dealer is the unofficial leader of this town. If anyone can point us in the right direction, it'll be him."

Bianca checked her knives and made sure she could whip them out without snagging on anything. Darius had noticed that anytime she became nervous her hand flew to her waist, even when she was unarmed. "No need for that," Anastasia said witnessing her sister's nervous tick. "He's one of the good Venator. I've met him and he's an honorable man. He wouldn't kill a fly."

Darius raised an eyebrow. "Somehow I'm hesitant to trust him. Seeing as the last two Venator we've met have been murderous lunatics."

"The Wolf was trained by the Venator," Bianca interjected. "He's not a murderous lunatic."

"You don't get to lead a revolution without a significant body count on your hands," Darius countered.

"If context doesn't matter then we're all murderous lunatics," Bianca said.

"Go team," Anastasia said sarcastically.

The group went up the stairs. Darius took it step by step, careful not to shake the bar with his weight. Once they reached the top floor, they came upon a group of men smoking and playing cards in silence. A few of them looked up when they realized they had visitors. "You kids need help?" one at the front asked. He was shuffling cards with such ease that they looked like they were dancing.

Darius knew he was a Venator upon first sight. He had that razor sharp focus in his eyes and mahogany brown hair. He also had an immaculate pair of muttonchops that fed into an even more immaculate handlebar moustache. It was facial hair so excellent that Darius felt jealousy welling up in his chest. All of Darius' facial hair grew in blonde and was unsightly for the first couple months.

"We're here for Barlow Venator," Darius said.

Barlow's eyes flickered over to Anastasia. "Hey Ann," he said.

"Hello," she said as she curtseyed with an imaginary dress.

"Ann?" Darius asked quietly enough for no one to hear him.

"Is this urgent?" Barlow asked.

"It is," Darius interjected. "Someone very close to us is in trouble."

"Very well," Barlow said.

He collected the deck from the center of the table and a few men groaned in displeasure. He stood up and bowed. Before anyone could respond, he was throwing cards at lightning pace. It was silent for a moment. In unison, the men slumped over dead. Darius's mouth popped open and so did Bianca's. Anastasia somehow looked unsurprised. "He wouldn't kill a fly?" Darius breathed.

"You're right," the Dealer said as he collected all of his cards. "I wouldn't kill a fly. But I sure as hell would kill four Imperial spies in my bar."

"How does that even work?" Bianca asked. "You can kill with playing cards?"

"If you throw them right." He tossed one into the wall behind them to illustrate his point.

He assembled the full deck and inserted it into a holster by his side. Anastasia approached without worry, and Darius fought the urge to start throwing punches. He definitely didn't want her to be next. "Why are there Imperial soldiers in your bar?" she asked.

"I've heard rumors that Quintus is in town," the Dealer said. "Word is he's come to Arkney to lay low where there's no chance of rebels finding him."

Anastasia cursed under her breath. "You shouldn't have killed these men."

"I had a losing hand," he replied. "Something had to be done."

"We're looking for Quintus," Bianca said. "We need information from him. Those men could have led us right to him."

"I see," Barlow said. "Well, I was looking to take a stab at him as well, so I guess this all shakes out."

"You want him too?" Bianca asked.

"This is a peaceful town," Barlow said. "It also happens to be my region to protect. I do my best to keep politics out of it. Even if I have to force them out."

Anastasia beamed. "Excellent!" she said as if she weren't standing in front of four bodies. "Looks like we have a new friend!"

Darius eyed him. "Yeah," he said with apprehension. "He seems real friendly."

Chapter Fifty-One

BRIGHTBOW
LILLY CELERIUS

IT DIDN'T TAKE LONG FOR THE REBEL FORCES TO ASSEMBLE. IF THEY EVEN could be referred to as a force. Including the Wolf and the Jacobson brothers, they were eleven strong. They'd all gathered in the attic of a bakery the eldest rebel owned.

"These bombs were assembled by the Jacobsons," the Wolf was dictating. "One in each cart should do the job. The fuse isn't long so you need to be far away from the supply carts by the time they blow. We estimate... five seconds?" He turned to the Jacobsons.

"Six seconds," they said together.

"Six seconds," the Wolf repeated.

"Why aren't they the one's setting the bombs?" one rebel asked. "They know them best."

"James and Jack aren't fighters," the Wolf said. "And you're likely to run into some well-armed guards. In addition, once the supply carts are destroyed you need to come back to the mayor's house and defend the entrance until we're able to wound Carlin. This can't happen in daylight, so we'll have one hour to prepare. Hopefully we can get there before Carlin hurts anyone else." The Wolf's eyes were sunken and he'd been shaking involuntarily. Lilly knew that the murder of innocent citizens would never have been allowed in his day. She could see the wheels turning in his mind. Exactly how far had the Imperial Military sunk under Carlin's rule?

The other rebels gave a small murmur of consent and began to ready their weapons.

The Wolf pulled the Jacobsons and Lilly aside. "Time to set our plan into motion. Jacobsons, come with me downstairs. We've got to loot this bakery for a wardrobe change."

"What about me?" Lilly asked.

"Get an ounce of shut-eye and prepare yourself mentally," the Wolf said. "Tonight won't be easy."

Lilly smiled at him disingenuously and fell into a sitting position against the wall. The Wolf and the Jacobsons exited. She closed her eyes slowly. She wanted to fight the urge to sleep, but had to admit that she was at the end of her rope. She clenched the hilt of her sword hard and prepared for the inevitable nightmare that was sure to come.

It was back. Lilly turned in circles trying to figure out where her nightmares were dragging her now. She appeared to be in the entry hall of the Celerius estate, but something wasn't quite right about the walls. They dripped with wine pooling at her feet.

Through a doorway came her youngest brother, Thomas, brandishing his rapier. He was running from something. Lilly tried to call to him, but her voice came out in an unnatural groan, as if she were despondent or drunk.

He turned to face the doorway as General Carlin jogged in wielding his massive broadsword and his even larger grin. "There's no honor in running, kid," he cackled.

Thomas stared deeply into Carlin's crazed eyes. "You killed Anthony!"

Carlin opened his arms wide, challenging the young boy. "I've heard about you. Tommy, right?"

Thomas was silent.

"You read minds? Or parts of them? What good does that do you in a fight?"

Carlin lunged forward and Thomas parried. Swing after swing was dodged. Thomas was getting visibly tired. Carlin's sword was now only missing him by inches.

"It means I can tell where you're swinging from next," Thomas grunted as he blocked a blow and retreated a few steps back.

Carlin advanced with insanity creeping into his expression. "What happens when you know where I'm coming from and you can't do anything to stop it?" Carlin brought blow after crushing blow against Thomas's thin rapier.

Lilly tried desperately to move or step in, but she found the wine soaked carpet pulling at her feet as if she were sinking in quicksand.

"There's so much hatred in you. You want us all dead because you're jealous. All you want is to impress your father!" Thomas began rattling off whatever he could use to distract Carlin, but nothing worked. Carlin kept swinging until eventually Thomas couldn't keep up. His rapier clattered to the floor. Thomas stared at it, and then turned back frightfully to Carlin. "You wouldn't kill an unarmed boy," he whispered.

"You're not as smart as you think," Carlin said plunging his sword into Thomas's chest, slightly grazing his fragile heart. Carlin twisted the sword and sneered. "Knowledge is power, Thomas Celerius. But power doesn't always mean security."

Thomas screamed and lashed out with his hands, trying desperately to claw at Carlin's face. Lilly was now sinking up to her waist in the wine soaked carpet. Carlin twisted the sword a bit further and shushed Thomas. He lowered the boy to the ground as if putting him to sleep. "Look into my mind," Carlin said quietly. "See what good that knowledge does you."

Thomas stared at him, eyes wide and horrified until he went still. Lilly could only gape at her brother while the carpet swallowed her neck and, eventually, her whole head.

Chapter Fifty-Two

BRIGHTBOW
VIRGIL SERVATUS

"YOU CAN'T DO THIS TO US!" HOWLED AN OLD MAN. VIRGIL AND HIS squadron tore through his house looking for secret doors or compartments. "We are friends of the crown!"

"I'm sorry, sir," Virgil said, "but we're searching for an enemy of the crown."

The man was flustered, but didn't exactly know how to respond. He watched in awe as the men tore apart his house. "Do you have anything to declare?" Virgil asked. "Secret compartments? Basements?"

"There's a basement," the old man said resignedly.

"Find the basement, men."

It didn't take long for the hatch down into the basement to be revealed. Virgil pulled it open and stared down into the darkness. "Someone find me a candle or an oil lamp," Virgil said. "Is there anything down here that could hurt me?"

The old man rubbed his balding head. "Depends on how much of it you drink."

Virgil swung his legs over and hopped down to the basement below. It was nearly pitch black and larger than the entire house above. His view was obstructed by what looked like shelves and shelves of barrels. "You come down here often?" Virgil called up.

"Old legs," the man responded. "Can't really take the jump. I've got a kid who comes by and checks on the ale."

"Down here!" Virgil called to the men above. A dark basement of this size would be the perfect place for an ambush and there was no way he was going to fumble around in the dark alone. One by one the five soldiers dropped down into the dark room until they could create a defensive formation. One man handed Virgil a candle. "All right men," Virgil said. "Follow my lead. Be prepared for one of them to jump out or surprise us."

He drew his sword and took a few steps forward into the dark. His candle went out. "What the hell?" Virgil said.

The men began to teeter back and forth anxiously. "Lieutenant Virgil and company," a cold voice said, "you are a danger to the one I am sworn to protect. For that you must die. Make peace."

There was silence for a single second. Virgil cried out first and the men began to scream. They lashed out viciously and without mercy, all in vain. They couldn't see their attacker. He cut through them fluidly as if he were sliding his sword through water.

The bodies thumped to the floor. Then there was silence.

Chapter Fifty-Three

OCEAN'S JAW
NEIL VAPROS

THE TRIDENTI FIGHTING PIT WAS SMALL AND BUILT LIKE AN IN-GROUND campfire. It was outside the back door of the mansion and about thirty feet across. The floor was made of sand and small rocks formed the edges. Neil stood with Alex and Serena as the rest of the islanders gathered around to watch. "Avoid the body slam," Alex said. "I cannot stress that enough."

"Yeah," Neil said, "I got that part." He glanced over and realized Haxon had a surprising number of supporters. Three or four men were whispering advice and prepping him for battle. He noticed Neil looking over. "You want some of this?" he screamed as he tore off his shirt.

Neil wanted none of that. "Don't answer," Alex said. "Let him rile himself up on his own."

Neil turned back one last time. Without his shirt it was impossible to determine where Haxon's neck ended on either side. His head was simply smeared into his body as if he were a clay sculpture made by a toddler and the neck had simply been forgotten. Neil also noticed, to his dismay, that Haxon had a lot more muscle than he had previously thought. Neil, on the other hand, had been shedding weight like crazy, mostly because of his hatred of fish. He made the silent resolution to eat more if he survived. Mama Tridenti approached the edge of the pit. "Ready?" she asked Haxon.

He screamed violently and beat his chest like an animal. "That means yes," someone from his crowd yelled.

She turned to Neil. "Ready?" He nodded. "Enter the pit, gentlemen," she commanded.

Neil turned back to look at Alex and Serena. She was giving him a thumbs-up and he was rubbing his palms together anxiously. "Go for the neck," Alex said.

"What neck?" Neil murmured. He stepped over the rocks and into the ring.

Haxon looked like he wanted to tear Neil into tiny edible pieces and turn him into a post-dinner snack. Neil squared off against him and raised his guard. "Begin!" Mama Tridenti boomed.

Haxon sized up Neil and circled him. Neil did the same, even though sizing up Haxon was a far greater task. He looked even larger standing, and Neil felt like a child in comparison. "Ever fought anyone as big as me?"

"I've never even seen anyone as big as you."

Haxon slapped his giant belly and a sickening ripple travelled across his midsection. "My mama used to call me her big beautiful baby!"

"You are one of those things," Neil said quietly.

Haxon leapt at Neil with his famous body slam. Neil spun out of reach and Haxon recovered remarkably quickly. Despite the weight he lugged around, Haxon was surprisingly athletic. Neil blocked Haxon's next swings and jabbed him in the nose. Haxon stumbled back and Neil used the moment to slam his hands on either side of Haxon's head. Haxon squealed and grabbed his ears, as Neil had just done serious damage to his eardrums. Tears welled up in Haxon's eyes and he swung harder this time. This strike was too strong to block and Neil only succeeded in spraining his wrist.

Things weren't exactly going as planned. Haxon was faster and stronger than he looked. Neil was already getting tired. Haxon head-butted him next and Neil fell to his knees. Before Haxon could slam his full weight into him, Neil threw a handful of sand into his eyes. Haxon swung blindly and Neil used his blindness as an opportunity to make it to his feet and out of range. "You fight like a coward," Haxon said as he cleared the grains of sand from his eyes.

"I've got to make up for the five hundred pound weight difference somehow."

"You think you're real funny, huh?" Haxon roared in fury. "I'm big boned!"

"I didn't realize that bones jiggled!" Alex called from the side of the ring.

In his infuriated state Haxon swung faster, but these were less accurate. Neil realized he needed to end this fight while Haxon was busy thinking about something other than pummeling him. Neil landed a few punches, but they practically bounced right off of Haxon's chest. Whenever Neil made contact with Haxon's flesh it sounded as if he was punching his hand into wet sand. "Go for the eyes!" Serena called from the sideline.

"Can't reach them!" Neil said exasperated.

Haxon tackled Neil and this time he wasn't able to squirm away. Haxon began to beat him senseless. Neil took a heavy blow to his eye and cried out in pain. Haxon reeled back for another strike, and Neil lashed out with his fist. By some miracle he found a vulnerable part of Haxon's non-existent neck. And the beast rolled off of him, gasping for air. As Haxon recovered, Neil turned to his compatriots. "Any ideas?"

"Knees?" Alex suggested.

Haxon stood upright and glared at Neil. He was clearly done playing around. Before he could tackle Neil again, Neil delivered a swift ankle breaker and quickly followed with a roundhouse kick to the inner thigh. This was a trick from somewhere deep in his memory. That's where all the nerves connected. Haxon's weight forced him to drop to his injured knee. Neil leapt forward with all his might and brought his knee straight into Haxon's nose. A stream of blood erupted and Haxon blinked slowly as if intoxicated. He fell to all fours and Neil finished him off with an elbow to the temple.

The behemoth collapsed onto the ground and the crowd burst into applause, all except Haxon's friends. They just shifted between sympathetically staring at their friend and glaring at Neil. Neil smiled weakly and looked to see Mama Tridenti's reaction. She gave him an evanescent smile and raised her arms. "Back to the dining hall!" she said. "It's time to celebrate our new friend, Mamba."

Neil trotted over to rejoin Alex and Serena for the walk back to the mansion. They patted him on the back and his heart swelled with pride. This could be a real home for him.

Chapter Fifty-Four

ARKNEY
DARIUS TAURLUM

Barlow Venator was different from the Marksman in every observable mannerism. He was funny and lighthearted in a way that Victor never was. They'd been offered cots to sleep in above his bar. Darius was tired of sleeping in bars, but luckily no longer had to worry about being caught by the Empire. Here he was a fugitive, but so was everyone else. "I'm heading out for the night," Barlow said to the group the night after their arrival. "I'll bring us a new spy."

"Perfect," Anastasia said. "This needs to get done quickly."

"I'm curious," Barlow said. "I know Ms. Bianca Blackmore is part of the revolution, but why are you all so intent on finding the Bookkeeper? He's not exactly the most important figure in the Imperial military."

"No, but he's the key to finding the Imperial Doctor," Darius said.

Barlow's smile fell and he stared at the group. Darius got the feeling that he'd said something he shouldn't have. "I see," Barlow said. "What makes you think the Bookkeeper can lead you to the Doctor?"

"The Bookkeeper is in charge of getting the Doctor his money. He manages every coin the Empire spends on assassinations. He sends money by courier to the Imperial Doctor. It stands to reason that he'll know where to find him," Anastasia said. "This plan is well thought out."

"I've seen a lot of people go after the Doctor," Barlow said. He didn't need to say the rest. They didn't come back.

"We don't have a choice," Darius said. "He's captured one of our best friends."

Barlow stared at them. "How much do you know about the Doctor?" he asked. His voice was quivering.

"We know enough," Bianca said. "He's a monster and he's methodical."

"He's also superstitious," Barlow said. "If this is what I think it is, your friend is in grave danger."

"What do you mean?" Darius asked.

Barlow dropped his bag and walked over to his table. He sat down and pulled out his cards. It made Darius nervous, but all he did was shuffle them. "The Doctor used to be a part of the official Venator Lodge. He was expelled for torturing students that he'd kidnapped from the libraries around Volteria."

"Why would he do that?" Darius asked, concern welling up in his throat.

"He used to be a scholar but was tortured into insanity," Barlow said. "I've always assumed he was just insane, but he told everyone that would listen that the experiments had turned him into something else. He thought that the spirit of the man who tortured him had become his own."

"That's unsettling," Bianca said.

"It's also not the worst part," Barlow said. "He thinks he can transfer the spirit to someone else."

"That doesn't make any sense," Darius said.

"Tell that to him," Barlow muttered. "He's always believed that by torturing someone with an especially strong mind he can make them into the new Doctor."

An unnatural silence covered the room as the group imagined the horrors that Rhys must be going through. "We have to get there," Bianca said. "We have to stop him."

"I've always thought the Doctor was insane but he's been known to commit medical miracles in the name of scientific advancement," Barlow said. "You have to get there before he can break your friend."

"You don't actually believe that, do you?" Darius accused. "You don't believe he can transfer his spirit?"

"No," Barlow said, "of course not." He paused and gulped. "It's just... I've learned not to underestimate evil."

He waited for someone to respond. When no one did he pocketed his cards. "I'm going out to find a spy. You need every second on your side."

He descended the stairs and left the others to dread what might be happening to Rhys. To dread the small possibility that the Doctor might have found the supernatural powers he'd been seeking.

※

Everyone was asleep except for Darius. He usually waited for everyone to nod off and then he would attempt to finish *A Rough History of Lightborns.* He'd managed to convince Bianca and Anastasia that bringing it on their journey would be helpful. He was getting quicker but still had to sound out the words one at a time. Barlow was out hunting spies and the Blackmore sisters were asleep. Darius flipped through the pages to find a Taurlum to read about. There were nearly a dozen pages on Nikolai Taurlum that detailed his life up until his assassination of the old emperor. Darius picked an entry at random. *"After his fallout with Charles Vapros (See page: ninety-four.) Nikolai Taurlum thought it best to lock himself inside the mansion."*

Darius thought hard. He'd heard a lot about Charles Vapros but he didn't remember exactly who that was. He flipped to page ninety-four and read through Charles Vapros's aliases and connections. The Wolf had recently scribbled in Neil's name, along with another one that he couldn't read. It dawned on him that Charles Vapros was Neil and Rhys's father. He wrinkled his nose. Sir Vapros certainly didn't look like a Charles. To Darius he didn't look like anything other than an assassination machine. There were quite a few pages dedicated to Sir Vapros. Apparently he and Nikolai had tried to kill each other many times as a result of a dispute at a ball. Neither had succeeded. Darius wished there was something after his uncle Nikolai had escaped into the sewers. That was the greatest question in all of Altryon and the subject of many Taurlum dinner discussions. Where was Nikolai Taurlum?

Darius scanned the pages about Nikolai. He'd known the man in life. Maybe the Wolf knew things he didn't. Maybe there was something he could add to the book. Darius envied Nikolai's advanced ability. As he'd grown bigger and stronger, the weak points on his body had disappeared one by one. Darius would kill for that ability. The Wolf estimated that Nikolai only had one weak point left, but he didn't know where it was.

Darius brought the candle closer to stare at the sketch of his uncle. Nikolai's battle armor was incredible. His helmet had giant curved horns that made him look like a metal bull. Darius's brother, Michael, once wore a similar one. Although Michael's didn't cover his neck and chin like Nikolai's did. It must have been hard to breathe in that thing.

"So you really can read," someone said behind him.

Darius tried to act like his heart wasn't beating out of his chest. He closed the book. "Of course I can."

Anastasia sat across from him and gave a knowing smile. "Rhys sure is a great teacher."

"I wouldn't know," Darius said. "I was taught by a Taurlum tutor."

"How long ago?" she asked.

"When I was around five years old."

"Then why do you still move your lips when you read and sound out letters?" she asked.

He stared at her, trying not to sweat. "I'm a light sleeper," she said.

Darius drummed his fingers on the book. "Got me," he said. "Laugh if you want to."

She cocked her head. "I only learned to read a few years ago, when I went off on my own and left my father. It took me years to get it."

He didn't know what to say. She noticed and continued. "Lilly and the Vapros might make fun of you, but they were born nobles. Not everyone out here is a scholar."

"What did it for you?" he asked. "Did something click?"

She went into her bag by the cots and pulled out a small book. "I kept this," she said. "They don't teach you that every letter has several different pronunciations. So I wrote down every word that used a letter differently than I was used to. It really helped to read through this every day."

"I'll have to make one of those," Darius mused.

She tossed hers to him. "I can read all right now. You can have mine."

"Really?" he asked.

She passed it to him as a way of answering. He couldn't believe that less than a year ago this girl had attempted to assassinate him three times. She looked to be thinking the same thing. "Is there anything you want help with?" she asked. "We could go through the Lightborn book. It would go faster if I was there to help you."

"Why are you doing this?" he asked.

"Guilt, probably," she said candidly.

"For helping Michael?"

"Yes."

He stared at her and she stared back unwaveringly. "All right," he said. "Pick any page. Let's read something."

Maybe it was minutes or maybe it was hours, but they took turns educating themselves on the family history in hushed tones, careful not to wake Bianca. She actually laughed when he made quips or told stories that weren't included in the book. "Your friend Barlow is in here," Darius said as he curled up the edge of the page to show her.

She peered at it expectantly. "Apparently he and the Wolf trained together. He's got a lot to say."

Darius was interested in hearing what the Wolf had to say about their new friend and landlord. Darius wasn't exactly a reading prodigy, but he knew how to spell "arrogant." It was written all over the page. "He's made an impression on the Wolf," Darius said. "That can be said for sure."

"The only thing stronger than his affinity for alcohol is his affinity for liberty. He is a drunk and an idealist of the highest caliber," Anastasia read. "That's true." She continued on, *"However, he is the one thing keeping Arkney from slipping into Imperial hands. He believes in the people's ability to govern themselves above all else. He's not a rebel. He's a libertarian."*

"Is he really that much of a drinker?" Darius asked.

Anastasia gave him a look that said: *You have no idea.* "He's actually constantly under the effects of it. He thinks it's the only way he can aim perfectly."

"He's an alcoholic who owns a bar?" Darius asked.

"That's the thing about Arkney. No one judges here. People just go about their business. If he wants to drink himself to death, that's his business."

"A Venator does not indulge," Darius said. "That means no alcohol right?"

"It means no getting drunk," Anastasia said. "Barlow takes about one serving per hour. He's constantly buzzed and somehow that doesn't stop his powers from working."

Darius tried to sound casual as he posed his next question. He even leaned back slightly to show how uninterested he was in his own words. "How do you know him so well anyway?"

She looked at him the way she always did, as if she saw right through every game and every wall. "Arkney has always been a good place to lay low in-between jobs. Or it was."

"It's not anymore?"

"Once the Doctor has you in his service things change," she said. "You don't ever stop moving. He's always in control. You're always on a clock."

Darius took his hands off the book. "How are you on a clock?"

"I don't want to discuss it," she said a little too quickly for Darius to be comfortable. "I'm nervous about Rhys. I don't want to speak about the Doctor right now."

Darius realized his reading light was getting brighter and brighter and noticed that they had been up all night. The sun was rising. "You're up early," Barlow the Dealer said as he lugged a hogtied body up the stairs.

Darius noticed what the Wolf had been talking about. He hadn't been looking for it earlier, but now he saw that Barlow swayed slightly with every step. His eyes also drooped in a clear indication of intoxication. He hid it well, like a man who had never been away from the bottle for more than an hour. "Darius was reading me a story," Anastasia said through a yawn.

"Well, guess who else is gonna tell us a story?" Barlow whispered as if he were telling a ghost story of his own. He pushed the man into a chair and ungagged him.

"Please, I don't know.... I don't know what you've been talking about..." the man said.

At this Bianca awoke. "What's happening?" she groaned. "It's early."

The Dealer pulled a card from his deck. "Any knowledge of card throwing, friend?" he asked. The man just stared at him. "You've gotta throw it just right. It helps that my deck has been specially made with steel tips. I reckon that I could hit the back of the chair through your head. I've done it before."

"Please!" he screamed. "I'll do anything!"

"Where's Quintus, the Bookkeeper? I won't ask twice," Barlow said.

The spy looked around the room fearfully as if the Bookkeeper were with them. "Quintus knows everything. He'll know if I rat him out."

"You're in the right place to be a fugitive of the Empire," Barlow said.

The spy was on the verge of tears. "He's running the boxing parlor!" the spy screamed as Barlow pulled his hand back to throw a card. "He's rigging fights."

Barlow stared at him. "No way."

The spy's lower lip quivered. "He puts spies in the ring and weights their gloves. It's how he gets rid of anyone who's onto him."

"What do weighted gloves do?" Darius asked.

"They make it easier to beat people to death," Anastasia said.

Barlow looked beyond upset. "But I fight there every other night," he said to himself.

"You've been fighting men with weighted gloves for weeks. No one can hit you."

Barlow grinned at Darius. "Guess I really am the best."

Anastasia laughed. "It's just like you to not even realize you're fighting a losing fight."

"It's me," Barlow said. "I don't lose fights. Right, spy?" The spy wept like a small child. "That's the Imperial way of saying 'Right.'"

The spy didn't seem to get the joke. Barlow turned to face his friends. "So we've got a place, who's got a plan?"

The room was silent for a moment as the fugitives collectively rubbed their chins. Anastasia leaned back and a smile ghosted over her face. "I've got an idea," she said. "Darius remember when you were talking about your sister?"

"Cassie? What about her?" he asked.

"You said she used to infiltrate boxing competitions. I recommend you do the same."

"Yeah," Barlow said. "Skin of steel probably helps a good deal in a dust-up. Right, Blondie?"

Darius wanted to flex but didn't. "I don't know of anyone who could beat a Taurlum in a fist fight. But I don't see how me winning fights does anything for us."

Barlow was getting excited. He seized Anastasia's idea and ran with it. "No, no this is perfect." He laughed like a mad man, but stifled it when he realized his compatriots were staring. "You get in the ring, Darius. You'll win a few fights and they'll send in some guys to cheat. You'll keep knocking them down. Quintus won't take that. He'll either pull you into the back room to kill you or offer you a job. Doesn't matter. We'll know who he is. What he looks like, and that'll be enough."

"So I'm bait," Darius concluded.

"You're bait with iron flesh," Anastasia said. "Stop whining."

"So what happens when I get in front of the Bookkeeper?" Darius asked.

"We'll be there," Barlow said. "We can capture him, take him wherever and have a little fun. You'll find out where the Imperial Doctor is."

Darius tilted his head back and forth as if weighing the options. He looked over at Anastasia and she met his eyes. She trusted Barlow and it looked like she trusted this haphazardly assembled plan. He looked next to Bianca. She'd been quiet through most of this and he couldn't tell if it was because she was concerned about the logistics of the plan, concerned about Neil, or that she was still waking up.

"What do you think?" he asked her.

"We can't waste time," Bianca said. "It took us ten days just to get to Arkney. I'm going to be at Misty Hollow in twenty days and ideally Rhys will be there too. If this is the quickest solution I'm all for it. How soon can we go to the Boxing Parlor?"

Barlow absentmindedly pulled a card from his pack and spun it between his pointer finger and thumb. "The next fight is... tomorrow?"

"Tonight," the spy whimpered.

"Thanks buddy," Barlow said. "We can go tonight unless you all want to stick around and check out the sights." Bianca opened her mouth to protest. "That was a joke," he interrupted.

Darius could see her patience running thin by the way her jawline tightened. She was gritting her teeth hard. "I'm stressed," she mumbled. "Jokes are not appreciated."

"I'm very sorry about your boy toy," Barlow said. "But if you don't have humor what do you have?"

"Killer aim and about seven knives," Bianca said almost too quietly for anyone to hear.

He held his card up. "I wonder whose aim is better."

He was being condescending and as a Venator he was probably used to getting away with it. However, if Darius had learned anything about seeing Bianca interact with Neil, he knew that she didn't care if someone came with superhuman powers. She certainly didn't take to being talked down to either. "So do I," she said unwaveringly.

"I hate to interrupt," Anastasia said. "But we have one last problem to deal with." She pointed her head to the hogtied spy.

The spy realized what she was saying and dissolved into a miserable mess. He curled up further into his own self-pity. Barlow looked at the card in his hand and spun it between his fingers once more. "I've got fifty-two solutions to that problem. Don't you worry."

"Hold up," Bianca said. "There are fifty-three solutions by my count. What will the Bookkeeper do to you if he knew that you sold him out?" she asked the spy.

The man was sobbing too hard to answer. "Come on," Barlow said. "This is easier. He looks like a five of clubs guy, right?"

"Let him talk," Bianca said with more force this time.

"He'd kill me," the Spy slobbered. "He'd have me beaten to death."

"Problem solved then," Bianca said. "Set him free. He won't be running to anyone for help."

Barlow's lips slid into a smug smirk. He opened his arms wide and looked to Darius. "What about you tough guy?" he asked. "Are you all right with letting this one run straight back to his boss?"

Darius realized it had been a bit since he'd spoken. "Rhys is in danger. We have to get this guy."

"I won't say a thing!" the spy yelled. "I'll flee to Shipwreck Bay. Or further. I'll sail from the mainland. No one you know will ever see this face again."

"You've got nearly perfect aim," Bianca said to Barlow. She approached the spy and slit the ropes binding his hands. "So you know what's important when it comes to hitting a mark. You need to understand the weight of your knife… or card." She grunted as she cut the binds on his feet. "You need to understand the air, the wind, the speed at which your target is moving…"

The guard, after realizing he was free, sprung up and fled on all fours until he reached the stairs. "But the most important thing, by far, is knowing when not to strike."

Barlow tossed a card and it embedded itself into the Spy's head. He hit the ground face first and twitched a few times before going still. "I like you guys," Barlow said. "I really do, but I'm not willing to sacrifice the safety of Arkney for anything." He collected his card and wiped it off before re-pocketing it. "If you want my honest opinion, you all don't kill enough."

"We try not to get into the habit," Bianca said. She was clearly disappointed. She'd wanted him to live.

Barlow bowed his head slightly. Bianca sighed and lay back down on her cot to sleep. Darius found his own cot and winced as it creaked under his weight. Anastasia walked around him to her own bed. They made eye contact one last time before they shut their eyes. He felt his heart swell but he pushed the feeling away. Sure she'd been different since he'd met her outside the wall. How much of the old assassin was still in there? Would she cut him down now and claim it was just business? Despite the kiss, and the banter, and even the all-night reading session, he had trouble trusting her completely. No matter how much he wanted to.

Chapter Fifty-Five

BRIGHTBOW
LILLY CELERIUS

LILLY STARTLED AWAKE. IN HER CONFUSION AND FEAR SHE LASHED OUT viciously. James Jacobson scrambled backwards with a new black eye and horror in his expression. Lilly blinked and rubbed the bridge of her nose. "Apologies, James," she sighed. "I didn't know who you were. You shouldn't sneak up on a fugitive."

He was hyperventilating loudly, but she could hear him attempting to apologize. "It's okay, James," she said. "Calm down."

The Wolf and Jack were there too. The Wolf watched with mild amusement. Jack was looking concerned for his fallen brother.

"Where did they all go?" Lilly asked referring to the revolutionaries.

"They're went off to set the bombs," the Wolf said. "We have ten minutes before we have to leave."

"Is there anything else we have to do?" Lilly asked.

The Wolf loosened his collar. He seemed anxious. "What do you suspect Carlin thinks the Celerius move in this situation is?"

Lilly stared into space. "I bet he thinks it's to approach him and challenge him to a duel one-on-one. Right?"

The Wolf removed his sword. Lilly looked at him quizzically. He then pulled a pair of goggles out of his pocket. No doubt it was one of the ones from earlier. "Remember when I told you that we need to abandon old honor?"

Lilly cocked her head. "Yes?"

"Well there's one final thing we should do. You're not going to like it, but it's absolutely paramount to tricking Carlin."

She looked at the sword, then back at the goggles. "Carlin's going to invite us in…" she repeated slowly. Her eyes widened as she realized what the Wolf had been talking about earlier. "You're being serious?"

One look into his eyes told her he was. "If he realizes who we are we'll be killed before we can lay a hand on him. We need to do the last thing he'd ever expect from us."

Lilly groaned and stood up. She unsheathed her sword and looked hard at her uncle. "I'm not happy about this."

"I'm in the same boat," he said.

He pulled a small tin from deep inside his coat and tossed it to her. "Boot polish," he said. "In case you want to go the extra mile."

"Boot polish? I hate you."

"Don't be dramatic. Do you want to put a sword through Carlin or not?"

"I want to," Lilly said. "I really do."

"Then let's get to work."

Chapter Fifty-Six

BRIGHTBOW
CARLIN FILUS

CARLIN PACED THE ATRIUM OF THE MAYOR'S HOME. HIS GUARDS WERE clearly nervous he would throw a tantrum and kept a safe distance. "People in this village clearly don't care about their citizens," he said as he approached an older looking hostage. "What do you think, old man?"

The old man opened his mouth to express some sentiment, but was quickly dealt with before any words could leave his mouth. Carlin swiveled and faced his men. "That's all right!" he yelled. "Because I don't care about them either!"

He laughed loudly and his men nervously pretended to laugh as well. His position was well armed. He had five archers surrounding him and they were more than willing to turn any intruders or hostages into pincushions. He couldn't see the Celerius getting in without having to face him directly. He was confident in his ability to defeat Lilly Celerius in a sword battle, but the Wolf was another story. Not only was he a lightning quick swordsman, but also news was spreading quickly of The Howl, his new advanced ability.

"You can't do this," said a weak murmur in the corner of the room.

Carlin laughed loudly at the mayor. "I can't? And why is that?"

"This city has famously been supportive of the Empire in times of turmoil. We have done nothing to deserve this radical mistreatment. We are nothing but loyal to the Empire!" the mayor cried.

Carlin approached him. "What an interesting statement." His voice was as calm as death. "You are nothing but loyal... However, four hours ago I requested that the Lightborns be brought to me. Have they been?"

The mayor was silent. Carlin gleefully kneeled in front of him and placed the mayor's head between his hands. The mayor struggled, but Carlin held him in an iron grip. "Not only that, but no one has even spotted them. No one. So either they've adapted the ability to turn invisible... or..."

"Someone is hiding them," the mayor whimpered.

Carlin glared at him without breaking eye contact. "Exactly. Someone is hiding them. So when you say your village has been nothing but loyal... Well that strikes me as a bold faced lie."

He removed his hands from the mayor's head. Before the mayor could respond, Carlin slapped him across the face savagely. The mayor fell onto his back, groaning in agony. A small guard entered the room from the kitchen. Presumably he'd come from the back door of the building. "Sir," he said breathlessly. "The rebels are destroying supply carts!"

Carlin turned around and stared at him. "What? That's... unusual. That's unlike the Celerius."

"Maybe they're trying to break the occupation?" the small guard said.

Carlin clenched his fists. "Probably. Where is Virgil? He and his men haven't checked back have they?"

"No sir," the small guard said.

Carlin glared at the floor. "Send a few guards out to look for him."

"Really?" the small guard asked. "We can't spare many."

"Send two then," Carlin said.

The small guard saluted and then retreated back through the kitchen. Carlin faced his men who looked at him expectantly. "This strategy is tactically genius," he said confidently. "It will be met with resistance, but the Lightborns are merely prolonging their deaths. How pitiful that they don't understand how many they will hurt in attempting to avoid their fate."

His men stared at him. "Don't look at me," he hissed. "Look at the doors, morons."

His men readjusted and he continued his pacing, silently trying to decide which hostage would be next. There was a young boy. Maybe he would be inspiration for the townspeople.

The small guard reentered from the kitchen and saluted again. "I told you to find Virgil!" Carlin said in his strictest general voice.

"I've sent two men, but we have good news!" the small guard said. "Two bounty hunters have collected the Celerius. They have them tied up and bagged outside the back door."

Carlin's heart leapt with glee. "Bring them in!" he yelled. "Bring them in this instant."

He drew his sword and his entire body began to shake. This was it. It was finally about to be over. He wrapped both hands around his sword and tried to focus himself. There was nothing to worry about now, aside from where to pin his medals and where to hang Lilly's sword on his wall.

Chapter Fifty-Seven

OCEAN'S JAW
NEIL VAPROS

"I NEVER DOUBTED YOU FOR A SECOND," ALEX SAID AS HE FINISHED OFF YET another drink.

"Really?" Neil asked.

"No," he said. He and Serena shared a chuckle. "We were a few seconds away from preparing your rowboat."

The dining hall had mostly emptied out by now. All of Haxon's friends had refused to attend the celebration in solidarity and Mama Tridenti had left early to take care of some late-night errands. "Honestly, I thought he'd have a heart attack the second you two started fighting," Alex said. "At least that's what I was waiting for the whole time."

Neil smiled. "You're slurring your words pretty heavily."

Alex scratched his head and grinned his snow-white smile. "Guess I'm sleepy."

"Sleep it off then," Serena said.

"Best idea of the night," Alex said as he laid his head on the wooden dining table.

"It's certainly a better idea than 'Hey Mamba, fight the giant,'" Neil said.

After a few moments quiet snores drifted from Alex and it was clear that he was out for the night. Serena patted him on the head gingerly. She stood up and skipped through the door. "Follow me," she sang.

Neil didn't argue. He trotted after her and through the front doors of the mansion onto the beach. "You're gonna learn how to swim tonight, Mamba," she said and she waded out knee deep into the water.

"You're serious?" Neil asked. "It's been a long day."

"Don't be a guppy," she said as she gestured for him to come closer. "You won't drown, I promise."

With a slow exhale, Neil pulled off his shirt and followed her into the warm ocean. It felt almost as warm as the bath he'd taken earlier. She waited patiently for him to approach. "Okay," she said. "We're gonna start with the easiest thing to do: Jellyfish."

She lay on her back and slowly brought her extremities towards her head and then used them to propel herself forward, imitating a jellyfish. There was something surreal about the Tridenti when they made contact with the water. Serena was simply lying in the water and doing a leisurely stroke, but she naturally glided through the water faster than any fish Neil had ever seen. "If you can manage to drown doing this one then maybe you really are hopeless," she said as she rejoined him.

He spent a few moments floating on his back and transitioned to actually moving. He paddled around her a few times and then stood. She clapped modestly. "Happy?" he asked.

"Very. You're excellent at floating around aimlessly."

"That's what they tell me."

"Are you ready to try something a little more difficult?" she asked.

"Absolutely. Bring it on."

She glided over to him. "Okay," she said as she grabbed his wrists. "You're going to move them in big circles."

She rotated his arms around in large circles. He looked down at her as she continued to mimic the motion he should make while swimming through the water. She stopped when she noticed how he was looking at her. She dropped his right wrist and placed her hand on the side of his neck. He stared into turquoise for a fraction of a second and then they were kissing. Neil's heart swelled with happiness and adrenaline as he pulled her closer. However, guilt began to rise up in him and they parted.

She smiled at him. "You all right, Mamba?"

"I have a strange feeling that someone would be very upset with me for doing that," he said despite how much he enjoyed it.

She cocked her head. "There's someone else?"

"I have no idea," Neil said with a vague gesture to his temple. "Can't remember."

She hummed to him softly and the feelings of guilt subsided. "Well, until you figure that one out, why don't we just stick to swimming?" She beckoned him deeper into the ocean.

He followed and practiced his other strokes for a while. They swam around for almost an hour even though she was a million times faster. "This must feel like teaching a child to walk," Neil said.

"It's more like teaching a child to crawl. Walking comes later."

They swam until Neil got tired and then he paddled himself to shore awkwardly. He watched as she dove in and out of the water effortlessly. He felt the forces of lust and confusion battling inside his chest. Serena had an unmatched beauty and Neil liked her as much as he could remember liking anyone. Still, a strong sense of guilt welled up in his chest. As if he should be kissing someone else instead.

Chapter Fifty-Eight

ARKNEY
DARIUS TAURLUM

B IANCA WRAPPED D ARIUS'S HANDS ONCE WITH A ROLL OF CLOTH. "I'M
not gonna bother wrapping your hands twice. It's not like you're
going to hurt your knuckles."

Darius grinned. He threw a look over his shoulder. In Altryon places like these were underground and fiercely regulated by the
Empire. Arkney, as always, was the exception. Their Boxing Parlor
was well lit and on the ground floor. It appeared that every ruffian in
town was in attendance. Darius actually loved Arkney. It reminded
him of the chaos of a bar fight, but instead of being broken up it had
consumed the entire village. There were no rules here and no author-
ity to answer to. Especially in the ring.

His hair had been wrapped and it made him look like a ruffian. He could see the fear in the eyes of the man across from him.
Darius lifted his fists and faced his opponent to the sound of uproarious cheering and screaming. They sure were passionate about their

boxing. He pulled off his shirt and his opponent did the same. He wasn't going to let anyone pull him to the ground or get an unfair hold. Barlow and Anastasia were in the crowd somewhere looking to see if anyone distinguished themselves as a leader to the poorly hidden guards.

Darius ended his first fight with one swing, much to the shock of the crowd. The cheering stopped instantly and Darius looked at his fist in surprise. The crowd cheered again as his opponent was pulled from the ring and a new fighter stepped in. He squared off against Darius and the match ended the exact same way: with one Taurlum swing. Darius raised his arms as the crowd showered him with praise. Darius caught a look at Anastasia. She looked proud of him and he winked at her. "Hey," Bianca said from the side of the ring. Darius looked over. "Maybe you're fighting a little too well."

"Can't help it."

"I'm serious," she said, careful not to alert anyone in the crowd. "He's gonna figure out exactly who you are if you finish matches that fast. Also knocking people unconscious is super bad for them, if you didn't know."

"Really? Isn't it like forced sleep?" Darius said as she rewrapped his hands.

"With brain damage."

"Damn. I knock people out all the time."

"Better stop doing that."

Darius faced his next opponent. He raised his fists in a solid guard. The man swung at his flank and cracked his fist against Darius's skin. He screamed in horror and pain. Darius kicked him over and he didn't get up again. The crowd looked at him again and tried to think of an excuse as to why people were breaking their fists against his sides. "Guess he hit a bone?" Darius said.

The crowd, fickle as ever, burst into reinvigorated applause. "One more opponent!" one of the men working at the Parlor yelled.

Darius saw Anastasia at the edge of the ring and he walked over to her. "Enjoying the show?" he asked.

She smiled at him and for a moment he thought she looked down to glimpse his bare chest. "Yes. And so it seems are the men who work here. They're running in and out of the back. If you win this fight, you'll be sure to meet the boss."

"Then wish me luck," Darius started to say until he turned and came face-to-face with Victor Venator, the Marksman.

Victor never smiled. He had the power to portray all his smug confidence with a straight face. He raised his arms far apart and his muscles rippled. Darius tried not to worry. "You want a rematch?" Darius asked. "Last time we did this you had seven shots to finish me. I don't think you'll do as well with zero."

The Marksman scanned his opponent. "I've been studying up on your kind. Your weak spots, in particular."

Darius looked over at Bianca. She looked as afraid as he felt. Anastasia did as well. Before he could turn back around to attack, a newcomer jumped into the ring. It was Barlow. "Victor!" he said. "This man has had enough. Let him have a break."

"I need an opponent," the Marksman growled.

"You've got one," Barlow said as he removed his holster and his shirt. "Come on, Victor. Haven't you always wondered who would win between the two of us?"

"I don't need to wonder," Victor said. "You're a drunk and you've slowed over the years."

"You wouldn't mind proving that, would you?" Barlow asked.

The Marksman replied with his first strike. He lashed out with a right cross, but Barlow bent out of the way just in time. Darius leapt over the wall of the ring and into the crowd. He found Bianca. "I'm going to stay with Barlow. I don't want to know what happens if he loses," she said.

"Okay," he said. "Anastasia and I will hopefully find the boss."

Darius grabbed his shirt and circled the ring until he met back up with Anastasia. "Stay close," he whispered. "The guards are eyeing me."

He started for the door. A man approached and stopped him right before he was out of the building. "Sir, someone would like to speak with you," he said as he laid a hand on Darius's shoulder. "He'll make it worth your while."

Darius did an excellent job of pretending to consider the offer thoughtfully. "What does he want with me?" he asked in his best simpleton voice.

"He's got a job offer for you," the man said.

Darius smiled like a moron. "Great! Lead the way!"

The man took him past the ring and down a small staircase. Darius had to turn sideways just to fit. He was led down a hallway to a comically small doorway. "Seriously?" he asked.

The guard ignored him and opened the door. Darius shoved his way through. It took him almost a minute. The room was larger inside, but not by much. The two guards on either side of the door didn't help with the cluttered nature of the room. A stout man with curls and thick spectacles sat behind the desk. He probably weighed more than the desk in front of him. He peered over his glasses. "I hear you're quite the ruffian," he said in a voice that was unnaturally whiney.

"That's what they say," Darius said. "You have a job for me?"

"I might."

Darius didn't want to look impatient but he needed to be sure that this man was Quintus, the Imperial Bookkeeper. "I need a little information first," Darius said. "Who are you? What would I have to do?"

The man removed his glasses. "You'd fight anyone I asked you to and take care of anyone who is causing too much trouble."

"You own this place?" Darius asked.

Quintus didn't stop working. "I move... money through here. As is my right."

"People don't talk about rights very often in Arkney," Darius said.

The man narrowed his eyes. "Well every man has the right to property."

Darius planted his hands on the desk. "Last I checked the Empire didn't have the right to operate within Arkney."

"Who says I care where the Empire can operate?"

"That seal on your papers for one," Darius said. Quintus looked down and realized his papers were in full view and bore the stamp of the Empire.

The Bookkeeper glared at him. "Listen here you ignorant brute. Not that it's any of your business, but the Empire can operate everywhere. Arkney is on the landmass and therefore it belongs to us. Remember that."

Darius stood upright. That was enough to prove his identity. Anastasia burst through the door and whipped her spike through the first guard's chest. She rolled behind Darius and swung her fist into the second guard's neck. Quintus yelped and tried to escape over the table. Darius threw him back into his chair. "Where's the Imperial Doctor?" Darius asked.

"You can't ask to me to disclose that information," Quintus gasped.

"I'm not asking. Where is he?"

The Bookkeeper glared at him. "I won't talk. He's the last man on Earth I'd ever dream of selling out."

Darius turned to Anastasia. "Should I pull off his fingers?"

"Oh you Lightborns are all the same!" Quintus moaned.

Anastasia smiled like a viper and approached the Bookkeeper from the other side of the desk. "Remember this?" she asked as she pulled a pouch from her side. "Nature's Scream?"

The Bookkeeper heard what she said and his face lost all color. "Please…" he whispered.

Anastasia wrapped her chain around him in an instant. He flopped like a newly caught fish. "No!" he screamed.

"Darius, hold his hands."

Darius latched onto the poor man's hands and locked them in place. She pulled the string on the bag and poured a small bit of the red powder into his screaming mouth. He coughed as it entered and Darius let him go. "That wasn't much," he said.

Quintus's face turned crimson. Sweat poured down his face and into his agape mouth. He looked like he was trying to scream, but evidently the powder had sucked every ounce of moisture out of his mouth. He fell to the ground and rolled around as if trying to extinguish imaginary flames. "Quintus?" Anastasia said sweetly. She grabbed the pitcher of wine on the table lodged into the corner. "Would you like a drink?"

He crawled to his knees and begged at her feet silently. "Before you get a single drop…" she said as she began to pour it onto the floor, "we want the Doctor." The tiny man scrambled toward the puddle but she pushed him away with her foot. "I'll pour the whole bottle out," she warned.

He pointed at his mouth. "He can't speak," Darius said.

"Write then," Anastasia spat.

He crawled to his desk and through his tears scrawled out a short message. *"Abington,"* Anastasia read.

"Where in Abington?" Darius asked.

Almost delirious from pain Quintus scrawled another message on the paper. *"Library."*

"Abington has a library?" Darius asked.

Quintus nodded and his beet red tongue flapped up and down in his mouth. He reached for the bottle. Anastasia smiled and tossed the bottle into the air. It shattered on the ground and he scrambled to the resulting puddle. "I forgot to mention. That won't help," Anastasia said. He licked up the wine despite her warning. "If I come back to Arkney and you're still here, I'll give you the rest of the pouch."

She walked out and Darius followed. "That was pretty brutal," Darius said.

"So is preying on liberty," she said. "Come on. Let's go get Rhys."

Chapter Fifty-Nine

ARKNEY
BIANCA BLACKMORE

Bianca watched helplessly as Barlow and the Marksman went to battle. Victor was much quicker, but constantly being on the move denied him the necessary muscle density Barlow garnered eating and fighting every night. Barlow only landed half as many punches, but it was clear to Bianca that they were far more effective. Victor went for his trademark holds and pressure points. Barlow could anticipate these without difficulty. The Marksman was clearly getting desperate as Barlow moved in with more vicious attacks.

"You're strong," Victor said as he ducked under a right cross. "But you're slow."

He jabbed Barlow between his ribs and the Dealer stumbled back out of range. Victor cocked his head and studied Barlow with his soulless eyes. "I wonder," he continued as he advanced. "If you'd be quicker without all that alcohol in your system."

"I'd be a lot more irritable," Barlow said. "That's all we can know for sure."

Victor lunged forward more quickly this time and brought his knee up into Barlow's stomach. Before he could recover the Marksman drove his palm into his nose. Blood squirted onto the Marksman, but he didn't seem to be bothered. He leapt into the air and round-house kicked Barlow across the head. With a mighty thump Barlow fell to the ground, seemingly unconscious. Bianca was tired of watching. She leapt into the ring and snap kicked the Marksman's feet out from under him. He expertly somersaulted backwards and onto his feet again. He threw an arm against Bianca and she hit her head hard on the ground. Stars appeared and when they cleared, Victor was standing over Barlow. "With every sip you dull your senses," Victor accused. "You get slower. Venator do not indulge and every single time you do, you make it a little easier for someone to damage the land."

"Says the bastard who hunts in packs!" Barlow said. "And kills for sport."

"Not for sport," Victor said. "For money."

He slammed his heel into Barlow's face a few times silenced him. Bianca stood and raised her fists. "Did you kill him?" she asked.

Victor leaned his head closer to Barlow. "His heart still beats faintly. A few more kicks should solve that. Like I said before, the foolish don't deserve mercy."

He raised his foot, but Bianca kicked it away from Barlow. She swung at him and he deflected it with his elbow. After taking a step, he slammed the back of her head with his other elbow. She fell to the ground and he kicked her in the stomach for good measure. "You'd make a good assassin Blackmore," Victor said as he retrieved Barlow's cards. "You're talented for someone so young. With discipline and time you could be great. It's too bad that you chose to get in my way."

He selected a card at random and flung it at Bianca. Luckily Anastasia's chain spike impaled it in mid air. The spectators recognized the danger in a fight that was turning bloody and most had already escaped out of the open double-doors. Victor blocked Anastasia's attacks as she flung herself into the ring. Her attacks almost seemed half-hearted, as did the way he easily fought her off. Victor seemed to realize his odds were worsening. He leapt from the ring and joined the fleeing crowd. Bianca wanted to follow him, but her stomach roared in protest. The Marksman clearly knew where to hit his enemies to make it hurt. That was his skill: exploiting weakness.

"Grab Barlow," Bianca told Darius who had just entered. "He's critical."

"And me?" Anastasia asked.

"With me," Bianca said. "I'm going after Victor."

"He'll kill you," Anastasia said. "You don't stand a chance."

"He can't beat the both of us."

Anastasia didn't look convinced. Bianca didn't argue further. She leapt out of the ring and chased Victor into the streets. He hadn't brought his guns so Bianca was at least hopeful of her chances. She saw him darting down the street toward the edge of town. Bianca followed him with a knife. He must have heard it coming because he whipped around and caught it by the handle. "You could have lived past tonight," he called.

She followed up his comment with two more knives. He blocked both and flung one back. She dodged it. Anastasia joined them in the street and hurled her spike. He ducked and caught another one of Bianca's knives. He chucked it at Anastasia and she was forced to drop her chain to deflect it. He grabbed the chain and expertly flung it at Bianca. It scraped her collar and she fell to her knees howling in pain. The Marksman looked over to Anastasia and dropped the chain. He fled down the street and Anastasia ran to her sister. She sat her up. "You'll live," Anastasia said. "Let's hope the same can be said for Barlow."

Chapter Sixty

OCEAN'S JAW
NEIL VAPROS

WHEN NEIL HAD DEDICATED HIS SERVICE TO THE SHORE HE DIDN'T REALIZE that his vow meant life would consist of manual labor. The Tridenti children favored him, of course, so he was allowed to do less than the others, but he still had to spend several hours per day doing whatever was needed for the night's feast or for the general upkeep of the island. Today that meant retrieving the day's haul of food from a Tridenti fishing boat on a rowboat. His job was rowing while two other men were to collect the nets and make sure they stayed in the boat while Neil rowed back. "You know Haxon was a good man," one of Neil's crewmembers said when they were in the bay. "A lot of people liked him here. There was a lot to him."

"There certainly was," Neil said.

This only prompted glares from the other two men. Neil didn't care. The Tridenti liked him. As long as they did, he wouldn't be harmed. "You know Haxon's brother is on this island, right?"

"No," Neil said. "I didn't know that. Who is Haxon's brother?"

"His name is Earnest Haxon," one of them said. "I'd be worried. He's the violent type."

"I wonder if it runs in the family," Neil muttered.

They retrieved the nets full of fish and Neil rowed back to shore. The three of them pulled it in and Neil surveyed the beach. "Someone's supposed to come and help us bring these inside, right?"

"Yeah," one of the men said. Slyness began to creep into his voice as a crewman bounded toward them. "Here he is now."

The new crewman had a rather distinctive mustache and even more distinctive muscles. He brushed by Neil violently and Neil quickly realized whom he was dealing with. "Earnest Haxon, right?"

Earnest turned around and finally made eye contact with Neil. "Yeah."

"I hope there are no hard feelings about your brother."

"You'd better believe there are hard feelings," Earnest said. "George was my best friend. Now he's rowing off to god knows where. I loved my brother."

"Not enough to row with him," Neil pointed out.

Earnest glared at him. "You might have the favor of the Tridenti, but they don't watch you everywhere. I swear by the Golden Light that if you stray from their gaze...." He didn't complete his threat.

"What?" Neil asked.

"I'm just saying." Earnest picked up a net filled with fish. "I hear you're not too great a swimmer. Would be a shame to see the ocean take you away from us."

"That would be a shame!" Alex said from behind them.

Earnest jumped as he turned around. Alex was knee deep in the water and stood there expectantly with his arms crossed. He must have swum up while they were talking. Neil hadn't even noticed him.

"If Mamba finds himself in the water, I expect one of you courageous gents to paddle him to shore. We look out for each other here at the Ocean's Jaw."

Earnest said nothing as he shouldered his net of fish and walked off toward the mansion. Neil saluted Alex and he laughed. "Men, take these fish inside. I've got to have a word with Mamba."

The men complied and Alex waited until they were out of earshot. "Hopefully that won't be too much of a problem. The Tridenti love you, but a few crewmen are bound to be upset. You can never please everyone."

"Then I guess it helps to please those in charge."

"Smart thinking," Alex said. "Just wanted to let you know you're relieved for the rest of the day. Tonight's dinner is kind of a big one so you should rest up."

"Don't tell me I have to fight someone again," Neil said.

"No, it's going to be a giant celebration. In the Tridenti family you lose your guppy name when you can swim out into the ocean on your own and bring back an animal larger than yourself. A seven year old cousin of mine brought in a shark, so tonight there's gonna be a party."

"Awesome," Neil said. "I'll wash up and see you there."

Alex saluted and dove back into the depths of the water. Neil walked to his room with leisure, careful to avoid the men unloading fish. They wouldn't be happy if they knew Neil had been released from work early. He already wasn't the most popular fellow on the island. He rounded a corner and almost walked straight into Mama Tridenti. He backpedaled as not to get in her way. "Mamba," she said.

"Ma'am," he replied.

"I've heard many interesting things about you recently."

He paled thinking of the previous night with Serena. "You have?"

"You're from the Industrial City?"

"That's what I'm told. But I really can't remember. My memories are scattered."

"I've heard that too," Mama Tridenti said. There was an unusual connotation in her voice. As if she were suggesting something. Whatever it was Neil didn't know. "So you're quite the mysterious fellow."

"I suppose so."

She smiled at him and continued on her way. The smile was fake, of course. "Oh and Mamba," she said over her shoulder. "You listened to my speech last night, right?"

"Of course," he said. "It was inspiring."

"So you know how protective I am of my children. Remember that. They really seem to like you. It would disappoint me, and them, if you weren't what they expected."

"Um... Alright," Neil said. "Understood."

"It better be."

With that she turned the corner and disappeared. That was odd. As Neil continued to walk to his room a strong feeling of anxiety settled in his chest. He had a seat at the dinner table, but in no way did he feel truly safe.

<hr />

Dinner was fish again. "What kind is this?" Neil asked Serena.

"Carp. All of it tastes the same though. So get used to the texture."

Neil sighed and consumed a forkful. Alex and Serena shoveled it down. They didn't seem to care at all about the taste, table manners, or that fish had dead eyes. That's how they were about everything. They had no burdens and no worries. They were lighter than air.

A silence descended over the hall and Neil turned his head to see Mama Tridenti standing at her table. She had her wooden cup in her hand and she swirled it lightly. "I'm glad we have these dinners," she started calmly. "Because when there's only twenty-five of us it means a lot to be a cohesive family. A unit. So these dinners are useful. I also now have the opportunity to address everyone on this island at the same time. So let me begin by telling you all a little story."

Neil glanced at Alex and Serena. They looked thrilled to be getting a story from their mother. Neil, on the other hand, was worried. Her words were light and calm, but there were undertones of hostility in her voice. "Do any of you still remember Hector?" she asked.

A light chuckle went up among the crowd. Serena smiled. "Oh, I love this one," she whispered in Neil's ear.

Mama Tridenti continued. "When my husband passed away I was very lonely for a great while. Sure, I had my beautiful children, but my nights felt empty. So when I was out foraging for food with the parties one day I found a friend out in the swamps. It was a snake."

"What's a snake?" Neil whispered to Alex.

He laughed and rubbed his forehead. "Umm…. Imagine a long, slithery land fish with big teeth. No fins."

Neil stared at him. "Like a tube?"

Alex popped a bite of fish into his mouth. "Yeah, like a living tube with big, mean teeth."

Neil realized he was being rude. A few people at their table were staring at him. He went quiet. Mama Tridenti continued. "He was friendly. So I named him Hector and brought him home. Many people were concerned about me, saying a snake was not a compatible sleeping companion and all that. But I didn't care. He'd roll up into a ball next to me while I slept, and that was that. I'd feed it with anything I could find and he gobbled it all up. Hector was always hungry."

She chuckled dryly. "Always hungry," she said it again, slower this time. "So we had a wonderful arrangement, he and I. He was a nice snake. But then one day he stopped eating. No matter what I tried to feed him, he would keep his jaw clamped tight. He wouldn't consume a morsel. What was even weirder was that he no longer slept in a ball curled up next to me. He stretched himself way out so that he ran parallel to me. We used to have someone on the island that claimed to be an expert in animals. I asked him about Hector's new condition. Was Hector sick? Was he depressed? What was wrong with Hector? The man told me that Hector wasn't sick. You see, Hector wasn't starving himself... He was fasting."

Neil felt his stomach lurch.

"The reason he was stretched out... was because he was measuring me. He wanted to know how many meals he should skip so that he could safely eat me whole."

The dining room was silent. No one was eating or drinking anything anymore. She laughed. "I was so foolish. I told him there was no way Hector was going to eat me. So I continued to sleep with the snake. All was well until the night after, when I felt him try to wrap his body around mine. The bastard was trying to strangle me to death. I grabbed his head in one hand and his body in the other and I snapped his stupid snake spine."

She crushed the wooden glass that was in her hand and splinters went flying. Someone in the dining hall squealed. "It was sad. I loved Hector. But he was a snake first and friend second. So he had to die." She pointed above their heads. "There he is. Stuffed."

Neil looked up and saw what must have been Hector hanging from the ceiling. It was a long speckled tube with an unnaturally twisted neck and dead eyes. Neil assumed a snake with a non-broken neck looked slightly different. Mama Tridenti stepped around the table and approached the center of the dining hall. She stood beneath the snake. "Today we were attacked by the Empire. They found the location of one of our hidden coves and open fired on our ships. Also, a few of our carrier pigeons are gone. Someone sent word to the Empire about our location and our secrets. Someone in our home is not who they say they are."

A few too many people turned to look at Neil. He was the newest recruit. He tried not to gulp noticeably. "I invited that snake into my bed," she said as she pointed at Hector. "I trusted it and I let it get close. Now it seems I've done it again."

She glanced at Neil. He stared back unwaveringly. "So whoever you are, spy. Look up. Look up and see what happens to snakes in this house."

With that she returned to her seat. Neil had no trouble eating the carp after that. There was nothing like a little fear to make one forget the small stuff. He no longer thought about dead fish eyes. He thought about proving his innocence. Because if Mama Tridenti thought he was a snake, there was only one possible outcome. He looked up at Hector again. He had no doubt that someone was going to have their stupid snake spine broken. Maybe they'd end up stuffed, right next to Hector.

Chapter Sixty-One

BRIGHTBOW
CARLIN FILUS

THE TWO BOUNTY HUNTERS ENTERED THE ATRIUM OF THE MAYOR'S HOUSE with their trophies in tow. If not for the blue Celerius coats the two prisoners would have been unrecognizable. Their limbs were tied and their heads bagged.

Carlin looked the bounty hunters up and down. One was large and bald. The other was a good deal smaller and had neck length black hair. Their outfits were the kind that had clearly been assembled out of bits and pieces. Aside from their large goggles, which were visibly nicer than any of their other clothing.

Carlin grinned at them in an odd fashion, as if showing every single tooth was necessary in expressing gratitude. "Want your gold now?" Carlin asked. "How did you catch them?"

"Caught 'em crawling around by the roof next door. Trying to get in a window," the large bald one muttered in a gravelly tone. "We pushed them off and they broke a few bones. Tied them before they could recover."

Carlin laughed. "Idiots!" He signaled to one of his archers. "In a second I want you to take these men to be weighed and paid in full! No! Pay them double!"

Carlin kneeled in front of the larger figure and pulled him to a sitting position. "I've dreamed of this moment for so long, Wolf." Carlin said. "Five years together in the Imperial Hunting Squadron and every day all I could imagine was having what you had. I wanted that title. I wanted the respect you had. How does it feel?" He gestured with his sword. "Do you feel like I felt? Do you covet my title? Does it make you feel small to be facing a general? I want you to see it coming. I want you to look into my eyes."

He pulled the bag off of the hostage and came face to face with James Jacobson. He gasped and scrambled to a standing position.

The Wolf nodded at Lilly and planted his feet. "There isn't a title in existence that could make you any more of a man, Carlin."

Carlin's eyes widened in fury as he realized who the bounty hunters really were. He sputtered a few times trying to comprehend his situation. The Wolf opened his mouth and released the cry that had inspired legends. Luckily the Wolf had been right. Lilly was unaffected by his advanced ability. Carlin roared in pain and tried his best to block out the sound by pawing at his ears. The archers followed suit and dropped their bows. After cutting the Jacobson's bonds, Lilly was across the room and made short work of the archers. The Jacobson had ears full of candle wax to block them from the worst of the Howl. The Wolf ceased his scream and staggered slightly. Carlin recovered inhumanly fast and charged him. The Wolf raised his sword and blocked the first swings, but it was clear that his howl had taken a lot out of him. He wasn't even at half strength. Lilly leapt to her uncle's aid and the two swung at Carlin viciously. He dodged swing after swing and dealt out his fair share of blows. Sparks flew from the blades as Carlin somehow managed to match their Celerius speed.

The Jacobson's crawled away from the brawl and began ushering hostages out the back door. They were through the kitchen before Carlin could stop them. James lingered behind and pulled the wax from his one ear. "Should we…?"

"Go," the Wolf grunted. "Meeting place," he managed through swings.

James didn't wait for a second order before bolting out of the room.

Carlin kicked the Wolf hard as he was preparing for a swing. In the same motion he spun around and jabbed at Lilly hard enough to make her retreat. He earned himself a moment's break and used it to scream with rage. "You cut your hair!" he cried in disbelief. "You actually cut off all your hair."

Lilly removed her goggles and tossed them to the ground. "Survival takes precedence over fashion," she said, "It was time to abandon old honor."

Carlin spat on the ground. "You've also abandoned your chances of an honorable death."

Chapter Sixty-Two

ARKNEY
DARIUS TAURLUM

AGAINST ALL ODDS, BARLOW AWOKE IN THE MIDDLE OF THE NIGHT screaming. "What happened?" he finally managed after Anastasia was able to calm him. Darius held him down until the thrashing stopped. That was a benefit to Taurlum strength: not even the most frantic of men could overpower him.

"You're at your bar. Victor gave you a beating," she said. "I remember you being quicker."

"Did you kill him?"

"No," Anastasia said.

"Then I guess he was too fast for you as well," Barlow said.

He tried to sit-up but groaned and gripped his head. His headache must have been unholy. "Stay," Darius said. "You need a drink?"

Anastasia gave him a look. Clearly she didn't recommend this solution. Usually Darius wouldn't either, but Barlow looked like a nightmare. His face was swelling and cut in various places. They'd have to stitch up his forehead when he calmed down. "No drinks," Barlow said.

"Really?" Anastasia asked.

"Really," Barlow said. "Victor is the worst kind of scoundrel, but he was right. I'm getting much slower. Maybe I'll quit for a few weeks." He paused. "I'll quit for a few days."

He rolled over and planted his face on the wooden table where they set him. They heard snoring within seconds. Bianca pulled him up by the hair. "You can't fall asleep with a head wound."

"What…?" he asked. "Why?"

"I don't know," she said. "But some people do it and they don't wake up."

Barlow crossed his arms and sat up. He looked like he wanted to argue but didn't. He swung his legs over the table and, with a pouty look at his compatriots, stood and began pacing the floor.

"How long will it take to get to Abington from here?" Darius asked Bianca.

"Two weeks at least. We'll have to cover a ton of ground." She was right. Arkney was as Far East as someone could travel without falling in the ocean. Abington was west.

"Can we leave tonight?" Anastasia asked. "I don't want to give him time to move."

"What about him?" Bianca asked as she jerked her head towards Barlow who swayed like a drunkard as he walked soberly.

"He's a strong fellow," Darius said.

"I agree," Anastasia said. "He'll be okay. Rhys is the priority."

They made the silent agreement to leave that morning. Darius went upstairs to pack his things. He heard Anastasia's quiet footsteps behind him. "That was an exhilarating evening," she said once they reached the top floor.

He gathered his meager belongings and shoved them into his bag. "I'm not sure if that's the word I'd use." Something was weighing on his mind. "The Marksman took down you, Barlow, and Bianca tonight. He could have killed any of you but he let you live. Any idea why?"

He looked back at her. She was eerily calm. "Maybe when Bianca and I attacked him together he realized he was outnumbered."

"From what I hear, that's not really a problem for him."

"Stop dancing around what you really want to say," Anastasia said.

He slung his bag over his shoulder. "The Doctor wants us to get to him at some point. It's not about the money anymore. He wants to toy with us. He wants us to attack him on his home turf again."

"What can I tell you?" Anastasia asked. "He's a sadist. Of course he wants to fight us on his home turf."

Darius nodded slowly as if asking for more. She looked like she wanted to tell him more, but couldn't let the words out. "You worked for him," Darius said.

"I did."

He was sure her eyes were moist. "Would he trick a group of us into going after him?" Darius asked. "Are we walking into a trap we couldn't possibly hope to survive?"

She didn't say anything for a while. It almost seemed like she was going to confess something. "Darius... I..." She took a deep breath. "I don't think we have a choice. Rhys is in trouble."

"I was thinking the same thing," Darius said as he brushed past her and descended the staircase. As he left her he couldn't fight the feeling that she was keeping something from him. It had always been like that with her. She always had information he wanted; ever since the day she'd broken him out of prison to kill him. She always knew a little bit more than he did.

Chapter Sixty-Three

BRIGHTBOW
LILLY CELERIUS

BEFORE THE TWO CELERIUS COULD OVERTAKE CARLIN, LILLY HEARD A window break behind her. Focused on the combat, she didn't hear the Hyena approach. By the time she heard his snickering it was too late. He tackled her to the ground and away from the duel. Her sword slid away from her. He planted his feet on her ankles and began snapping at her neck viciously. "Sorry I'm late," he said between bites. "I stopped at a hospital for something to eat."

Carlin took the moment's distraction and disarmed the Wolf with a mighty swing. Before the Wolf could escape, Carlin stabbed him through the stomach. "Do you know what I realized when I killed Anthony?" Carlin asked as he plunged his sword into the Wolf.

Steven crumpled and Carlin stood over him, continuing to push his sword deeper. "I had a religious realization," Carlin said slowly as if pushing his words out at the same rate that he pushed the sword into the Wolf. "I realized something incredible. A god sent you, didn't he? You were bestowed upon the people, right? You were destined to protect the people of Altryon, weren't you? But look at this." He gestured with his free hand to the sword. "My blade slices right through you. You're flesh. You're blood. I had no reason to look up to you because you are what I always suspected: a false god."

The Wolf tried to stand, but Carlin kicked him to the ground and began sliding his sword up toward the heart. The Wolf grabbed the blade desperately and tried to stop it from cutting him in two. "You weren't meant to protect us! We were meant to kill you. You are a test for us to prove who the real heroes are! Why else would any god send such fragile heroes? He wanted to protect Altryon by teaching it to burn and to break the petty, selfish, Lightborns." Carlin laughed to himself. "Well, here I go. Doing his bidding."

Carlin's sword was mere inches away from the Wolf's heart. He was slicing through ribs slowly and maliciously. Lilly wanted to run to her uncle's aid, but she was no better off. The Hyena snapped viciously at her neck and inched closer with every bite. She pushed on his neck desperately, but he was strong, even stronger than he looked. She could hear the Wolf calling to her from far away, but she couldn't understand him. The Hyena finally reached her neck and grazed the surface with his razor sharp teeth. She screamed louder.

The Hyena laughed. "What happens if I chew through the spinal cord?"

She knew exactly what would happen. She would die. Decapitation was one way to kill a Celerius, and the Hyena's teeth, although an unconventional tool, were probably sharp enough to accomplish it. Suddenly the Wolf's voice could be heard clear as day. "Lilly! Fight! Go for the eyes!"

She tried desperately but was tiring and her neck was struggling to recover as the Hyena's teeth made deeper cuts. "Come on," the

Hyena persisted, frustration creeping into his voice. "Just a little off the top."

Lilly was amazed the Wolf could focus or talk with a sword in his chest, but he kept calling to her. "Who are you, Lilly?" he asked. "Are you a girl petrified by nightmares? Or are you the nightmare?" His voice grew weaker. He was swinging his fists desperately at Carlin, but Carlin was out of reach.

The Wolf persisted. "Are you a victim? Or are you a force to fear? Abandon Lilly the lady. She has no place here. Abandon old honor. This isn't a sword fight."

The Hyena giggled with glee. "You have nightmares do you?" he whispered into her neck, "Do your nightmares involve traveling through my digestive tract?"

Lilly's eyes met the Hyena's and his smile dropped. Something was different about her. She slammed her forehead into the Hyena's nose. He growled and attempted to snap at her throat again but she slammed her head into his again. She beat his face senselessly with her own until she felt her skull fracture and heal itself over. The Hyena rolled off and groaned in pain. He tried to stand, but Lilly was on her feet in an instant. She slammed her foot into his stomach and, despite his hard muscles, he yelped. Before she could do it again, he scampered to his feet. "No more jokes, eh?" he said maniacally.

"You want a joke?" she asked.

She closed the distance between them in an instant and delivered a lightening fast kick to his ankle. As he tried to correct his footing, she punched him hard in his neck. He dropped to the ground and she placed her foot on the back of his head. "What's stronger than a Hyena's upper jaw?"

"What?" he choked.

"His lower one," she said.

With that she stomped on the back of his head. She heard the telltale crack that told her his metal teeth had fractured his jaw. He would have been howling in pain if his mouth hadn't been crushed shut. She didn't have time to relish her victory though. The Wolf needed help. She grabbed her discarded sword from the ground and charged Carlin without mercy. He ducked under her swing, but was forced to backtrack away from the Wolf. She pulled the sword from his chest and he breathed in relief. His wounds began to sew themselves shut, but she knew it would be a while before he could stand.

Carlin took a few more steps back as Lilly advanced. "You wouldn't kill an unarmed man," Carlin said. "That's your Celerius honor at work."

She clucked her tongue. "Sorry, Carlin. The lady Lilly Celerius is gone. I am the warrior Lilly Celerius. Honorable men deserve honorable deaths. You deserve nothing."

She jabbed her blade at him but as always, he was quicker than he looked. He used her moment of confusion to leave sword-fighting distance and enter combat distance. He brought his elbow across her face. She hardly seemed to notice it as she slammed her sword hilt into his chin. He stumbled backward. Even in his dazed state he was able to duck under her next swing. "I do admit," he breathed. "Something's different about you. You're less stuck up. Less arrogant."

She caught him in the leg and he howled. A sudden opening of the doors drew her attention. The rebels guarding the doors must have fled. Carlin seized his opportunity and kicked her sword out of her hand. He pulled a knife and jabbed it into Lilly's flank. She still managed to catch a glimpse of Virgil entering. He was covered in blood and looked worse than the Wolf.

Carlin was momentarily distracted and Lilly broke his grip on the knife. She pulled it out and sliced into his arm. He cried out in pain. Across the room, Virgil pulled a knife from his belt. "Carlin!" he yelled.

Lilly saw the knife coming and ducked under it easily. It impaled itself into Carlin's chest and he howled loudly. Lilly used the distraction to kick Carlin off his feet and bolt to her uncle. They'd accomplished their mission. Not only was Carlin wounded, but so was his second-in-command. She could also hear more troops and their heavy armor clanging as they arrived to their general's aid. Lilly pulled the Wolf to his feet. "We need to go," she said.

Without so much as a backward look, they fled out the back doors with their Celerius speed. The Wolf had reclaimed his sword and used it to cut down the soldiers standing directly outside. They found themselves in the dark streets of Brightbow. "Horses," he breathed as he pointed down the road to an inn.

As he'd indicated there were two horses tied up out front. They commandeered them and rode off. They could hear soldiers yelling "The General's injured!" They spurred their horses on harder and harder until they were past the limits of the village.

"Where to?" Lilly yelled above the hoof beats.

The Wolf peered into the darkness. "Seeing as I have no idea where we are, I was going to suggest forward. We'll circle around toward the meeting point when we're sure we're not being followed."

"Forward is good," she called back as they rode deeper and deeper into the wilderness.

Chapter Sixty-Four

THE DOCTOR'S WORKSHOP
THE PACK

*R*HYS *ALWAYS SCREAMED WHEN THE BUCKET OF WATER HIT HIM.* T*HAT MADE* sense though. He'd been awake for days, and at his every attempt to flee into sleep the Doctor would pull him right back. "It's probably very hard for you to express what you're feeling." the Doctor mused as he lowered his bucket to the floor and examined his captive through the bars. "But if you could rate this exhaustion, this discomfort on a scale of one to one hundred, where would you place it?"

Rhys clenched his jaw and closed his eyes tightly. The Doctor cocked his head in response. "You can't tell me that I haven't piqued your interest. Don't you long to know how it all works? Don't you long to understand how our bodies measure pain? We can measure temperature, distance, time, but pain is just outside of our reach… Don't you long to be enlightened?"

"I long to…" Rhys paused. "Be free. And that's all."

The Doctor looked at him with renewed interest. "You were about to make a threat," he deducted. "You were about to threaten my life, weren't you?"

Rhys was silent. He bowed his head in reservation and shame, then curled into a ball, receding further into the corner of the cell.

The Doctor paced away from the cell slowly. He'd leave the boy alone for now. Breaking him would consist of giving out punishment in doses. In between he would finally have time to take care of some other rudimentary business. His son had sent him a letter by pigeon, but he'd spent the day exercising restraint. He was almost certain of what it said. There was no use in worrying about the oncoming attackers. All that mattered was securing his legacy; besides, he had Anastasia and his pet to keep him protected. He tore open the letter and skimmed it. "You're not going to like this," the Doctor said to his prisoner. "But our timetable has been advanced. It's important for me to know... do you feel the urge to kill me? Torture me? Finish my pain index?" Rhys was silent. "Good," the Doctor said.

In the last few weeks he had concentrated on breaking Rhys's mind without hurting him physically, but now he would have to move quicker. He'd have to resort to more barbaric methods. "Time to start the real stuff." the Doctor said. "I'm so excited to see how your rankings compare to mine."

Rhys screamed, of course, as he had for the last few weeks, but the Doctor knew that soon that wouldn't be the case. He wouldn't try to alert anyone because he would believe it futile. He would believe that he was truly alone and adrift. Soon the only thing to latch on to would be the mantle of the Doctor.

The Doctor pulled a saw from his toolkit and was surprised to hear a laugh coming from the boy. He spun around. "What?" he asked infuriated. "What's funny?"

"That letter is from the Marksman, isn't it?" Rhys asked.

The Doctor wiped a cloth over his saw to clean it. "And?"

"And my friends are coming for me," Rhys said.

The Doctor said nothing this time. He gritted his top teeth against his metal jaw. Rhys smiled at him. He actually smiled, and the Doctor felt rage burning in his chest and face. "There's a difference between me and you," Rhys said. "You were alone, completely alone, when you became the new Doctor. But me, I've got tons of people who care about me. I won't have to kill you. They'll do it for me."

The Doctor stared at him stunned.

"Do whatever you want to me," Rhys continued. "Kill me if you want, but don't deceive yourself. Your legacy ends with me."

The Doctor knew that every second of silence exposed weakness, but he couldn't decide on a response. He narrowed his eyebrows and glared at his experiment. "You should hope that they kill me, Rhys," he whispered. "You should hope."

With that, he lowered the saw back into the box. His passion was missing. It had been replaced by something far harder to act on: fear. For the first time since he'd taken the title, the Doctor feared death.

Chapter Sixty-Five

OCEAN'S JAW
NEIL VAPROS

THE REST OF DINNER HAD BEEN QUIET WHILE EVERYONE MADE AWKWARD eye contact. Neil could feel several eyes on him. "Maybe we shouldn't have named you after a snake," Serena whispered.

Alex looked at his plate guiltily. "I forgot that Mama had a thing against them."

"You guys know I'm not the spy, right?" Neil asked.

"Frankly Mamba, I'm surprised that you know what a spy is," Alex said suppressing a giggle.

"You guys are taking this way too lightly," Neil said.

"No we're not," Serena said. "No one would accuse you without proof. If there's a spy, Mama will find him eventually. Just be good."

Neil ate another bite of carp. *Just be good.* He didn't feel reassured despite their attempts to soothe him. He wasn't exactly beloved on this island, between Haxon's friends and Mama Tridenti. Mama Tridenti was still on her throne eating moderately. Despite the fury and power in her speech, she dined without worry. Neil couldn't wrap his head around why she'd tell the spy that she was onto them. Tactically, the smarter decision would be to set traps while the spy was confident that he or she was working in secret. Neil watched her curiously as he finished his dinner and tried to comprehend her thought process. It was possible that she trusted the island and its inhabitants enough to let them take care of it. Or maybe she thought the spy would quit reporting if they knew how dangerous it had become.

"Why let the spy know she's onto them?" Neil asked. "I can't wrap my head around that."

Alex pondered the question. "Mama Tridenti is smart. She doesn't do anything without reason."

"She might be trying to stir the pot," Serena said. "Now everyone will be on the lookout, not just her."

Whatever her logic was, she clearly had a plan. "I guess that makes sense."

The rest of dinner passed in silence. Neil walked back to his side of the house with the Tridenti trailing slightly behind him. They made it just beyond the dining room when Mama Tridenti caught up to them. "Alex. Serena." she said. "I'd like to speak to you for a moment."

Neil hung around for a moment and she cleared her throat. "Just them, Mamba. It's captain stuff."

"Yes, ma'am," Neil said, unconvinced.

They were near enough to the next corner for Neil to hide behind it. He kept stepping lighter and lighter until he was sure they thought he was gone. He needed to hear this. "How much do you two trust Mamba?" Mama Tridenti asked.

"Completely," Alex said.

"And you?" Mama Tridenti's voice asked.

"With my life," Serena said.

Mama Tridenti sighed loud enough for Neil to hear. "At the moment he's my only suspect. There is an overwhelming body of evidence against him."

Neil's blood went cold. "What kind of evidence?" Serena asked.

"Of course it's all circumstantial," she said. "But honestly. You pull a mysterious man out of the ocean underneath the Cliff, an Imperial base, and he doesn't remember a thing? That's convenient."

"I'm sure if you ask him he'll tell you that it's anything but convenient," Alex muttered.

"Those Imperial guards we fought said he was a fugitive of the Empire," Serena said. "Explain that."

"They're covering for their spy," she said. "It's an excellent way to get you to trust him."

"I don't buy it," Serena said.

"The first pigeons must have been sent around his time of arrival," Mama Tridenti said. "Whether you like to believe it or not, he's our best suspect."

"We're not going to turn on our friend," Alex said.

"Don't," Mama Tridenti said. "But don't let him get too close either."

Neil's friends sighed. "We'll keep it in mind."

Neil could sense that they were almost done with their conversation so he crept down the hall and darted around the next corner to his room. He wished he could have materialized, but the band on his wrist made it harder than it had been in the past. Judging by the speed at which his friends reached his door they were curious to see if he'd been eavesdropping. They pushed open the door and he sat up with mock surprise on his face. "What's up?" he asked.

They looked surprised to see him waiting patiently. Serena said, "Mama Tridenti wanted to talk about—"

"Captain stuff," Alex said.

Neil and Serena both looked at him completely understanding the implication. Even Alex was suspicious of Neil. Neil felt a pang in his chest, but he understood. There wasn't much he could do to prove his innocence without a memory or anyone to vouch for him. "Want to go swimming or something?" Serena asked.

"Absolutely," Neil said with relief, but his mind was somewhere else.

If he really wanted to be safe he knew what he had to do. He had to find the spy before Mama Tridenti could act on her suspicions. Otherwise, there was only one possible fate for him, and it looked alarmingly like Hector's.

Neil's next days on the island were strenuous. His friends weren't asking him to abandon his work early anymore. That meant one-on-one time with several crewmembers, including Earnest Haxon. Neil did his best to ignore the brute. He had bigger problems. For instance, he'd heard through the grapevine that another pigeon had gone missing despite the entire island being on high alert. The spy wasn't quitting and also happened to be clever enough to avoid capture. "It could be a Tridenti, right?" a crewman asked on break one day.

"Absolutely not," Neil said. "'The shore holds strong' is their thing. I can't imagine any Tridenti putting their ability to protect the shore in danger for any reason."

"They shouldn't be released from scrutiny," the crewman replied. "All I'm saying."

They were sitting out on the docks dipping their feet in the water. Walking barefoot on the hot sand all day was an acquired taste, but they still needed to cool off every few hours. "Well, who would you suspect?" Neil asked.

"If it were a Tridenti, I'd suspect Alex. He's way more ambitious than people give him credit for."

"I'm done considering that it's a Tridenti," another one said. "This is their home. I'd suspect the person who has the reason to be angriest at the island."

Neil raised his eyebrow. "Who's that?"

The crewman gestured down the beach to Earnest Haxon who was pulling in a haul of fish. "I'd be pretty upset if my brother had been kicked off the island. Maybe he's taking revenge against everyone."

That was the best theory Neil had to go on so far. Maybe Haxon was even trying to steer Mama Tridenti in his direction in way of retribution for his brother. Earnest seemed to feel Neil's eyes on him. He looked up from his haul to stare at Neil. He grinned slightly and Neil's throat tightened. What reasons did Earnest have to be grinning? "Time to head back to work," one of the crewmen said. The rest of them groaned.

After gathering coconuts for an hour, Neil heard the doors to the mansion open. "Mamba!" Alex called.

Neil jogged over with a coconut tucked under his arm. "Hey. Need something?" Neil asked.

"I need you to come inside," Alex said.

He seemed grim. "Uh…Okay," Neil said. He chucked the coconut and walked up the steps. Alex ushered him inside where Mama Tridenti and Serena were waiting for him. The door closed behind

Neil and his body flooded with adrenaline. "What's going on?" he asked.

"We found this in your room," Mama Tridenti said. She held up a dead pigeon by the neck expectantly.

"You found a dead bird in my room?" Neil asked.

"No," she growled. "We found a live bird in your room. We can only assume you were preparing to give it a message and send it off."

Neil looked from Serena to Alex. They appeared to be serious. "Why would I keep a pigeon in my room?" Neil asked. "If I were a spy, wouldn't I just send it from the coop?"

"I'm not sure," Mama Tridenti said. "But for now you can't be allowed to walk free."

"You can't be serious…" Neil said.

"We're just being careful, Mamba." Serena said quietly.

Neil considered running for a second, but he knew how that would look. Alex shackled Neil's arms and directed him down a hallway he hadn't seen before. Neil made eye contact with Serena for a long moment. She looked conflicted. Neil wanted to believe he saw more hope than fear in her eyes, but he couldn't be certain. Alex pushed him through the door and they walked down a stone staircase. "Earnest Haxon," Neil said as soon as Mama Tridenti was out of view.

"I was thinking the same thing," Alex said.

"So why are you locking me up?" Neil asked. He realized they were in a dungeon.

"Mama Tridenti wants what she wants," Alex replied. "And she wants to make sure you're not the spy. If spy activity continues, she won't kill you."

"Charming," Neil said as Alex directed him into a cell. Neil stepped behind the bars and Alex locked it.

"Don't worry," Alex said. "I'm about to do some investigating of my own. Hang in there, Mamba. This'll be over before dinner."

Alex trotted up the stairs and Neil was left alone with his thoughts. He turned to the right and realized that there was a skeleton gripping the bars of the cell next door. Hopefully he'd have a more promising fate than that poor man.

Neil crossed his legs and cleared his mind. If he was going to be here alone it would help to search his mind for clues. Dungeon or not, he was going to put all his brainpower toward discovering this spy.

Neil eyes flickered open. He had no way to know how much time had passed but something in his chest told him that it was night. He rubbed his eyebrows while wondering how long he'd be staying here. How long would it take Alex to prove his innocence? And would it be enough to validate his freedom? Mama Tridenti didn't strike him as the type to be convinced easily, except when it came to the matter of his guilt.

The island shook suddenly and Neil bolted upright. *What was that?* Another explosion sounded and he realized that the sound was familiar. It was cannon fire. He heard the door open and realized someone must be coming to get him to help fight whoever was firing at them. He heard multiple pairs of footsteps trailing down the stairs and someone speaking in a gruff voice. "In and out," the voice said. "We need to get back quickly."

Neil quickly realized the kind of danger he was in. The men entering the dungeon weren't here to rescue him. It was Earnest Haxon and some friends. Neil looked around the cell for something to defend himself with, but only found the bones of his friend next door. Neil reached through the bars and began fumbling.

A few second's later, when Earnest approached his cell, Neil appeared to be sleeping. He fit the most likely stolen key into the lock and opened the door silently. He crept up on Neil, but before he could finish the job Neil clobbered him over the head with a femur bone. Earnest reeled backward and Neil smacked him across the face with the bone. Earnest fell backwards onto his backside and spat out a tooth. His friends started to run to his aid. "No!" Haxon screamed as he waved them off. "This is between me and him. You're not going to weasel out of this one," he told Neil.

"You put the bird in my room," Neil accused.

"I did," Haxon said. "I needed to get you alone."

Neil opened his arms wide. "Here I am."

Earnest stood and picked up his knife from the ground. The two danced around each other for a moment. Neil made sure to stay clear of the bars as Earnest's friends were also armed and could easily stab him through them. Neil lashed out with the bone but Earnest blocked it with his knife and lashed out fast enough to nick Neil's thumb. Neil scowled in pain, but dodged the next strike. He snap kicked Earnest in the side and followed up with a swing of the femur. The kick knocked Earnest off balance and the blow from the femur was enough to knock his head into the bars. He fell to the ground, unconscious. His friends tried to run to his aid, but Neil knocked them both out before they could assist him. They were already stirring, but Neil didn't give them a chance to rejoin the fight. He bolted from the cell and up the stairs. He was worried about what would happen if the Tridenti saw him walking about, but that was preferable to sharing a cell with Earnest and his lackeys. At first Neil was worried about how he'd get through the giant main doors. But upon reaching the atrium he realized that the front doors were in shambles. Evidently someone had fired a cannonball through them. It was certainly more effective than knocking.

Neil darted through the threshold and came face to face with an Imperial soldier. He clobbered him with the femur while he still had the element of surprise. The soldier's helmet rang like a bell when Neil struck it and the guard collapsed. Neil grabbed his sword and surveyed the beach.

Two Imperial ships were right outside the stone teeth of the island and several rowboats transported soldiers to the mainland. Alex was knee-deep in water and disposing of soldiers left and right, but they looked close to ganging up on him. Mama Tridenti was fighting three guards on the sand near the fighting pit. He looked around for Serena but she was nowhere to be found. "Mamba!" Mama Tridenti screamed. He turned to her. "Serena is wounded and being chased through the swamp! She needs help!" She grunted as she fended off yet another soldier ganging up on her.

Neil wanted to ask her why she'd had a sudden change of heart, but he knew there wasn't time. Even if she believed that he was a spy she couldn't risk leaving her daughter alone. He darted around the side of the mansion and through the trees of the swamp. He could hear Serena faintly singing through the underbrush and he tried to resist turning into putty. He reached the area where she was and cut down one of the soldiers who was cornering her. She was pinned against a tree, swinging a small dagger to fend off the soldiers. Her voice was growing fainter and the soldiers looked like they were regaining their motor skills. One of the guards turned his attention to Neil and Neil disposed of him quickly. The other was getting dangerously close to Serena. Neil tackled him from the side. He didn't put up much of a fight and it was clear that he was still recovering.

Neil was just about to run to Serena, but the guard he'd tackled regained his wits and swung his armored fist against Neil's face. An edge found Neil's cheekbone and it sustained a deep cut. Neil rolled off and winced in pain. The soldier stood and raised his fists. "You Lightborns are going to get what's coming to you," he spat.

"Probably," Neil said. "But not from you."

The soldier swung at Neil and he dodged it handily. That was the advantage to being without armor. The soldier swung a few more times unsuccessfully, so he lunged for his discarded sword. Neil didn't have time to stop him. He backed up until he was against a palm tree. He had an idea. The solder rushed him and swung the sword without fully planting his feet. Neil ducked as it imbedded into the palm tree. In the same motion he spun around and slammed the guard by the back of his head into the sword hilt. The guard's eyes lost focus and he collapsed. Neil ran to Serena. "Can you hear me?" he asked.

She was pale. He realized that she had a deep wound in her stomach. "The sea…" she managed before she lost consciousness.

Neil began to sweat. He knew he couldn't carry her all the way to the water before she succumbed to her wounds. Unless… "Serena," he said trying to spur her awake. It did no good.

The guard who Neil had knocked unconscious began to stir and another plan arose in his mind. He glanced down at the bracelet attached to his arm and knew that his only hope was removing it. He pulled a sword off of a soldier's body and slid it across the swamp floor to the awakening soldier. The soldier looked at it skeptically and grabbed the sword as he stood. "Big mistake," the soldier said.

Neil was hoping that he was wrong. As the soldier swung at him he leaned back and raised his wrist. The sword connected with Neil's iron bracelet and the sound of the clash echoed throughout the swamp. Despite the sound it didn't break. The soldier kicked Neil to the ground and brought the sword up as if to cut Neil down the middle. At the last second Neil grabbed his hand and held it tight. The sword connected with the bracelet squarely and it fractured. As the bracelet broke, Neil felt a surge of power rush through his hands and he launched a fireball at the solder. It sent him flying off into the distance, and Neil knew he wouldn't be a problem anymore. Neil scooped up Serena in his arms and channeled all his energy in a way he never had before. Fire burst from his feet and launched the two of them into the air. Neil directed them as best he could until he was sure they'd land in the ocean. He surrendered to his dizziness and his fire extinguished. The two plummeted into the water and Neil sank like a rock. He tried to fight, but the energy used had exhausted him. His last thought as the sea consumed him was a single hope: that it had been enough.

Chapter Sixty-Six

BRIGHTBOW
CARLIN FILUS

CARLIN SLAMMED HIS FIST AGAINST THE FLOOR AND SCREAMED FOR THE tenth time. He'd lost the Celerius girl. Again. "Sir," a soldier whispered as he approached. Carlin stood slowly. "Orders dictate that we must bring you to the nearest military outpost immediately. Furthermore, if we don't get Virgil to a doctor soon he's going to die."

Carlin turned to face him. He grabbed the soldier's head in his hands and with a clean twist the young man fell to the ground, dead. "Leave me," Virgil moaned. "They escaped because of me. This is what I deserve."

Carlin stared at him. Virgil was slumped up against the wall bleeding profusely from his chest wound. "What happened?" Carlin demanded.

"We went to search a basement," Virgil blubbered. "Someone was down there waiting for us. He told us we were a danger to someone he was protecting. We didn't stand a chance. I couldn't see anything. I couldn't fight him."

Carlin's blood went cold. He still remembered his encounter with the masked man months ago in Altryon. Was the man protecting Lilly Celerius? That was the only thing that made sense. "Leave me," Virgil whispered.

"No," Carlin decided. "I won't let you die, Lieutenant."

"Back to the outpost for medical attention!" he called to his men waiting outside the door. "Make sure Virgil doesn't bleed out on the way there."

A few soldiers ran in and pulled Virgil through the doors. Another came to offer Carlin assistance, but he waved him away. Carlin placed his face in his hands and breathed deeply. After a few moments he heard laughter from across the room. Carlin tried to tune it out but it only grew louder. Carlin lowered his hands and glared at the Hyena.

"She got the jump on me," the Hyena cackled through broken teeth. "She literally got the jump on me."

Carlin limped over. "What's so funny?"

"She got the jump on me. She jumped on my head." The Hyena chuckled. He gestured to the floor beneath him. "You ought to try this marble floor, General. It needs seasoning, but it tastes better than you might expect."

Carlin grabbed Lilly's discarded sword and placed it up against the Hyena's neck. The Hyena stared at him quizzically as if he were waiting for the punch line to the joke. The Hyena's broken smile faded as he realized that Carlin was serious. "You're gonna kill me? You really want to find out what the Imperial Doctor will do to you for that?"

"No," Carlin said. "Lilly Celerius killed you. She kicked out all of your teeth and then she slit your throat."

The Hyena chuckled. "Oh…" he whispered. "I get it."

Carlin stared at him. The Hyena burst into uncontrollable laughter and shook his head at Carlin. "You do everything you do to make your father proud right? You do it to make him love you, right?" He measured his next words carefully. "You can't pay for love in blood, trust me. I've spilled my fair share. And you especially can't buy love from someone who's in the… state that your father is in."

"What do you mean?"

"I've met your father, Carlin. I came when the Doctor met him quite recently. And I get it. I get the joke that you don't get yet."

Carlin pressed and blood began to dribble from the Hyena's neck. The Hyena continued to laugh. "I get the joke, General! And it's funny. It might be the funniest thing about you. You don't get it yet. But you will. You're going to cut through this nation with a bloody sword only to realize that the joke was on you the whole time."

The Hyena laughed again and Carlin stared at him. After a few moments the General couldn't contain his fury. "Stop!" he demanded.

The Hyena couldn't stop though. He was far too satisfied with himself. Eventually Carlin just wanted the sound to stop clawing at his eardrums. He wanted silence. With a swift flick of Carlin's wrist the laughter stopped. The Hyena's head rolled across the floor, even with his teeth shattered and his eyes empty, he looked absolutely thrilled. *You don't get it yet. But you will.* The words continued to bounce around in his brain.

Carlin dropped the sword on the Hyena's body and walked out the exit of the hall. He rejoined his men and gave the silent order to move out. Carlin silently cursed their order to protect him at all costs, as it would deter him from chasing after the Celerius and the hostages. As he and his men exited the city he receded into his mind, trying desperately to understand the joke that the Hyena was referring to. What could possibly be so funny? "Are you all right, sir?" asked one of his sergeants.

"I'm fine," Carlin said. "Just some stupid joke." He stepped onto his carriage and prepared for the journey back to the outpost. "It wasn't even funny," he whispered, more to himself than to anyone else.

You don't get it yet. But you will.

Chapter Sixty-Seven

OCEAN'S JAW
NEIL VAPROS

NEIL AWOKE BEFORE HIS EYES OPENED. HE COULD FEEL THE SAND caressing his body as if he were a baby and the beach was his blanket. He awoke fully and knew at once that along with his powers, his memory was returning piece by piece. The bracelet must have stopped his mind from coming together fully after his materialization. Serena lay next to him. Relief crossed her face when he looked up and met her eyes. "Looks like those swimming lessons didn't sink in," Neil whispered through his salty lips.

"Ha. Sink," she said. "Get it?"

"Boo," Neil said as he rolled forward and into a crouching position. "Let's get back to the front of the island. Your family might still be in danger."

She shook her head. "Hear any cannon fire? I guarantee that there are two new Imperial ships at the bottom of the ocean."

"What if they're done firing because they won?"

"Trust me, Mama Tridenti would have used her advanced ability if things were that dire."

They trudged back to the front of the island. Serena had been right. According to Alex, shortly after Neil ran after Serena, Mama Tridenti created a whirlpool that spun one of the ships and it actually fired on the other ship accidentally. Then she'd pulled both under. Neil made a silent resolution to get back on her good side. The three of them reentered the house. Mama Tridenti was standing in the same place she'd been doing yoga on the day that Neil arrived. This time she was standing upright with clenched fists. From what he could see, her skin was turning red with fury. A paper was clenched in her hand. Earnest Haxon was lying at her feet sobbing. "It looks like we know how you escaped your cell, Mamba," she said, voice booming.

"Please..." Earnest whispered. "I'm not—"

Mama Tridenti stepped on his neck and his words ceased. Without turning to the face the three teens, she held up the crumpled paper in her hands. "I had his room searched when I found out that he tried to kill Mamba. It's a letter to the nearest military outpost. We've found our snake."

Earnest squirmed desperately and small bursts of air escaped his lungs as he attempted to breathe. Mama Tridenti removed her foot and grabbed him by the neck with her free hand. He squirmed and tried to escape as she lifted him above the ground, but it was no use. Her grip was iron. Eventually he stopped and she dropped his body to the floor. Neil watched his body for any traces of life. There were none.

"Nasty business," Mama Tridenti said. "But he knew the risks when he decided to betray me."

She stepped over his body and through the doors to the dining room. The remaining three spent a moment staring at Earnest Haxon's body. "I guess it goes without saying that we're sorry for accusing you," Alex said.

Neil gulped. "I'm just glad to not be him. Are we just gonna leave him there?"

Serena crossed her arms uncomfortably. "Mama Tridenti will want people to see him as they come inside. He's an example now."

Neil stared at the body until Alex ushered him along into the dining room. Despite the damage to the island, apparently regrouping was most important. Mama Tridenti must have had something to say. They shuffled in along with the other survivors of the Empire's attack. It looked like all the Tridenti were still alive, not surprising given their powers, but five crewmen were gone, not including Earnest and his lackeys. So the island was down eight people. The rest of the islanders joined them in the dining room and sat, waiting for Mama Tridenti to speak. "The shore holds strong…" she said as if in a trance. "That's our purpose. We live by it. Keep anyone from monopolizing the sea and attacking the mainland from it. Without us the demons could fire on Misty Hollow or Shipwreck Bay with the full force of their cannons. Our purpose is for Volteria."

Neil looked over and saw that Serena and Alex were nodding passionately. Their mother had the ability to stir something powerful in them. "That was always our purpose," Mama Tridenti continued. "But we have to ask ourselves, with the Empire in its current state, will the shore ever be safe? How long will it be until they come back with more ships? Can we stand up to their numbers? They've always been our enemies, and time has only made them more aggressive."

An unnatural silence settled over the room. Everyone was nervous. Alex and Serena stopped nodding. "I have made a decision about the future of this family," Mama Tridenti said. "The Empire crossed a line by placing a spy in my home. They crossed a line by injuring my daughter. Tomorrow we make preparations to cripple their navy at its source. There are ports connected to one side of their Industrial City. They will be underwater within a month."

"What about the shore?" Neil heard Alex whisper to himself.

"So long as that Empire exists we will never be able to truly realize our potential," Mama Tridenti said as she pounded her fist into the wooden dinner table. "We will crush their ports and starve them out. Maybe the Venator would even agree to a truce. Either way, it's time to expand. For my children and for my family, I will create an empire of my own. The shore is not enough anymore. When we finish with the Empire of Altryon I assure you, that all of the realm will be safe, even if I have to sink their entire dammed city to assure it."

The room was silent. She smiled distantly and left the hall with their new mantra. Alex stared at the table as if his world were falling apart and Serena looked off as if in a trance. Neil couldn't blame them. Who could be expected to react rationally in a situation like this one? Their entire purpose had been ripped from them and replaced with a far more ambitious one. And it didn't even look like they wanted it.

Chapter Sixty-Eight

ABINGTON
DARIUS TAURLUM

DARIUS, ANASTASIA, AND BIANCA MADE IT TO ABINGTON AT THE END OF the predicted two weeks. As the days of travel went on, Anastasia seemed to come down with something again. She coughed more often and slept longer. Dark bags developed under her eyes and her complexion worsened. She denied it, of course, but it was almost exactly as it had been before. Darius interpreted it as a sickness that developed the closer she got to the Doctor. Maybe it was induced by panic. He was sure if panic could make him sick, he'd be right there with her.

They bought two rooms at an inn and turned them into their armories. Anastasia and Bianca sharpened knives and spikes and trained while Darius went into town for armor. He made sure to keep his head down. Abington, after all, had the strongest Imperial presence. After haggling with a blacksmith for almost an hour, he was able to obtain a breastplate that would hopefully cover his weak navel. Once back at the inn, he butchered a plate of leather armor to make protection for his flanks. After living in the Taurlum mansion for so many years, he'd learned everything that could be learned about armor. His craftsmanship was admirable and he felt confident in his chances against the Marksman. He hoped that the thick strips of leather could stop a bullet. He left his room and went into the one next door. Anastasia and Bianca were armed to the teeth with sharp instruments and fierce grimaces of determination. "Looks like we're ready," Darius said. "Now the only question is when to attack."

Anastasia wrapped her chain around her arm experimentally. "The best time to ambush is just before dawn. It's when people sleep deepest."

"He knows we're coming," Bianca pointed out. "The Marksman must have told him. No one will be sleeping."

"Still," Anastasia said. "That would give us time to rest. If there's a chance that we could catch him off his guard, it's worth taking."

"All right," Bianca said. "Before dawn it is."

They broke silently and Darius returned to his room. He could see the sun beginning to set, and the fading light of dusk passed over his face. It had been a long time since he'd taken time to actually appreciate anything. In his first days outside the wall he'd been awestruck by unobstructed views. He'd spent hours in the dead of night watching the rolling plains and mountains, perplexed by the absence of a giant wall closing him in. Now all he ever thought about was rescuing Rhys and killing the Doctor. Of course, Anastasia also drifted into his mind every so often.

He heard the door open behind him and gripped the windowsill, ready to tear it off and pummel the intruder. "My, you look tense," Anastasia said.

He settled and let it go. He spun around to face her and was struck by the way the light from the window filtered by him and over her. It almost distracted from how sickly she'd been looking recently. "Aren't you?" he asked.

She sat on his bed. "I don't want to think about it. I just know one thing and one thing only. The Doctor has hurt too many people. There are too many people caught in his web. Tomorrow he's going to die." She shuddered and held her breath for a second. "I can't imagine a world in which he can keep doing what he's doing."

"If Barlow was right and that monster is torturing Rhys, then I'm right there with you," Darius said. "We'll finish this tomorrow."

Anastasia seemed satisfied. She lay across the bed horizontally. Darius could hear her breathing shallowly. "You sure you're all right?" he asked her. "We could see someone before tomorrow."

"I'll feel better when I'm free from the Doctor." She opened her eyes and quickly amended. "When we're all free from him."

Darius sat next to her until he was sure she was asleep. It was hard to tell with the shallow and quick nature of her breathing. He went to his bag and removed *A Rough History of Lightborns*. Before the first page had been turned Anastasia was awake again. "Trying to read on without me?" she prodded.

Darius rolled his eyes. "There's no way I'm going to be able to sleep tonight. Might as well educate myself."

"You'll be useless without me," Anastasia teased as she pulled it out of his hands. "Let me go first."

They shared in their second reading session until well past sun down. Through the pages they trekked until they were out of pages to skim and they reached the blank ones. "Looks like you're onto your next frontier," Anastasia said.

"What's that?" Darius asked.

"Writing," she said with a mischievous smile.

"I wouldn't even know where to begin," Darius said.

"Letter by letter." She went to his bag and retrieved the little reading book that she'd given him. "It's just like reading but with a few more steps."

Together she helped him trace the letters over and over in the blank sheets of her former book. Even after she went to sleep, he kept at it, stubbornly trying to convince his muscles to remember good penmanship. He flipped through the tiny book and after a while was writing his own words. His handwriting looked infantile at best. It grew easier but not much. It was clear to him that he'd have to spend endless hours practicing to make any improvement. Anastasia awoke again. "Why'd you let me sleep?" she asked.

"Because you need it. You don't want to be tired or just a little bit too slow. That's what happened to Barlow," Darius murmured as he roughly attempted to sketch a Q in the book.

"Barlow was drinking. I won't let Victor get the better of me," Anastasia said. "What are you writing?"

"Just practicing," Darius said. "I wouldn't know what to write."

Anastasia stood up and leaned over to look at his progress. "And I'm not sure anyone would be able to read it," she giggled.

He'd never heard her giggle before. It sounded unnatural coming from her lips. It made him swell with emotion but, as per usual, he suppressed it. "Write me something," she said.

He looked up. She was serious. "What if you can't read it?" he said as he tapped the pen against his chin. It made an unnatural sound against his skin.

"Write it anyway."

He didn't answer because he wasn't sure what he could possibly say to her in writing. He turned to a new page. She gave him a satisfied smirk which almost made it hard to see her as the same girl who giggled earlier. There were many sides to Anastasia, but to Darius it seemed as if she was actively burying many of them. He wrote on and on, even well after she'd fallen back asleep. He saw the slightest bit of light peer over the horizon and he knew it was time to go. Luckily, he'd finished his letter to Anastasia.

He reached out to shake her awake, but his hand only hovered over her shoulder for a moment. Part of him didn't want to leave the serenity of the room in order to enter the chaotic pits of the Doctor's domain. He wanted to be the kind of person who could sleep next to someone. Despite his desires, he remembered Rhys and the danger he was surely in. He pushed her gently and her eyes flew open. "It's time."

She rubbed her eyes. She appeared to dread what was coming as much as Darius. He helped her up and they went next door to get Bianca. When she awoke she reached for her belt first thing, as if to attack whoever had startled her. The fugitives awoke in fear. Always in fear.

They gathered their weapons and everything useful before leaving the inn and travelling down the abandoned streets. Bianca had asked around and found out where the Library was located. She led the group to the outskirts of town. Darius was surprised by the height of the Abington Library and realized with a more wary eye that it was clearly old and abandoned. The outsides were decaying and the doors eaten by rot.

Darius's shoulder brushed Anastasia's shoulder and he found that she was shaking. "I can't do this," she said in a hushed tone.

"What do you mean?" Darius asked.

She buried her face in her hands. When she pulled them away it was soaked in tears. "I've lied to you," she said. "Both of you."

"What are you talking about?" Bianca asked.

"I undersold my involvement with the Doctor. He owns me. He owns all the assassins. I led you to the cliff because I knew you didn't stand a chance... He... I knew he had traps waiting... I'm the reason that Rhys is..." Anastasia began shuddering.

Darius wanted to be angry, but he was too busy being confused and terrified. "He gives us injections once a month," Anastasia continued. "Until our bodies become addicted to the chemicals. Then we need it every month or we'll..." She knew how to finish the sentence but didn't.

"That's why you've gotten sicker as the weeks have gone on," Darius realized.

Anastasia stared at them, crumbling under the weight of her own actions. A boy was being tortured in this building, and she'd seen worse done. "You injected yourself back at the Cliff, didn't you?" Bianca asked with a realization.

Anastasia didn't move. "He was the only one who could patch me up after Rhys stabbed me that night, but when I went to him to get stitched up he also made me one of his servants."

"I don't understand," Darius said. "Why poison his assassins?"

"It's so they can never leave him," Anastasia said. "They can never escape. He's the only one who knows the recipe for the injection."

Darius wanted to hate her, but sympathy flooded his veins. "He knew we'd have to get here before the month was over..." Darius said. "He knew you'd die if you didn't."

"I'm sorry," she said. "I had no choice. But I didn't come here to prolong my life, I came to end his."

"More importantly..." Bianca said. "He's going to be prepared for us. Anastasia, you should have told us."

She looked on the verge of collapsing. "I know... I..." She couldn't find words to continue.

"It's all right," Bianca said. "We have two objectives now. We're here for Rhys and we're here for the injection."

Anastasia stared at her gratefully. Darius remembered how complicated their relationship had been. He could see how badly Anastasia wanted Bianca to care for her. "But it also means we should change our plan of attack," Darius said. "What does he expect?"

"He probably expects Bianca and me to go after Victor. If I remain in his control, I would never kill Victor. It would be suicide. So he will expect me to fake an attack on Victor," Anastasia said, recovering. It helped her disposition to be planning for battle. "So what if you go after Victor, Darius?"

"He said he'd studied me," Darius pointed out. "But I think I can take him."

"Then I'll go after Rhys," Bianca said. "Anastasia can go after the Doctor."

"Thank you," Anastasia said.

Chapter Sixty-Nine

OCEAN'S JAW
NEIL VAPROS

NEIL'S MEMORY HAD COME TOGETHER THE WAY ONE MIGHT GLUE together a broken vase. Sometimes he was only able to pull out microscopic shards from his experiences. Occasionally entire fragments appeared at once. In recent days he'd seen a young boy holding a book bigger than he was and everything associated with his younger brother came rushing back. Rhys was still out there somewhere and needed his protection. One day he saw Hector the snake's broken neck and a memory of his sister, Victoria, came back to him in a powerful flood that caused tears at dinnertime. Memories of others came slower, one piece at a time. He remembered fighting with Darius after hearing the sound of metal on metal. Despite the pace at which his mind was re-forming, Neil felt that someone important was missing. The largest piece of his mind had yet to come together. And that's exactly why he had to leave.

"You're sure about this?" Alex asked dejectedly as he watched Neil pack up his meager possessions from the end table in his room.

"Yeah," Neil said. "The feeling that I have to be at Misty Hollow soon is only getting stronger. Maybe that's where I'll find whatever's missing."

"Are you ever going to come back?" Serena asked hopefully.

"Of course," Neil said. "As soon as I know what's out there for me, I'll come back. Maybe we can head out on another voyage."

Serena giggled. "And we'll finally get you to swim. For real this time."

"Exactly," Neil said.

Alex didn't seem as okay with it. Clearly he'd been wrestling with something since his mother's announcement about going after the Empire. Losing Neil was probably just another change in his unpredictable life. "It won't be the same without you," Alex said as he shook Neil's hand. "You're one of us, Mamba."

Neil smiled. "It might actually be weird to hear people call me Neil again."

"Maybe you could be Mamba on the mainland, too," Serena joked. "Although you'd have to tell everyone you know that you've got a new name. You'd have to have some serious dedication."

The word stuck in Neil's mind like a splinter. *Dedication.* He rubbed his forehead. "Something new?" Alex asked.

"Maybe," Neil said. "That word triggered something."

"We'll let you get some sleep, Mamba." Alex said. "You'll have to leave early tomorrow in order to get back to the nearest port without capsizing."

"Comforting," Neil said.

"What are you worried about?" Serena asked. "You can fly."

Alex hugged him and walked out of the room backwards. "Don't forget to say goodbye before you leave tomorrow."

"I won't," Neil said.

Serena lingered for a moment. "Any chance you've remembered that 'someone else' yet?"

Neil didn't exactly know how to respond. "Sort of. I think there's a missing piece. It's a big part of why I'm headed to Misty Hollow."

"Right," she said and took a step toward him. "I just want you to know that there might be more here for you than you think there is."

Neil stared at her. "What do you mean?"

"You might think that there's this huge purpose for you out there. I don't know what you'll find, but there's always another option."

"And what would that be?" he asked.

"I'm a hell of a navigator," she said. "And I have an entire fleet of ships. If you don't want to fight in this revolution or you don't find what you're looking for, we could go anywhere."

"I..." he trailed off. "You're family's getting involved in a war as well."

"Maybe it's not what I want either," she said.

He wanted to respond but was silenced by her stare. Her turquoise eyes drilled into his and he knew she wasn't kidding. He opened his mouth to tell her that it wouldn't happen, but the words wouldn't come. He really did feel more for her more than he could express, but something was stopping him. "I don't want you to tell me I deserve better or that I shouldn't wait around," she said. "I just want you to tell me that you'll think about it. It could be a life free of worry. Free of pain. Free of whatever will come of this war." Without waiting for a response she added, "Just think about it."

She kissed his cheek and turned without saying goodbye. That was all right though. He'd see her in the morning.

Neil grabbed his rag-tag assembly of things and left his room before the sun could awake the island. It was time for him to go. If Serena and Alex were awake, he'd say goodbye. Otherwise maybe it would be best if he just left. Serena's offer had shaken his spirit. A life without worry and without pain was all he wanted. Every time he looked at Serena he wanted it more, but there was something out there for him. He knew that.

He walked through the house. When he reached the door to the dining room he realized that farther down the hallway was a room with light pouring out of it. Curious, he crept over and pushed the door ajar. It was a study of sorts, piled high with books and papers. A small desk was tucked into the corner and a large candle was alight on top of it. Someone must have forgotten to put it out before heading to bed. It was a miracle that the house was still standing and not in a burned heap given that it was completely made of polished wood.

He put the candle out with his hand and a small drop of wax dripped onto a paper in prominent view. The paper looked familiar so he picked it up and examined it. It was Earnest Haxon's letter to the military outpost regarding the location of the Ocean's Jaw. Something tugged at Neil's mind. Why would he write a letter to the Empire about the location of the Ocean's Jaw? It was clear they knew where it was based on their siege. Neil read the letter twice. It was what he'd expected; the Tridenti had betrayed him by sending his brother away and deserved to be punished. Haxon had incredibly neat handwriting. He hadn't struck Neil as a calligrapher, but sometimes people had hidden talents and Neil didn't feel like judging. It was always harder to nitpick someone after they had been killed.

Underneath the letter were dozens of documents detailing ship locations and other logistics. This must be Mama Tridenti's office. She had excellent handwriting as well. He dropped the letter back onto the desk and watched it fall lazily. His eyes widened as it fell next to the other documents.

The handwriting on the letter and on the documents was identical.

"Mamba," Mama Tridenti said.

Neil wanted to leap out of his skin. He turned slowly. She smiled at him, but it didn't reach her eyes. "I thought you were leaving this morning."

"I am," Neil said with his vocal chords quivering. "I just wanted to thank you for your hospitality."

She smiled but kept him gripped with her iron glare. "I appreciate that."

He walked past her and bowed slightly. She nodded slightly back to him. Once in the hallway he darted through the dining room and toward the front door. He had to tell Alex and Serena. When he glanced back at the office, she was looking after him. He reached the front door when he heard her footsteps behind him. Instead of running to Alex's room, he ran out the front door. That's where she caught him. Mama Tridenti pulled him off his feet and threw him to the ground. "You're a lot smarter than I've given you credit for," she said standing over him. "That's changed now. I know how intelligent you are. I know you're smart enough to realize I can't let you live, Mamba."

Neil glared at her. "I don't understand. Why would you do this? Your daughter almost died during that siege."

Mama Tridenti put her hands on her knees and brought her face close to Neil's. "I did it *for* my children, you insolent child," she hissed. "And for their children."

"What good does selling out your ships to the Empire do? What good was blaming Haxon?"

She stood and shook her head sympathetically. "What kind of life could the Tridenti live if nothing changes? Protect the shore? We compete in a meaningless turf war with the Empire's navy in the hopes that it will make the lives better for those on the mainland. Their lives will never be safe. Not until the entire Empire is destroyed. I've suggested this many times and have always been greeted with the same response. It's not our place. It's not what was meant for us. Those are weak cries from infants and they needed incentive." She paused. "You were such a gift, Mamba."

"I was a… gift?"

"My children brought you here, and I realized what a perfect opportunity you provided. You were a boy from the Industrial City with no memories or family to speak of. We had every reason not to trust you."

"So then why did you end up blaming Haxon instead of me?"

She laughed humorously. "He showed disrespect to this island and to me. He tried to kill you for winning a contest against his brother. So he became an unwilling martyr. Because of his sacrifice I now have this family stirred up. For once they're finally angry. Angry enough to sink the entire Industrial City."

Neil was conflicted. He hated the idea of Mama Tridenti per-verting the purpose of the Tridenti, but also knew that the Empire needed to fall. "You can't just replace the old Empire with your new one. There needs to be something else. Something for the people. And there are good people in that city. You can't just destroy the entire thing. Taking that many lives will just force the people to hate Light-borns. You'll just create more enemies who want to see us extinct."

She went to the water and dipped her hands. Neil didn't want to know what she would do with that newfound strength. "My position as matriarch has long been threatened by those who say I am too ir-rational to lead. They say that I am too angry. I hope you understand the position I am left in."

"What position?"

"I either send you off into the ocean in hopes that you'll never come back, or I kill you here and now and tie up all of my loose ends."

Neil stood and faced her. "I wouldn't take the first option even if you offered it. Your children need to know the truth."

She stared at him. "I did this *for* my children," she said once more. "Do they really need to know how their better world was created?"

"Have you considered that they might not want to be a part of your better world?"

"I've considered everything."

She leapt at him and wrapped her hands around his neck. He tried to pull her off, but she was far too powerful. His hands ignited and she pushed him off. "My flesh won't burn," she said as she kicked him off of his feet. "The sea is on my side."

She stepped on his neck and pushed down. Neil felt his neck on the verge of cracking and he materialized out of her hold. "I've known Vapros before," she said. "Your family is especially talented at prolonging death. Not avoiding it, but prolonging it."

An idea struck Neil. He couldn't possibly win this fight while her hands were dripping with seawater. He couldn't burn her, but the water wasn't immune to evaporation. When she lunged at him again he leaned in instead of trying to fight it. He grabbed her hands in his and ignited them. She tried to pull away but as her hands dried her power faded. "I won't let you do this," she hissed. "The means don't matter."

Neil held her tighter. "Your daughter almost died."

"She would have died for something greater!" The words escaped her like the steam escaping her hands. "I'd watch her die a thousand times to forge the new world."

She shook free of his hands and landed a solid punch against his jaw. Neil let fire stream from his hands and tackled her with the extra boost from the fire. She collided with the front steps of the mansion and Neil heard her spine snap. She howled in pain, rolled over, and crawled towards the ocean. Neil tried to hold her back. She was nearing the water and he knew that if she reached it she would kill him. He didn't want to be responsible for killing Alex and Serena's mother. He heard new footsteps walking down the steps of the mansion.

Mama Tridenti collapsed mere inches from the water and Neil realized just from looking at her eyes that she was dead. She had fish eyes, eyes without a soul, eyes that had just had the life ripped from them. Neil fell to his knees and let the horror of what he had done wash over him. He looked to his side and realized that Alex was there with him. Every last bit of air escaped from his lungs.

He expected to be killed, or attacked. But nothing happened. Neil tried to form a few words. "Don't," Alex said. "I heard what she said at the end there. About watching Serena die."

Neil stared at the sand. He didn't know what to say. "She…"

Alex was crying, but he didn't look surprised. Neil felt so bad for him. "She was the spy."

Neil didn't have to say anything. The truth was evident. Alex sat down. "It's what she always wanted, to crush the Empire. Make it her own."

Neil didn't remember killing anyone in the past, but with horror he wondered if he'd done it before. Did it always feel like this? As if you'd torn off a piece of your own heart? They sat there until the sun was almost up. Neither had words to say that would do the situation justice. Neil wanted to speak a hundred times, but what could he possibly do? Apologize? Nothing would be enough.

"I want you to do something for me," Alex said after a while. "Feel free to tell me I'm insane."

"Okay." Neil's voice didn't sound like his own. It was filled with horrors.

"I want you to carry this," Alex said. "This burden." He stared off into the ocean.

"What burden?" Neil said.

"I have uncles who want to take control of this family," Alex said. "They'll do it, too, if they know their last leader was manipulating them for power."

The realization dawned on Neil and he felt a weight settling on his shoulders, something that he'd never felt before. "You want to tell them I was the spy. That she found out and I killed her."

Alex's head didn't shift. He looked off. Maybe it was easier to ask for something like this without looking at his friend. "I do." He put his face in his hands. "I believe in our purpose. The Man with the Golden Light told us to protect the shore, nothing else, and I believe in that." For the first time he met Neil's eyes. "I need to steer the family back toward that purpose. That won't happen if I'm ousted for being the son of a murderer and a liar."

Neil remembered once again that the right thing wouldn't be the easy thing. It was hard to think of something that sounded so terrible to be the right thing. "Serena too?" he asked.

"Would you rather she know that her mother offered her up for sacrifice?" Alex asked.

Neil had never wanted to fight anything more. He could feel energy in his fingertips looking to ignite, but there was no enemy. Serena and he would never be together. The fantasy that they'd had, sailing away into the unknown, was dead. He knew she would hate him for what he'd done. He knew her offer wouldn't stand. And he knew that he would never be able to look back.

"I'll do it," he said as his heart broke.

Alex rubbed his eyes and Neil could hear the tightness in his voice. "I'm sorry to have asked it."

"You have no choice. I see that."

They sat in silence for what felt like hours. It was probably a minute, but Neil couldn't tell the difference. "You're going to need to go soon," Alex said. "Seas are only gonna get rougher."

"In my experience they always do," Neil said.

Alex helped him up and led him to a rowboat. Neil climbed inside and paused. There wasn't anything that could possibly fit a situation like this. "You've been like a brother," Alex said for him.

"Lead this family well," Neil said. "Protect the shore. Make a better world the right way."

"I will," Alex said. "You'll have to go north. There's an island midway between here and the mainland. Set up camp there for the night so you don't have to row through rough waters."

Neil took control of the oars. He got one last look at Alex, a boy thrust into leadership and on the verge of a new order. Neil rowed off and channeled his pain into the physical labor of rowing forward.

He closed his eyes so that he wouldn't have to look at a life that he was leaving behind. There was nothing left for him on those sands, despite how badly he wanted there to be.

Chapter Seventy

ABINGTON LIBRARY
DARIUS TAURLUM

THEY APPROACHED THE DOORS AND DARIUS PULLED THEM OPEN. HE looked at his friends. They all shared the same look. *Unlocked.* They stared at each other silently. He was waiting for them. They entered back to back-to-back in order to prepare for any ambushes. It wasn't planned, but done out of instinct and fear. It appeared to be an ordinary library aside from the fact that it was abandoned. Thick layers of dust covered everything in sight. It was clear that people in today's world weren't as interested in reading as they had once been. Revolution beckoned and the people had answered. Simple pleasantries had fallen away. "Do you hear that?" Anastasia whispered.

Darius craned his head and listened. Beneath them a mechanical whirling noise floated through the cracks in the floor. "That's a familiar sound," he whispered.

"The Imperial Doctor's sword sharpener?" Bianca asked.

That was it. Darius remembered the shrill wailing that had filled the Doctor's last workshop. He was in the basement. Darius remembered the Wolf telling him the Empire had overtaken several buildings in Abington and had started turning them into secret fortresses. "The only question is, how do we get down there?" Bianca asked.

"Look for a staircase?" Darius asked.

They fanned out hesitantly. The Marksman could be hiding behind any one of the bookcases. "Over here," Anastasia said almost immediately.

Darius trotted over with Bianca and it was apparent what she meant. The dust was cleared away in an arc in front of one particular bookcase, as if it could swing away like a door. "Our tax man in the Industrial City had a secret door that looked like a bookshelf," Darius said. "You have to pull out the books in a certain order to open it."

Bianca ran one finger down the spine of a random book. "I robbed that guy once." Darius gave her a look. "You had to pull out all of the ones by William Cartwright."

"Didn't he write *Little Billy*?" Darius asked.

"You read *Little Billy*?" Anastasia asked.

"No," Darius said as he examined the bookshelf closer. "Any idea what the Doctor reads?"

"I've never seen him read," Anastasia said. "He's a fan of puzzles though."

Darius read the spines of the books and found nothing that obviously leapt out as a solution. He pulled on the side of it with his Taurlum strength. The wood creaked but didn't budge. Whatever this door was made of, it was well anchored and meticulously constructed. Either that, or it had been built with him in mind.

He took another look at the books. "Here's one by Cartright," Darius said. "It's not *Little Billy*, though. It's the *Wight of the Cliff*."

Anastasia looked at it. "There's also a misprint. Isn't Cartwright spelled with a *W*?"

Darius pulled the book out and something behind the bookcase clicked. "W?" Bianca asked. "Maybe there are spelling errors on the spine and the missing letters spell something?"

"Something that starts with a W?" Darius asked.

"Web," Anastasia said. "He's obsessed with building his web."

"Look for the missing E then," Bianca said.

After a little searching they found a book entitled *The History of Abington* with the E left off of "the." Darius was thankful he'd practiced his reading and writing the night before. He was the one who found *Arkney and its Rebels* with a missing B.

Nothing happened. "Damn," he said. "I thought we had it."

Bianca shook her head. "These books, each one represents a place we've been in pursuit of the Doctor."

"What?" Darius asked. It dawned on him. "*The Wight of the Cliff.* That's the military base that was in the cliff."

"*Arkney and its Rebels* and *The History of Abington* are obvious." Bianca said.

"This is a taunt." Anastasia whispered. "Everything we've done... It's all been part of his plan. He knew we'd go to Arkney. He knew we'd find him here."

"So we pull them out in order," Darius said. He didn't want to admit that this was a death trap.

He pulled them out in order now. *The Wight of the Cliff* first, *Arkney and its Rebels* next and finally, *The History of Abington*. As he pulled it down, the sound of shifting gears echoed throughout the library and Darius realized how modern and impressive the door was. It opened as if controlled by a spring mechanism. Behind was a deep stone staircase that amplified the sounds of the Doctor's personal forge.

"You first," Bianca said quietly as she pushed on Darius's back.

He glared at her, but proceeded down the staircase with his friends behind him. He knew that they were descending into the Doctor's web. It didn't matter. That's where Rhys was. He could only hope they'd be strong enough to tear through the strands.

Once they made it to the bottom of the stone staircase Darius, Bianca, and Anastasia stepped into a sandy pit that was so far around it probably encompassed the entire library above. The space reminded him of the Taurlum coliseum. They were in the fighting pit now. Where seats would normally go was the Doctor's workshop. The only way out, foreseeably, was a giant gate on the opposite side of the arena. Darius suspected he could climb up given enough time to punch into the wall to make holds, but in order to escape to where the workshop most likely was, he'd probably have to boost the girls up and climb out on his own. Darius took a moment to look back at Anastasia. She appeared sicker than ever, and Darius wasn't sure how much more time she had left. "You're here earlier than I had expected," the Doctor's metallic voice rang down from the upper area. "Despite this, I am so glad you are here." He sounded overjoyed to have them in his company. "Are you ready, Darius?"

Anastasia and Bianca looked over at him, and he looked up into the shadows above. "Let Rhys go and you'll be imprisoned, not killed," Darius said.

"You expect me to believe that?" he snorted. "Besides, Rhys is so close to achieving his destiny. We cannot stop now."

Darius was almost sure that he could hear muffled cries for help coming from the upper ring where the Doctor's voice was coming from. "I'm going to get you guys up there," Darius said low enough that the Doctor couldn't hear him. "I'll deal with whatever he has planned for me down here."

Without warning, Anastasia jumped up and he boosted her easily over the side of the ring. She leapt into the darkness and was gone. Bianca followed closely behind her. "Victor," the Doctor commanded. "Take care of them."

Darius was now alone in the Doctor's ring and he could hear something behind the gate growling. Presumably it was his opponent. He pounded his fist into his palm and the thud echoed throughout the Doctor's makeshift coliseum. "Come on!" Darius cried. "I'm ready."

"Nothing could prepare you for this," the Doctor's voice said. "I'm curious. Do you remember your childhood, Darius?" The Gate began to open one click at a time, operated by a crank somewhere. "What about your role models? Did you look up to any family members in particular?"

Darius's heart began to pound and he could hear his blood pumping in his ears. He couldn't find the proper response to answer the Doctor's question. "Follow up," the Doctor said. "Do you understand what it means for something to be feral?"

Panic seeped into Darius's chest and he wanted to flee. He didn't have to see his opponent to know that something was very, very wrong. Darius remained silent.

"When a creature is feral, it is untamed. It is wild," the Doctor said. "The term may also apply to a human who has abandoned all civilization and has become an animal in its own right. This is normally brought on by extensive trauma."

One step at a time the beast lurched out of the gate. It was about seven feet tall. Darius had never seen anything like it before. "Imagine living in the sewers for years, Darius. Eating rats to stay alive. It must have quite the effect on a man's psyche."

"No…" was all Darius could manage when he realized that the monster had human eyes.

"That's right, Darius." The Doctor was cackling now. "Once I captured him it only took a few weeks for him to learn to like the taste of human flesh. And then it was only a matter of time before he turned completely into an animal. He speaks and understands no language. Did you look up to your uncle, Darius? Do you admire him now?"

The beast stepped fully into the light. What had once been armor had been molded to his skin and had become a thick exoskeleton. His nails had been filed into claws. Darius was sure that beneath his scraggly facial hair his teeth were just as sharp. His eyes lacked understanding and were instead filled with a dark hunger. "Darius Taurlum, meet your opponent!" the Doctor thundered. "The Sewer Man, your uncle!" The monster stood upright and prepared to charge. "Nikolai Taurlum!"

VOLTERIA

Chapter Seventy-One

THE DOCTOR'S WORKSHOP
BIANCA BLACKMORE

ANASTASIA LANDED IN THE UPPER RING AND IMMEDIATELY DODGED A bullet fired by the Marksman. Bianca was next over the side and threw a knife into the barrel of his second pistol as he drew it. Bianca was finally able to see the full extent of the Doctor's workshop. He had enough room to work on any possible project. He had four work-benches covered in sharp instruments and vials of chemicals. His forge roared, unwatched, and sprayed sparks into the air. The man himself was on the other side of the ring and Victor surely wouldn't make it easy to reach him. She peered through the low light and realized she could see Rhys tied to the doors of the cage he was im-prisoned in. She gasped audibly. He looked to be on death's doorstep.

Victor grinned for the first time at Bianca. "Are you ready for round three?" he asked as he pulled another pistol out and spun it around his finger. "I assure you, this will be the last one."

"Get Rhys," Bianca told Anastasia.

Anastasia looked on the verge of collapsing, but she slid past the Marksman as Bianca distracted him with two more knives. He fired a bullet through both knives and they shattered into tiny shards of metal. Bianca grabbed a knife in her hand, and instead of throwing it, she lunged at him. She managed to cut his hand and he dropped one of his pistols. His multiple weapons method proved effective against the common target, but Bianca was not a common target. He jabbed with his right hand and struck her arm hard enough to paralyze it. She dropped it, undeterred and snap kicked him in the stomach. The force pushed him back, and she dodged his next strike. "Have you gotten quicker?" he asked.

"No," she said as she pulled another knife from her belt. "Angrier."

He pulled out his other guns and dropped them. This was a bare hands fight and they both knew it. She dropped her knife and they circled each other. He ran forward suddenly and roundhouse kicked her. She blocked it barely and as soon as he dropped his foot she drove her front facing foot into his groin. He yelped and dropped to his knees. She tried to knee him in the face, but he ducked to the left and she awkwardly stumbled. He sprung up to his feet and head-butted her in the face. She saw stars and darkness seeped into her vision. He elbowed her across the face and she dropped like a sack of bricks. She was awake, but he'd nearly knocked the consciousness out of her. He stomped down where her head had been a second before as she regained her wits and rolled out of the way. "I was on the verge of feeling impressed," the Marksman said. "And I don't feel that often."

She raised her fists. "You're going to feel this."

He didn't spend any time acknowledging her quip. He tackled her and, although she staggered, she held her footing. In her moment of surprise, he pulled one of her knives from her belt. His error was thinking he could defeat Bianca Blackmore in a knife fight. She dodged his first swing and pulled out her own knife. He tried to stab her again and this time she anticipated his attack. She sidestepped his advance and with one blow sliced his hand clean off of his wrist. The Marksman screamed inhumanly and stared at his new stump. "My hand…" he screamed.

"Good luck aiming with that," Bianca said.

"I'll cut you apart with your own knives," he hissed, collapsing to his knees. "Then Anastasia… And I'll slaughter everyone that you…"

She front kicked him and focused all of her power in the center of his forehead. Maybe it was from her strike or from blood loss, but the Marksman passed out. She dropped the bloody knife. "Fools don't deserve mercy," she said to his body.

Chapter Seventy-Two

THE DOCTOR'S WORKSHOP
THE PACK

THE DOCTOR WATCHED AS ANASTASIA SET HIS PRISONER FREE. DESPITE what these fools thought, this was part of his plan. If Rhys were to assume his identity as the new Doctor, he'd have to confront the current titleholder. Anastasia picked the lock and undid the knots that tied Rhys to the inside of the bars. The Doctor watched her from afar and laughed to himself as she reeled in horror at the appearance of the young boy. She probably noticed the missing foot first. The Doctor had amputated it perfectly, then sterilized and cauterized the wound. It didn't make the act less horrific.

He approached Anastasia from behind and caught her in a sleeper hold. The poor girl was already on the verge of passing out so he needed little force. Rhys escaped on his one leg past the Doctor. The boy ran to the workbenches and hobbled around it to put it between the two of them. The Doctor laughed. "You can't escape this workshop without dealing with me first, boy," he said. He pointed to the sharp instruments on the table. "Use those. End me. End your own suffering."

"I will never kill anyone," Rhys said. "I made that choice a long time ago."

The Doctor glared at him and selected a knife from the table. "You will. And when I die I will be courteous enough to rate my pain on a scale for you." He spat. "Don't deny your destiny. Don't deny me."

Rhys seemed to see something off in the distance. He chased the boy until they reached the workbench next to the forge. The Doctor's fury was growing. Why couldn't the boy understand what he did? Why couldn't the boy just answer his call to a higher purpose and to science?

Rhys was clearly running out of energy. The last few weeks had taken its toll on his health and motor skills. Rhys grabbed a bottle of chemicals and sniffed it. He looked conflicted about holding it. The Doctor raised his knife. "Maybe you weren't the heir I was hoping for."

The boy splashed the chemical in the Doctor's face and he recoiled expecting it to be acid or something corrosive. He waited until he realized that the liquid was nothing but acetone. "Foolish," the Doctor accused him. "You thought acetone would hurt me? It's not corrosive."

"No," Rhys said almost sadly. "But it is flammable."

The Doctor's eyes widened as he realized how close he was to the forge. As if on cue, a small spark flew from it and settled on the top of his head. For an instance silence, then flames engulfed his body. The fire consumed him and he ran in a newfound terror that he hadn't felt since childhood. He fell to the ground and smothered the flames in his coat. Before he abandoned consciousness one thought sprung into his fading mind. *The boy had done it. He'd tried to kill him. That would be enough. It had to be.*

Chapter Seventy-Three

THE PIT
DARIUS TAURLUM

*D*ARIUS *LEAPT OUT OF THE WAY AS* N*IKOLAI SLAMMED THE SANDY FLOOR* where he'd once been. Darius couldn't grapple with the horror of what his uncle had become. "Listen to me…" Darius said on the verge of desperation.

Nikolai roared and charged him. Darius swung at him hard and dented his scales. Nikolai raked his claws down Darius's arm and the sound of sharp metal on metal caused him to recoil. He kicked Nikolai off him. "Listen. Uncle Nikolai… It's me, Darius. Remember me?"

Nikolai stood upright and cocked his head to the left, considering him. He shook his massive head and body slammed Darius, all the while swinging his giant claws. Darius was backed into the wall and managed to escape being crushed by pushing off with his legs. Nikolai was strong, perhaps even stronger than Michael had been. His new sinister diet, no matter how evil and repulsive, had only enhanced his legendary strength. Nikolai's next vicious swing missed Darius's head and carved a block of stone out of the wall behind him. Darius crumpled to escape being backed into the corner again. He scrambled out of Nikolai's reach and retreated to the other side of the coliseum.

Despite his panic and fear Darius knew one thing, and he knew it without compromise. He didn't have it in him to kill another family member, no matter what Nikolai had become. His uncle turned and faced him again. With a mighty roar he leapt across the room with an incredible leg strength that had remained hidden until that moment. Darius didn't have time to react and was brought to the ground as his uncle pounced on him. He tried to buck him off. Nikolai clobbered him across the jaw and Darius's vision went funny. Nikolai struck him twice more and then tossed his body to the other side of the ring, clearly confused as to why his meal wouldn't shred into pieces like they usually did. Darius rolled over and Nikolai nudged his body experimentally. Darius tried to sit up, but a two-handed slam from Nikolai discouraged that behavior. He waited patiently for Nikolai to circle him and get closer. When he did, Darius kicked his legs upwards and nailed Nikolai beneath his chin. He roared in pain and held his head in his hands. He dropped to all fours and roared again in a register Darius had formerly considered to be out of a human's range. He wasn't sure if Nikolai counted as a human anymore biologically. He'd clearly been the subject of several experiments by the Imperial Doctor. "I'm your nephew," Darius said back. "You used to take me to see fights in an arena a lot like this one. My father, Gabriel, is your brother."

At the mention of his brother's name Nikolai stood taller and blinked his crazed eyes. "Yeah?" Darius asked as he tried to control his panic. "You remember Gabriel Taurlum?"

Nikolai actually looked like he did, for a moment at least. Nikolai approached him more slowly this time, and Darius's heart pumped hope through his blood. Nikolai leaned one hand out and held it experimentally in front of Darius. Darius reached to touch it and when he did Nikolai grabbed him by the arm and hurled him into the nearest wall.

The wall crumbled on impact and Darius groaned in pain. Nikolai made a loud screeching noise that could have been laughter. Darius stood and realized with horror that his elbow joint was bleeding from Nikolai's claws. Once a Taurlum's weak point was exploited the skin became soft enough to pierce. He was mortal now...

Darius stood and truth enveloped him. There was no hope against a monster of this size and strength without his impervious skin. Nikolai dug his foot into the ground repeatedly to prepare for a charge. Darius backed up until he was against the wall and waited for death.

Nikolai bashed Darius against the wall and he exhaled in pain. Nikolai seemed to realize his attacks were more fruitful now and began striking with more force. Darius struggled to avoid being completely annihilated under Nikolai's crushing blows.

He raised his arms in one last desperate attempt to save himself and felt a peculiar energy flowing through his fingertips. He pushed it out of his arms and it traveled through him like a current. Nikolai tried to tear Darius to pieces, but the beast found himself restrained by the armor melded to his skin. Darius realized with relief and elation that he could move the armor holding Nikolai. Darius had never put too much thought into an advanced ability since he already stood confidently against most enemies, but this was a welcome surprise that brought tears to his eyes. He didn't have to kill his uncle. There would be another way. Darius could now control metal with the mere wave of his arm.

With his newfound power, Darius pushed Nikolai back with his mind, much to the creature's fury. At times he found Nikolai fighting him, but he focused his energy on the wrists and elbows, where his uncle would have less force to fight him.

Even though his new ability was strong, Nikolai flailed too hard for Darius to control him. He needed to be sedated, or at least worn out. Something tugged at Darius's memory as he fought against Nikolai's struggling. Nikolai only had one weak point. Where was it?

Nikolai was breaking free of his control. Darius was sure it wouldn't take many more hits for his uncle to finish him off. Darius examined his uncle's armor. Taurlum armor usually had gaps so that the skin could breathe. Where had Nikolai tried to protect himself? Certain parts of Nikolai's armor were gone, so it was hard to tell. He was missing one shoulder plate and his helmet had a metal chinstrap.

Wait. That was it. That's why he had the metal chinstrap. He was protecting the underside of his chin. All Taurlum shared that weak point, apparently even the biggest, strongest ones. Nikolai tore free of Darius's hold and charged at full speed. He had to be right. There was no other option. If Darius was wrong he would die. Nikolai leapt through the air and Darius delivered a super-human uppercut to the under side of his jaw.

Nikolai Taurlum flopped onto his back, dazed and defeated. He babbled a few times, but it was clear he'd lost what little wits he had.

After struggling for a time, Darius used his ability to push Nikolai back into the cage. Before his uncle could escape, Darius pulled the gate down, effectively imprisoning him once more. Darius buried his head in his hands in relief. He'd been spared another great emotional pain. He'd also gained the ability to move metal with his mind.

He flexed his arm and silently measured his new strength. He felt a power, once dormant, running through his blood.

After clearing his head of his self-involvement, Darius heard the Doctor screaming in the ring above him. He climbed out of the coliseum using one of the indents Nikolai had made. Once he reached the upper ring, an unpredictable scene greeted him: Bianca was helping up her weary sister, the Marksman was unconscious and without his right hand, the Doctor was on the floor, smoke billowing from his body, and Rhys Vapros was hunched against the wall with a bandaged stump where his left foot had once been. Darius ran to him. Rhys had his face buried and shook every couple seconds as his sobs rattled him. Darius scooped him up and hugged him tightly. "No worries, little buddy," he said. "We've got you. You're safe."

"Is he okay?" Anastasia asked.

"Are you okay?" Darius asked Rhys.

Rhys shook violently and tears streamed down his face. "Far away from here," he pleaded.

Darius turned to carry Rhys back through the ring, up the stairs, and through the library. But when he turned the Doctor was standing once more. His body was charred beyond recognition, including bits that were already half missing. "I've had just about enough of this!" he roared through his red-hot jaw.

Darius could hear the links on Anastasia's chain spike rattling as she prepared to throw it. "You may think you are in control, but you forget who I am and you forget where you are." His jaw creaked as he talked. "Without my formula Anastasia will die. It will be painful and I can assure you, it is fast approaching. There is none in this workshop and only I have the knowledge to create it."

Darius wanted to run over and snap his neck, but one look over at Anastasia proved the Doctor was right. She teetered back and forth even now. He could feel Rhys quivering in his arms and he knew that something had to be done about the spider. Anastasia took a few shaky steps toward him. "You'll never stop," she whispered. "What you did to Rhys, to Darius's uncle…" She paused. "To me… You'll do it again." She looked over at Rhys. "This was all my fault."

The Doctor straightened his spine. "I fail to see how any of this is your business. Now if you want to live through the evening I suggest you—"

Anastasia hurled her chain spike straight through his forehead. He stood for a few seconds, then he fell forward and his metal jaw rang like a church bell as it struck the ground. "Rate that on your pain scale," Anastasia whispered through pained lips.

She followed him to the ground and her friends ran to her side. Her face was completely devoid of color and her eyes were fluttering. "Stay awake," Bianca said. "You've got to stay awake."

"I haven't been a good sister," Anastasia murmured. "Betrayed you… Ignored you… Lied…"

"It's okay," Bianca said. "You're not allowed to talk like this at the end. It's not the end… We just…"

Anastasia mustered a sarcastic look. She looked like she was on the verge of screaming with pain.

"We just found each other again." Bianca was sobbing. "I just got you back."

Darius laid Rhys down gently and grabbed her hand. "Maybe he has something lying around that we could…" he started but he remembered the Doctor's warning. She'd known the consequences of her actions. "Look you have to stay." He was getting desperate. "I've still got a letter to read you."

She and her hand went limp in his. "You can read it to me," she said, voice fading. "I really hope I'll be able to hear it."

With that she left them and Darius felt his iron heart tear. They sat over her, rigid with disbelief, until Rhys's shivering called them back to reality. Darius couldn't imagine standing now. He couldn't imagine taking a single step. But, despite her sacrifice and their loss, someone still needed them. Darius hauled her over his shoulder. He held her gently and grabbed Rhys with his other arm. To their dismay, the Marksman was no longer lying where he had been. A blood trail led out of the room through a back door designed to look like a work shelf. "Do you want to go after him?" Darius asked.

Bianca looked five years older when she peered up from her hands. "Today has been enough," she said. "He's not as much of a threat without the right hand."

"He might come after you," Darius said. "In revenge."

"If he does, I'll take the other one," Bianca vowed.

Darius had no doubt she meant it. He held the two broken things in his arms and carried them out of the workshop. He took one last look back at the dead Doctor. His limbs fell behind him and twitched with the absence of life. The spider had been crushed. "What about your uncle?" Bianca asked Darius as they left.

"Tomorrow night I'll come back," he said. "I'll take him deep into the woods and release him. Perhaps he'll find something for himself."

Bianca didn't respond. He knew that it was dangerous to let a monster like this free, but he didn't care. He'd take Nikolai far away where he couldn't hurt anyone and the world would cease to hurt him. "We can also find a nice place to bury her," he added quietly, as if asking for permission.

She nodded and that was enough. Darius didn't remember the walk back to the inn. All he could think about was Anastasia and what she'd been through. She'd been extorted and forced into her life as an assassin, forced to betray her friends. Despite her situation, in the end, she managed to make things right. She would forever be complicated for Darius. She would forever be someone who he'd only known bits and pieces of until their final moments together. The world had lost her, but it had also lost the Doctor. There was no sanity in keeping score, but he knew that Volteria was better off because Anastasia gave her life to eliminate the Doctor.

Before he knew it, they were setting Rhys into a bed and Bianca was checking his vitals. She told him that he had a fever and would need several days of rest. Darius doubted that Rhys was even listening. The boy was sleeping the moment his skin touched the sheets. Darius pulled the Lightborn cuffs off of Rhys's arms and he groaned in relief. Darius waited until Bianca was preoccupied and pulled a single page from Anastasia's notebook. It was his letter for her. For a terrible instant fury filled him and he considered tearing it in half. At the last moment, he folded it and placed it in his pocket. He'd written it for her and no one else would read it. Except for Darius. Darius would read it every night.

He walked out of his room and down the stairs once the other two were asleep. He approached the woman who owned the inn and tried not to think of Josephine. "Do you have gin?" he asked.

She placed her hands on the bar and looked at him. "It's not even time for breakfast."

He didn't waver. "I won't be a problem."

She pulled a bottle out from one of the cupboards. "I'll kick you out if you make yourself a disturbance," she warned. "You want a glass?"

Darius remembered the Wolf's warnings about his overweight friend and his lack of self-control. Darius rubbed his forehead. "I'll take the bottle."

"That's too much," she said.

He put all of the money he had on the bar. "I know. That's the point."

Chapter Seventy-Four

ANIMA ISLAND
NEIL VAPROS

BY THE TIME NEIL REACHED THE ISLAND HALF WAY BETWEEN OCEAN'S JAW and the mainland, Neil felt like his arms were going to fall off or his heart would drop into his stomach. As he rowed toward land, he saw the Man with the Golden Light on the beach.

Neil pulled his boat far enough ashore so that it wouldn't float away during his exploration. The Man was already fading by the time Neil reached him. "Wait!" Neil said. He needed guidance now more than ever. "Was that it? The right thing?"

"Onward, Neil," the Man said as he dissolved. "You'll never know what was right until you see the repercussions of your actions. Look inside that house," he said as he pointed up the beach with what remained of his form. "Learn about repercussions."

There was something very wrong about this island. Neil could feel it in the air. The sand beneath him turned to a mixture of soil and soot as he walked. Roughly a hundred feet up the beach was a giant stone house overgrown with vines and coated in the soot that covered the ground. If it were cleaner and larger it would have looked similar to the Taurlum mansion. Neil jogged to the front door and was nearly floored by the smell of what was undoubtedly inside. Neil pushed open the half-unhinged door and braced himself for the worst. He found it.

The entry hall was littered with skeletons that looked to have been impaled by silverware. Some were stabbed through and pinned to the walls and others were lying in heaps around the room. One was even attached to the ceiling by a series of forks. The floor was decorated with dried blood. The next thing that Neil noticed was the carvings that adorned the walls. These walls were stone. It would have taken an immense amount of force to write on them, and yet here they were. Neil approached one and rubbed his elbow over it to clear the dust. *I AM NO ONE'S SLAVE* was the inscription. Neil scratched his head. That was odd. He found another inscription and cleared the dust off once again. *I AM NO ONE'S SLAVE.*

Before Neil could clear off another he heard a voice behind him. "Was he your father?"

Neil turned with a start and his hands ignited by instinct. The old man didn't look phased. "Was who my father?" Neil asked breathlessly.

"Barrick," the old man whispered frightfully. "You look just like him…"

Neil stared at him questioningly. The man clearly wasn't a threat. It looked like his skin was made from wet paper merely wrapped around bones. "I don't know what you're talking about," Neil said as he extinguished his hands. "I don't know anyone named Barrick. Someone told me there could be answers here."

The old man sighed. "Well you'd have to get them from me. I'm the only one left on this island."

"What is this place?" Neil asked.

The old man hobbled by Neil and through the entry hall. Neil followed him into what looked to be the kitchen. They passed by four more bodies on the way. The old man pointed to a window on the opposite wall. Neil approached and peered out. "It was a mine?" Neil asked.

"Yes," the old man said. "Silver."

Neil turned back around. "I still don't understand."

"Some unequaled crimes against humanity were performed here." The man cleared his throat. "My son. Such a sweet boy. Broken. Taken from us."

"What are you talking about?" Neil asked.

The old man gestured around him. "Read the walls around you. He wrote them hundreds of times."

Neil looked around to notice that this room also had engravings on the walls and ceilings. "I am no one's slave," Neil recited. "Do they all say that?"

The old man shook his head. "All of them but one. The last one he wrote."

"Show me," Neil said.

The old man took him into the connecting dining room and pointed to the wall. Surrounded by hundreds of inscriptions that read, *I AM NO ONE'S SLAVE* was one written larger and inscribed deeper than any others. *I AM SAEWULF ANIMA.*

Neil's heart stopped and he gripped the table to keep from falling down. "This is…"

The totality of Saewulf's memory had been eluding Neil, but in an instant it returned. He remembered the glowing eyes, the raspy threats, and the way he'd killed Victoria without hesitation.

"This is where my sweet boy was turned into a monster," the man said with his voice full of pity and regret.

"You're Saewulf's…"

"I was his father," the man said. "You sound like you knew him."

Neil didn't respond. He stopped himself from igniting a fireball in his hand. This was the man that had spawned the Emperor's Psychic. Saewulf had killed his sister, after all. "Saewulf killed everyone here?" Neil asked.

The old man sat down at what used to be the dinner table. "They killed him first, boy. Killed his soul." He looked like he was tearing up, but it was possible that he was just an old man with moist eyes. "Years ago, we were living on the other side of this island. There's a small village there. We were peaceful. Friendly. No one suspected we might be Lightborns. Until one day when someone lost control of a cart and it rolled toward a young child. Saewulf stopped it with his mind. He was praised as a hero by all. Except for John Dalton, who owned the mine. He saw this pure boy with powers as an opportunity. This is where his opportunity brought him, " the old man said. He pointed to a body in the corner that was adorned with silks and precious looking jewelry.

"So Saewulf was forced to mine?"

"Yes," the old man said. "They slaughtered his mother and kidnapped his sister. They'd send him out to toil in the mines and once he was done, they'd let him in the house to sleep. I couldn't do anything. His mother was the Lightborn and she was dead. I had no powers to use to help him. Dalton had an army."

"What was to stop Saewulf from killing them all the moment he walked in?" Neil asked.

"Barrick Vapros."

Neil cringed at the mention of his own family name. "Who was Barrick Vapros?"

"A Lightborn from the Industrial City," the old man said. "He was exiled and by chance ended up on this island. He had an unusual ability to block other people's powers. That is, when he was around Saewulf, the boy was unable to use his gifts. It's also how they managed to capture him and kill his mother. So Barrick was paid a fortune to stay with the boy at all times whenever he was inside. Barrick was a cruel individual. He beat the boy and his sister constantly in hopes that it would motivate Saewolf to work harder. After years of this pain and abuse, Barrick took it too far. Whether they'd forgotten to feed her or they'd been too ruthless with her, I'm not sure, but Saewulf's sister, my daughter, was dead. They tried to keep it from Saewolf, but the boy was smart enough to realize what had happened. He murdered Barrick in his sleep with a shard of silver. Then he pulled the silverware from the cupboards and well…" he gestured around him.

Neil rubbed his forehead and tried to breathe. "And then?"

"We don't know. Everyone assumed that he walked out into the surf and drowned. That was a common rumor."

Neil shook his head. "He didn't. He died inside the walls."

The old man sighed. "I hope he rests in peace."

Neil didn't want to share any of the details about Saewulf's life once he was on the mainland.

"How did you know what happened after he was kidnapped?" Neil asked.

"A few young men escaped Saewulf's onslaught and came to the village to warn us. Most climbed into rowboats in fear that he would come for us next. I stayed, hoping he never would."

"And he didn't?"

"No," the old man said. "Sometimes I wished he would. We knew what John Dalton was doing with my boy. But he was too powerful for me to do anything about it. Some people on this island simply stated that it wasn't their business. Can you fathom that? That it wasn't their business? Imagine the sins committed because they couldn't be bothered to step out of their way." He held his face in his hands. "There's so much blood on their hands. My hands."

The old man sobbed while Neil was stared at the walls. It made sense now. Saewulf's hatred for Lightborns and his desire to destroy the families was a result of his enslavement and his encounter with Barrick Vapros. Saewulf had been a crucial part of planning the Emperor's attack on the Lightborns. He realized that Bianca had been right when she'd said it wasn't about power, it was about extinction. Saewulf had been trying to rid the world of people like Barrick Vapros. He'd been trying to make sure no one would suffer what he'd suffered ever again.

Neil stared at the final inscription on the wall. *I AM SAEWULF ANIMA*. Neil shook his head. "So that makes six families in all." He groaned. Things were complicated enough when there were just three of them.

"I only ever knew one family. My family," the old man said.

Neil placed his hand against the inscription and shuddered. It felt as if all his bones had scraped each other at once. "The Anima family has the power of what?"

"Power of the mind" the old man whispered from behind his hands. "It always manifests in a different way. Saewulf used his to move things."

Neil was afraid of the answer to his next question. "Are there any others left?"

"If my boy is dead, then that really might be the last of them. We've been hunted and used for our powers time and time again."

Neil turned to the entrance and walked toward it.

"I really do hope he rests in peace," the old man said to himself. "He is owed some peace."

Neil had something else to say, but didn't. He left. He kept his eyes locked forward when he left. He didn't want to see the carnage. He pushed off of the shore and continued rowing toward the mainland. He'd rather drown than stay on that island. Saewulf's father's words rang through his head. *I hope he rests in peace.*

Neil wanted that to be true, he really did. But he was filled with doubt. After all, evil never rests.

Chapter Seventy-Five

ABINGTON
DARIUS TAURLUM

It was amazing that Darius was able to fit Nikolai through the doors of the library, and even more amazing that the creature didn't awaken the entire village with its roaring. Darius's concerns grew less pertinent as they entered the woods outside of Abington. Darius was still swaying from the drinks he'd had earlier, but his powers held strong. He held Nikolai at the joints again with his advanced ability, and after an hour or so the creature stopped struggling. He carried him long into the night until he found a small lake surrounded by a ridge. He dropped his Uncle and Nikolai settled on the mossy forest floor.

Darius focused with all his might and began peeling off the armor piece by piece. Nikolai screamed in the beginning, but as time went on he began to sigh in relief with each removed piece. Eventually he was a man again, dressed in nothing but a thin undershirt and pantaloons. Nikolai collapsed in what looked like pure relief, alone in his newfound freedom from his scales and from the armor that had restricted him. Darius knew he no longer had control of the beast, but he had a feeling his temperament had changed. His uncle rolled on the ground as if to scratch an itch and Darius approached. "I'm sorry this happened to you."

Nikolai sat up, confused and then bounded into the water. Everywhere he went in the clean lake, dark pools of dirt surrounded him. Darius wondered how long it had been since his uncle's last bath. He watched Nikolai, living in bliss for almost an hour. He'd never be the same, and he'd probably never be human again, but he would be happy out here away from the cages and human sacrifices. When Darius finally left, Nikolai slept on the soft grass.

Darius walked through the forest and met Bianca closer to Abington in a clearing. She looked as terrible as he felt. She had two shovels with her and a small coffin. Darius proved to be far more effective at digging than she was, and before long they had an adequate resting place for Anastasia. They set her down lightly in the grave and covered it with dirt. All of it was done without a word. Darius was thankful for it. What could he possibly offer Bianca at a time like this?

He found a sizeable flat stone to use for the epitaph and brought it back to Bianca, who was kneeling at the grave. "Will this work?" he asked.

"What do you want to say?" she asked.

"I don't know. I thought I'd leave that up to you. She was your sister."

"I wish I had something," Bianca said almost in a whisper. "I only just reconnected with her. I wish I had gotten to know her like you did."

Darius blinked at her. *Like he did?*

"You two spent a lot of time together. And there was something in her eyes, whenever she talked about you. I don't know how much of what she said was real, but the way she felt about you… that wasn't an act."

Darius turned away from her to get another rock to make the inscription, but also because he didn't want her to see the pain in his eyes. He used his Taurlum strength to carve her name into the headstone. He sat with Bianca until he knew what he wanted to write. *Anastasia Blackmore. Her last act was a selfless one.* He turned the stone over and showed it to Bianca. She squinted to read it, then looked at him when she did. "I think she would have liked it."

He placed it at the head of her grave and sat next to Bianca. He'd never connected with Bianca as well as the others did, but he felt a connection to her now, through Anastasia. "I guess it must say something about us as people…" Bianca said.

"What?"

"Every time we lose someone it still hits us so hard. We've seen so much death, and it never gets any easier."

"I don't think us being soft changes anything," Darius said.

She shook her head. "When you go to war, you see death. You see it everywhere." And some people get used to it, eventually. The fact that we haven't… I don't know. Maybe we really are the good guys."

Darius stared at Anastasia's grave and then into the distance to where he'd left Nikolai. "You saw what the Doctor did to Rhys, and to Anastasia. He didn't value life like we do. Any doubts that I had about this cause are gone. The Empire isn't justified. It's evil."

Bianca stood and tightened her belt. "Thank you, Darius. For all of this." She indicated the grave. "Thank you for being there for her. I need to head to Misty Hollow to meet Neil before it's too late."

Darius stood and shook her hand. His dwarfed hers, but she still had a firm grip. "Good luck," he said. "Tell Neil his brother needs him. We all do."

Bianca shifted a lock of ashen hair away from her face. "Keep Rhys safe."

She turned and headed over a hill, leaving him alone with the grave. He bowed to it and then headed back to Abington.

When Darius reentered his room at the inn Rhys was awake and sitting against the wall. He looked traumatized. His short hair was standing on end, and his right eye twitched every couple seconds. Darius tossed him Anastasia's notebook and it seemed to pull him out of his trance. "What's this?" Rhys asked.

"Anastasia made me a book to help me read."

Rhys smiled faintly and flipped through the pages. "She was smart. I doubt she knew it, but she was discovering something called phonetics. It's a way of classifying how letters can sound."

Darius thought he saw a bit of Rhys's old excitement in his eyes, but it was overshadowed by a look of fear and shock. "Hey," Darius said uneasily. "Are you going to be okay?"

Rhys blinked a few times and laughed. It was fake and they both knew it. "Yes." Rhys said. "It's just…" He was quivering. "It's going to be a while before anything feels like it used to. I lost a foot, Darius. I don't even remember most of the torture. He kept me awake and without water for days at a time."

Darius tried not to cringe. He was more than ready to never hear about the Imperial Doctor ever again. "Well, now you've got all the water you could ever want." Rhys stared at the floor. "And we'll teach you to walk again!" Darius said. "There were guys in town that had missing feet. There are ways to give you a fake one. Maybe out of metal."

Rhys smiled, but it didn't reach his eyes. "I'll be okay. I'm not easily broken. I just need time." He closed his eyes and leaned his head against the pillow. "It'll be a while before I stop hearing his voice in my head," he said in a sad tone.

Suddenly Rhys bolted upright and stared at Darius in horror. "Why would you say that?" he asked.

"I didn't say anything!" Darius said uneasily.

"Oh," Rhys said. "That's odd. I thought you said *Good luck with that.*"

"I didn't," Darius said with his arms outstretched. "I promise."

"Okay," Rhys said as he lay back down on his pillow and sleep overtook him again. "It must be my mind playing tricks on me. It's just…" Rhys drifted off with his final words before resting. "It even sounded like his voice."

Chapter Seventy-Six

MISTY HOLLOW
NEIL VAPROS

NEIL TRUDGED INTO THE SQUARE OF MISTY HOLLOW AND PEERED THROUGH the dense fog. Whatever he was searching for was here. He knew it. It had to be. Small lanterns littered the square. Some were stationary and occasionally a citizen of the town would drift by holding one. The light reflected off the fog and created a warm and artificial glow.

Neil tried his best to feel optimistic, or at least comfortable, but there was something in the air aside from the fog. There was an unseen tension. Neil shook his head to clear it. And then there she was. Directly across the square stood his oldest friend. Through every waking moment she was his rock, even when he failed to be hers. Bianca stood anxiously tapping her belt and glancing around expectantly. Memories flooded his head and threatened to overwhelm him. He remembered years and years of friendship. He remembered their jokes and their younger years. He remembered the fights and kissing her on a mountaintop. He remembered every time he'd ever seen her face and heard her laugh. The final piece of him was back, and it was her.

He wanted to call out to her. He wanted to scream her name and tear through whoever was in his way of getting to her, but the second his mouth opened, he noticed the fog. Small wisps had stopped their motion. It began pooling against what looked to be an invisible wall of sorts. Its form tightened as it neared some unseen barrier. Neil's eyes widened. He tried to summon a cry to call out to Bianca, but it died in his throat as he felt an invisible force wrap around his throat. He tried to run, but found his feet cemented to the ground. He desperately tried to move a single muscle. Maybe if he could shake an arm or leg Bianca would notice. She could run.

He pooled his energy in his stomach and attempted to materialize out of the shadowy grip. He only managed to break out of his human form for less than a second and he immediately found himself choking as the force tightened around his neck.

Savagely and all at once, he felt the force rip him off his feet and away from the center of the square. Through the fog he glimpsed one last look at Bianca who waited there for him to arrive. As the force pulled him into the depths of an alley, Neil desperately dragged his fingernails down the side of the nearest building. They fractured on the brick and warm blood was left in their absence. Neil's body was lifted up into the air and then slammed mercilessly down onto the hard ground. Over and over again, he was pummeled against the stable earth until his ribs cracked. He tried to spit blood into the street, but instead it ended up dripping down his chin. His body was pushed up against a nearby wall. Neil knew this feeling. He knew of this empty coldness and he knew of its merciless nature. He also knew the hand behind the force, he'd felt it before. "Sae…" he managed.

He tried over and over again, but all he could push through his lips was that word. "Sae..."

"You're so close," Saewulf Anima rasped as he exited the shadows, one arm raised and glowing with a black aura.

Burns stretched from his left hand all the way to his face. The pattern almost resembled a hand clawing at him, as if his burned flesh were trying to claw his face off and lap at his burnt orange hairline. The left side of his lips was burned away and his teeth shined through in a grim smile. "Say my name, Vapros," Saewulf hissed through his mangled mouth. "Do you even recognize me?"

"I watched you die," Neil said when he felt Saewulf's grip loosen. "Jonathan died for it."

Saewulf shook his head violently. "The slave died for nothing. He was close. Very close. But I had just enough time to shield myself."

The grip tightened again and dark spots appeared in Neil's vision. "You know what else, Vapros?" Saewulf whispered as Neil felt his consciousness slipping from his grasp. "You may find comfort in the idea that your death will mean something else..."

Neil's head drifted without his will and Saewulf leaned forward so that their eyes could meet. Saewulf's eyes looked as they always did, desperate, starving for something. "Your death will mean a safer world, a safer existence for Altryon, a brighter future, and an end to this fruitless revolution."

Neil's head slammed back into the wall and his vision left him. His body collapsed onto the ground.

Saewulf chuckled as he placed a foot on the back of Neil's body. "In the end, the sum of your existence could never possibly be more important than your death."

He turned and trotted down the alleyway with Neil's body slowly being dragged behind him. Neil's mind clung to one thought as he felt his wits leave him. Bianca was waiting for him. She was alone. In a way, he hoped she didn't long for the same reunion he did. Because he knew that day would never come.

ABOUT THE AUTHOR

Kyle Prue is an award winning author and teen advocate. He wrote *The Sparks*, the first book in the Feud series, at just 16 years old. The Sparks has won numerous state, national and international awards for Best YA Fiction. Prue is also an actor, improv comedian and popular keynote speaker.

To book an event, visit kyleprue@kyleprue.com.

Prue is also the founder of Sparking Literacy, a non-profit dedicated to lowering the high school dropout rate by inspiring teens to read, write and follow their dreams. You can learn more at sparkingliteracy.org.

CONNECT WITH KYLE

Follow Kyle on social media:
Facebook: KylePrue
Twitter: @KylePrue
Instagram: KylePrueOfficial
Website: kyleprue.com and sparkingliteracy.org

If you've enjoyed this book, sign up for our newsletter at www. kyleprue.com. Members receive free gifts and updates about new releases.

If you would like to connect with other fans of the Feud series, join our Facebook group at www.facebook.com/FeudTrilogy

One more thing, if you liked this book, please leave a review. As a young author, I really appreciate your help to spread the word about my books. Thank you so much!

ACKNOWLEDGEMENTS

This book has been two years in the making, and I am so grateful for the help of so many people.

The team at Cartwright Publishing has been amazing and I am so happy that we are taking this journey together. A big shout out to Samantha Paxton who started as an intern and has quickly become indispensable. I want to thank my agent, Veronica Park, for always believing in me. Also thank you to Ashley Ruggirello for the awesome cover designs for the series and the interior layouts. Also a big thank you to Sari Cicurel, my incredible PR agent, who is so great about helping me to share my message about literacy and helping to get my books into the hands of readers.

I have to thank my editor, Julie Mosow, for always getting what I'm trying to communicate and giving me great notes to improve the story. A special thank you to Howard Schott who is the world's best copy editor. You were the first person to encourage me to get published so in a way you are responsible for this amazing journey. Teachers have the power to change lives, so I am so happy that you are now Head of High School at Seacrest Country Day and inspiring the next group of kids.

I am also grateful to Julia Basile for being an early reader. A special thanks to Owen Gemmer for always being the first person to read my drafts, giving incredible notes, and for always getting my inside jokes.

Thanks to the University of Michigan Class of 2020 for being a constant source of inspiration and for keeping me humble.

A special thank you to all the teachers and students that I met on my year-long book tour. You were all amazing and I loved meeting each and every one of you. I know you've waited a long time for *The Flames*. So thanks for your patience and I hope you enjoy it.

I would like to extend my greatest thanks to my parents. Over the last couple years you've been readers, collaborators, advisors, and the best of mentors. I'm incredibly proud to be your son and I'm so incredibly grateful to be learning from you every day.

Thanks to all my family and friends for your incredible support. A very special thank you to all of our donors and volunteers at Sparking Literacy. Because of you, we are making a positive impact and lowering the high school dropout rate. Thank you for helping us to make a difference.

Made in the USA
Columbia, SC
09 April 2018